The Sins of my Fathers

How three family relationships attempt to deal with generational curses so prevalent in their family history, and struggle to overcome the battle of unbelief, family secrets, disparagement and suspicion.

A book of fiction

By

C. Anthony Sherman

authorHOUSE®

AuthorHouse™
1663 Liberty Drive
Bloomington, IN 47403
www.authorhouse.com
Phone: 1-800-839-8640

First published by AuthorHouse 8/26/2011

ISBN: 978-1-4634-5267-4 (ebk)
ISBN: 978-1-4634-5268-1 (hc)
ISBN: 978-1-4634-5269-8 (sc)

Library of Congress Control Number: 2011915367

Printed in the United States of America

Chapter 1

The best chance for success in working his way back into the dynamics of his brothers routine was for Dexter to agree to play golf with them starting on the next Saturday morning. By now, he had run out of excuses for not being available when he received a call to join them. Dexter was an open and gregarious brother-much friendlier than his two younger siblings, but he was not a golfer. After a moment of hesitation on the phone conversation he had with his younger brother, Dexter finally agreed.

"Alright, but you guy's better take it easy on me. Can I tee off from the ladies markers?"

"You know Dex; you don't give yourself enough credit. I'm telling you for sure, you've got a sweet swing. I'll bet you shoot under 80 Saturday," said Adam, the younger brother.

"Well I don't know about all that. I am going to need some help."

When Adam and Dexter finished their conversation, Adam called Brian, the middle brother. They spoke.

"Hey B.B., he's coming with us!"

"Who?"

"Dex, man."

"Oh...he is?"

"*Yep, I just finished talking to him. He said he wants to tee off from the ladies markers.*"

"*Not the way he can hit that ball. He might not be accurate every time, but you know what happens when he gets hold of a good one, right?*"

"*Oh yeah, I know. No, no, we're going to make him earn what he gets. You know I never believed him when he said he only played two or three times a year, did you?*" asked Adam.

"*Naw, not at all, but that's fine. Listen, let me get back in here and finish this painting before my wife gets mad at me and I can't go Saturday,*" said Brian.

"*Okay, later, B.B.*"

"*Later!*"

Saturday was not the best day to play two rounds of golf. The weather turned out to be the worst it had been in three months. In the mind of Dexter, this might be just what he needed. He was nervous about his brothers showing him up in what he considered to be 'their game'. He left his clubs in the trunk of his car as he scrambled to get inside of the clubhouse where Brian and Adam had been waiting for fifteen minutes. By now, the rain was coming down in a steady heavy pattern. It began to thunder and lightening roared intermittingly. All play had stopped, and some golfers had sought shelter from being drenched under some of the majestic old pecan trees, ringing the manicured and curved fairways.

"*Hey Dex, over here,*" directed Adam.

Dexter zigzagged his way to the table where his still seated brothers extended their hand to shake his hand as he arrived. In Dexter's mind, since the rain continued, he would have a chance to sit with his brothers and have a nice conversation with them about their lives, their wives and especially, their spirituality. He spoke.

"*You guy's really picked the perfect day to play golf, didn't you?*"

"*It must have been your magic that brought this on,*" said Adam.

"*Yeah… black magic at that,*" responded Brian.

"*Well, I don't know about you guy's, but I don't believe in that magic*

2

stuff," explained Dexter. "I believe everything happens for the good of those who love the Lord."

"Oh boy," exclaimed Brian. "I'm not sure I want to play golf today, if I got to listen to a sermon."

"Naw, there won't be a sermon, my brother. Just an expression as to my state of mind, in spite of the conditions around me," said Dexter.

"Do you want something to drink, Dex?" asked Adam. "Maybe some coffee, or do you want a beer?"

"No, I'm fine. I'm okay."

Dexter sat down with a mind of ambivalence as to where this conversation was going to lead them. After all, Dexter was in a strange world, owned by his brothers. He had reentered their lives after being gone from them since he graduated from high school, when Adam, his baby brother, was only thirteen years old. As kids, Dexter was always the leader in all their daily activities. He was strong in his creativity, and his ideas were the ones most often acted upon by them, and their friends in the neighborhood. However, after Dexter went away to the military and later to college in Chicago, their relationship with each other had taken a dissimilar course. Dexter returned to the city of his youth some twenty-five years after graduating from high school, only to find that the position he had held as the leader among the friends of his youth, was taken over by his brother, Brian. Dexter looked upon the situation as normal, considering his absence from their lives for such a long period of time. It was not his intention to try to reconnect in the way they were as teenagers. He simply wanted to become a part of their lives as grown men, who shared the same DNA. He sought no position of hierarchy with them-just to be the older brother that he was.

Putting his advanced education aside and his strong, deep roots with his God; Dexter wanted to simply have a relationship with their families as any other family system would have in a functional way. Notwithstanding others, he wondered if it could happen with this family. Could there be a relaxing of the tenseness between them, that he was sure each of them felt? What would it take? How far should he go in trying? What compromises needed to be made, and by whom? Many questions remained open, and no concrete answers were forthcoming—at least, not in Dexter's mind.

"*You know, since we have this time, why don't we try to get reacquainted with each other. It really has been a long time since…*"

"*Ah cut the bull, Dex. Man, you don't get it, do you? Look, you are the one that went away, okay? We have been here all the time. If you expect to come down here and try to change the way things are…you got another thought coming,*" explained Brian.

"*What are you talking about, B.B.?*" asked Dexter.

"*You know damn well what I'm talking about, Dex. You go away to the service; and then to the big city of Chicago; You get all those degrees, and make the big bucks working for the man; Buy the big house and cars and you decide to move down here to tell us how we ought to run our lives. Well, big brother, I for one, am not interested in listening to your religious lectures about how we live. So you'd best not go there, okay?*" Brian lectured.

"*Hold up B.B.! I don't think Dex was going there. Let's not jump to conclusion too soon,*" said Adam.

"*Thanks little brother. I am amazed that YOUR big brother has such strong feelings about my moving back here. I thought…*"

"*I don't have strong feelings about your moving back here. I just don't want no bull from you about how you think we ought to live our lives, that's all,*" said Brian.

"*Brian …hey little brother…*"

"*And don't call me little brother. Hell, I weigh more than you do, and I can hold my own as well. It ain't like it used to be, Dexter- Do you feel me?*"

By this time, the rain had subsided to a trickle. The sun began to peek through the heavy clouds that covered the skies. Adam was eager to change the subject, ease the tension, and get out there to play some golf. He was not in favor of the way Brian had attached Dexter, but he reasoned that Dex had brought it upon himself. Adam was always the one to ask for a time out between his brothers as they were growing up as teenagers. Dexter knew how things were while they were young, but he cannot imagine what brought on this poison from Brian at this time.

Dexter spoke:

"Listen fellows. We don't have to continue this. I apologize for anything I have said or done to cause you to respond that way, Brian. The Bible tells me to do good to those who despitefully use me. I ask for your forgiveness. Now if you will excuse me...I will..."

Adam interrupted.

"Come on guys! I came here to play some golf, not to get into all that religious stuff, or to go back in time. Come on back Dex.—sit down, man."

"You want to know why I get so upset?" asked Brian.

..."Tell me you want to know!"

"You got the floor, Brian-go for it," said Dexter.

"If you really want to know, I will tell you," said Brian.

"I repeat... go for it," said Dex.

"Alright! Do you remember when you and your wife came down here for the family reunion two years ago? Do you remember when your wife cornered my son in the den and told him that he was not very smart?

"What are you talking about, Brian?" asked Dexter.

"You know damn well what I'm talking about. My son told my wife exactly what your wife said to him," said Brian.

"You got me totally baffled, Brian. I don't have the foggiest idea what you're talking about. Please tell me what happened," pleaded Dexter.

"Did you ever wonder why he stopped coming around you guys when you came home earlier this year? Huh?"

"Do you want to tell me or what?"

"Your wife told my son that she thought he was dressed like a thug, with his pants 'saggin'. Did she tell you about that?"

"As a matter of fact, she did!"

"Well what the hell business is it of hers? What does it matter to her

that MY son…MY son has saggin pants? It is none of her business how he dresses…NONE!"

Adam spoke.

"I heard about it too. I think it was over the line, Dex."

"Like I said, I knew she told him that, but I am truly sorry that that conversation even had to take place," said Dex.

"You are sorry it HAD to take place? …That it HAD to take place!" Man you got to be out of your cotton pickin mind! That it had to take place…Your WIFE was out of place, big brother! She had no business telling MY son that. In fact, she should mind her own damn business and leave my family alone. I don't need her putting bad thoughts in my kids' head. Why don't you exercise control of your wife and tell her to leave my family, the hell alone," demanded Brian.

"You know, this is truly amazing! I never knew you guys took that statement so personally. Do you even know what that word 'saggin' mean? What do you think it means when you spell it backward?" Dexter hesitated and then proceeded when he didn't get an answer. "Yeah…that's it! Is that what you want for your son, Brian? Is that how you want the world to view your son, my nephew? I don't think so. I can tell you; Norma wanted to help Greg to see what others see when they look at him. She did that out of love for him, Brian. Can't you see that? This is a cruel world out there. I know how you might have mistaken what she meant, but she certainly meant him no harm."

Silence filled the air. Dexter pleaded his case for understanding, as Brian looked away. Adam Stood up and reached out his hand to Dexter.

"Hey, I understand what happened, Dex. Let's go play some golf now."

"I understand what happened too, Adam. It's unfortunate that we could not discuss these things with our family members without everything going to pot. I don't understand why you guy's could not have discussed this matter with us when it happened. Why would you even think we would do or say anything to hurt one of our loved ones? How could you hold this in for all this time and allow others to get infected with such poison, Brian? Even though we had our sibling rivalry when we were young, I never expected this thing would continue into our adulthood. Listen to me, Brian... I harbor no animosity towards you or your family. It is over, man. The competition is over. I don't have to win any more. I am not trying to win anything, but your hearts. Can you understand that? Can you guy's accept that? Can't we just be brothers again? Can't we just …get along?"

Dexter stood and shook Adams hand. He reached out to shake Brian's hand but Brian was still looking away. They were silent. Brian turned to see Dexter's extended hand. He looked up. Dexter was smiling. Brian looked again at his outstretched hand, and then at his smile. They all embraced each other with the strength of a bear, as they laughed and cried at the same time. They were brothers again. Brian spoke.

"What do you guy's want to do? Stay here and mop the floor with your tears, or get out there and rip the skin off that damn ball?"

"That's why we came here isn't it?" said Dexter.

"LET'S DO IT!" commanded Adam.

For the next three hours, the three brothers managed to get in at least 12 holes of golf. Hampered by the weather and the slow play of others, they pushed through the puddles of water and the fallen debris, to be able to finally call it a rap. All of the brothers felt relieved that they were able to salvage some play, and to vent their building emotions. It's funny what a good game of golf could do to a hardened position taken by strong minded men, thought Adam. With all of them being in their forties, there was little room or time to change their way of thinking—especially the way they felt so protective about their families and their family secrets.

Chapter 2

Brian arrived home shortly before 7 PM. His next door neighbor was visiting with his wife Sharon. As he entered through the kitchen, the neighbor spoke to him, and moved towards the front door. Brian invited her to stay if she liked, but Sharon explained that she was just leaving.

"I'll be sure to tell him what your husband said Betty," Sharon responded.

Sharon closed the door behind Betty. Brian moved to the dining room table waiting for his wife to join him as she normally did.

"What was she here for, baby?" asked Brian.

"Aw, I don't pay much attention to that girl," said Sharon. "She always has something to gossip about—especially when it comes to the leadership in her church."

"What is that supposed to mean?" asked Brian.

"Well, she said that her husband was supposed to go to work for the church as a musician. When the pastor found out that he was a married man, he refused to hire him."

"WHAT? ...What did you say?"

"You heard me right. ...He refused to hire him," said Sharon.

"I know there has to be something wrong with this picture. Are you telling me that the preacher is gay?" asked Brian.

"I am not telling you anything except what she told me. But, like I said, I don't pay much attention to what that girl has to say. I don't believe that was the reason he didn't get the job. I think she is trying to make something up because he was not good enough as a musician," said Sharon.

"Naw, I bet there is something to her story. I bet that she's telling you the truth about that preacher. I bet you his church is full of them, too."

"Honey!"

"I'm serious! I remember I had that feeling ever since we visited that church back in May. You remember when we were walking out of the church, and we were introduced to him by Betty? You remember what he did, don't you?"

"What?"

"You remember that he refused to shake my hand and instead he grabbed me and hugged me? ...Remember?"

"Brian, how could you think that about a man of God?"

"Are you kidding me? He don't impress me as a man of God, the way he acts. No man of God is supposed to act like that. Buy the way, is he married? I bet he's not even married is he?" asked Brian.

"I don't know what he is," said Sharon.

"You know what, baby?" There was a preacher, who called himself a Christian, when I was a kid. This guy was going around the neighborhood on weekdays visiting members of the congregation...or so we thought. He was actually visiting the single women of the church, and having sex with them. He had it going on until one of the women caught him coming from another members' house at 10 at night. That sister was all over the neighborhood telling everybody about old Rev. They kicked him out of the church right away. That's why I have little respect for preachers. They only want you to give them money for this...money for that!" As far as I am concerned, they can go to..."

"Brian! Don't say that! ...Not all preachers are that way. I do think there are some who are testing God's patience and his grace. But..."

I wouldn't make a broad statement like that about them ALL." said Sharon.

"What about that preacher they caught with a prostitute in his car in California. What about that Jim Baker? What about…"

"Brian, I am sure you can find many who have sinned against God. We need to be washed ourselves!" said Sharon.

"Baby you can't put us in the same category as preachers. They are supposed to be perfect …sort of. I mean, they are the shepherds of the flock. How are they going to lead the people, if they are walking around with sin dripping off their backs? You don't think God is going to forgive them like he forgives the flock, do you?" asked Brian.

"The Bible say's we have all sinned and fallen short of the grace of God. We are not supposed to judge each other. That is for God to do."

The telephone rang. Brian went into the kitchen to answer it.

"Hello"

"Hey Brian, its Dex."

"Hey Dex, what's up?"

"I was just calling to tell you how much I enjoyed the play today, and that I was sorry for the misunderstanding about my nephew."

"Yeah you got it Dex. Everything's cool," said Brian.

"Say, Norma and I would like to invite you and Sharon to our church next Sunday. We attend this…"

"Hold it right there, Dex. Man I told you we do our own thing. We have our own routine on the weekend. That's our time together with our family… my grandkid and my daughter and son-in-law. Now, I appreciate the fact that you played golf with us today, but that's about all the time I got." said Brian.

"Okay Brian. I thought we kind of talked through that situation earlier and we were getting past the…"

"Yeah, we did! …We did. But, like I said, you are the one that was away Dex. We have been here all along. You are the one who has to adjust to us. You have to adjust to what's going on here. The fact is, I work during the week, and I play golf on Saturday, and I spend the rest of the weekend with MY family. I don't have time for anything else." said Brian.

"Wow! I am truly amazed, 'lil' brother," said Dex.

"I told you not to call me that, Dex."

"Oh Yeh, you did, didn't you! Well, it is true what they say, isn't it Brian?"

"What's true?"

"It is true that no matter how things change…they do remain the same," explained Dex.

"What is that supposed to mean?" asked Brian.

"It's real simple, Brian. I came back home with my family, expecting that I would find that we have grown closer as a family…not further apart. We were once very competitive in our youth, but we were also close. It seems that you have held on to your competitiveness. I told you brother, I have changed. I only have the love of Christ in my heart now."

"Oh boy, here we go again," said Brian.

"Brian, in my youth, I was a sinner who was lost. Now I am a sinner who has been saved by the grace of God. I have been set free from the bondage of Satan who came to deceive, steal and destroy us."

"Well, you need to save that sermon for someone who needs it my brother. Right now, I got my own sermon to preach. By the way…speaking of preachers…let me ask you something. You can answer this, I'm sure," said Brian.

"What's that?"

"Do you think it is a 'bigger' sin for a preacher when he sins against God? I mean, will he be punished harder than his congregation if he does something wrong?" asked Brian.

"Well, I would say that God knows all our hearts. God knows that we are subject to temptation and can fall from time to time. I will also say that because of the victory that we have in Jesus, we can be forgiven for our sins, if we repent," explained Dex.

"You are not answering my question about the preacher though. What responsibility does the preacher have as the head of his church? What if he sins? Isn't he supposed to be the leader of the church? Shouldn't God hold him to a higher standard than the rest of us?"

"Brian, I am not fully matured in the faith as of yet. I still have much growth to do. However, I can tell you that I think that a preacher does have a special place in the kingdom of God. IF God has called him into the ministry, and he fervently seeks the will of God for his vision for the Church, God will supply all his needs. As long as the pastor stays in the will of God, God will protect him from the guises of Satan. That does not mean that he will be immune from temptation, however. He is still human. But the thing you must remember is, we are all sinners. All of us are subject to sin, including the preacher. But when we do, and Christ is in us, and we are in Christ, he is the mediator for us. In him, we have an advocate with God to forgive our sins and cast them into the sea of forgetfulness. He does not hold our sins against us. But we must have a relationship with Christ first," explained Dex.

"You sound like a preacher yourself," retorted Brian. "When are you going to start?"

"I already have. When you receive salvation through Christ, you become a minister of Christ's gospel," said Dex.

"Well, I just thought you would tell me that preachers would go to hell first because they hold a higher position in the church," said Brian. "Are you sure you know what you are telling me?

"Why not come with me and Norma to the next bible study at our church and let's find out what the Bible say's. ...Can't hurt you, that's for sure. How about it?"

"I have to get back to you. I...I have to check with my wife. I'll get back to you later," said Brian.

Brian hung up the phone. He stood silent for a few seconds before turning towards his wife who was awaiting a response from him. He spoke.

"Ooo... k a y..."

"Okay what?" asked Sharon.

"This guy will not give up. He simply will not quit!"

"What happened now?" asked Sharon.

"Ah...do you want to go to Bible study with them Wednesday night?"

"Sure, why not?"

"WHAT? You do?"

"Sure, why not?"

"Baby, I told him I didn't have time to go to no Bible study... and for what? You go to your church on Sunday. What do you need to go to somebody else's church for Bible study?" asked Brian.

"Actually Brian, WE need to go together, to somebody's Bible study. You know, the last time we studied the Bible together was when my mother came over last year. I don't have a problem with going to their church. I really don't." said Sharon.

Brian stood silent watching his wife speak words he was not comfortable with. He felt strange listening to anyone who brought up the subject of church, or Christianity, or religion. He began to search his soul for evidence that he could do this. He reasoned that his life was just fine as it was before Dexter came to town to stir up the nest that he had made for himself and his family. Now, his wife is showing signs that she was assisting Dexter in stirring up his settled spirit.

How was he going to handle this situation? He could not let Dexter maneuver him as he used to when they were younger. Yet, if he went along with Dex's invitation that was exactly the way things would turn out. Brian spoke.

"I think YOU can go, if you want to. I'm not going!"

"Baby, I do not want to go without you. Why can't we go together?" asked Sharon.

"Because!"

"Come on, Brian... why not? ...Let's go together."

"Listen baby. You don't understand. It's really not that I don't want to go with you. I have no problem with that. That's not it at all."

"Well, what is it then, Brian?"

"You know I told you about Dex always wanting to be the one in charge when we were teens. It was always what he wanted to do. We all followed him in whatever HE wanted to do. Now, he's trying to do the same thing again. He's trying to come here after all this time and turn our routine up-side-down. I don't like it. I don't like it at all. He's the one that was away. That was his choice. Now he's back here trying to do the same *thing he was doing before. I am not going to let him get away with it...not anymore," said Brian.*

"I really think you are taking this control thing too far, Brian. My sense is that Dexter's thoughts are far from trying to show some sort of control over you as he used to," said Sharon.

"You might think so but I know him better than you do. The point is, I am not going to give in and let him talk me into joining somebody's church."

"Don't you think you should join somebody's church, honey? We've talked about this so many times...You need to accept Christ for yourself. I can't do it for you. This is a personal thing. It is not about pleasing a person or even a preacher. The Bible says..."

"I don't want to hear about what the Bible says, Sharon. I don't need you preaching to me, too. Just let me take my time on this. I am not ready to start giving my money to some preacher who goes out and buys that big house with an elevator in it, and that big Rolls Royce that he trades in every year for a bigger one," said Brian.

Sharon moved closer to Brian and placed her left hand on his right shoulder as she leaned forward. She spoke softly.

"As many as received him, to them He gave the right to become children of God, even to those who believe in His name. That was from John 1:12. Honey we must all receive Christ through faith in him. When we do, we are saved by God's grace. There is nothing we can do to deserve his salvation or to earn it through our works. It is a 'gift' from God. You remember my pastor said that in his sermon on the first Sunday last month?" asked Sharon.

"Yeh, I remember. Any way... Like I said...you can go to Bible study with them...I am not ready. Listen Baby, I need to go to the store to pick up a few things. Do you need anything?" asked Brian.

"No, I don't need anything. You always have somewhere to go whenever this subject comes up!"

"I'll be back in a little bit," said Brian.

Chapter 3

B rian left for the convenient store at about 8 pm. He made a mental
note as he backed out of the driveway, that his son Greg had not
taken the empty trash cans in from the curb. He promised himself
that he would talk to that boy, again when he returned. At 8:10 pm, Brian
pulled up to the stoplight, a distance of 2 blocks from his favorite store. As
he waited for the light to turn green, he was unexpectedly surprised by a
hooded figure that appeared in his rear view mirror. The figure, appearing
to be a homeless man, walked briskly towards the drivers' side--his hand
reached out silently--asking for money. Brian's window was rolled up, but
he felt threatened by the boldness of the person. He thought to himself,
'don't roll down the window'. Hurry up light so I can get out of here…
The intruder to Brian's space knocked on the window with his fist. Brian
motioned his hands to tell the intruder to move away from him. He became
more and more agitated, as he began to predict the light changing to green.
Within a flash, he saw another ominous figure approaching his car from
the rear passenger side. Brian's emotional state became increasingly excited.
His adrenalin flowed like a rocket reaching the outer bounds of the earths'
atmosphere. He refused to become a victim of a carjacking. To sit stoically
like a sitting duck, was against all rationale. He decided finally, to drive
through the red light to remove himself from the threat he perceived. He
pressed the accelerator pedal and catapulted the car into the intersection.

The lights of an oncoming vehicle loomed large. With the lights getting larger by the millisecond, Brian was blinded temporarily, and tried to escape an impact by leaning forward and tensing every muscle in his body. He panicked and held his breath in anticipation of the collision about to happen. It appeared to him as though the oncoming car was trying to deliberately hit him. He reacted within his reptilian brain, which told him to turn loose of the steering wheel and protect his face. He yelled!

"OH GOD, NOoooo!"

The oncoming driver's brakes were heard squealing as it slammed into Brian's car, with the force of a tank. Brian had his seat belt on, but was thrown with great force against the driver's side door, and then into the passenger seat. The car was pushed onto the curb on the right side of the street and crashed into a metal traffic light pole. The impact was so strong; it bent the pole from four feet above the ground. It sent the fixture crashing down on top of his car. Brian was knocked unconscious and suffered lacerations and deep cuts all over his face. He was bleeding from his mouth and ears. Blood flowed down the back of his head. The intersection resembled an Iraqi battlefield with metal and glass sprawled across 40 yards. The truck that slammed into Brian was wedged into the driver's door panel, with his lights still shinning. The driver exited his truck with fear and concern.

"HEY! …ARE YOU ALRIGHT?" yelled the driver of the truck. HEY…Oh my GOD; SOMEBODY HELP…HELP!"

The smell of gasoline was strong. The engine was not running but steam bellowed out of the pick up trucks' radiator. The driver felt his life was threatened by the spillage of gasoline, and possible fire. He yelled!

"SOMEBODY CALL 911… CALL 911."

Several drivers approaching the intersection, hurried to the accident to offer help. A teenager driving behind the damaged pickup truck called 911 for help. The two homeless men who had approached Brian's car and caused him to speed through the red light, also approached the scene. They surveyed the damage they knew they were responsible for, and decided to vacate the scene. Partly because they saw Brian was not moving, and because the police were arriving within 30 seconds or so, they left in different directions. The EMS and Fire Department arrived on the scene shortly thereafter.

"Get these people back. Are there any witnesses' here?" ordered the senior officer at the scene.

Brian was extracted from the passenger side of the car. The EMS checked his pulse, as they worked to secure him to the transport gurney, before he would be taken to the nearest hospital.

"Are you guys ready? Do you have it, or do you want an escort," asked the officer.

"I think we'll be okay. It's about a five minute trip for us to the County hospital. That one will be better for this guy-- He's pretty banged up." answered the EMS driver.

"Okay, here we go—hit the lights Phil!"

The trip took only five minutes because of the light traffic. As they entered through the entrance of the Emergency Room, two trauma doctors and two nurses met them. The lead doctor spoke.

"Hi, I'm Dr. Albright! Tell me what you got."

"We have a 47 year old male 'MVA' patient with multiple lacerations; head trauma; massive internal bleeding; pupils fixed and dilated," reported the head EMS Technician.

"I got it. What have you given him?" asked the doctor.

"I started an 18 gauge IV with 1000 cc's of normal saline infusion, and a hard collar. His vitals are 90/60 with pulse of 40."

"Okay, let's get X-rays of the skull and c-spine, chest and pelvis. Let's move it people…STAT!" ordered the doctor.

Brian was rushed into the emergency room with great speed. His fate was now in the hands of the doctors, and in the ONE who could answer the unhindered prayers of the righteous. One of the doctors told a nurse to call the Chaplin on duty, and to call Brian's wife. The head nurse Donna, went to her station and notified the Chaplin of the arrival of the new patient. She then called information for the number of Brian Simon, and called his home. When someone answered, she spoke.

"Hello is this Mrs. Simon?" asked the nurse.

""Yes it is. …Who is this?"

"Mrs. Simon, this is Donna. I am a nurse at the County Hospital."

"Yes, what is it? …What is it?"

"Mrs. Simon, your husband has been in an auto accident. You should get down here right away!"

"NOOOO! Oh God no! … No, no!"

"Mrs. Simon, can you get here right away? You need to get someone to drive you here right away, hon," said the nurse.

Sharon dropped the phone to the floor as she continued crying, uncontrollably. Greg came out of his room to see his mother on the floor on her knees and in pain.

"Mom, what is it? What's the matter, mom?"

Sharon tried to talk but she could not. Her mouth made motions, but no words came out. Greg began to panic when he saw the phone on the floor next to his mother. He picked up the phone and said…

"Hello, who is this? Who is this?"

"This is Donna at the County Hospital. Are you a family member of Mr. Simon?" asked the lead nurse.

""YES! I'm his son. What is it?"

"Your dad has been in an accident. Please, can you get your mother here as soon as possible? You need to get here right away, okay?"

"Okay, okay…okay. Mom, come on! Mom, we got to get to the hospital! MOM, come on…Oh God…Mom, get up…we got to go, okay?"

Sharon rose slowly with Greg's help. She continued to hold her hand over her mouth as she wept. Greg was nervous and shaking while grabbing the keys to his mother's car. He managed to get her into the front seat on the passenger's side and hurriedly backed out of the garage. He sped down the street as fast as he could while driving through several stop signs before he reached the freeway entrance. Within fifteen minutes, they arrived at the hospital. As they arrived, the EMS, which just transported Brian to the Emergency Room was about to pull out. Greg spoke.

"Mom, wait here while I ask these guy's if they know where we should go."

"Excuse me sir, do you know anything about a man who was brought to this hospital after an accident a few minutes ago?" asked Greg.

"Yes, are you looking for Mr. Simon?"

"Yes that's him. That's my Dad," said Greg. "How is he, sir? Is he going to be alright?"

"You can go through that door right there. When you get inside, ask for the lead nurse on duty. They will let you know how he's doing, okay. Keep the faith son! … Keep praying!"

Sharon was still speechless when Greg returned to the car. She was in total shock at what has happened to her husband. All she could think about now is, whether Brian will make it through this alive. He has to make it. She begged for that blessing in her mind. She knew there was nothing she could do to save him now. It was all up to the doctors. More important than that, he was in God's hands, if he was going to survive. God knows how much she has prayed for her husband's Salvation. He knows that he is a good man who had not accepted Christ as his savior. Would God be forgiving of his stubbornness? Would he give her another chance to try and convince Brian that God is in control of his life, and not Brian? What if he didn't make it? How would she go on? What is God's will for her and her family? Greg spoke.

"Mom, come with me. The driver of that EMS truck told me we can go in through that door over there. Are you going to be alright? Can you talk to me, mom?"

Sharon shook her head…no. She appeared to be in a daze without the ability to communicate with anyone. Greg led her into the emergency room entrance where they were met by one of the nurses.

"Are you Mrs. Simon," asked the nurse.

Sharon nodded her head…yes.

"Come with me Mrs. Simon. Your husband is in surgery now. Let me get you to a comfortable area so you can wait," said the nurse.

"Can you tell us what is happening with my Dad, nurse? Is he going to be okay?" asked Greg.

"I will find out what the status of the operation is for you as soon as possible. Mrs. Simon, can I get you something to drink? What would you like, some coffee or a coke?" inquired nurse Donna.

Sharon grabbed the arm of the nurse.

"SAVE MY HUSBAND! ...SAVE MY HUSBAND! That's what you can get for me!"

"Excuse me," cried a voice from behind the nurse. It was the Chaplin for the hospital.

"Mrs. Simon, my name is Pablo Gutierrez. I am the Chaplin here at the hospital. May I have a moment with you? ...Please have a seat."

Sharon sat down while looking into the face of the Chaplin to try and find a clue as to what news he had about the condition of Brian.

"Greg, go call your uncle Dex. and Adam. Tell them what's happened, and tell them where we are."

The Chaplin spoke...

"Mrs. Simon, do you wish for me to pray with you at this time?

"Yes I do." said Sharon.

The prayer took a few minutes. Sharon cried during the time of prayer by the Chaplin. The nurse stayed with them and said 'Amen' when the prayer ended. She turned to leave when Sharon called for her to wait.

"Please let me know something. When can I see him?"

"I will, Mrs. Simon. I will be right back."

The Chaplin settled down in a chair next to Sharon. He engaged in conversation about what she did for a living and where she was raised. He wanted to know where she went to school and how long she and Brian had been married. Sharon wanted to get some news from the nurse about Brian's condition. She was anxious to have the nurse return as she looked towards the hallway where she last saw her. She spoke.

"I appreciate your conversation Pastor, but I'm sorry. I need to know what's happening... I'm sorry."

"I understand, my sister. Would you like for me to wait here with you, or would you like to be alone for now?"

"You can wait, Pastor. Please stay with me."

Greg returned from making the two phone calls to his uncles. He reported to his mother that his uncle Dex. was on his way to the hospital with his wife Norma, but he was not able to get in touch with his uncle Adam. The nurse returned and spoke.

"Mrs. Simon, your husband has been stabilized. While he is still in critical condition, we are optimistic that he will come through the operation. He did suffer a lot of trauma to his head and chest area. He does have a strong pulse and his pressure is better. It looks like about another 3 to 4 hours before we will know how things will look. Keep your prayers going!"

"Thank God! ... Thank God! ... Thank you God! He's going to be okay," said Sharon.

Chapter 4

Back at the accident site, the police had cordoned off the area around the intersection, and had begun to interview the driver of the pick-up truck. The driver assured the police that he had a green light when the car he hit, violated his right of way. While the interview was going on, the young lady who called 911 entered into the accident zone to report that she saw a couple of guys leaving the scene after they checked the driver in the car. She reported that they looked suspicious as they left the scene. One of the police officers spoke.

"Why do you say they looked suspicious, lady?"

"It was the way they approached the car; looked in at the driver; and then they ran away in different directions. But, I think they both wound up behind that service station over there. I think they were there before the accident happened."

"Why …have you seen them before on this corner?" asked one officer.

"I pass this way every day, going to work and back. I have seen two guys on this intersection everyday, asking for money. That could have been the same two guys," said the woman.

"Which way did you see them go, again?"

"Over there, behind that service station."

"Okay partner, I'll check it out," said the junior officer.

"Okay, be careful. ...Maam let me get some information on you. May I see your drivers' license?"

The Officer heard the sound of a cell phone ringing. The sound was coming from the wrecked car. The officer walked over to the vehicle and picked up the phone. He pushed the talk button and spoke.

"Hello.". ..."This is Officer Harley. Who was it you were looking for?" ... Are you his wife? Well he has been in an accident... Yes ...he is at the County Hospital...I couldn't tell you that Maam...You will have to call or visit the hospital. Yes maam...you're welcome."

Officer Harley's radio carried the voice of his junior partner.

"Charlie 14 to 21."

"21, go ahead"

"I got 2 suspects that fit the description of the men in question behind the Mobil station ...clear."

"Okay 14, I'll be right there."

"Mam, sit in your car for me until I check this situation out. I might need you to ID these two for me. ...Dispatch, this is 21."

"Dispatch, go ahead!"

"We are going to check out two possible witnesses to the accident. Witnesses are behind the Mobil station. 14 has them in detention. ... Clear!"

"21 standby." ... 21 you're clear!"

Officer Harley drove to the rear of the station to assist his partner investigating the two men. He exited his patrol car, slowly.

"Okay Neil, what you got?"

"I got no ID for either of them. I got this one here with the hood who say's he never been at this corner before now. He said he came here to get a pack of cigarettes."

"You got anything on the other one?"

"No, not yet! You want to take him?"

Harley escorted the second suspect to his patrol car, located about 25 yards away from his partner.

"Sir, come over here for me," asked Officer Harley.

"*Sir, what's your name?*

"*Huh?*"

"*What is your name?*"

"*Alvin Dotson*"

"*Alvin, you got some ID for me? ...How do I know you are who you say you are?*"

"*I lost my wallet. But that's my name, though.*"

"*You hold on for me ...What's your date of birth?*"

"*May 5, 1975.*"

"*Okay, hold on ...21 to Dispatch...*"

"*Dispatch, go ahead...*"

"*...Run one for me on a black male; date of birth 'Mary-Adam-Young 5, 1975 ...clear*"

"*Dispatch to 21...standby!*"

"*Okay, Mr. Dotson. Tell me what were you doing here at this intersection tonight?*"

"*I came here to git a pac a cigarettes.*"

"*How much do cigarettes cost?*" asked Officer Harley.

"*Dey cost a couple 'a bucks.*"

"*Let me see what's in your pockets, Mr. Dotson.*"

Mr. Dotson reached into his pockets and turned them inside out. They were empty. He looked at the officer. Officer Harley looked at him and asked the burning question on his mind.

"*What were you going to buy the cigarettes **with**, Mr. Dotson?*"

"*Okay...Look... Officer, I had nothin to do wit dat accident!*"

"*You had nothing to do with WHAT accident, Mr. Dotson?*"

"*I mean, I didn do nothin to dat guy. It wun't me.*"

"*You didn't do WHAT, Mr. Dotson?*"

"*I didn spook dat guy! Wayne wus da one dat rapped on his windo. I never said nothin to da guy. ...**He just took off!** ... We wus goin ask him for a couple of bucks ...dat's all. We didn do nothin...He just took off like a bat outa' hell,*" declared Alvin.

The dispatcher called Officer Harley...

"Dispatch to 21."

"21, clear."

"We have a black male with a DOB 5-5-75; he's 5'-10" approximately 170 pounds, medium build... His name is Alfonso Dobson... He has an outstanding warrant for parole violation...clear!"

Officer Harley called his partner over, after handcuffing and placing Alvin (Alfonso) into his car. Harley spoke...

"Hey Neil, I think these guys are the ones who spooked the driver and caused him to panic. It looks like the two of them need to be taken down to the station. This guy gave me an incorrect name, and we got a warrant on him. I think we got enough probable cause here. Go ahead, cuff that one, and let's take 'em in."

Chapter 5

Meanwhile at the hospital, Dexter and his wife Norma had arrived. They were sitting with Sharon when the nurse returned for more news about Brian's condition. She reported...

"Things are looking better. They are getting him stabilized and he will be in ICU in about 2 hours. You won't be able to talk to him because he'll still be out. But you can see him in a couple of hours, okay?"

"That's wonderful! Thank you nurse," said Dexter.

He hugged Sharon, Norma, and Greg at the same time. He was excited that the report was positive and couldn't wait to see Brian, even if it had to be in the ICU. He asked about Adam.

"Did anyone call him yet?"

"Yes, I called him but he wasn't home. I didn't have his cell number," advised Greg.

"I got his cell. I'll call him now," said Dexter.

After the officers took the two men in for questioning, and turned them over to the desk Sergeant, Officer Harley decided to take the cell phone that was left in Brian's car, to his wife at the hospital. This was not standard procedure for an officer to even answer a cell phone call. Harley knew he was beyond his authority, but the softer side of him led him to do so. When he walked in, he greeted Sharon, and offered his condolences for their suffering. Then he explained that the phone rang while it was on the floorboard of his car. He went on to explain that he spoke to a woman who had inquired where Brian was.

"Did she say who she was?" asked Sharon.

"No maam …and I didn't ask her when I found out that it was not you, his wife."

"It could have been one of our sisters!" said Dexter. "Perhaps you can take a look at the call register on the phone, and then you may recognize the number."

Sharon gave the phone to Dexter. She felt that he could get right to the feature on the phone much faster than she would. Dexter did the search and found the last call made to that phone. The officer saluted Sharon, wished her the best and left. Dexter spoke.

"Okay, here it is. Let's see…the number is 333-331-3131…. Does that ring a bell to you?"

"333 is the area code?" asked Sharon. "I don't know anybody in that area code."

"Well, you can call back if you like," said Dexter.

"Wait," said Norma. "Do you want to do that right now, Sharon?"

"I don't know, Norma. I can't think about that right now. But in the back of my mind, I do want to know who it was? …That's my question. … Who was it?"

The lead nurse Donna, came in to report that Brian will be moved to ICU, room A115. Sharon, Norma, Greg, and Dexter got up and headed to the wing where he will be moved to see him. After they found the room, Dexter asked Sharon if they could pray first, before Brian would be moved to the room. She agreed. Dexter led them in prayer.

"Father, we honor you as the living God who knows all, and the one true God who hears our hearts. Give us strength dear God, to stand in the midst of enormous trials, and to be able to stand for those who are weaker than we are, during this time of pain and suffering. Forgive us father for our sins, and keep us within your will, as we seek to walk according to the direction of the Holy Spirit. We thank you for our dear brother, father, and husband, whose life you have spared. We give thanks to you in Jesus' name…Amen."

Dexter felt that he was a man of principle. He had invested a great deal of his personal reputation in showing his family that he was the leader that he has always been. Only now, Dexter would be put to the test of helping to sort out the direction their future would take, since Brian will require a lot of his time and attention. Never before has he been challenged to step up to the plate of taking on the leadership role, as this time would require. He felt that he could not rely on their past experiences to dictate their future relationship. Instead, a new one had to be forged, and he must step up to lead the way. To date, Brian and Adam largely rejected his spiritual leadership. The direct approach he pursued was not totally effective. While he contemplated his next move, Adam showed up, wide-eyed and nervous. He was alone as he spoke.

"Is he awake? What's up? How's he doing Sharon?"

"I'm okay, Adam. He's still in the operating room."

"What happened? Do we know how this happened to him? I mean…was it his fault…did he do something that he shouldn't have, or was somebody else at fault?" asked Adam.

Dexter spoke.

"At this time, we don't know what happened. All we know is that he got hit from the drivers' side of the car. Now that means he either ran the light, or somebody else ran the light and hit him. The person that hit him must have been going pretty fast to do the damage they did to him. He's in pretty bad shape Adam."

"Man, I can't believe this happened…We were just together a few hours ago," said Adam.

"He was only home less than an hour before he left to go to the store," said Sharon. "It must have happened within ten minutes after he left."

"Excuse us, Sharon. Norma, we will be right outside and down the hall," said Dexter. "Let me talk to you Adam."

The two of them walked to another waiting room down the hall. Dexter placed his left arm around Adam's shoulder. They walked while Dexter talked.

"Adam, Brian will need all the prayers we all have in us. I am concerned *about what he will be like when the recovery starts. I mean, his injuries were so extensive, there might be some concern that he might not have full mobility, and have the full capacity of his mind."*

"Did the doctors say that?" asked Adam.

"No, we have not spoken to the doctors yet. I am basing this on what he was like when he came in, and how long the operation is taking. I didn't want to say this around Sharon. She is going to need some very strong support when she sees him, I'm sure. He will no doubt be swollen and disfigured, with tubes and the like. Can you imagine?"

"Oh man, this is unreal! We just saw him a couple of hours ago, Dex. How can this happen? …Just like that, he's gone from full health to lying on an operating table, within hours."

Adam could not hold on to his emotions any longer. He slumped down onto a chair and cried. Dexter placed his hand on his left shoulder, but did not speak. Adam could only ask a rhetorical question…Why?

"Brian is a good guy, Dex. He didn't deserve this. Why did God let this happen? He's a good guy…he is a good guy…"

Dexter tried to remember the right words to say to Adam at a time like this. Should he try to remember a quote from the bible, or should he just let him vent? Is this the time to talk about having life through the spirit? Would Adam be accepting of the explanation of a compassionate God who has compassion on whom he chooses? What should we say then, (Romans 9:14) Is God unjust? For God said to Moses, "I will have mercy on whom I have mercy." Would Adam understand that God is a sovereign God, and answers to no one? What should he say to console his younger brother, who loves Brian as much as anyone else could? The sudden ring of the cell phone he was holding since the officer delivered it to Sharon, broke silence from Dexter.

"Oh, it's Brian's phone! You want to answer it?" asked Dexter.

Adam reached out his hand, took the phone, and pressed the talk button.

"Hello, who is this? … Who? … This is Adam, Brian's brother… Who did you say you were? …Tara? …Simon? Do you mean Brian's other

daughter? …Are you calling about your father? I am not the one to say…
I think you should wait until his wife is not around. I understand that, but
she doesn't know you…I know you should be able to see your dad, but not
now, Tara. It would not be the best right now. He's not out from surgery
yet. Here's what I will do…I will keep you informed about his status…
and…No, I will…I will call you and let you know his condition…Okay…
Okay, I will. Bye!"

"Adam, what in the world was that all about?" asked Dexter.

Dex., you DON'T want to know, man. You really don't want to know!"
said Adam.

"But did you say…Brian's other daughter? … What other daughter,
Adam?"

"Dex., Brian never wanted to talk about her…I would rather not go
into it, man."

"But you might have a disaster of catastrophic proportions," said Dexter.
You did say that Sharon doesn't know about her, didn't you?"

"Yes I said that. She doesn't know!"

"Well, did YOU know about her Adam?" asked Dexter.

"I knew her since she was two years old. But, I forgot about her, since
Brian stopped talking about her when she was about 6 years old."

"How old is she now?"

"She should be about …16r or 17, now."

"That's how old Greg is, Adam."

"I know, Dex., I know."

"Well, obviously, this cannot come out right now. There is no way
Sharon can handle this bombshell. I think you've got to protect her from
this. She's pretty fragile right now… You agree Adam?"

"I have never said anything, Dex. Remember that I knew about her for
some time. Why do you think you have to tell me that?"

"Okay…okay. I apologize. I think this thing could affect the relationship
of the whole family and how we will interact with each other in the future.
Just think of it Adam… All these questions surrounding her age; who is her
mother; how long the relationship went on, etc, etc. etc.," said Dexter.

"Hey Dex., none of us are perfect, right? We have all sinned, right? So, let's not get on some high horse and castrate Brian for some 'affair' he may have had sixteen years ago."

"Does it sound like that's what I am doing, Adam?"

"Yes, it does. And I don't give a damn what anybody says…none of us can criticize him about this girl. I can tell you one thing; he always took care of her. He never let her go wanting for anything over the years. I know that for a fact!"

"I applaud him for that Adam. But what's going to happen now that we know she wants to see her father here in the hospital? You know Sharon will never leave Brian's bedside. If he stays here for six months, she's going to be right there by his side 24/7. What's going to happen then? What do you see Adam? It sure sound to me as if this other daughter will not leave things along. Sounds like she wants to see her father and she couldn't care less who knows what …right?"

"Like I said Dex, I am not going to be the one to stand in her way, but I am not going to go running in there to announce who she is either. I guess we will have to see how this thing plays out. I will keep her advised of Brian's condition. Maybe that will keep her away …for now.

Norma came down the hall to find Dexter. Dexter and Adam stopped their conversation to acknowledge her presence. She spoke.

"Honey, I need to get back to the kids. Did you want to stay here until Brian gets into the room and maybe call me when you are ready to come home?"

"Sure baby, that would be fine. Let me call you!"

"You guys don't have any kids," said Adam.

"Oh…I mean the dogs…the miniature Schnauzers. Believe me; they act worse than kids when we are gone too long. They tear up everything in the house," said Norma.

Norma went back to the waiting room to touch and say goodbye to Sharon. Dexter and Adam accompanied her. Sharon had been given a sedative to quiet her nerves while she waited. She acknowledged Norma's show of care and concern by giving her a hug before she left. Greg had *taken off his coat and placed it over his mothers' chest to keep her warm. Sharon settled back down into her chair and closed her eyes. She tried to imagine what it would be like when she gets to see her husband. She knew she wanted to show him she loved him by giving him a big hug and kiss. She thought better of that scenario however, because of his injuries. For the moment, she was pleased to know that he was going to make it through this ordeal. She said a silent prayer for the doctors, and nurses who attended to him. She was thankful for the family who was giving her support. She especially appreciated the involvement of her brother-in-law (Dexter) who was so sincere in bringing the word to his brother. He really has tried hard, she thought.*

Perhaps, when Brian recovers, he might appreciate the words Dexter had spoken to him so many times in the past. It was now midnight, and the doctor who performed the microscopic surgery to clamp off and repair the leaking blood vessels in Brian's brain, entered the waiting area. He spoke.

"Hello!"

"Oh hello doctor," said Sharon.

"How are you holding up?"

"I'm doing the best I can…how's my husband, doctor?"

"Well…let me say that he is a lot better than several hours ago. I think we got the inside sealed off from the outside," the doctor said, humorously.

"Dexter said, "That would be important wouldn't it?"

"To put it in laymen's terms, he is out of the woods right now, Mrs. Simon. But, there are acres of forest all around him. In less than forty-five minutes, he'll be sent to ICU. We will be monitoring him constantly, to see if there is going to be any infection. Actually, we need 24 hours…that will tell us what we need to know right now. But, he's a pretty strong guy. You must have been feeding him some strong Louisiana foods, huh?" asked the doctor.

"He loves my mom's Gumbo." Greg explained.

"I would too," said the doctor. "Well…let me get back in here and help them rap things up so you can get to see him. He does have some swelling,

especially in the head area. That is normal after this type of trauma. So, you need to know that when you see him, okay?"

"Okay, thank you doctor," said Dexter.

"Dexter, would you use that phone to call Brenda and her husband for me. I just realized that I did not tell them what happened since they are out of town. They went to my son-in-laws family in East Texas, and supposed to return later tonight. I just want to leave a message for her to call me on her dad's phone," said Sharon.

"I can do that. What's her number?"

"Greg, do you remember your sisters cell number...I keep forgetting it," said Sharon.

"Yes, its' 203-231-2233."

"I got it. I'll call her now."

"By the way, did you find out who made that call to Brian's number earlier?" asked Sharon.

"Well, yes...and...no."

Silence filled the air. Dexter started dialing Brenda's number. Sharon looked at Dexter from the corner of her left eye. She waited for Dexter to answer her. Dexter turned away from Sharon as he placed the phone up to his right ear. He began to slowly walk away from her without answering her question, or even looking at her. Sharon was quiet in her speech, but her mind had a lot of activity racing through it. She could hear Dexter leaving a message on the cell phone for Brenda, as he instructed her to call Brian's cell number. He hung up-He spoke.

"Listen guys...everyone's been here a long time now, and I'm getting hungry. I have an idea. Adam and I will go get something to eat for everyone, since there is no cafeteria open at the hospital. How does that sound Sharon...Greg?"

"Sounds good," responded Greg.

"Okay," said Sharon. "But I don't want any chicken. Maybe if you can find a Chinese food store open. That would be fine for me. If not, just get me a salad at Wendy's."

"Okay, let's go Adam," prompted Dexter.

Chapter 6

Adam and Dexter left at a fast pace. They both knew the importance of getting away from Sharon and her questions about that cell phone call. They inquired at the nurses' station how to exit to the parking lot at the rear of the hospital. As they exited the rear entry of the hospital emergency exit door, Adam slowed his pace of walking to fix his eyes upon a figure walking towards the hospital in a brisk manner. Dexter turned to Adam and signaled for him to catch up. Adam reached his right hand out to Dexter to attempt to slow his walk as well. Dexter spoke.

"Why are you slowing down Adam?"

"Just wait a second Dex…Hold on just a few minutes."

Adam continued to fix his gaze upon the moving character making its way through the parking lot. He resembled a lion in Africa, as it was stalking its prey. Dexter looked in the direction Adam was looking in to see what caught Adams attention. He could tell it was the image of a female that caught Adams eye, but he himself did not recognize her. He reasoned that Adam must think he knows her, even from this distance.

Dexter spoke again.

"Do you see somebody you know, Adam?"

"Dex., …if I am not mistaken, …I think you are looking at Brian's other daughter, coming through the parking lot."

"NO!" said Dexter. "It couldn't be her, Adam! You told her NOT to come to the hospital...right? Didn't you say...?"

"YES!" Yes, I told her, but that don't mean a damn thing, man. I have not seen that girl in a while, but... it... sure... looks ...like ...that could be her."

"Adam, lets go over there so we can get a better look at her. Lets head her off before she gets into the hospital...before she..."

"Okay, come on!" said Adam.

They walked briskly at an angle to intercept the young girl before she entered the entry door to the hospital. As the two of them gained ground on the young woman about to enter the hospital door, she realized that she was being approached by them, and began to panic. She caught their movement out of the left corner of her eye, as they appeared that they were headed in her direction. She stepped up her pace. Adam, with Dexter following, was thirty yards away from her when she began to run.

Adam yelled...

"Hello...Ma'am...Ma'am...Excuse me! ... Tara is that you?"

The young woman whirled around to face the men, just as she reached the door. She spoke through her excited breath...

"Who the hell are you? ... What the hell are you chasing me for? ... Don't come any closer, or I will spray you with this mace I have!"

"No, no...we are not trying to hurt you. Are you Tara?" asked Adam.

"Yes, I'm Tara...**who are you?**"

"Tara, I'm Adam! ...Remember me? I'm Brian's brother, your dad, remember? ...This is our oldest brother Dexter. I talked to you on the phone earlier, when you called."

"Oh, okay, right ...I remember you from when I was younger. You came by my house with my dad when I was about 8 or 9 years old," said Tara.

"Listen, I told you this was not a good time to see your father, Tara. His wife and son are in there waiting on him to come out of surgery, and it would not be a good idea for you to be there, right Dexter?"

"Tara, we were just going to get something to eat. Would you join us? We will be right back."

"Alright! But I'm telling you, don't try to talk me out of seeing my dad before something happens to him, and I don't get the chance to tell him I love him," demanded Tara.

Tara joined Dexter and Adam in Adams car. They drove three blocks before they spotted a Chinese restaurant. It was closed. Continuing on another four blocks, Dexter spotted a Wendy's drive-thru. The inside restaurant was still open. Dexter suggested that they go inside and order their food. Tara went along with the suggestion because she wanted to find out what both of them wanted to tell her about her father. Although she was only sixteen years old, she had a lot of 'street smarts', and would not accept any attempt to short circuit her getting in to the ICU, this night. Adam was stoic and remained low-keyed. Adam wanted the usual hamburger, fries and chocolate shake. Funny how some things never changed Adam thought; that was his favorite fast food meal when they were younger. Adam proceeded to the counter to stand behind a long line of others waiting to satisfy their midnight cravings. Tara declined anything. Dexter felt that he should open the dialog concerning Tara's desire to see her father.

He spoke.

"I am delighted to meet you, young lady."

"Why is that? You never wanted to meet me before… None of you guys ever wanted to meet me… I ain't no fool now. …I always knew what the deal was with you Simons," said Tara.

"Well… please tell ME …please!" pleaded Dexter.

"I know how you guy's have always been secretive about everything. You guys never did anything to reach out to others. You have been protective of each other to the extent that you never wanted to know anything about me, or what interests I have. Nobody ever reached out to me or my mother to make us feel welcome. I can understand about my mother…but what about me? Why couldn't I have been included in the 'family's' affairs, get-togethers or reunions?"

Tara's' eyes began to tear. She began to tense in her jaws as she spoke. She had held in this feeling for a long time. She was upset that she was not raised by her father. She never had a father to sit on his lap, and rub *his head, and investigate his ears, just as she had imagined girls do to their fathers. Why the hell did he bring me into this world, if I couldn't have the love of a father AND a mother, she thought.* Adam returned with his order and sat down. He hoped that Dexter had resolved the issue at hand. He was unnerved to find that Tara had gotten very emotional about the situation they found themselves in. Since he was the only one who knew of her, he felt that he should seek to smooth over this encounter. Adam sat down next to Tara in the booth they were in, and began to rub his hands together to warm them. He spoke in a softened voice to Tara.

"Listen Tara, I know Dex told you about the situation going on inside that hospital. Now every since I met you some 8 or 9 years ago, I knew there would come a day that this type of encounter might happen. In fact, your dad had some concerns as well. Actually, he had more than concerns…he was scared to death that his wife and kids would find out about you. He just didn't know what to do about it. … See, the way I understand it, your mother threatened to expose your dad to the family, if he didn't marry her when you were first born," explained Adam.

"My mother has her own life. She is happy raising me as a single mother. She don't need a man in her life," said Tara.

"I'm sure that's true Tara. I don't dispute that. All I'm saying is your dad could not have a relationship with you or you mother, the way you would have wanted it, because he was in fear of what your mother would do to him if he continued it. She wanted him to leave his wife and new baby."

"Yeh, I heard that he had a son about the same age as I am."

"That suggests that my brother committed a sin against the teachings of the bible, Tara. The bible tells us that we should not commit adultery. Is your mother a believer in Christ and his teaching?" asked Dexter.

"She believes in Christ, yes!"

"You see, if she had sex with a person who was married, then she committed adultery and he committed fornication with her. They are both sins which can be forgiven. The Holy Spirit knows their hearts, and can bring them to repentance. Has your mother forgiven Brian for his sin against her?"

"I have no idea!"

"I am not asking you to speak for your mother...I'm just explaining how this whole forgiveness thing works. What about you, Tara? Have you forgiven your father?"

"Hell no! ...Why should I forgive him?"

"...Because forgiveness benefits you, sweetheart...not him! Unforgiveness does more harm to you, than it does to any person you have not forgiven. Have you ever considered that maybe your dad only wanted to have sex with your mother...and not have a baby? Suppose your mother decided she wanted to have a baby by him, to get him to leave his wife and marry her? I am definitely not saying that that was the situation, because I knew nothing about you or his affair with your mother until today. ...But, who should be held accountable here? BOTH! That's right, both. That's something you need to also talk to your mother about. But you can't go into that ICU room and confront a person who can't even know that you're there; to tell him you have not forgiven him for not being your dad, Tara... That's all I'm saying. Am I making sense?" asked Dexter?

"I understand what you're saying," said Tara.

Adam interjected.

"I would feel as you do too, Tara. But Dexter is right. I mean, if you went in there with the attitude that you want to confront those who you have not forgiven or have a problem with, how do you expect them to respond. And, what good would it do, AT... THIS...TIME?" That's all I'm saying. And you know what, I think we can work to get the family to begin to know who you are and make you feel a part of what's going on. Hell, I think Brian would like for his kids to know each other. But Dexter and I need to work on that. You follow me? You understand where I'm coming from?"

"Yes, I do. I understand what you're saying. I will say this...I want to see how you guys are going to act when you get to know me better. I want to see if you will turn your back against me...again. "

"What makes you say that, young lady? What should we expect to hear when we find out more about you? ...Do you have Aliens in your room?" asked Dexter, smiling.

Chapter 7

When Dexter and Adam returned to the hospital, they were alone. They had managed to convince Tara to wait until a more appropriate time to visit her dad in the hospital. Although they were gone for more than an hour, Sharon and Greg did not miss them because they were asleep when Dex and Adam returned. Quietly, Adam announced their arrival.

"Hey you guys, we're back."

Sharon awakened by stretching and yawning. She reached to touch Greg to awaken him. Dex removed the food from the bags and placed the containers on the table. He inquired about Brian.

"What's happening? Has anyone said anything yet?"

"The nurse came back about a half hour or so. We should be hearing something soon," said Greg.

"Okay, come and get it before it gets too hot or too cold," advised Dex.

"Oh oh…I think I got a call on Brian's' vibrating phone. I'll take it outside."

"NO! Give it to me, Adam…" said Sharon.

"Are you sure…?"

"Give me the phone, Adam."

"Hello, who is this?" asked Sharon.

"Oh hey baby...I am so glad you called...You guy's made it back okay?
...Listen Brenda...we are at the County hospital... yes ...your daddy had
an accident ...yes ...he's going to be okay ...he's going to be okay, sweetie...I
know...I know...but he's going to be okay. He should be in the recovery
room any minute now. ...Yes...you can come on down. ...We're in A333
in ICU. Okay... see you soon."

Sharon wiped the tears from her eyes. She felt emotionally drained.
She hugged her son as they released their emotions within each other's
arms. Greg held his mother tight as she quivered and squeezed out a
tiny prayer.

"Lord Jesus, please give us strength to bear this burden."

As they sat down to eat, no one spoke. They simply felt drained
of energy and needed to replenish their strength. The hospital seemed
unusually quiet. There was activity from the nurses and assistants,
including housekeeping. Only one other patient had passed their
waiting area since they had been there. Perhaps that was a good sign
for Brian. That meant that all available doctors were attending to him.
The nurse, who had kept the family up to date on the progress of the
surgery, returned. She was smiling as she came into the waiting area.
She spoke.

*"Well, he's in his room now. We are getting him situated with everything
now. It'll be just a few minutes, and you can go on in and see him. Are
you happy?"*

"Thank you nurse Donna," said Sharon. *"Thank you so much. You
bet we are happy...you bet."*

Sharon, Greg, Adam and Dex slowly walked into Brian's room.
Dex had both of his hands on Sharon's shoulders. Greg walked in
ahead of them all, as Adam brought up the rear. Two of the nurses
who assisted with the surgery were completing the adjustments on the
IV, and the oxygen tank. They offered their blessings to Sharon as she
approached the side of Brian's bed. She walked as if she did not want to
wake him. Her eyes were fixed on his eyes, which were closed. He was
breathing with the assistance of a machine, which took the pressure

off of his lungs. Brian's face was swollen, as Sharon knew it would be. However, she could not have imagined that it would be disfigured to the extent that it was. He simply did not resemble the husband that she knew and loved so much. Except for his chest cavity moving up and down because of the breathing machine, Brian was motionless. Sharon moved next to his left side, placed her hand over his forehead, and began to stroke him. Even though he was still unconscious, she whispered to him that she loved him. Greg and his Uncles walked up to the right side of the bed. Greg touched his right arm. He held back his tears as he surveyed his dad. Dexter said a silent prayer of thanks for the sparing of Brian's life. He felt relieved to see Brian as he turned to Adam to get a reading on his emotions. Adam stood motionless, crying within. This is really too much, he thought. This is my brother and my buddy. This in not supposed to happen, he thought. They all were content to just stand and look. No further communication needed to take place. As they continued in their vigil, Brenda and her husband entered the room. Brenda was emotional as she scrambled to get to her mother on the opposite side of the bed. They embraced as they both continued to release their emotions on each other's shoulder.

Brenda finally looked up, and at her father. She covered her mouth as she continued to cry. Her husband came to console her as she walked closer to the bed. There was not a dry eye in the room. Dexter reached out to clasp the hand of Greg and Adam. Adam reached out to touch Brenda and her husbands' hand, who touched the hand of Sharon. Sharon touched the forehead of Brian. Sharon prayed.

"*Precious Lord, take my hand, lead me on, and let me stand. I am tired, I am weak, I am worn. Through the storm, through the night, lead me on to the light, take my hand precious Lord, and lead me on. Father God, I can do nothing without you. You are my provider, my savior, my counselor, and my healer. Father God, your word says that you are a Spirit, and they that worship you must worship you in spirit and in truth. I surrender to your Holy Spirit, the only true God. Father forgive us for our sins, and draw us nearer to your son Jesus. Heal my husband, dear God, and save his soul.*

Father as you have raised others from the dead, I ask that you raise my husband from this hospital bed, that he may proclaim Jesus as his Lord and Savior. I pray this prayer in Jesus' name…Amen."

"Momma, he don't look the same," said Brenda.

"I know, honey. Your father is in bad shape. It was a terrible accident," explained Sharon.

"I feel so helpless. I feel like I can do something for him, but I don't know what. What can I do, mom?" asked Brenda.

"You can only pray for him baby. That's what we all can do, right Dexter?"

"You're right…let's just keep praying for him."

Chapter 8

For 11 years, Allison Tate was a legal assistant at a Law Firm that had been established for over 22 years. She had been recruited for her expertise in personal injury filings, and was considered one of the best assistants in town, thereby commanding a hefty salary. Allison liked her position of high esteem and carried herself accordingly. She worked out at the gym at least 3 times a week, and tried to eat healthy. She and her daughter lived in a condominium in an upscale part of town. By all accounts, Allison had a lifestyle that suggested that she was successful. She had devoted the past 16 years raising her daughter so that she would not have a need, or want for anything. She kept her in the best of clothing, and provided her with a one-year-old car just this year. She attended a private high school, with future plans to attend a university in the East when she graduates. It was late when Allison arrived home, but she could tell that her daughter was still up. She parked her car in the garage and entered the house through the kitchen area. Her daughter met her at the kitchen counter and spoke.

"Mom, you are not going to believe this…Well, I'm sure you will but let me tell you…"

"Tell me what, Tara?"

"My dad…my dad…he was in a accident!"

"*Your dad? …Brian?*"

"*Yes, mom…and he is not doing well at all!*"

"*How do you know that, Tara?*"

"*I was there mom, I was there, but I didn't see him!*"

Tara rushed to her mothers' arms as she cried. Allison was stunned at the news. She wanted to know more.

"*What happened, baby? Is he okay? How did you find out about it?*"

"*It was weird, mom. I called his cell phone number to talk to him, and wish him happy birthday. A policeman answered the phone and said he was in an accident, and that he was at the County Hospital.*"

"*How did you get…*"

"*Wait…mom; let me tell you the rest. Before I went to the hospital, I called the number again to see if it was true, and my Uncle Adam answered.*"

"*What?*"

"*Wait. There's more. He tried to tell me not to come to the hospital because his wife was there with him. Well, I went there anyway, and he and another Uncle I never heard of before named Dexter, got to me before I could get into the back door. They talked me into going to Wendy's and basically they talked me out of seeing him.*"

"*Baby, I am sorry about your dad. Did you find out how he's doing?*" asked Allison.

"*Not really!*"

"*Well here, let's call the hospital and find out. Even though I have not seen him in years, that does not mean I can't show some concern for his health. Do you think it was bad enough to threaten his life?*"

"*Absolutely! I think he almost DIED. That's why I wanted to see him before anything happened.*"

"*Tara, you can understand what they were trying to protect, right?*"

"*Oh Yeh, I understand that mom. But that's my DAD!*"

Allison called the hospital and found out that Brian had been moved into ICU. She explained that she was his daughter and wanted to know what his condition was. A nurse at the nurses' station informed her that his condition was listed as critical. The nurse also told her that he had other members of the family in the room with him. Allison hung up the phone. She wanted to be sure Tara was going to be okay with the information she was just given. She thought she would just wait a day or so, and call back. Tara spoke.

"Mom, can't your company represent dad in this accident?"

"Oh, no baby. That couldn't happen!"

"Why not? Why couldn't you give it to one of your investigators, like Marvin? He probably can find who did this and maybe dad can get some big bucks."

"Tara, this would not be right for a company I work for to represent your dad. No…no. That won't work!"

"Well, why should anybody else get the lawsuit, when that is what your company does?" asked Tara.

"There's more involved than just giving it to someone to investigate, honey. His family would have to come into the office and there would have to be interviews… No baby, that would not work," advised Allison.

Monday morning, Allison went to work at the usual time. She usually works until late in the evening, so she reports for work by 10 AM. It was a rainy morning and the weather was cool in the 60's. She removed her coat and placed it on the coat rack located near her desk. She spoke to the receptionist as she walked past her, heading for the coffee pot. As she approached the coffee pot area Marvin Klein, the top investigator for the firm, met her there.

"Good morning Allison."

"Good mornings Marvin-how are you?"

"Tired, had a busy weekend."

"Me too," said Allison.

"What did you have going on, to be so busy," asked Marvin."

"Just dealing with my daughter, mainly. Her father was in an accident Saturday, and he's in the hospital."

"He was in an accident? An auto accident…Who's working his case? Come on… tell me no one…tell me!"

"You right...no one!"

"Ohhhh yeahhhh! ...I got it! Can I work this one? I realize it's your husband, but I could work this for you for a discount. Nothing up front... In fact..."

"Marvin...he is NOT my husband! I said it was my baby's father... we were not married. Besides, I don't make those kinds of decisions. That's for his wife to do. I don't know who caused the accident, or whose fault it was. I don't know anything, okay!"

"You do know his wife's name and how I can get in touch with her, right?"

"My daughter tells me they are at the County Hospital. That's all I know. Listen Marvin, this is not going to work, because his wife don't know about me, or my daughter. I have not seen him for years, but I had his daughter. You understand where I'm coming from. I can't have her coming here where I work. I don't have a problem with her. It just won't work if we represented him. It would be best to let some other firm handle this one."

"Allison sweetheart, you know me...it don't work that way. This is strictly business. Nothing personal here. ...We can handle the case, if there is one, and nobody has to know anything about anything. You just have to stay away from the office when his wife comes in, that's all. ...Let me check it out... Maybe there's nothing here. I need to pull a police report, and find out what they say. But I need to get to the family to be sure they have not contacted anyone else. What do you think?" asked Marvin.

"I will have nothing to do with it. You don't have to have this one, Marvin. I am sorry I even told you about this," said Allison.

"Just let me check it out, Allison. That's all I'm asking, okay? That's all I'm asking. If there's nothing there...we won't be going anywhere. Okay? Just...let me ...check... it... out."

Chapter 9

Two and a half days after Brian was placed into the intensive care unit, his vitals had stabilized enough for his condition to be upgraded to Serious. Although he had not regained consciousness, the attending physicians were satisfied that he was 'out of the woods', and that he was on his way to satisfactory recovery. Sharon had remained at his bedside from the start, as she spent her waking moments holding Brian's hand and silently praying for him. Sharon felt so relieved that Brian had improved in his condition so quickly. Even though she saw improvement each day, she thought it would be many more days before he was truly out of the danger of loosing him. At 8 Am on Monday morning, the head nurse entered into Brian's room to take his vital signs and to check his fluids. Sharon, sleeping on the couch in his room, woke up at the opening of the door. The nurse spoke.

"God morning Sharon, how are you feeling today?"

"Oh, I'm a little tired and stiff, but otherwise...I'm fine."

"I understand! Well, let's see how your man is doing this morning...he is making good progress, though," said the nurse.

"I was wondering, nurse...what does it mean when his eyes seem to be rolling around a lot?" asked Sharon.

"Actually, that happens all the time. I think it has to do with him *dreaming. When the doctor comes in a few minutes, ask him. He can explain it better than I can. Sometimes it has to do with the level of sleep he's in-whether he's deep sleeping or not, okay?"*

Sharon assisted the nurse in raising Brian's head in order to change the pillow. Sharon wiped his mouth and nose. She always pampered him in little things at home, and wanted to get back to it. She went to the sink to wet a towel to complete the grooming on his face. The nurse could not help but feel the warmth coming through from her, to Brian.

"How long have you two been married?" asked the nurse.

"Twenty-two years next month."

"Wow!"

"Yep, it doesn't seem like it though. We've had a good life so far. (Silence) I have no idea...what... what the future holds... I am praying God will restore my husband to me...whole!" said Sharon.

The attending physician entered the room.

"Hello!"

"Hello, doctor."

"I'm Doctor Watanabe, how are you?

"I'm fine doctor. I just need to get my man together so I can take him home," said Sharon.

"Well, as long as we all do our part, he does his part, and God does his part, that should be the result real soon," said the doctor. *His chart is looking good. His vitals, color, breathing, and lungs...all look good. So... do you have any questions for me?"*

While the doctor pulled back the sheet to check his stomach and ribs, Sharon asked the question she had asked the nurse, previously.

"Doctor Watanabe, what causes his eyes to roll like they do?"

"A lot of research has been done on this over the past decade or so. With all that money and time spent in research, they still have not found any conclusive answers. However, what we do know is that there are different levels of sleep we all go through. The kind of sleep that manifests itself with

the eyes fluttering is a deep one that signals a fast forward of the past…sort of as you would a VCR tape."

"It does not mean that he is in pain, does it?" asked Sharon.

"No, no. He's medicated pretty good and is not in pain right now. That will come later when we ease him off some of the medication. That has nothing to do with his eyes, however."

"Good! I wanted to be sure."

"Not a problem. He's doing better than he was a couple of days ago. We are optimistic about his recovery right now. Keep praying…!"

"Thank you doctor, I will."

Both the doctor and the nurse left Brian's' room together. Sharon decided to follow them to go down to the cafeteria for some breakfast. As she entered the elevator to go down to the first floor, she passed by a young person who spoke to her, and went directly to the nurses station, as the door to the elevator closed. Perhaps due to her woman's intuition, Sharon wondered silently who that was she spoke to, and where was she headed? She surveyed her mind to make a connection, but there was no connection made. The person was not familiar to her. She shrugged her shoulders and brushed off the thoughts she had, as she continued toward breakfast. Thirty-five minutes later, Sharon returned from the cafeteria. She casually walked towards Brian's room, while talking on her cell phone. She was talking to Adam, who was on his way to the hospital to see Brian. When she approached the entrance to Brian's room, she could hear a faint female voice speaking softly. The sounds came as a surprise to her, as no one was there when she left him. She moved cautiously into the room. As she entered, she saw a female person leaning over Brian. She was the same person Sharon passed on her way to the cafeteria. Sharon's heart began to beat faster. The food she just finished eating felt like it was coming back up, because her muscles had tensed up all over her body. She felt protective of her husband, and she wanted no outside intrusion. Who is this? She thought. What is she doing in my husbands' room? What is she saying to him, as she leans over him? It was time for her to interrupt!

"*Excuse me! Who are you? What do you need?*" asked Sharon.

The visitor stood up. She looked at Sharon withholding her speech. Their eyes were fixed on each other as emotions began to build. Sharon moved closer to Brian's bed while keeping her eyes on the young lady. Sharon spoke again…

"*You are the person I spoke to getting off the elevator, right?*"

"*Yes, Ma' am,*" answered the young woman.

"*Well, why are you here? Who are you? I have never seen you before. What are you doing here in my husbands' room? Did you make a mistake? Are you looking for someone else?*" asked Sharon.

"**No Ma' am!**"

"*What do you mean? Who are you young lady? Why are you here?*"

"*I came…I came…to see…I came to see my dad,*" **responded Tara.**

"YOUR WHAT?

"*…My dad!*"

"*WHAT THE HELL (excuse me Lord) DO YOU MEAN? WHAT DAD? …Who are you talking about, young lady? What the HELL (Lord forgive me) are you talking about?*"

Sharon was visibly shaking. She clenched her fists and tightened the muscles in her jaws as she spoke. She could see that the person sharing the space in her husbands' room felt that she belonged there. She also knew that she was about to loose her religion, based on the statement this person has just made. She never suspected that there was a child born outside of her marriage to Brian, and she prayed that she was not hearing things right. She could see that this girl was about the age of her son, and yes, she seemed to have a face that resembled her husbands. She felt hopeless and afraid that she could not maintain control of her emotions. She felt as if she would scream. Her skin started to crawl with electrical impulses all over it. She felt as if she had dealt with all she could with her husband being in the shape he was in. She braced herself for some rough news of who this girl really was. She stared at her from the outside of her skin all the way to her soul. Time was rushing past her by the millisecond. It was time for her to speak. She needed to confront the news head on and boldly. She moved closer to her as she pulled up the words she needed to say, to establish her position of strength and power in the situation.

"Young lady, I have no idea who you are, or where you came from. I really don't have the time to explore all that right now. I know that at this time, you better find yourself some other place to call your home, cause this one is not yours…In other words, I need you to LEAVE THIS ROOM. Do you understand me?" demanded Sharon.

Tara stood motionless while fixing her eyes onto Sharon's mouth. She could not look into her eyes any longer. She knew Sharon could have been old enough to be her mother. She heard her words. She heard the angry rejection coming from her heart. She knew that words, which came from a persons' mouth, was the most damaging way to hurt a person. She felt hurt that Sharon was speaking to her with such venom. What was she supposed to do, she wondered. How was she supposed to respond to a grown woman who just showed the backside of her religion? Tara decided to respond directly to her. She would not let Sharon chase her from her fathers' presence, in spite of the tenseness of the situation.

"I got as much right to be here as you do. You don't own exclusive rights to Brian Simon. **I happen to have his blood in me, which is not something you can say!"** She yelled.

Tara could not believe that she said that. Her body tensed up with fear, wondering what would be Sharon's reaction to that statement. She knew that she was loud, but she wanted to push back at the woman who was treating her as if she was something other than a human being. Just because this was the first time Sharon had heard about Tara, that was no way for her to treat her, she felt. She stood her ground near Brian's bed as she spoke. She moved closer to the foot of the bed. Sharon moved closer to her as she spoke.

"Maybe you didn't hear me before, young lady. You better get the hell out of my face and out of this room, RIGHT NOW! This is not your father, so you get out of here before I call security. Now MOVE!" shouted Sharon.

"*You can call whomever you want to call; I am not leaving my father.*"

"**Shut up! That's not your father, girl!**"

"**How do you know that**? *Huh? How can you say that, when you never met me before? I know all about you, and your family. You just never heard about my family and me. But that don't mean that we don't exist! You have that attitude because you never knew your husband would have another child, outside of your marriage, right?*" asked Tara.

"*You are definitely out of line, little girl!* **You are way out of line!** *Your mother should have taught you how to talk to grown-ups. Now like I said, you need to leave.*"

The head nurse supervising Brian's condition at her station, noticed that the monitor showed a sharp rise in Brian's heart rate. She also noticed that a louder conversation was going on, seemingly coming from his room. As she left her station to check on Brian in person, Brian's brother Adam, exited the elevator and was fifteen feet behind her. When the nurse arrived at Brian's room, she noticed that Sharon had Tara by the arm, attempting to escort her from the room. Tara was resisting and had grabbed the foot of the hospital bed with her right hand, where Brian was resting.

"*Get out! Get out!*" shouted Sharon.

"*Mrs. Simon, what is going on in here?*" asked the nurse.

Adam heard the scuffling and loud noises as well. As he entered through the door, he was stunned at all the commotion.

"*What the hell is going on?*" he asked.

"*GET HER OUT OF HERE!*" shouted Sharon. "*You better get her out of here before I loose my religion!*"

"*Please turn the bed loose young lady. You are disturbing Mr. Simon. Please! It'll be alright, just turn loose, okay.*" asked the nurse.

"*Tara, what are you doing here? I told you this would not be the right time to come over here. Didn't I tell you to wait and I would let you know how he was doing?*" asked Adam.

"*You know this girl Adam? You've seen her before?*" asked Sharon.

"Yes, I know her. I have known her for sometime," explained Adam.

"Well, will you please explain who she is to me, and what is she doing here? Why would a stranger come down here to visit MY husband while he is in the hospital, Adam? Please tell me!"

"Sharon, let's go outside and let the nurse get Brian settled down. Do you see he's disturbed with this loud talking?" insisted Adam. "You come with us too, Tara. We're sorry for all this noise, nurse. We will be in the waiting room while you do your job. Please Sharon and Tara, come with me."

"Will he be alright nurse?" asked Sharon. "I'm sorry."

"I must get the doctor in to check him out. I think he was affected by whatever you guys were arguing about, though...as a matter of fact, this might be a good sign!"

"Okay...okay. I'll get out of the way so you can find out what's happening to him. You are saying it's all good, right?" asked Sharon.

"I'll let you know Mrs. Simon. I'll be right back. You can leave now. Yes...try down the hall...I need to get the doctor!" encouraged the nurse.

"You coming Sharon?" asked Adam.

"I guess...I guess!"

"Come on so we can talk... about this...this situation!"

"Yeah, Adam, I want to hear this...I want to hear this!"

Chapter 10

At the end of a long line outside of The Bunker restaurant, Allison and her exercise partner and friend Quin Parker, were waiting to be seated for lunch. Allison's cell phone rang. She answered it. It was Marvin from her office. He wandered where she was, so he could discuss the new information he found out concerning Brian Simon. By the time he arrived at the restaurant, Allison and her friend were being seated in the outdoor section. Marvin was anxious to talk.

"*Tell me what you know about your boyfriend, Allison,*" said Marvin.

"*What are you talking about, Marvin?*"

"*Come on, what do you know about him...about who he really is... what kind of person was he in his past?*"

"*I thought I told you he was my baby's father. Doesn't that say I knew him pretty well?*"

"*Did you know about his involvement with drug trafficking?*"

"*Get the hell out of here Marvin. Where did you get that shit?*" Don't come up in here trying to stir up no shit like that about my baby's daddy. That is not necessary, okay?" demanded Allison.

"*Listen Allison, you must not know much about this guy's past. I checked him out. You know me! This guy is not an innocent person. Here...I got it right here in this briefcase. This is real, Allison. This guy may not have been as innocent as you think he was. He may have been in an unfortunate accident, but this guy has some history that is bound to stir up some questions."*

"So what are you saying Marvin?"

"I'm saying, if this information is true, you might want to stay away from him as far as you can, because an insurance investigator will eat him alive...if he makes it."

"Why?"

"Because his record would be devastating for any personal injury lawsuit."

"You mean his wife should not file a suit against anyone, to try to collect? Well, I need to see what you got in that briefcase. I have no idea if they thought about filing a suit, but I suppose they need to know the facts. But wait, Marvin. We don't even know who caused the accident yet. Suppose everything was his fault. If we knew that, all this talk about his past would not even come up, right?" asked Allison.

"I already know who hit whom. He was the one that ran that light. The question was why he did it. That's what I'm working on before we go any further. But I'm telling you, this guy is dirty. I can smell a dead rat in this case."

"Marvin, I wish you wouldn't talk about Brian like that; especially ... to me" said Allison.

"Let's see where the water flows... let's see!" Said Marvin.

Allison and Quin continued with their lunch. Allison glanced at her friend who sat wide-eyed Marvin ordered a sandwich to go. He felt that he was on to something much more involved than what he originally saw in this case. Allison was afraid that Marvin would lock onto this case like an angry bulldog. The only question was, where would all this lead to, and to what extent would it involve her and her daughter. She really had no feelings left for Brian. They had settled that a long time ago. She knew the relationship with Brian was against God's law, but she felt she loved him enough early in their affair to risk the punishment that might come their way. She never wanted to get pregnant, but when she found out that she was, having his baby was the only way she could be a part of his life, forever. She knew he bought stolen goods from street thieves who stole from convenient and electronic stores, during the time they were together. She even knew of his gambling over the years. However, she thought he gave all that up after her daughter was born. In fact, if he was involved in selling anything else like drugs, it all happened after she stopped seeing him when her daughter was six years old. That was about the time they agreed to be friends only and she was starting to date other men. She had gradually weaned herself and her daughter from involvement with Brian. She made no demands of him over the years, as she wanted to get her life on an independent track, free from drama and demands for support for her daughter.

Although she never married, she resigned to have a life alone, at least until her daughter was finished with college and out on her own. Involvement with him, even through this tragedy, has brought back many of the feelings she once freely shared with him. She knew she had to closely guard her feelings for many reasons. Major among them was the possibility of Brian's wife finding out about Allison's involvement with him during the time of their marriage—Involvement she is not proud of, but could never erase. How far could she allow herself to get involved in his plight now? This is a new chapter in her life. What should be the title of it? How should it be played out? More importantly, how would it end? Many questions remained and begged to be answered. If it was left up to Marvin however, everyone would have the answers. The question then would be…what should be done with them? Allison needed to explain something to her friend who sat stoic and animated at what she just heard. She wondered if she should explain everything about her previous relationship with Brian, or whether to just leave it alone. She decided to leave it alone. She spoke.

"I appreciate you not asking about what you just heard from Marvin, Quin. I don't have the foggiest idea what that's all about myself. Let's just finish this lunch and get out of here. I know we need to get back to work."

Chapter 11

The pattern of dealing with investigations was always the same for Marvin-always let the information drive the investigation. That was his motto. How far he went to get the information was sometimes questioned by his office. He left no stones unearthed, and was as thorough as anyone in his profession. A mere week after Brian's accident and Marvin has discovered something about his past that may be worse than a hornets nest. Marvin was now in the local office of the DEA, and requested to see his longtime friend and confidant, Zack Powder.

"Hey Zack, what's up dog?" asked Marvin.

"Dog? Marvin, I told you before, you don't know a dog from a wolf. I am wolf man, dog!"

"Okay, okay. You're right. Listen wolf man, you got a couple of minutes?"

"I got exactly two minutes, Marv. I got a new shift coming in. I got to get ready for them. What you got?"

"I need some info on a case I'm working. It's for a friend, so I'm just trying to save her some heartache…you know what I mean?

"Come on back to my office. Let me see what I can do for you. How's your business? You keeping busy, Marv?"

"*Sometimes more than I want, Zack. You know how that goes. You changed your office around?*"

"*I just moved it closer to the main floor where most of my people have their desk. Okay, here we are. Have a seat. Now, what are you looking for Marv?*"

"*Can you run an ID on a Brian Dwayne Simon for me?*

"*I can run a name search and see if he's in our system. Let's see...S... i...m... O...k...a...y. I do have a Simon, Brian D.; Address on Palmdale. Is that the one?*"

"*Yeah, I'm sure that's the one. What you got?*"

"*This one is sealed Marvin. Can't get you much on it because it's been kicked up to the top floor.*"

"*What for?*"

"*Well, it looks like a ring of...a ring of tow truck drivers...towing cars that come in from Mexico...that breaks down on the freeway...and they are full of 'contra'. It looks like the drivers were taking them to a storage garage that was owned by a Brian D. Simon.*"

"*Aha!*"

"*Yeah, that's why it got bumped upstairs. This one is complicated, Marv.*"

"*That's what I thought. I really don't need much more, but is this still ongoing?*"

"*I can't tell you. I don't know the current status. I just can't tell you any more than I told you already.*"

"*Okay, okay...that's all I need, really. That's ...all...I need!*"

"*Okay, I need to get back to work, dog. You take care of yourself. Don't forget me when you come into that million*", reminded Zack.

"*You'll be the first one to know wolf man... the first!*"

Chapter 12

The rains had not let up in more than a week. Getting around the city was cumbersome and slow. The skies were gray and the temperature hovered around the middle forties. Allison and Tara decided to stay home this midweek evening. It would not be long before their conversation involved Brian, Tara's father. Tara spoke first.

"Mom, why didn't you and Brian get married?"

"Girl, please!"

"Well, what happened after I was born? Did you want to marry him?"

"At one time, I did."

"Why didn't you then?"

"It was a matter of him being married already, Tara."

"But did you want him to marry you?"

"Yes, I can't tell a lie…I did at one time."

"Did you think it was wrong for you to have an affair with a married man?"

"Tara, why are you asking me these questions?"

"I really want to know mom."

"I knew it was wrong, Tara. Let me be clear about this…It is wrong to commit fornication. The Bible is very clear about that. I should have cut it off when I found out that he was married."

Allison sat back against the couch with the pillar she had placed on the floor. She felt that Tara would continue the questions so she wanted to get comfortable to fully discuss the situation. She felt that she owed it to her daughter, who seldom brought up the subject of her father, throughout her entire life.

"*Baby, one day you're going to get serious about a man.*"

"*Mom!*"

"*Seriously, Tara. That very special person will come along and you will not be thinking about his status, as much as you will be thinking about how much he pleases you. He will make you feel as though you are the only person in the world. You will feel as though you were made for him and he for you. Now, you will think that you are as mature as any other person, but your thinking will become as selfish as it can be. All you want to do is have him as often as you can. You will want to please him in every way.*"

"*But mom, you knew he was married?*"

"*I found out for sure after we were together for over six months.*"

"*How did you find out?*"

"*It was Thanksgiving, and he just wasn't available for me. I wanted to take him to my Aunt Doris' place for dinner.*"

"*How did that make you feel?*"

"*I was crushed! I could not forgive him for that. In fact, I started trying to separate myself from him from that moment on. I knew he was married, even though he denied it for weeks after that. He tried to prove that he single, by spending the next weekend with me.*"

"*How did that go?*"

"*That was when you were conceived, baby.*"

"*That's when you got pregnant with me?*"

"*Yep!*"

"*Did that freak you out?*"

"*It sure did! I knew it would not work out though. I knew he would not leave his wife, and I did not want him to.*"

"*I thought you said you wanted to marry him!*"

"*I did. But I did not want him to leave his wife to make that happen.*"

"I don't understand, mom. How could you WANT to marry him, but you didn't want him to leave his wife for me?"

"I knew it was wrong to even look at him in that way...I knew I should have checked him out first, before I started seeing him."

"How did you meet him?"

"I used to work with his younger brother, Adam."

"What? You used to work with Adam? Doing what?"

"We both worked at a dealership. He was a salesman, and I worked in the office. He was married too, but he knew his wife would kill him if he even thought about another woman. He never told me that Brian was married, and I didn't ask."

"Did you think what you were doing was wrong from a spiritual point of view, mom?"

"Absolutely! God knows everything we do baby. The Bible tells us that adultery is a sin...I sinned against God because I committed fornication. Brian committed adultery."

"So I'm just a mistake?. I feel like I was born by mistake...out of fornication... whatever that means."

"Baby, you were NOT a mistake! You were born because God wanted you to be born for his purposes...for his will...if God did not want you to be born, believe me, you would not be here now."

"But I was born out of a sinful act, mom. How could God accept me as the result of that act?"

"The Bible say's we have all sinned, Tara. None of us are without sin. But God forgave me for my sin a long time ago."

"What about Brian? Do you think God forgave him for his sin?"

"I can't answer that for him. All I can do is pray for him."

"Yeah, the way he's banged up, he is going to need a lot of prayers. You know mom, he may not be able to walk or talk, or even work...nothing! He may turn out to be a vegetable. He is going to need some big money from a law suit or something."

"We need to talk about that too, Tara! Your father does not have a *problem with money. He may not look it, but he's got money…plenty of it. You should not bring that up again."*

"Why mom?"

"There are some complications around that lawsuit thing. You need to just let 'them' handle what ever they feel they should handle, and leave us out of it."

"Mom, what are you talking about? Why are you saying that about my dad? Don't you care even just a little bit?"

"Baby, I just don't want us to get involved in anything that has to do with them…I mean concerning helping them file a lawsuit, okay?"

"But you work for a law firm. Why can't your company represent him?"

"WE CAN'T… *We can't baby. I'm sorry for yelling…I'm sorry, but we can't get involved in this accident at all. They will have to find someone else, that's all. They can do it on their own. Now you just have to trust me on this Tara. I would not be telling you something that was not true, okay?"*

"No, it's not okay. I want to know why we…your company can't help them file a personal injury lawsuit against whoever crashed into him. Why can't you do that? You did it before for other people. Or, do you still hate him for not marrying you?"

"YOU HUSH YOUR MOUTH, TARA! You just zip it young lady. You don't know what you are saying. You just stay out of this. You don't need to get involved in this lawsuit thing. We never know what people will find when they start investigating folk. We just don't need to be a part of any investigation. That's all I'm saying, baby."

"Why would WE be a part of any investigation?"

"I'm not saying we would be a part of any investigation, but you never know where these things will lead. You heard me say I had an affair with him for six years. His wife does not know me. She never knew me as far as I know. Nevertheless, you never know how sharp PI's can dig up all kinds of stuff. Let's leave that accident investigation thing to them."

Tara could hardly sequester her emotions. She felt that her mother was holding back on information that she needed to connect the dots-to complete the puzzle. Why was her mother treating this case as if it was filled with a virus? Why is she suddenly shielding her from her dad who has not had the ability to defend himself? What could it possibly be, that would make her want to run 180 degrees from her father and any possible future he might have? All she could do was to change the subject and hope that her mother would revisit it at a later date. But for now, she would let it be. Her curiosity would surface again.

"I will let it go mom…for now."

"Okay, I will see you in the morning, baby. Goodnight."

"Goodnight, mom!"

Chapter 13

Dexter and Adam had not seen each other since Brian's accident. Dexter wanted to get together to discuss what could be done to assist Brian's family, who had spent most of their time at the hospital. Dexter wanted to solicit Adam's support for what he wanted to do for them, in order to forestall any hard feelings that might erupt later. Adam lived close to their mothers home on the east side and suggested that they meet there, while visiting their mom. Mrs. Simon had been a widow for over 15 years. She lived alone in the family home that was built by her husband in the early fifties. There, they reared their nine children. Mrs. Simon was quite independent for being in her eighties. She had repeatedly refused to go to the nursing home, and insisted that she could take care of herself, in spite of her frail health. She had in-home care provided by Medicare and was blessed to be in her right mind. When Dexter and Adam came in, Mrs. Simon was getting ready for bed at 5:30 in the evening.

"What you boys doing out here in the rain?"

"We came to see you momma," said Adam.

"Well, I'm glad to see you boys. What ya'll want? Come on in here and sit down on the end of the bed if you want to."

"Mamma, have you been to the hospital to see Brian?" asked Dexter.

"Naw, I ain't been there yet. How's he doing? His wife told me he is still in a coma."

"Yes...he is still in serious condition. We got to keep praying for him, momma," explained Dexter.

"Dexter, you don't know how much I been praying for that boy. That's about all I've done since he was born. I pray for all my children, but Brian's been a different child...ya'll know that. He was always the sickly one all his life. But that don't make him no different in how much I pray for each of my children."

"Momma," **said Dexter, "**Can we pray for him now?"

"Come over here and hold my hand you two...bow your heads..." She prayed.

"Lord God...I am your child...You are my creator...I worship no other god but you...You are a holy God...I am not worthy to even call upon your name...Forgive me for my failings and mistakes...Forgive me for not always honoring you in all that I have done...But right now, I come before your throne on behalf of my son, Brian...You know how I have prayed for his full recovery...You know that I have prayed for his salvation... I have prayed that he would accept the Lord Jesus as his savior...Give him another chance to hear your call...heal his broken body, align his cells throughout his body...restore his health and sustain his mind...Give me back my son... Have mercy on him Heavenly Father...Have mercy on him...In Jesus' name I pray...Amen."

"That's good mom, that's good," said Dexter.

"You boys remember what your dad told you a long time ago, don't you?" asked Mrs. Simon.

Adam answered. "I remember, mom. How can we forget?"

"What is she referring to Adam?"

"She's talking about the sticks."

"The what?" asked Dexter.

"You know how dad wrapped the 9 sticks together and..."

"Oh yeah, I remember. I had to remind myself for a minute," explained Dexter.

65

"I need to put it on your mind again...Your father wanted all you children to stay together. That's why he bundled nine sticks together and gave it to each of you to break. None of you could break the sticks when they were together. But when he took them apart and gave one to each of you, you broke it easily. That was his way of showing that there is strength in the family when you look out for each other, and don't let anyone come between you. It was very important to us that you kids stayed together. I know he is looking down on all of you now. Just stay together like your daddy wanted, okay? Ya'll need to stay together 'through thick and even razor thin,' okay?"

With her voice shaking as she began to cry, Mrs. Simon held her sons hands tightly. Her senses told her that there was some distance between her three boys. She knew that the words she planted would be taken seriously but she would leave it up to God to provide the increase. As she settled onto the soft fluffy pillar in her bed, Adam and Dexter covered her with the thick blanket she had quilted for herself over ten years ago. It was time for her to go to sleep for the evening. They kissed her gently and turned the television off as they left the room. Dexter led Adam into the den. Dexter wanted to talk to Adam alone and confidentially about their hospitalized brother. Adam was guarded about his knowledge of Brian's business and he did not want to share any more information than he already has. Dexter spoke.

"Adam, you know what's going on around here, not me. I'm not trying to get into anybody's business, okay? My problem is that everyone's so secretive about their lives. You've seen it...Brian never talks about anything that has substance, right? What has he been hiding? Why can't we just relax and be a family?"

"Dex, the best I can tell you is that Brian has a business he's trying to protect. Nobody knows about his business, and everybody is cool with that. We just don't question him about his business, not even his wife Sharon."

"You mean she don't even not know about what he does for a living, Adam?"

"Sharon knows that Brian has a tow truck business. She knows that *he runs about 4 trucks. He has a storage garage and a shop. That's all anybody knows, Dex."*

"Why don't you know what's going on Adam? You're his best friend, aren't you? Why is there such secrecy? Who's running the business now? Do we know? Is it still a business? What's going on Adam?" asked Dexter.

"Damn you Dex! I ain't telling you nothing about Brian. His business and how he runs it is his business, man. I don't give a damn what you think about it, okay?"

"But Adam, that's what I'm talking about. Why can't we, as family, step up and help out when one of our family members are in trouble? That's what other cultures do. Why would you let his business go down the drain?" I am willing to get over there and help out in any way I can. What about the employees? Does he have any left? Are they getting paid? How much? Adam, can anybody answer these questions? Where is his business located? Do you know?"* asked Dexter.

"Yes, I know where it is," answered Adam.

"Would you show me where it is, Adam?"

"Maybe we should let Sharon know what we're doing before we go poking our noses into his business, don't you think?" advised Adam.

Dexter spoke.

"Right now, I don't think we should go poking into anything just yet. I think we should go over to check things out first."

Dexter parked his car on the front curb at their mother's house, and climbed into the passenger side of Adam's car. Adam had to move a stack of papers from the seat before Dex could situate himself and fasten his seat belt. Adam was not a very neat person and the shambled appearance of his auto reflected that.

"Adam, can you understand what it is that I am saying about being a family?"

"Hey, that's just the way it has always been around here. Nobody wants to get into nobody's business. Where do you get this cocka mamie idea that we are some sort of tight knit family? Hell, I never see anybody else on a regular basis but Brian, before you came down here. None of our sisters

are interested in anything we do. There is no "family" as you think it is, or ought to be, Dex."

"Isn't that what mamma is talking about, Adam? Do you think that she is living in a fantasy about her family? Do you think she would still be talking about togetherness if that was not what she wanted? Adam, this togetherness is a process, man. I'm not saying that we have it now...but I am saying that we need to work on coming together for the cohesiveness of the entire family. We need to start working on it, brother. Do you follow what I am saying?"

"I am not deaf or dumb Dex. I understand what you are saying. But, what I am saying to you is, you don't know how things are down here. We don't hate each other, but we are NOT off into each others business either."

"But I think Brian needs our help now. He needs us to be in his business since he can't be. What do we do about that?" asked Dexter.

"Alright, alright. I will take you out there, okay? But I am telling you Dex, I am not going to get into his business...I am NOT going to do it!"

For 30 minutes, Adam and Dexter drove to find the location where Brian housed his business. The weather had been unusually rainy and the clouds had not gone away in over two weeks. The grounds were saturated with moisture while the temperature hovered around fifty degrees. Adam didn't want to talk much, as he didn't know what they would find once they arrived at Brian's garage. Instead, he followed Dexter's conversation, with the intent to keep the talk light and without much depth about this business of togetherness. For Dexter's' part, no amount of silence from Adam would thwart the desire to get to the bottom of the unfolding mystery. He wanted to probe Adam for all he knew, and offer logical reasons for what he didn't know. One thing was clear to Dexter...He wanted the truth to set all of them free. Freedom from secrecy and concealment was his aim, and Adam would have to go along with what ever was uncovered.

"Okay, we are getting near the turn off we gotta take. There's an old

abandoned service station and coffee house on the corner, with lots of weeds grown up around it. Keep looking on your side…it's just up her…"

"Is that it there, just ahead?" asked Dexter.

"Yep, that's it!" replied Adam. "Now, I'll turn right here… and it's down about a quarter mile on the left. I got to be careful cause these roads are like the country roads…they only allow for one lane going both ways."

"This place looks creepy Adam. What would Brian be doing back here?" asked Dexter.

"Man, like I told you…that's Brian's business."

"Watch for that car coming towards you, Adam. It looks like you're going to have to move over onto the right side, 'cause that guy's coming fast…move over Adam…WATCH IT!!!"

"SON- OF- A- %$#@*!!!"

"What was that guy trying to do?" asked Dexter.

"That was one of Brian's trucks! I know that truck…that's one of his… that bastard tried to run me down, didn't he?"

"I believe he did, Adam. But why?"

"I don't know."

"Let's drive on ahead, and see what's going on," suggested Dexter.

The two of them sat up in their seats as they drove slowly down the muddy road. Up ahead, they could see the lights on at a business where several trucks were parked in front. By this time, it was almost dark, and Adam decided not to turn his lights on. Instead, he drove slowly up to the front of the business which stood alone at almost the end of the road. Adam could see that he would have to turn around within fifty yards of the business, in order to get back to the main highway. No one was outside of the business which looked like a storage lot and behind it was several other buildings which were not visible from the street. As the brothers drove past the front of the building, they could see the lights were on inside of the front building. Dexter spoke softly.

"Adam, I think we should pull up to the front and go inside."

"You must be crazy Dex. This damn place looks too spooky to me. I am not going in there. I going to turn around and get the hell out of here."

"No, no Adam, I think we'll be alright. What can anyone do to us? Huh?"

"Are you asking me?"

"Yeah…what are you afraid of? It's Brian's business, right? Right?"

"Yeah, this is his business alright. At least this is where he told me it was. I ain't never been out here before." explained Adam.

"Just turn around here, and let me go inside. Turn around, you can stay in the car, okay!" assured Dexter.

"That's fine with me. Let me turn my light on so I don't run over something in this grass… There, I made it…there you go big brother. I'll be here when you get back…I think!"

"No matter what, you better not leave me here Adam. Turn the engine off and wait for me."

"Wait Dex, wait!"

"What is it, Adam?"

"The light just went off."

"I know, I told you to turn 'em off and wait for me."

"I'm talking about inside that house." said Adam.

"Are you sure? Were they on when we came by here just now?" asked Dexter.

"Come ooonnn man. I know they were on just a minute ago. Get in the car Dex, let's get the hell outta here, come on, and get in."

"Let me at least knock on the door, Adam. Hold on a second!"

"Man…this thing don't look right Dex…hey Dex, come on…Dex… Let's go man!"

Dexter hurried up to the front of the business. He politely knocked on the door and listened for any sounds. He heard nothing. He reasoned that perhaps they were seeing things when they went by the first time. He knocked again. He decided to reach for the door handle to see if the door was locked. As he turned the handle, the door opened. Dexter turned towards Adam still sitting in the car. Adam was frantically motioning for Dexter to come back to the car. Dexter slowly opened the door while peeking inside. He wanted to yell out a greeting before entering, but decided not to. He was soon swallowed up by the darkness inside of the building. Adam sat petrified in his car. His thoughts went back to when they were younger, when Dexter always displayed bravery in the darkness, while he and Brian held on to each other in total fear. Dexter was now inside of the building and the door was still open. As he slowly walked through the building, he was able to make his way towards the back room, where a dim light cascaded down from under a cabinet in the kitchen.

Dexter was conscious of the fact that someone could be in the house and hear him as he tipped through the front room and into the kitchen area. He listened for any sounds that might give him a clue as to the nature of the activity out back. Since Adam was unable to see Dexter and was afraid to stay in the car alone, he decided to join him in the house. Surely, he thought, Dexter had the power to protect him in whatever situation that came up. As Adam approached the front door, he instinctively reached for the door bell. He was able to check himself before that happened. He entered the house while softly calling out Dexter's name.

"Dex...Dex...Dex, where are you man?"

Dexter had made his way to one of the windows located at the rear of the house. He heard Adam calling for him, but he felt that he was too close to the back of the house to answer him. Dex peered through the uncovered window and saw several men walking around, exiting one building and entering into another. Adam slowly made his way to the Dexter's hiding position. His eyes were bucked wide open as they were when he was a frightened kid. Adam whispered softly...

"Dex, I don't know what the hell you think you're doing man, but we are illegally entering into somebody's house. We can't do that, man!"

"Shhhhh! Keep it down Adam. Take a look out there. What do you see? What are those guys doing? Can you see?"

71

"Yeah I see people…guys walking, but I don't see what they are doing." replied Adam.

"See, every time you see one, you see another. The second guy looks like he has his hands tied behind his back. See!"

"Yeah I see. Dex, I'm begging you man, let's get the hell out of here before somebody comes back in here. Let's go…let's go!"

"I will, but I am going to find out what is going on over here. Are you sure this is Brian's place? Are you positive?"

"This is his place. Now let's go."

Adam started to walk away with Dexter following behind him. As they entered into the front area of the house, the sound of a heavy thump broke the silence. It came from the back window they had just vacated. Adam grabbed and squeezed Dexter's right arm. They both stopped. Dexter turned to investigate. He saw the large head, and shining canines of one of the huge Rotweiler guard dogs. The dog spotted Dexter as he crouched over to avoid being spotted. The dog started barking as though he had spotted prey. He continued to jump up to peer into the window, while turning around. Adam ran for the front door without uttering another word. Dexter was six feet behind him. The dog continued to bark when more than eight or nine men from the back of the house stopped their activities to investigate the disturbance going on, highlighted by the dog. The dog continued to jump up and bark, while the two snooping brothers had made their way to Adam's car. Adam turned the key to start the car. Dexter jumped in and slammed the door. The men retrieved wrenches and one had a shotgun as they entered into the back door of the house. Adam floored the car while leaving his lights off. By this time, it was totally dark outside, and therefore it was difficult for him to see the narrow road. He swerved left and right as he left a spray of mud trailing behind him. The men at the house heard the noise of the escaping automobile, and hurried to the front of the house in enough time to see only the mud. Two men jumped into their tow trucks parked in front of the house to chase after them. Adam floored the car all the way to the main highway. He noticed the traffic was moderately heavy. He stopped momentarily, and sped to the inside lane, avoiding colliding with several cars, which were traveling above the speed limit of 60 mph. Although Adam was traveling in the opposite direction to his mother's house, it did not matter to either of them, as long as they could escape being caught by the pursuing 'bad guy's. Dexter was holding onto the dashboard and gazing at the speeding traffic to try to catch a glimpse of the tow trucks in chase.

Adam blurted! *"Are those bastards still behind us?*

"This is no time to loose control of your car, nor your mouth Adam" shouted Dexter. *"Just keep going as fast as you can without getting a ticket."*

"You're the one that caused this shit any way Dex. I didn't want to go down that road—are they still there?"

I can't see them, but I do see some blinking lights coming this way.

"What?" shouted Adam. *Is it the cops?"*

"I can't tell. How fast are you going?

"I was going 80. It's 65 now!"

"What are the colors of the lights on a tow truck?" asked Dexter.

"I think they're white!"

"Oh no!"

"Oh no, what?"

"Those are the lights of a police car."

"Ah sh#@!"

"Just take it easy Adam. Just wait 'till he stops us. We can explain. In fact, let me do the talking."

The flashing lights maneuvered through the traffic until they were flashing behind Adams car. Adam had slowed to 50 mph by the time the police car reached them. Dexter motioned for Adam to pull off to the left side of the road, next to the fast lane. The police car creped to the right middle lane with his turn signals indicating that he wanted to turn right. All traffic behind him had slowed to allow the vehicles to clear to the right shoulder. Adam recognized the intent of the officer in the car and exited to the right shoulder.

He pulled to a stop. They both sat stoic to await instructions. As they waited, Adam reached for the glove compartment to retrieve his insurance information. The officer flashed his bright lights through the rear of the car onto the back of Adam and Dexter.

"PLACE YOUR HANDS ON THE DASHBOARD AND LEAVE THEM THERE DRIVER!!!" ...PASSANGER, GET OUT OF THE CAR WITH YOUR HANDS UP!!!

The officer turned his spot light on Dexter as he opened the car with his hands in the air. The officer had drawn his weapon and aimed it towards Dexter.

"OFFICER... IS THERE SOMETHING WRONG? DID WE DO SOMETHING WRONG?"

"JUST KEEP YOUR MOUTH CLOSED AND PLACE YOUR HANDS ON TOP OF THE CAR...NOW!!!"

"But officer, if you stopped us for speeding...I can explain what happened! But you don't need you gun, 'cause we can tell you why...

"SIR, I WILL TELL YOU ONCE MORE... PLACE YOUR HANDS ON TOP OF THE CAR AND SHUT UP!!! ...DRIVER, GET OUT OF THE CAR SLOWLY AND BACK UP TOWARDS ME! ...SLOWLY!!!"

"What the hell's going on, officer?" asked Adam.

"You do like I told you and keep coming back here to me. Passenger, I don't want to tell you again to keep your hand on top of the car. Keep coming...keep coming. Now you place your hands on the trunk. If you do it nice and easy, nobody will get hurt. Put your hands back here for me."

"WHAT FOR, OFFICER?"

"I TOLD YOU BOY! ..."

"BOY! Who the hell you calling a boy? This ain't the 40's Judge Roy Bean!" yelled Adam.

"Okay, you boys are going to give me trouble, huh!"

"NO...no, we are not officer! We WILL cooperate. Put your hands on the trunk Adam. ...JUST DO IT, ADAM!"

"I am going to place these handcuffs on you for yours and my protection. Now you just hold still as I get...these...on."

"OFFICER," yelled Dexter. "Would you take a minute and listen to what we have to say? Just let us explain why we were speeding. Please, just give us a second to explain."

"You just place your hands behind you first. I will let you talk in just a minute. There will be an opportunity for you to tell me what you want in a few minutes. There...one second...now...what is your explanation?"

Before Dexter could speak, Adam was speaking to him in a language unknown by the officer. It was a gutter language (Pig Latin) they learned as children and spoke it anytime they didn't want anyone to understand what they were saying.

"Exterda, ontda ellta attha oolfa anyha-angtha!" (Dexter, don't tell that fool anything)

"Iha ontwa imha oota ona eha antca eattra usha ikela imenalscra." (I want him to know he can't treat us like criminals)

"If you got something to tell me, you better speak English," demanded the officer..."I'll tell you what...you just wait here till I get some assistance. Perhaps you two will need to go down to the station where we have an interpreter. How's that?...

24 to base!"

"Base, come in 24."

"Officer we were speeding because we were trying to get away from some guys who were chasing us in a tow truck" explained Dexter.

"Base, I need a supervisor to assist in a probable cause," requested the officer. "Excuse me! They were in a what?"

"There were some guy's chasing us in a... wait! ...There they are now! ...Those guy's right there,...in that tow truck. They were following us," explained Adam.

"What have you boys been smoking?" asked the officer.

The tow truck identified by the brothers drove by them slowly, as they peered at the scene on the side of the road. Inside were two males, whose eyes surveyed the action with keen interest. Dexter took note of the slight smile the passenger had on his face as he seemed to be writing something on a pad. Dexter wondered in his mind if these were the men they spotted back at the old house as they made their escape. They seemed sinister and seedy. If only this stupid officer would give them a chance to explain what they had just witnessed. He was not quite sure what is going on, but something was not right about this whole episode.

"Okay, take us to the station, Officer," demanded Dexter.

"Atwha areha ouya alkingta aha-outba, Exterda? Iha aintha oing-ga oota ona ationsta. Orfa atwha? (What are you talking about, Dexter? I ain't going to no station. For what?

"Attha isha oha-aka, Adamha. Iha ouldwa atherra aketa yma anchesha ithwa omesa-odyba ithwa omesa inha-ellenge-ta." (That is okay, Adam. I would rather take my chances with somebody with some intelligence.)

"Listen officer, we will corporate with you if you let us talk to your supervisor," explained Dexter.

"You boys just relax. He'll be here in a minute."

Dexter could envision a scenario where the rookie officer could commit an act of violence against them, due to his misunderstanding of their intentions. There was no doubt that they were speeding, but there is no cause for them to be hand-cuffed and made to endure the stares of passersby. What could he do to keep the situation calm for his brother, who seems to be getting irritated by the moment….? What would the guys in the tow truck be recording as they passed by? Were they in fact the guys chasing them, or were these guys just passing by to see if they needed towing? Dexter thought about the possibility of them being in a smuggling operation with illegal aliens. He also thought that these guys might be part of a gang. But none of those scenarios made any sense. He believed with all his heart that his brother Brian could not be involved with something so diabolical and illegal. But, on the other hand, Brian has been very guarded about his business. So much so, that he didn't even let his best friend Adam, in on the nature of his business. How this could be true, he thought. Family secrets could sometimes prove deadly, he reasoned. The possibilities were hard to imagine. His mind raced through them all with blinding speed. He dismissed them as fast as they came. He refused to believe that Brian got involved in anything against the law. On the other hand, he finally realized that he really didn't know him as well as he thought he did. Now, he could see that Adam was in the dark as well. Adam had always been led by Brian in his thinking, and even though they were grown men now, none of that has changed.

"Listen officer, you either take us to your station, or cut us loose if you refuse to believe that we are telling the truth," demanded Dexter.

The supervisor in charge of the evening shift pulled up behind the officers' car with his emergency lights flashing. At the same time of his arrival, Adam noticed that another tow truck was approaching them driving slowly, just as the other one did a few minutes earlier. This time, the driver was alone. He pulled in front of Adams car on the side of the road and turned on the emergency lights atop his truck. Dexter felt relieved that the supervisor was there. Perhaps he could make his point and get out of there. Dexter spoke.

"Thank you for coming, Sarge! Listen, I thought I would…"

"Sir… excuse me for a moment! I will be with you in a moment. What you got here Payne?"

"I got two Black males who are brothers, speeding… doing 82 mph in a 65 mile zone."

"That's bullsh…"

"ADAM! Adam, just chill brother. This officer here is going to take care of this situation. Let's just give him a chance to hear us…it'll be alright," assured Dexter.

"Did you run their info on the computer, Officer Payne?" asked the supervisor.

"*No not yet. They were acting suspicious, so I had to cuff them first. I'll run them now.*"

Officer Payne captured both of the brothers wallets, and walked back to his police car. After checking their numbers in the police records. Meanwhile, the tow truck driver exited his cab, and was leaning against the drivers' side door. The Supervisor walked over to him and held a conversation for a few minutes before returning back to the brothers. He spoke.

"*Now, tell me…what were you boys doing out here spying on these independent business owners? What were you looking for?*"

"*Sergeant, we never said anything about any business…where did you get that from?*" Asked Dexter?

Dexter looked at Adam about the same time a light went off in Adams head. Where did that officer get information about what happened before they were stopped for speeding, Dexter asked himself. None of this was adding up in their minds.

"*Okay Sergeant, I ran their info and we don't have anything on either of them. I guess we can give them a ticket for speeding and send them on their way.*"

"*Let me see the report,*" said the Sergeant. .."*Okay….last name Simon…address is 1209 W. Adams… Wait a second…last name Simon! Your last name is Simon? Do you have another brother?*"

"*Yes we do,*" answered Adam.

"*Was he in an accident a weeks ago?*" asked the Sergeant.

"*Yes he was…he is in comma as we speak. That was what we were trying to explain to you guys. That's why we came out here to check on his business and…*"

"*ADAM! It's okay. Let's leave it alone. Let's leave it there, okay? We don't need to go any further, okay? Okay?*"

"*Come with me Mr. Simon. Step back here by my car. I will get those handcuffs off of you, okay?*" assured the supervisor.

"*Okay, good… It's about time.*" agreed Adam.

The supervisor took Adam to the rear of his car near the trunk.

Dexter could see that he was questioning his brother about something. Adam was animated as if he was trying to deny something that the officer did not believe. Without warning, the supervisor sucker punched Adam to the stomach. Adam bent over trying to catch his breath. Dexter yelled!

"HEY! ...HEY! *What are you doing to my brother, officer? What is your supervisor doing? WHAT IS HE DOING? HEY, OFFICER...YOU KNOW THAT IS ILLEGAL WHAT YOU ARE DOING!*" yelled Dexter.

The supervising officer appeared to be on some sort of mission. He would not ease up on the questions he was asking Adam. Each time he asked a question, and Adam shrugged his shoulders, he was punched in the stomach until he was beaten to the ground. Officer Payne kept an eye on Dexter while Adam was being interrogated. The supervisor assisted Adam in getting on his feet with the cuffs still on. Adam was so weak, he could hardly stand. When the supervisor thought he had not made any progress with Adam, he assisted him back to Officer Payne's squad car. Dexter was about as mad as he had ever been. He knew this was not right, and he knew the officers knew they were wrong. But, what were they trying to extract from Adam? Why was the supervisor so intent on questioning him concerning a traffic violation? In his heart, he knew there was something about this situation that was much bigger than it looked on the surface. Now, he wondered if he was going to be the next one in line to be beaten. Is this what Rodney King went through, he wondered? How far will these "protectors" go in violating their own universal slogan..."To protect & Serve"?

"*Sergeant, what is going on here? You have no right to abuse my brother like that!*"

"*I would suggest you get the hell out of here and never come back, do you understand?*"

"*We will leave, but you better believe we will report this to the NAACP, the Urban League, and anyone else who will listen. What is your name and badge number, sir? Sergeant H.. a.. r.. l ..e ..y! ... I got it!*"

"What you got is… exactly ten seconds to get in your car, you and your brother, and get the hell out of here. I BETTER NEVER SEE YOU AROUND HERE AGAIN…NEVER! Is that understood? If I do…I won't take you to jail, but it will be the last time you'll see your brother again."

Dex reached for his brother who was still bent over from the sucker punch the officer gave him.

"Come on Adam, let's go home. You better believe he hasn't heard the last of us!"

Standing beside the officer was the tow truck driver who had remained there throughout the incident. He had a shameful grin of a smile on his face which puzzled Dex. With his arms folded and swaying from side to side, the driver shook hands with the officer as he whispered undistinguishable words that suggested an agreement between the two of them. Dex assisted Adam into the passenger's seat and closed the door. He walked around the front of the car to the driver's side and climbed in.

"What is it that you two were talking about? Is there something I should know," asked Dex.

"Come on Dex, let's get the hell out of here" said Adam as he groaned while holding his stomach. "Just take me back to Momma's house so I can drop you off. That son-of-a-bitch musta busted my guts, he hit me so hard."

"I can't believe what just happened, Adam. I wanted to jump in there and get him off of you. But…what would happen then?"

The drive to Momma's house did not seem to take as long as it did on the way out. Dexter wanted to get some answers on what had transpired at Brian's place of business, and on the road with the officer. As he pulled into the driveway, he turned the headlights off so he would not disturb his mother. He was mostly silent for most of the drive, trying to process the past couple of hours.

"Adam, I have watched television many times, when I saw the police abuse a citizen, but…"

"Dex, Dex, cut the bull man. Don't you realize this ain't no television? This shit is real, man."

"But that was not supposed to happen. We didn't do anything except maybe speed. What did we do that got him so mad he wanted to use violence?"

"Listen brother, I didn't like it one bit. But you don't know why he was so upset at us. It wasn't about the speeding, Dex."

"What was it about?"

"Come on Dex, don't you smell something rotten about this whole evening? You got to know what I'm talking about…you can't be that naive!"

"No, I don't know! What was it, please tell me!"

"I got to get home Dex. I don't have the time to talk about it now!"

"Adam, I need to know. Does it have anything to do with Brian?" I mean, are you connecting that officer with what we saw at Brian's business?"

"You're getting warm my brother. You're getting warm."

"Wait a minute, do you think that officer is involved with Brian, in the towing business, and he doesn't want us to know about it? How does he know we are related to Brian."

"Don't you recognize that officer, Dex?"

"Should I recognize him?"

"Man that was the cop who brought Brian's cell phone to the hospital."

"Oh my God, you're right! That was the same officer, who was so nice to the family!"

"Well what's his problem now? Why was he so upset over our speeding?"

"That's what I'm trying to tell you Dex. It ain't about the speeding. Can't you see, in some way, he was notified that we were there at that house. Someone notified him that we saw something there that we were not supposed to see."

"Who? Why? How?"

I don't know, man. All I want to do right now is get home so I can soak in a tub of hot water. I got to go man. I'm really hurting!"

"Okay, okay. But let me ask you this, what did you say that caused that officer to punch you like he did?"

"I can't talk about it right now, brother. I got to get the hell out of here and get into a tub of water, alright? I'll talk to you tomorrow. Tomorrow, not now!"

Dexter watched as Adam drove off from their mothers house. It was dark and dank as it has for over 2 weeks now. Dexter searched and found his keys in his jacket pocket. As he opened the door to his car, he looked up and saw a light on in his mothers bedroom. He hesitated for a couple of seconds before deciding to investigate whether she was having a problem. He stepped upon the front porch, quietly. He knocked on the door a couple of times so as not to frighten her. He waited. He knocked again a little harder, and called for her at the same time.

"Mom! Mom, are you up?"

He heard nothing! He was not sure if it was normal for her to turn the light on after she went to bed, or not. One thing for sure, he had to assure himself of her safety. He moved closer to the window to her bedroom and called out to her again.

"Mom, it's Dex. Are you up?"

He heard her respond through the tight walls of the house.

"Who is it?" she called out.

"It's me mom, Dex. Are you alright?"

Dex waited to hear more. After what seemed like five minutes or so, the front door opened, as Mrs. Simon appeared.

"Mom, are you alright?"

Dex moved to his mothers' side as he noticed that she had been crying.

"What's wrong mom?

Mrs. Simon turned her head and walked back into her home,

where Dex placed his arms around her shoulder and followed her back inside.

"*Mom is something wrong? Come on, now, you can talk to me. Let's sit down over here. You're not hurting are you?*"

Dexter had not experienced his mother's state of emotion such as she was displaying now. He wanted to speculate but thought not. Perhaps it's best to just sit and let her explain her emotions when she felt ready to do so. He waited as he sat across from her with his arms resting on his knees. He spoke.

"*I am not going to leave you, until you are ready for me to, mom. You take your time.*"

She spoke.

"*Dexter, my heart is heavy tonight. I couldn't sleep, so I got up and took another sleeping pill.*"

Dexter spoke.

"*But I thought you were not supposed to take those sleeping pills because they made you feel funny all day.*"

"*Yeh, they do, but I needed something to help me tonight.*"

"*Well tell me what's going on with you, why are you having such a heavy heart tonight, mom?*"

"*One day, the Lord might give you boys a 6th sense so you can see what us women see and feel. Maybe one day he will.*"

Dexter agreed with his mother and knew exactly what she meant. But he also knew he needed to go silent so she could share her feelings with him. Mom continued...

"*You know, one thing your daddy always told you children--become a leader and let somebody else follow YOU. Now he wanted you boys to take what you been taught, and carve a path to success by your own means. He always believed in helping yourself and not have to depend on nobody else for your success. That's what kept us here where we are now-my husbands gone, but I don't owe nobody for nothing- Never have. That's cause he made sure he worked and made money to support our family, and he made sure I had what I needed to raise all of you kids by leaving enough life insurance*" *when he died. Now I have used some of that money to put several of you children through college, 'specially you."*

"And you know how much I appreciate you helping me with my Undergrad studies, Mom."

"I know that. But, let me tell you this...I'm not having a heavy heart because of you. You are the only one of my boys who even wanted to go to College; so naturally, I was going to make sure you got what you needed. My problem right now, is I don't have a long time to live, and I feel I have not done all I needed to do to help all my children get off to a good start in life. All the girls are married and doing fine. It's your two other brothers that's bothering me now. Adam being the baby boy, just seemed to follow after Brian. They always were together, in everything. If Brian wanted to jump off the bridge, I 'sposse Adam would want to follow after him. Now they are grown...well all 'yall's grown...seems like they go away from what your daddy said about being a leader."

"Well mom, you know that boys have to somehow find their own way, as the saying goes."

"That's an old saying for sure, but look what's happening to Brian. That boy has had the hardest time of it and look what he's doing now. Driving those old tow trucks. I don't even think he's making much money, do you?"

"That I don't know, mom. I'm trying to find out. I hate to even ask about his business. Nobody wants to talk about it. You know he's got a nice house, and drives a nice car. But beyond that I don't know what he's doing with any money he might be making," said Dexter.

*"It's not just about making more money either, Dexter. It's about living right with God. God got to be number one. Now that boy's laying up there in that hospital, not knowing if he is here or there, and **he don't know the Lord!** That's what got me worried most of all. I'm praying God will spare him so he can decide to accept the Lord Jesus before the Lord takes him out of this world. Now I know what's happening between you boys Dexter, but you are the oldest, and you are a leader and a Christian. Your daddy always thought you had a good head on your shoulder. So, you listen to me..."*

"I know what you're gonna say, mamma!"

"Well, let me say it then, before I can't say anything anymore. You are the leader. You got to make the effort to help straighten out your brother's life, if he ever gets out of that comma."

"But that suggests that I have the power of the Holy Spirit mom, which you know I don't...nobody has that power, mom!"

"Jesus said, when you pray, and you believe in your heart what you pray for, it shall be done."

"Yes, I am familiar with that passage, but..."

"Naw, that's where your Faith comes in. If the Bible is the word of God, and God (Jesus) said it...it must be true! As believers, we must believe all of God's word...We must have Faith that his word is Truth! Use his word, Dexter...Stay true to his teachings and do what you know you need to do to save your brother from eternal damnation... from being lost forever... from destroying his life and his family. I'm counting on you... you can do it!"

Mrs. Simon appeared to be fading off to sleep. Her speech slowed. Her head lowered to her chest several times. Dexter felt he had a good understanding of her concerns for her family-what was bothering her-preventing her from having a restful night. He was conflicted about the assignment his mother was giving him. He knew in his heart he faced a mountain of opposition with the mere suggestion of salvation to both his brothers. He did not speak as he assisted her in going back to bed. He gently covered her again, and gave her a kiss on the forehead. He again, turned out the light and quietly, left the house.

Chapter 14

Friday nights were set aside for Dexter and Norma to have some private time together. As usual, Norma had arranged for them to take in a movie and grab a meal afterwards. Dexter left his mothers house around 9PM, and he thought Norma might take a rain check until next week. So he dialed home on his cell phone to tell her he should be home within the hour. They actually lived in the suburbs, some 25 miles away, but the weather was causing him to drive slower than normal. Norma answered the home phone with a sound of anticipation and excitement.

"Hellooo!"

"Hey, baby, it's me!"

"I thought I recognized that voice... you're my husband, aren't you?"

"That I am, sweetheart...that I am!"

"Are you on your way home?"

"Yep, I'm about 45 to 50 minutes away."

"It's gonna take you THAT long?" I don't think I can wait THAT long for you to get here!"

"Well, you can always meet me half way, you know!"

"You are funny, you know that? Listen, do you still want to get something to eat out, or do you want me to cook you something here?"

"Baby, can I get a rain check until tomorrow night? It's been one heck of a day for me, and I do **not** feel like going anywhere tonight. Do you mind?"

"Of course I do!" But I'll give you the check, though. Tomorrow night, right?"

"You got it!"

"Okay, see you shortly. Oh, I'll have a baked potato, if you don't mind—All the way!"

"Oh, you don't want a pota**to**, you want a pota**toe!**"

"You got it!"

"Thanks, babe! See you soon!

The relationship between Dexter and Norma was as loving and genuine as any Christian married couple could be. Dexter appreciated Norma's patience with him during the course of their 15 years of marriage. Considering all they had experienced in their earlier years, they both felt their relationship had grown to solid ground. Because of that fact, he felt he needed to share his deepest emotions and feelings about today's events with the one he trusted the most. No one else would understand the confusion, hurt and rejection he has suffered since he has tried to reconnect with his family of origin. No one else would understand his passion for serving Christ, and his mission he had been given to bring peace and salvation to his lost siblings. He knew she would be the one who would give him comfort and words of wisdom. His mother's words came to the fore-front of his mind. She had appointed him as the family leader. That responsibility loomed large and daunting. He knew the road would be long and hard. Proverbs 1:3 came to his mind. He wanted to be fair, just, and wise in all his relationships. That's what he needed to do tonight- he needed to read some scripture with his wife, before he closed his eyes to rest-before he closed his eyes to rest. He gripped the steering wheel with both hands and repositioned himself in the seat as he uttered these words:

"I TRUST IN YOU LORD! I TRUST IN YOU!"

When Dexter arrived home, Norma had his meal ready, and on the kitchen table. Dexter came in and greeted her with a kiss; quickly washed his hands, and sat down to eat. Norma sat across from him and leaned on the table with her elbows. She watched him as he raked through the potato, mixing the condiments into it. He made no eye contact with Norma, as she expected. She waited for his leadership in communicating with her. Something was going on that weighed heavily on him, but it was up to him to discuss it. After what seemed like an eternity, Dexter spoke:

"Are you feeling okay about our moving back here from Chicago, honey?"

"Yes, of course baby… why do you ask?"

"I want to be sure you are happy with being here… you know with everything happening with everybody, and the difficulties we are having fitting in with my brothers! I just wanted to know how all this is affecting you."

"You know the Bible tells us that because we have accepted the way of salvation by accepting Jesus Christ that we are going to suffer rejection, for his name sake. And…the Apostle Paul said we should count it as joy to be persecuted for Christ."

"You are right about that Norma, and I appreciate those words from my best friend. I really appreciate you, honey… I really appreciate your support as well, my queen!"

"Well, my king, I appreciate you, too! Oh, let me turn that television off."

"Wait! What's on? What are they saying about this weather?"

"More of the same for the next few days. I tell you, there's something going on with this weather. This is unusually bad weather to go on this long. It's depressing. Maybe we need a vacation to the Islands," she said jokingly.

"That might be a good idea. But, I need to get some answers to some questions I have before we can get away."

"You mean, about your brother's accident?"

"Yep, and a whole lot more. I can't understand the mess Brian seems to be tangled up in….. I mean, I would never believe…. what I'm seeing and hearing…. if somebody told me."

"Well, what is it, honey?"

"I haven't figured it out yet. It's all confusing and I don't know how much I want to know, either. Either way, if you smell a rat, there probably is one near by. I'm trying to determine how much I want to know. I would feel less of a brother, a man or Christian, if something was happening that should not have been happening, and I could have done something about it, but didn't. You following what I'm saying?"

"What's on your mind, baby?"

"I'm trying to figure out the plan…the plan for me, for you, for us, for my siblings… everybody. I mean, there has to be a reason for us to be offered a job, and our accepting a job, doing what I went to college for, right here in the town where I grew up. There's a reason… right?"

"Of course there is. I believe we are where God wants us to be, at the precise time he wants us to be, where we are. Does that make sense?"

"Okay, okay. Let me share this with you. All day long I have been with Adam. Now Adam is the kind of guy who is easy going, who can be trusted to keep tight secrets about anything you ask him to. Now, I persuaded him to take me out to Brian's place to check on his business. He didn't want to, but he relented and drove me some thirty miles out of town. Without getting in all the details, we found some things out there that do not look legitimate."

"Legitimate how?"

"We almost got run over by one of Brian's tow truck drivers, for one. Then, when we got to his office, somebody turned off the light inside. When we went inside and made our way to the back of the old house, we saw what appeared to be workers, but they were handling people who were handcuffed behind their backs."

"Wait a minute, wait a minute. PEOPLE WITH HANDCUFFS?"

"Yes! But we couldn't stay long because a huge dog spotted us, and we had to scamper out of there as fast as we could, with some of them chasing after us."

"Baby, this sounds like a plot for a television series!"

"I know! But wait, there's more."

"More?"

"We were being chased onto the main highway by some of the men (guy's) behind Brian's place. When we got on the interstate, Adam was going over the speed limit, and we got stopped by an aggressive police officer."

"Don't tell me... he gave him a ticket!"

"Worse than that, he called his boss on the radio."

"That was worse?"

"What happened when he came is the mystery to me."

"What happened?"

"The supervisor apparently has some connection with the men in the tow truck, who were chasing after us!"

"What kind of connection?"

"I mean they were apparently working together, in some kind of way."

"Well what did they do to...?"

Before Norma could complete what she was saying, Dexter interrupted.

"The supervisor took Adam to the side and was questioning him in a way that caused the supervisor to punch him in the stomach, several times."

"Oh... my... God!"

"I questioned the officer but he only told me that if I didn't shut my mouth, that I would get the same treatment. They would not explain why we were stopped in the first place and placed in handcuffs."

"They put you in handcuffs? Why?"

That's the mystery, honey. Here's where it gets real nasty!... it appeared that the supervisor was in with the tow truck driver, as he demanded that we stay away from that area, never to return. Now guess who that supervisor was?"

"You want me to guess who he was? How would I know?"

"Remember the officer who brought Brian's phone to the hospital?"

"Yeesss!"

"Officer Harley! He was the supervisor! He was the one who seems to be involved with Brian's business in some way.

"Honey, is Adam alright?"

"No, he's not. He's hurting right now, but he refuses to tell me why Officer Harley kept hitting him."

"You saw him do it?"

"Yes! I tried to stop him, but he hit him a couple more times. It was unreal, honey. It looked as if Adam was not giving him information the Officer wanted. He might have some bruised ribs, I feel."

"Oh my Lord, I think that's terrible, honey! I think that should be reported to someone as some sort of brutality!"

"To top all that off, when I asked Adam what caused the officer to assault him as he did, Adam went silent on me! I mean, he just shut down and refused to talk about it! I **saw** what happened, and yet, **he didn't want to talk about it!**"

"My GOD!"

"Listen Norma, I feel strongly, that I need to find out more about what's going on around here, don't you?"

"Oh baby, I don't know! I just don't know what good can come out of all this... this...!"

"This messed up... situation... complicated ... conflict! It's hard to describe. It's difficult to sort out when everybody is so secretive, **about everything!**"

"Honey, why don't you pray over it? Ask the Lord to show you what you should do. I don't want you to be stressed out behind anything that's been going on before we came. There's too much going on without seeking the Holy Spirit's eyes, protection and guidance.

"Yeh, you're right!... I need to pray about it, and ask the Lord to reveal the truth to me. **The truth shall set us all free, in all things.**"

"I'll pray with you. Why don't you take a shower when you finish eating, and I'll pray with you before we go to bed, okay?"

"Okay my Queen. Okay!"

Norma went ahead of Dexter into the master bathroom to get his bath towels ready for his shower. Dexter completed his meal and placed his dishes in the washer. He went to the den to turn off the television, to retire for the night. As he was about to push the power button, he paused to hear the following news flash:

"**This just in to our newsroom here at KLAC TV... there has been a huge explosion... we don't have all the details as of now... we do understand that an explosion has occurred on the outskirts of town... about 30 miles northeast of downtown... and our reporter Kitty Kincaid is headed out there now. Apparently she has not arrived as of yet. We will bring more details to you when she arrives and gets set up. In the meantime, a witness to the explosion and fire is on the line to our newsroom now... alright, alright, I am getting word now, that this was a person who was driving on the northeast interstate... who heard several loud explosions, and saw giant plums of fire climbing over 150-200 feet in the air... As I said, we will have some pictures and a report for you shortly, from our anchor, who is on her way to the event as we speak. Just to repeat, there has been an explosion, apparently a significant series of explosions, according to an eye witness who called in a couple of minutes ago... and that witness reported to us that they saw a very large fire ball, after hearing what they described as several loud explosions. Okay... we have a little more information now. The fire is at a business, located about a quarter mile off the northeast interstate, some 35 miles from downtown. Now that area is in an older part of the city, and very few businesses are located out there. Okay, reporter Kitty Kincaid is at the scene now, and has a report for us... Kitty, do you have a report on what happened out there on the northeast interstate? Has anyone been hurt, do we know?**"

Dexter called to Norma.

"*Honey come here and listen to this... there has been an explosion!*"

"*Where? Is anyone hurt?*"

"I don't know, yet…it just happened! Let's listen!"

"Yes Samantha, we are at the intersection of the Northeast Interstate and Old Simmons Road. We are near the scene of an explosion and fire at a business which has several warehouses at the rear of it. The business was actually housed in an old house, and the warehouses were unattached. That is where the explosion occurred, according to the Fire Captain in charge. Investigators are on their way to the scene, but the unpaved road to get to the business is very rough and muddy, making it difficult to get to the scene of the fire. We understand that there are Law Enforcement agencies here, including the FBI, Homeland Security, the DEA, the Sheriff Department, as well as the local Police. The Police have roped off the area at the Interstate, not allowing anyone to get near the scene. Samantha, back to you!"

The anchor continued her assessment of the situation as Dexter turned to Norma.

"Baby, did you hear her say they had the FBI, the DEA, and all those law enforcement agencies out there?" asked Dexter.

"Yes, I heard. Wow, it must be something pretty important going on, wouldn't you say?"

Dexter was listening intently to the TV anchorwoman.

"Kitty, before you go for now, can you tell us if we know the name of the business, or who owns that business, or even what type of business it is?"

"What we can tell you Samantha, is that it is, or was, a towing business. They had several tow trucks parked on the lot that were apparently destroyed. We have not completed our investigation on who the owner is, or what caused the explosion in the warehouses in the rear. As soon as we get that information, we will follow up with you … Samantha!"

"N o r m a!"

"Yes, "Yes, I'm right here!," Norma found herself shouting.

"Baby, are you hearing what I'm hearing? Did you hear that reporter say what type business it was?"

"I heard her say it was a towing business."

"Yes, and it's located off the Interstate... some 30 miles from downtown... with some warehouses in the rear... Baby, that's the description... of Brian's business!!!"

Chapter 15

I
t was early Saturday morning, when Dexter entered into the
YMCA to get in some exercise. Although he jogged two to
three times a week, lifting weights was reserved for the weekend.
Because of the rainy weather over the past couple of weeks, he had
not been able to work out at all-so he reasoned. He made his way to
the weight room, where several other men were grunting and straining
to work off the past weeks stress their bodies had accumulated. As
Dexter approached the stationary bike, he noticed another man, in
his forties- breathing heavily- and about to leave. On his tee shirt was
the name of a company called, "Klein Investigative Services." Dexter
toiled over whether to strike up a conversation with him, or not. In his
mind, the news report from last night was potentially devastating, and
could further tear his family system apart, if in fact that was Brian's
business. This fellow, he thought, might just be the one who could
help him find some answers he sought about his brother's business
involvement. Assuredly, any degree of investigation would shed more
light than he had, but how much did he really want to know? After
praying with Norma last night, he awoke this morning feeling as if
God had not yet answered him. He felt no compulsion to move in one
way or the other. The story ran again this morning, but with little,
new information. To avert loosing all contact with this man, Dexter

decided to greet him, and to ask if he had a business card. It would be good to have his information, just in case. Before the stranger reached the door to exit the weight room, Dexter spoke:

"*Good morning!*"

"*Good Morning,*" the stranger repeated.

"*May I interrupt you for a moment?*"

"*Of course... not a problem... how are you?*"

"*I'm fine, sir... just fine! I wanted to ask if that was your company there on your tee shirt..."Klein Investigative Service?*"

"*Yes it is... I'm Marvin Klein! ... I'm the owner!*"

"*Ah ha! Mr. Klein, do you have a card with you, just in case I know someone who may need your services sometimes...you know!*"

"*I do know, and I do have a card. Let me get it for you from my car. Just give me a minute and I will be right back with you.*"

This meeting by chance, with someone who was a professional investigator 'seemed' to be a Godsend. Could this be the answer to Dexter's prayer? Did God establish for this meeting to take place, at this time? Unquestionably, an investigator would be able to find answers Dexter could never expect to.

"*All right sir, here you are. I gave you several. Feel free to pass them out to someone else if you like. By the way, I didn't catch **your** name?*"

"*Oh, I'm sorry. My name is Dexter Simon.*"

"*Good to meet you, Dexter... Simon, huh? That name Simon, sounds familiar. But you don't sound as if you are from around here!*"

"*It's rather common for people born in Louisiana. But I spent most of my adult life in Chicago, Illinois.*" Said Dexter.

"*That's what I'm hearing... a Chi-town brogue,*" explained Marvin. "*It seems I ran across that name just recently. Huumm! Oh well, if I can be of any assistance, you got my card, Dexter.*"

"*I appreciate it, Marvin. Good to meet you! Take care!*"

Chapter 16

D
exter had promised Norma to take her out to a movie and to dinner on Saturday night. In view of the recent catastrophic event concerning Brian's business, and the horrific news last night, he thought it best to go by the hospital first and visit with Sharon and Brian. He had not talked to Norma about the chance meeting he had with Marvin Klein earlier that morning. Dexter was feeling the pressure mounting within him, to balance the reality he was facing, of some strange entanglements of his brother, and trying to advance his assimilation into the family. He traveled with Norma to the front parking lot. Norma noticed the cars parked at the entrance to the hospital. She commented to Dexter.

"I wonder what these cars are doing here on a Saturday night-so many of them. Oh, look honey; those are DEA, and FBI cars. I wonder..."

"You are absolutely right, honey. I see some police cars at the other end as well. Maybe we need to wait here for a moment to see what's going on."

Law Enforcement personnel were moving away from the hospital toward the outer perimeters of the parking lot. An Officer motioned for incoming cars to turn around as he stretched a yellow 'Police barrier' tape from light pole to light pole. Dexter and Norma sat motionless, watching the activity around them.

"What going on, honey?"

"Let me ask this Officer... EXCUSE ME, SIR! ... SIR, can you tell me what's going on?"

"Law enforcement business, sir. You need to back your car up and follow that Officers' direction over there!"

"But why? Just tell me what's going on! My brother is in that hospital... Can you just tell me?"

"Sir, I have to ask you to move this vehicle, now!"

"Alright, I'll move! I was just trying to find out what was happening in there! Honey, take my phone and call Sharon. She probably is in there with Brian. Do you have the number?"

"Yes, I have it. I'll call her! ..."

She dialed. The phone rang three times-then again. The voice mail came on. Norma looked at Dexter and said:

"She's not answering it!"

"Let me call Adam," said Dexter. "He might have heard of what's happening here!"

"Adam, hey man, how you feeling?"

"Like hell! My ribs feel like they've been run over by a tractor. What's up?"

"Listen, Norma and I are here at the hospital. Actually, we're in the parking lot-we can't get into the hospital. We tried to reach Sharon, but she's not answering her phone. Do you know anything? I mean nothing makes sense. Have you heard anything?"

"No, I've been sleep most of the day."

"Did you hear the news last night?

"No, I came home and went to bed. I need to go back to bed now... I need some rest. Did you check on the news today? There might be something on today about the hospital," said Adam.

"No I haven't. I'm going to turn the radio on now. Okay, you put a heat pack on your ribs. And Adam, if you're not feeling better, you really should get to a clinic to check it out. I'll call you later, okay!"

While Dexter searched for a news station, a couple with their child in the fathers' arm squeezed through the cars, passing by Dexter's car on the drivers side. He decided to ask them about the activity going on at the hospital.

"Hello sir …what's happening over there?"

"The Fed's, FBI and looks like everybody else, just came in and put everybody out. They went to all the exit doors and locked them, and I heard they went to the ICU floor, for some reason. I don't know man; it's weird in there with their guns, and that Rambo look!"

Norma found a news station on the radio. They listened as Dexter tried to find a spot to park a couple of blocks away from the hospital.

"**… And a spokesperson for the hospital reported that they have not been told the reason why the law enforcement personnel are there… she said they have been told to stay in their sections and not to move around within the hospital. As was reported last night, the FBI, DEA, Homeland Security and other law enforcement agencies were busy after an explosion and fire in Northeast part of the city, and now they are busy again this afternoon, at the Regional Hospital. Speculation is that these two incidents are related, but we reiterate, it is speculation. The visitors to the hospital, there to see their loved ones, are told that they must leave, without explanation. Stay tuned to this station for more information, which we will bring to you as soon as we get it.**"

"Oh my God, honey!" Brian is on the ICU floor. What on earth do you make of this?"

"You and I are in the same boat, honey. Just about the time you think everything's so confusing… it gets worse! The reporter say's the same enforcement agencies from the explosion, are here at the hospital! **And… and**, they are on the floor where Brian is located. This is too coincidental for it not to be relevant, or… for there to be NO connection!"

"Honey, are you saying you think Brian has something to do with all this?" I mean, he's in a comma! What are you saying?"

"I don't know what I'm saying! I'm saying… Brian might not be the skunk, but he's got the smell of one! Somebody got to have some pretty good evidence to the contrary, if there's no connection."

"Why do you think we can't get hold of Sharon? You want to try Brian's phone?"

"Try it. Let's see what happens!"

She dials. The phone rang three times. A male voice answers.

"Hello, who do you need?"

"Who is this?" asks Norma.

This is Officer Harley, what can I do for you?"

Chapter 17

Dexter and Norma were anxious to find some answers to the many questions they had. It has been about two weeks since this whole ordeal started and the mystery surrounding Brian's business; his possible involvement in some unlawful activity; and the unknown status of his health, weighed heavily on their minds. It used to be a simpler life when they lived in a suburb of Chicago, just three years ago. Dexter is beginning to question the wisdom of his own decision to start a new life with his wife and dogs, in a town she was not familiar with, which has come to be a distant memory for him. He rationalized however, that it was worth the efforts they put forward in trying to reconnect with his family of origin. Faced with the prospects of sinking even deeper into a morass of complications, Dexter wanted answers. He wanted more from his brother Adam. He felt Adam knew more than he was sharing with him, and wondered if he was also drawn into something he did not ask for.

"Baby, I need to go see Adam. There's just too much going on that surrounds him and Brian. I don't understand what it is, but I feel things are getting out of hand. I need to go talk to him. Do you mind? Do you want to go with me?"

"No, honey, I don't mind. But perhaps you should talk with him alone. He might feel free to open up with just the two of you."

"Well, I want us to go to dinner later, so what do you want to do?"

"Take me to the Mall, and I'll do some shopping for a couple of hours. Will that be enough time for you?"

"Okay, that'll be great! I'll drop you off and pick you up in front of that Jewelry store about 6, okay?"

Dexter decided not to call Adam on the phone until he was in front of his home. He wanted him not to make up an excuse for not seeing him, in spite of him not feeling up to it. After dropping Norma off at the Mall, he drove to an older neighborhood where Adam lived alone. It was a neat and tidy little neighborhood, with mostly elderly neighbors. It was the home where Adam's last wife had lived before she died in an auto accident. They had no children, but Adam had two with his first wife. On occasion, she would check in on him, and asked for financial assistance for the youngest daughter, approaching 13 years old. Dexter drove onto the driveway and parked. He walked up to the front porch and rang the doorbell. After the third ring, Adam came to the door and peered through the peep hole. Recognizing that it was Dexter, he unlocked the latch and walked away. Dexter could hear the noise made by the unlatching, but he waited for a greeting which never came. He opened the screen door, and grabbed hold of the door knob. He yelled for Adam while opening the door at the same time. Adam had moved to a queen Ann chair in the living room and turned on the floor lamp positioned next to the chair. Adam spoke.

"You couldn't let me rest could you?" You had to come over here and aggravate me, just for the hell of it, right? I mean, that's your calling ain't it Dex? In fact, I think your calling is to aggravate the shit out of everybody, am I right? ... Me ...Brian ...Momma!"

"Have you been drinking? You must've been drinking, Adam. You think I'm aggravating, huh? You think I am aggravating everybody, huh? Well brother, let me be clear... You have not seen the real me, if you think I've been aggravating! You just wait! ...Do you want to be the one that has to tell momma her son's are involved in something that made the news? You want to be the one that's responsible for cracking this 'brittle'

family apart because you know something is not right, and you refuse to do anything about it? You just wait until I get some answers on all this (Frickin) confusion around here! After I get some truth into what's happening; some clarity, then you will see some aggravation my brother! ...I have had about enough of all this secrecy!

"What **secrecy** are you talking about, Dex? Why do you get so worked up and sensitive about everything?

"You know what I'm talking about, Adam. **What's going on over there at that hospital? What kind of business was Brian really running?** Why does that Officer Harley always show up, and why was he beating on you last night? **What was he doing answering Brian's phone today?** Why are all those Cops and Feds swarming all over the hospital, and are on the ICU floor, where Brian is located? Can you answer that for me, Adam? What is it you're not telling me? What is Brian involved with? Are you involved with him, too? I need some answers, brother, and I need them quick. Because frankly, I know where to go to get the truth. ...Once and for all Adam, tell me what's going on! Tell... me... the... **truth!**"

"Are you sure... you can handle ...**the truth**, Dex?

Chapter 18

April showers were common in Northeast Texas well into the month of May. In fact, it was becoming that time of year, like no other, when its inhabitants held their communal breaths in anticipation of crisp, clean and oxygenated air invading their lungs, after a dreary, long and cold winter. Time-it seemed-had stood still, allowing freezing bad weather to hover over their socio/physical lives, infecting their psychology. Per capita, more babies are conceived in this area every year, than in any other area of the country. At least other weather systems allowed people to get out and clean up after a storm. But here, the weather was just plain old bad, for most of its climacteric weather seasons. In spite of these doom and gloom conditions, the Law Enforcement agencies assigned to the investigation of the explosion and fire Northeast of town, had to go on. The mere fact that there was some mystery about the cause of the catastrophe, Marvin Klein, The areas top Private Investigator, decided he needed to do a little investigation of his own. He determined that he needed to get to the sight, to get a sense of the enormity of the problems associated with the explosion. He reasoned that there must have been combustible materials, oxygen and something that created a spark. It would not be easy, however. The area would be cordoned off and protected by law enforcement officials from everywhere. This is the area to start his investigation, he reasoned, being prompted by the news reports from the weekend. He already knew about a seemingly average guy getting involved in a business which has attracted federal agents. What could there be out there, that might suggest something really big is going on out here-- or was? But what? Why are Zack Powders' people involved? Why is this so hush-hush? It's time for some answers. This might be his most shining moment-a moment of discovery leading to triumph.

Nightfall provided cover for Marvin as he approached the area where the explosion occurred. He was not certain of the exact location; therefore he needed to be stealth a half mile from the turnoff. Without lights, he made his way into the field adjoining the burned out property. The wet, grass weed was shoulder length and sliced across Marvin's face as he made his way through the thicket in a zigzag pattern. His shoes attracted ounces of mud with every step he made. He struggled to keep his footing as his breathing labored. In Marvin's mind, his instincts on this one were right. He felt certain he would uncover something that would be relevant to Brian and something he was involved in, that was illegal. The forces of intrigue and suspicion are powerful. They have always driven Marvin to a level beyond the probing done by an average investigator. His approach to investigating has been equated to that of a blood hound dog-so he nosed forward. The rains continued to fall, with intermittent thunder and lightning. Marvin heard noises up ahead. He heard sounds of truck engines and tractors as they moved debris around. Voices were heard giving instructions concerning the investigation. The blast was so powerful, it settled debris well over four hundred feet in diameter. Marvin was close enough now, to stop and take a survey of the situation. Although it was hard to see details, he was able to determine that body bags were being stuffed and placed inside of a refrigerator truck. What was that all about, he thought? Why are there dead bodies out here in the middle of nowhere; and why are they associated with this small-time business owner, who is lying in a state of unconsciousness in the hospital? What was it that Zack Powder couldn't tell him about the law enforcement investigation of one Brian Simon? Could this incident be a mere accident, or was it staged to cover something up on a larger scale? Is Brian a "player", or is he just a pawn being played by some sinister, evil individuals, with diabolical plans yet to be revealed?

It was time to maneuver to get in closer to the action, past the plastic tape barricade around the outer perimeter. Resembling a lion stalking its prey, Marvin crouched as he stepped slowly towards the muddy road in front of the old office. Except for the letters on the outer rain jackets the investigators wore, Marvin could not determine who was who. Perhaps, he thought, he could join in with them, and pretend to be one of them as well, without anyone realizing he didn't belong there. It was worth a try, he thought. Otherwise, what would be done to him, if they found out? Although he had not used it, Marvin pulled a flashlight from his back pocket and began to shine it in the muddy area, on the side of the old road, in front of the old office. He was trying to blend in by squatting and pointing at the ground. He found some debris which came from the explosion. He examined it with his flashlight. Two other inspectors passed by him with paper bags. He asked as he tried to hide his face:

"Do you fellows have another one of those?"

"What's that?"

"I mean an evidence bag…you got another one?"

"Yeh, sure-take this one", said one of the investigators whose jacket had the letters "ATF" on the back of it.

"Thanks…thanks a lot…I appreciate it," said Marvin.

"No problem…did you flag it?

"What's that?" Marvin asked.

"What category do you have there? Did you flag it yet?"

"Oh, no…No I'll get to it in a second…thanks a lot. I'll get it!"

Marvin felt weak in his knees. He was cold and wet and needed to take a leak. He didn't think he could hold it in until he found a restroom somewhere. More urgent than finding a place to take a leak, he needed to act as if he belonged there. He felt the gaze of the other two investigators who were fifteen feet away from him. There were at least 20 investigators fanned out to the perimeter of the site. Marvin tried to cover his head so as not to attract attention. He retrieved pieces of bloody, torn garments, as well as a severed, bloody finger. He grimaced!

"What you gonna do with it, inspector?"

"Huh? Oh...I got it! I got it!

The two ATF inspectors turned towards Marvin as he walked away from them. They were 10 feet away when one of them shouted:

"HOLD IT RIGHT THERE! DON'T MOVE... Place the bag on the ground in front of you! Put your hand behind your head... Put the cuffs on him, Gaylord! I got a feeling we got ourselves a terrorist here!

"WHO ME? No... you got me wrong... take a look... here in my pocket... my ID is in there! I'm an investigator, too," shouted Marvin.

"Take a look Gaylord! You couldn't be an investigator... you don't know what the hell you're doing out here, do you?"

"I admit, I am not one of you guys. But I am an investigator! I am working on a case that involves this explosion and fire. Here, take a look at my card!"

"Take his card Gaylord and call into the office. Man, you got a lot of nerves coming out here like this. How did you get past the control point?"

"I came a different way. But listen... what was your name?"

"My name is Stanton Cambria... what's yours?"

"Marvin Klein. You can call Zack Powder at the local police office. He can tell you who I am. I own my own private investigation business. Believe me, I am no terrorist!"

"I'm going to have to have you stay in the command center until we get this straightened out. We got a lot of work to do out here. We don't need to have all this evidence compromised by some cowboy investigator, trying to make a name for himself. So let's go over there for now."

"But if you make that call to Zack..."

"We'll make the call! You just stay put inside here until we do. Now that's the best I can do for you, short of locking you up for a few days for crossing the investigation barrier. Now just sit tight for a few minutes, okay? **Okay?**

"Okay, I will."

Chapter 19

Within twenty-four hours after the many law enforcement agencies shut down the hospital facilities, they released it. Both patients and their relatives alike struggled to make sense of it all. Even the news papers and broadcast stations were kept in the dark concerning the secrecy. Dexter was willing to obey the orders of the police, but he felt he had a vested interest in finding out what's going on in there, so he showed up-once again. When he arrived around noon, he was surprised to find a parking place, and no signs of police presence. He walked into visitors' entrance and walked up to the receptionist.

"Excuse me, maam! May I ask you a question?"

"Sure...how may I assist you?"

"I tried to get in here yesterday to see my brother... and I was turned back by the police. Can you tell me what happened?"

"It was just police work, that's all... routine police work! Is there anything else I can help you with?"

"What kind of routine police work? That didn't seem like 'routine' to me... I mean, is it 'routine' for the Police, and the ATF and the FBI and Homeland Security to come in here and completely shut down a whole hospital... **and put everybody out?**"

"Sir, is there something else I can help you with?"

"NO! There is nothing else you can do for me... thanks!"

Dexter worked himself into a state of agitation. He knew he was born at night, but he also knew he wasn't born last night. He made his way to the elevators. He paid particular attention the each hospital worker he came in contact with. Surprisingly, everyone seemed normal. Even the Orderly's scurried about with precision, with their usual friendly greetings. 'Well what was it?' Dexter asked himself. He continued to head towards Brian's room on the 3rd floor. When he arrived, he opened the door and poked his head in.

"Hello! Sharon, are you in here? Hello! ...Sharon!"

"Sir, who are you looking for?" asked the nurse.

"I'm looking for Brian Simon. He was in this room a couple of day's ago. Where did you move him?"

"Sir, there was no Brian Simon in this room."

"What! *Come on nurse... I know this was his room. His wife was in here with him... her name is Sharon."*

"Sir, are you sure you have the right room? I mean, is this the right wing and floor? Do you have the right hospital? Let me look at the computer for you. If he is here, we'll find him for you, okay?"

The nurse went back to her station with Dexter following after her. She made several entries into the computer. She shook her head and uttered an inaudible sound. Dexter looked at her. She shrugged her shoulders. Several more entries were made. She said...

"Sorry!"

"Wait a minute... wait a minute, nurse! I need to speak to your supervisor. **There is something terribly wrong here... do you understand that?"**

"Just calm down, sir! I will get somebody over here for you. Just have a seat right here!"

Dexter was furious! He paced back and forth in front of the nurses' station-desperately trying to figure out what was happening to his brother, and to himself. He retrieved his cell phone and tried once again, to call Sharon. He got no answer. He reached into his pocket and found the card of Klein Investigative Services. He dialed the number. The answer service came on. He hung up. On the other side of the card was a handwritten number, he hoped was his cell phone. As soon as the phone rang, Marvin answered.

"Hello, this is Marvin!"

"Hello Marvin, this is Dexter Simon, remember me?"

"I'm trying to place you… tell me more!"

"I actually met you at the YMCA last week. You were…"

"Oh yeh, yeh, I remember you! Sure do- what can I do for you?"

"Listen Mr. Klein, I need to speak with you, as soon as you have some time. I have some things happening to me and my family that has me totally baffled. I need to find some answers to some questions I have. Can you help me with this?

"Of course I can. When do you want to meet with me?"

"As soon as you are available, sir."

"I'm a little tied up right now. I'm completing an investigation which should only take another couple of hours. I can meet with you after that? Can you meet me at my office?"

"That's perfect, sir! That would be good timing for me!"

The head nurse returned to Dexter with an administrator next to her. She spoke:

"Okay Sir, this is Mr. Wayne Babanaux. He can answer any questions you may have."

"Thank you nurse. Mr. Babanaux, have you been here long?"

"Today begins my second week as the Assistant Regional Hospital Administrator, Mr.…."

"Dexter Simon is my name. Let me get right to it! My brother was in an accident over two weeks ago. He was brought to this hospital and operated on. He has been in a comma ever sense. His wife was in the room with him since he came out of surgery. Her name is Sharon. There was an explosion at his business and the next day, this hospital was shut down by law enforcement. Now today I came over to see my brother and nobody seems to know anything about him. Are you willing to step up and let me know where you transferred my brother? Just tell me where he is!"

"Mr. Simon, I'm going to try to work with you through this trying time. I understand how you must feel. Would you like to come down to my office?"

"I don't mind going to your office, but can you tell me where my brother is? Just tell me what you did with him?"

"Yes sir. I understand. Let's discuss this in my office!"

Both men walked to the administrators' office. Dexter was offered something to drink. He accepted water. For his part, the only discussion had to center around the whereabouts of his family member-assigned to the hospital. To him, it has become unconscionable to transfer a very sick patient, and no one has a clue as to his new location. If he ever had questions about anything in the past, nothing came close to being as complex and convoluted as this. There are too many "walls of secrecy" surrounding the family. How much of this, he wondered, was known by Adam, or any of his other siblings?" He was convinced that his mother has no knowledge of any of this. Now, he was about to open up the flood gates holding back secrets, and everything up-stream from it would flood into the consciousness of the general public. How much of this could be controlled? What would happen if all the connected dots were traced to Brian, and then continued into the "field of bad dreams?" Dexter felt certain he was about to embark upon a journey which afforded him no return path. With each answer he found, two more questions surfaced. There was no turning back now! He resigned in his spirit to accept whatever was to come.

"Now sir, you say your brother was a patient of ours as late as a couple of days ago, right?"

"That is correct... as late as two days ago when I saw him last. I came by to see him yesterday, but there were law enforcement officials all over the place, and no one could come in. In fact, those who were in here were forced to leave. Now listen, Mr. Babanaux, this can't be news to you if you've been here for two weeks!"

"Mr. Simon, let me explain something to you. This hospital has a special status. We are a trauma hospital who must respond to level 1 incidents.

Most of the time, we are at our maximum limit. A couple of days ago, our patient intake exceeded our capacity by over 30 percent, and we were placed under the control of the Homeland Security Department. In fact, we just resumed control this morning. What that means is… what happened between those times were totally without our knowledge or control."

"I don't understand how you can loose your patients who were here before they took control, however."

"Believe me when I tell you, that even the information that was on the computers for that period has been removed. So, I can't tell you where your brother is, nor could I tell you if I knew, because of the HS orders. I have already told you more than I was allowed to tell you, or anyone. The bottom line is, you have to find out what you need to find out… on your own. I can't help you…I'm sorry! I hope you have a blessed day."

Right about now, prayer seemed to the most appropriate thing to do, reasoned Dexter. As he sat staring at the model of a brain on Babanauxs' desk, he was reminded of the biblical passage that reads:

"Confess your faults one with another, that ye may be healed. The effectual fervent prayer of a righteous man availeth much." He prayed:

*"Lord, let your will be done on this earth; in this town; in this hospital, **and at this time**. There are no mysteries in your universe dear Lord- Your wisdom surpasses all our understanding. I fervently pray that you dispatch your Angels to this hospital to heal all these sick souls who believe in you—and those who **do not** believe in you. Perform a miracle, in the name of Jesus. Use me, dear Lord in any way you choose. Forgive our sins, and raise us above our circumstances. Take control of our lives and fulfill your purpose for us on this earth. In the precious name of Jesus I pray, Amen!"*

Babanaux repeated… "Amen!"

Dexter rose from his chair and walked out of the office. His steps were slowed as he headed towards the exit, on his way to meet with Marvin Klein. Others criss-crossed in front of him, going about their ways. He stopped several feet from the information desk and looked toward the ground. He saw a folded piece of paper lying near his feet. He was curious, and picked it up. He stood motionless while he unfolded the paper. The numbers, written in bold, black permanent marker read: "**333**" Dexter continued to stand still with a puzzled look on his face. What is this all about, he wondered. What is the meaning of three matching numbers? Was this placed on the floor for him to find it, or for anybody? He gazed towards the information desk. The receptionist was talking on the phone. She raised her head and met Dexter's curious eyes. She simply smiled at him and winked. She placed her hand over the telephone microphone and said:

"Have a blessed day, Mr. Simon!"

Dexter walked out of the hospital to retrieve his car. As he walked down the steps, he looked at his digital watch. It read: "3:33"

Chapter 20

Heavy moisture in the atmosphere produced hail damage over most of the downtown area. Dexter called his office to report that he would not be back until tomorrow. He also called his insurance company to report that his car had sustained hail damage. He was almost to Klein's Investigative Services office building when he reached his brother on his cell phone.

"Adam, where are you man?"

"I'm at momma's house. Where is Brian? …where are you? …what's going on Dex?"

"Listen, something incredible is happening, and I don't understand it all. Do you know about the lock-down at the hospital?"

"Yes, I heard about it. Where's Brian?"

"I just left there and I still can't tell you where he is. In fact, the administrator's are telling me they have no record of him being there."

"What the hell is that all about? We know they are lying!"

"We know he was there, right. But what we don't know is what happened to him after Homeland Security took over!"

"Homeland Security took over the hospital? I thought they learned their lesson after the big screw-up with hurricane Katrina!"

"Seriously, Adam, I'm worried about Brian and Sharon, too. Has anyone heard from her?"

"Momma told me they gave her some sort of sedative medicine at the hospital. She was sleeping all day, and was out of it for a while. She probably got an over-dose. She should be at the hospital with Brian, though."

"Adam, let me talk to Momma!"

"Hey Momma- How you feeling?"

"I'm in the hands of the Lord… so I'm doing alright."

"Momma, I want you to know that I'm working on finding out what's happening to Brian, Sharon and Brian's business, okay? I don't want you to pay a lot of attention to the television, or radio. I'm getting things checked out and I'll let you know, okay?"

"You're doing the right thing for your brother, Dexter. I know things are hanging by a thread… but you hang in there thru thick and 'razor' thin! God's on your side! Oh, by the way, your uncle Landry asked about you. Said he ain't seen you since the last reunion."

"I'm going to get in touch with uncle Landry. That's daddy's oldest brother, right? I'll call him in a couple of days. I do need to go down there to see him soon. Tell him I said so, the next time you talk to him."

"Alright, I will. I got you in my prayers, son!"

"Thanks mom… I appreciate that. Well, got to go…bye!"

"God be with you!"

Dexter rushed into the entrance to the office building which housed Marvin's suite. Tens of others packed the foyer awaiting their turn to rush out, and to their cars. Dexter spotted the marquee and confirmed the suite number he wanted. Few would admit the truth about it, but it seemed to him that most of the businesses listed, would not be considered as contributors to the manufacturing of income- rather support services to those who do generate productive income. Nevertheless, he had no doubt that they were necessary businesses for someone.

As he arrived at Marvin's office, he could now see that it was a simple "Executive Suite". There was no front and back office, with a receptionist or an assistant. There was just an office space, enough to house an old wooden desk and chair, and a wall flushed with file cabinets. Although few probably realize it, he thought, Americans should be aware that files are probably being kept on them in some form or another. How many businesses like this one, are keeping files on our bank accounts, credit cards, medical records and other personal and private information. It's the information that makes the commerce work, Dexter reasoned. Some good-some bad. The extent to which information is authorized for big brother to have access, has yet to be decided by the US Supreme Court. Parallel to the lack of clarity on the Constitutional Right to Privacy, is the issue of information mining. How far can you go; who is authorized, and under what circumstances?

"Mr. Simon, come on in and have a seat," invited Marvin.

"Thank you, sir!"

"Please, just call me Marvin."

"Okay Marvin. So this is it… your office?"

"This is it! I never needed much plaster and paint to do what I do."

"That's what I want to talk to you about Marvin. What is it that you do?"

"Well, I'm in the information business. I gather information on a wide range of topics, for any paying customer. Although I am the best at my craft, I always follow the law. But when I am hired, I work exclusively for my client. Now, sometimes there is information I uncover that may not be what my client really wants to hear. I don't have to give it to you, but I still have it. On the other hand, I work for you. You can fire me anytime you want. I work by the hour. You pay me when I submit my invoice to you. All the information I uncover is given to you in written form. I keep a copy of everything I do for 20 years. If I get a subpoena, and I have to go to court on your behalf, my prices double. If you don't pay, I don't work for you any longer-it's that simple! Does that help you?"

"Wow! That's simple enough. Gosh, I don't know if I can afford you, Marvin. I'm not sure if I really can afford your services. Let me ask you this, do you work in 'blocks'? I mean, can I pay for so much of your time with one check? When you use that up, I give you another check when I can afford it?"

"Sure you can! I work like that quite a bit. Do you want to get started?

"I think so... but I want to talk this over with my wife before I sign a contract. You do work by contract I presume."

"Absolutely!"

"Alright, I think we can work together to get some answers to some pressing questions I have."

"I am sure we can. What is the nature of the investigation you're looking to get information on?"

"I want to get information about a towing business about 30 miles outside of town. I want information on the nature of the business; who owns it; what else might be associated with it in the rear. I just think there is something happening there that's illegal and I need to find out."

"You want to know who owns the towing business that had the explosion a few nights ago?"

"That's the one!"

"That will be a free one... the fellow who owns that business has the same last name as you do. Now, I didn't really put that together until just now. But Mr. Simon, do you know your brother is in some deepwater?"

"That's what I'm trying to find out Marvin... how deep is he into it?

"That's going to cost you, Dexter. Do you have your checkbook with you?"

"Listen, if my wife agrees, I'm sure we can start off with five thousand dollars. We are not rich in any way, I hope you understand. But we need to clear up this confusion we are all suffering from. Let me be frank... I have no idea where he is right now; He's been in a comma since the accident. Is someone keeping him in that state of unconsciousness for some reason? Why does there seem to be a connection between him and that Police Sergeant, Harley? Even my youngest brother presents a mystery to me, although I don't think he's knowingly into anything criminal. Here's the kicker--why is the law enforcement agencies all over that hospital, and they have no record of my brother even being there? All of this is tearing the family apart. My wife and I struggle to become a part of a family who are seemingly on a different page than we are--with all this family secrets. Yet, I feel I have a responsibility to keep everyone together. The irony about that statement is we never really were together after we matured. Anyway... I'm venting to you as if you were a therapist of some kind."

"If you feel you need one, I can make a recommendation to you."

"Thanks, I'll keep that in mind. Listen Marvin, let me get back to you in a couple of days. I got to find my brother and sister-in-law first. I'm sure we can afford the five hundred, initially."

"That'll work! It'll get us started at least."

Chapter 21

Norma was a very supportive wife. She believed that her role should be to compliment her husband, and support the vision he has for his family. She had heard criticism voiced by one of his sisters that she seemed to go overboard at times. It was shared with the family, during one of their 'get-togethers', that she always served her husbands plate when they ate. In addition, she enjoyed giving him a back-rub after his evening shower or bath. It was no surprise to them then, when Dexter decided it was time for them to take some time off, and travel to his deceased fathers' hometown of New Iberia, Louisiana. Norma managed to take off work for a week, and they agreed to stay with Dexter's uncle Landry. Although she was not accustomed to the ways of the Old South, she wanted to give her husband full support on this decision as well.

"What should I expect when it comes down to cooking and washing the dishes, honey? I mean I don't mind doing it, but should I take the initiative?"

"I... I don't know about this one, babe. He's eighty- something and he stay's alone. I don't expect he will have the most tidy home, and cleanest kitchen. We are definitely going to have to wait for his moves."

"It'll be interesting to hear about the way he grew up ... you know the *way he grew up; what his youth was like! I'm just excited to spend some time with him and the other family members there."*

"I'm so pleased that you are into this trip, sweetheart. There aren't that many women today who find country living interesting. In fact, you hardly find anyone from the big city who wants to talk about anything in the past. I think that's a big problem in the black families today, don't you?"

"Oh no, not me! *I want to know. I want to know how he survived during the 'Civil Rights' era. I want to know how they interacted with white people during the old days. I want to know about their attempts to vote; to go to school; to spend their money and just how they managed to keep their sanity."*

"I love you for that, Norma! You don't know how much I appreciate your feeling that way."

She unlatched her seat belt and leaned over to Dexter. He leaned towards her as she kissed him on the cheek and said:

"The feeling is totally mutual, sir!"

"Okay, now put that seat belt back on before we both get in trouble," instructed Dexter. *"Maybe I better give you some additional info about how these people are down here."*

"Okay, good!"

"Well...many of them will refer to you, or me, as "Cousin" (coo-zan). "That's like a close relative-or a close friend. Many of the politicians in this area have a great desire to be known to his constituents as Cousin Theo, or Cousin Tina, and so on."

"Now... are you saying they call everyone that?"

"Unless you are a 'nainaine' (godmother) and a 'parrain' (godfather). The parrain & nainaine are expected to give the godchild gifts at special times, until they die. Of course they are expected to give them birthday presents until they are grown. If a mother or father dies, and the home must be broken, the parrain may assert a strong claim for the care of the child. But, there may be a 'nonc' or 'tante' (Uncle or Aunt), who may ask for the child as their right."

"Oh my God... look how these people take care of their own!"

"I am not necessarily saying that it's that way today. It has been that way in the past, even when I was a young man. We'll have to find out if things have changed, and if so, how much."

"What happened to his wife? How did she die?"

"She didn't!"

"Huh?"

"She didn't die…yet! …She lost her mind over 20 years ago, and they put her in Pineville, a mental institution."

"Oh my Lord!"

"They say she delivered a still-born girl for the second time in her life, when she was about forty. Apparently it was too much for her to bear, and she tried to commit suicide. Her youngest was 10 when that happened, and she went to stay with her oldest sister, who raised her."

"How old would she be now?"

"About thirty years old."

"Does she still live here?"

"The last time I heard, she was in New Orleans, finishing up her law degree at Dillard University."

"Alright! You go girl! Now that's what I'm talking about!"

"That **is** good news, isn't it?" asked Dexter.

"That's wonderful news. Did she earn a scholarship?"

"She was always a very sharp girl, but I don't think she got a full scholarship. I remember mom sent her some money when she graduated from high school. In fact, a lot of her cousins gave her money when she started college."

"Honey, do you see why I'm excited to come down here to meet the other side of your family? I just think God has placed all of us in special families to take care of each other, and support one another, with all our resources. That includes Physical, Spiritual, Relational and Financial. If you don't have a family set you can 'belong' to, there is something God intended for us to have, that we don't have. You can see how broken families miss out on blessings God intended for them to have? I just think this is *going to be a very special time for us over the next few days. I'm looking forward to it."*

For the first time in weeks, Dexter and Norma were enjoying some warm sunshine. It felt so good to put on shades to keep from being blinded by the bright sunlight. It appeared that Dexter's decision to get away when they did was the right one. For him, he would see this trip as a cleansing journey. He needed to flush out his mind, and give his body a rest. They approached the old house where Uncle Landry lived since he was twenty-five. It was not kept up as well as it could have. Dexter determined that some of his time would be spent helping to fix up the place. Norma was eager to meet Uncle Landry and just relax with him; doing whatever he wanted to do. Uncle Landry was outside in his tool shed. Several hens and a rooster darted across the yard.

"Hey *Nonc Landry...we're here,"* shouted Dexter.

"Hey... *ya'll come on in,"* answered Uncle Landry. *"I'm puttin up this rake. How ya'll doin?"*

"We're fine...just tired. *Nonc Landry, this is my wife, Norma."*

"Alright Lover-boy. You done gone up north and found you a Louisiana beauty. She sho' is pretty, Dex. Good to meet ya, sweetheart!"

"Well, she's from North Carolina, but I agree with you that she's pretty!"

They all laughed and hugged each other.

"Ya'll want some water?"

"Naw... we're fine Nonc."

"I'm just so honored to meet you Uncle Landry. May I call you Uncle?"

"Yes ma'am... you sure can!"

"Well, only if you call me Norma."

"I can't help it... I ben callin ladis lak dat all ma life."

"That's the way they are down here, honey. Everybody's so polite," explained Dexter.

"I appreciate that-make me feel like a special person when he say's that."

"You really are special to him-he really honors you and other ladies in that way."

"Okay, I accept that."

"Come on inside…ya'll hungry?"

"Don't tell me you cooked for us, Nonc!"

"Of course I did… you didn think I wus gonna let ya'll drive all da way down here and not feed you, did 'ya? I wun't gon hear dat mouth of yo mother, if she heard I didn have somethin for ya'll ta eat when 'ya got here… no sir, I didn want to hear it! Come on… come on in! You jus got to heat it up some. You ever had fried corn, okra & tomatoes, sauce picante with rice and cornbread? I stopped eating a lot of meat."

"What? …What is he speaking, honey? I have heard of corn and okra, but what else was that he said?"

"You'll have to trust me honey, it's all good!"

"Okay… I'm ready to try it. I do need to wash up first," said Norma.

"Look on dat shelf behind dat bathroom curtain … Get you one of dem towels from dere …dere's some soap on da sink …That handle on the left don't work.…You can only git cold water outa the one on da right," instructed Uncle Landry.

*"**Okay**,"* mumbled Norma …*"Work with me Jesus."*

The three of them sat down to eat. It was getting dark outside, creating a need for light around the dinner table. There was a small window above the kitchen sink, but light coming through it was diffused by curtains that needed to be drawn back. Both Dexter and Norma felt they needed more light but hesitated to be the one to suggest it. Their conversation was light, centering around Uncle Landry's health and daily routine. Norma started eating after Uncle Landry said the blessing over the food. Dexter wanted to make sure she would not show rejection in her facial expression when she tasted the food, so he quickly forked up some sauce picante and began chewing.

"Now that's sauce picante! That's the way I remember it when momma used to make it." said Dexter.

"*Shoot, we grew up on dis stuff. Yo momma won yo daddy-my brother-over to marry him, 'cause he liked da way she cooked dis picante.*"

"*It sure is good, Dexter. It tastes rich and spicy, too.*" Complimented Norma.

"*I told you so!*" Dexter said as he looked upon his wife with pride.

Somebody rang the door bell. Uncle Landry had a mouth full that he was trying desperately to chew since he was missing a few teeth here and there. Dexter asked if he should get it.

"*No... dat's okay... it's June-bug, probly. He'll come on in, in a secon.*"

"Hey old man! ...You in here? ...Your company come in yet?"

""*Yeh, June-bug... dey here. Who you got wit you?*"

"*How ya'll doing? This is my wife Winky.*"

"*Hello*"! said Winky.

"*I saw yo car outside, so I wanted to come over to say hi.*"

"*We eating now, June-bug. Ya'll want sometin ta eat, or you want to come back later?*" asked Uncle Landry. "*They gonna be here a few days.*"

"*No problem... I wanted ta see if he wanted ta come over ta play some dominoes wit me, Prince, Tea-spoon and Dale.*" We gon git it goin 'bout ten.*"

"*I appreciate the invitation June-bug, but I think I'll have to pass tonight... you know we're kinda tired, and I wanted to spend the first night with my uncle. You understand, right?*"

June-bug and Winky left to return later tomorrow. Dexter was relieved that it would be just the three of them for dinner tonight. For his part, he just didn't want to put up with company, who would want to stay up all hours of the night. As it was, most of the conversation seemed trivial enough. He wanted Uncle Landry to lead the conversation in any direction he wanted. Notwithstanding the age difference between them, Dexter knew the common denominator was to talk about the past. That would be his fall back position, if watching the TV no longer interested his uncle.

"*What time do you usually get up in the morning, Nonc?*"

"*Um usually up by 5:55.*"

"*Why 5:55? Why not 6:00,*" asked Dexter.

"*Ben lak dat for da las fifty yeas. I woked at da lumber yad fo 33 yeas. In fact hit was 33 yeas an 3 months when I retied. Hit took me xactly 20 minetes ta git dressed, and 15 minetes ta drive ta wok. Had ta be dhere by 6:30.*"

"*You know uncle, that's mighty curious that you worked for 33 years and 3 months, and you get up every morning at 5:55 AM. Have you ever considered those numbers to mean anything?...especially the 333?*"

"*Never even thought about it! It's been just some numbers to me. I can see why somebody could find something to them, though.*"

"*Yeh, it's strange how that works out ...I'm just not sure why! ...I just don't know why! ...I do get the feeling that somebody or something is trying to tell me something... with those matching numbers!*"

"*Maybe I'll play those numbers the next time the scratch off's come out,*" Uncle Landry said, laughing.

"*If you win, you better donate 10 percent to some charity,*" Dexter ordered, smiling.

Norma changed the pace and tone of the conversation by offering to remove the dinner plates from the table. She complimented Uncle Landry on being an excellent cook.

"*I wish we lived closer to you so we could enjoy this Creole food more often,*" Said Norma.

"*Ya'll can come down here anytime. Fact of da matter is, ya'll need ta spen yo time findin out 'bout yo heritage down here, Dexter.*"

"*That's one of the major reason I wanted to come here, Uncle. I knew that we had a lot of history in this town, and I always wanted to come here to do some research. For instance, I heard we had a lot of cousins here who are Broussard's, Guillory's, Fontenot's as well as Simon's, is that right?*"

"*Ya got lots of Broussard's... Lot's of 'em. In fact, dey named a town after dem 'cause there wus so many of dem. In fact, if you travel from Lake Charles ta here, you gonna know dat da majority of da people livin 'tween here and dere, are Broussard's. Now you got a few thousand Simon,*"

Guillory's, and Fontenot families in dere too but, dem Broussard's are mo dan a family...dey're a species by demselves. You seen 'em... dey're a good lookin species too--'specially deir women. Man, if ya got one of dem, you got yourself a good lookin, high yellow woman. But mo dan dat, dey are a family loving bunch; generous and kindly. Dey stick together and always help each other out.

Uncle Landry continued...

"One time, oh 'bout 10 years ago, it wus duck hunting season. Me, and a coupla other fella's from up north Louisiana wus makin our way 'long da bayou at da darkest hour of da night. Some of dem bends in da bayou git real shallo. After a while, we got stuck 'n coudn row no mo. It look lak we wus gon be dere for a long time-maybe all night. Dere wus no sign of any life nowhere 'round us in dat swamp-no lights-nothing!"

"How did you get out, Uncle?" asked Dexter.

"Well, dere wus five of us in da boat—three vistors, and a cousin, Ted Broussard and me. Well, he made his way to da back of da boat, and yelled out in da darkness. Some fifteen minutes later, here comes one man, den another, and den a third. Dey spoke (palaver) in Creole, and each of dem come 'long side of our boat in dey waders. Well, dey rocked da boat; dey pushed and pulled, til we got ta floatin again. Ol' Ted offer dem som money for helpin us out, but dey all shook dey head, and 'fused it. Each one climb back into his boat an dey paddle away."

"Did he know he was in the Broussard territory?"

"Yeh, he knew! But I didn know, 'cause it wus to dark out dre. He yelled, 'there is a Broussard out here stuck in da mud.' He said, 'If dre is a cousin out dre, I need sum hep'.

"Were they all three cousins of his?"

"No, only two of dem wus. Da other fella wus a foreiner, I guess."
Norma asked.

"Uncle Landry, is that the way most families are around here, today?

"I can't say dat's true, sugar! Dese families around here been influenced by too much television-you can't tell 'em what ta do or not ta do. Dese chirrin will curse ya out if you tell 'em anythin. Da momma havin babies when dey babies too. They can't make dem babies by demself, no! Dese young boys ain't got notin to do-no jobs-dey don wanna go to no school. Da police been findin weed and illegal drugs in dey cars. Where you think dem drugs come from? ...Naw... things ain't like it used to be, sugar. You can't tell what a real family look like no more. Half da future families in jail... $\frac{1}{4}$ on drugs... 'bout 1/8 in school... and dat leave 'bout 1/8 either goin in National Guard or get married. Hit's gon take a lot of praying to straitn dis mess out—a 'hole lot o' praying."

Chapter 22

After turning in for the night around 10:30 pm, Dexter and Norma thought it appropriate to study scripture dealing with protection from the evil one. It was no secret that the devil constantly scours the earth, looking for souls he could deceive, devour and destroy. They knew that there would be introductions, starting tomorrow, to individuals who were not believers in Christ, and would require some spiritual weapons to fight off many unforeseen attacks. It was apparent that this town was not unlike any other town or city where crime, violence and deprivation was part of the cultural fabric. So they devoted a half hour to study and prayer before going to bed.

Hearing some noise early the next morning, Norma was first to awaken. She didn't want to get out of bed until she was sure Uncle Landry was fully up and ready to go about his daily routine. Partly because she was not accustomed to washing up in a bathroom that had no door, and because the rooms were so small, there was virtually no privacy. She decided to move cautiously, to not disturb Dexter. She searched and found her watch. It was 6:10. Oh my, she thought. I don't have to get up this early... to do what? She laid back onto her pillow and fell asleep until Dexter started stirring. When he looked at his watch, he saw the time was 8:38.

"Baby, you awake?"

"*Almost!*" Norma answered.

"*It's after 8:30. Have you heard Uncle Landry stirring around?*"

"*I think I heard him earlier, around 6:00.*"

"*Okay, let me get up and do some scouting. You can rest until I see if the coast is clear for you, okay!*"

Dexter made his way through the house to the back door. Peering out, he saw his uncle feeding his chickens. He returned to his wife to inform her that it was safe to freshen up in the bathroom. When she finished, Dexter did the same. Together, they made their way out the back door and into the back yard.

"*Good morning Nonc,*" said Norma.

Dexter repeated the greeting.

"*How ya'll sleep?*" asked Uncle Landry.

"*Good! ...I know I slept like a baby,*" said Dexter.

"*I didn kno what ya'll want fo breakfast. I wus waitin fo ya'll to git up first.*"

"*We can wait till lunch time, Nonc. We aren't big breakfast eaters. Perhaps some coffee and toast would work out fine. But you do what you always do-don't let us stop you from that,*" said Dexter.

"*Shoots, I don already ate. I'm gon to finish feedin dese chickens. By dat time, you shoud be finish eatin. Den, if ya wan ta take yo time, you can drive 'round and see what dis place look lak. Later on, when you come bak, I will tak ya'll ta see som of yo cousins.*"

It remains to be seen if New Iberia, Louisiana would be classified as a 21st century town. As Dexter and Norma made their way through certain sections of the town, they quietly surveyed the surroundings. What is it, they wondered to each other, that was keeping these people living here? Was it the laid back style; the fact that most everyone knew each other, and many were related to each other? Could it be that they have grown accustomed to a life style that screams "slow down?" No one seemed to be in a hurry to get anywhere. As Dexter pulled onto the main street, he witnessed a police car cruising past them, with what appeared to be male in the rear seat. Norma commented:

"Do you see what I see, honey? Even the police are laid back. It just seems as though everybody just takes their time to get anywhere-even to the jail house."

"I agree. It looks like they are headed to that building across the street. Let's just wait here for a second to see what's going to happen."

Dexter and Norma were waiting at what turned out to be the rear of the police station. They saw the car park, and an officer exited. He opened the rear passenger door and reached in to retrieve the man in handcuffs. As he did, they witnessed the man raise his legs and kicked the officer in the face, knocking him backward. The officer fell to the ground, with a bleeding nose. The man attacking the officer scrambled to get out of the car, while the officer tried to upright himself. The officer reached for his gun as the man stumbled to the ground. The officer smashed the face of the still handcuffed man, as blood squirted from the man's eyes.

Norma grabbed Dexter's right arm, squeezing it with every frame of motion she viewed. Her mouth stood agape, in silence. Dexter was inclined to watch the action-as stunned as he was-rather than comment on what they were witnessing. Neither could believe what they were seeing. Help for the arresting officer soon arrived from inside the station. Three other officers broke the slow motion of the morning, and joined in on the attempt to control the arrested man. The man continued to struggle as the officers punched and kicked until they were able to finally subdue the arrested man.

Dexter was about to start the car to drive off, when Norma spoke:

"Oh my God! I can't believe what we just saw. That was terrible, honey!"

"I agree baby. That poor fella is really going to be sore in the morning. I wonder why he resisted by kicking the officer in the face?"

"I don't know, but I wonder why they had to beat him to a pulp like they did. That was terrible, for that many police against one little guy."

"I think we better get out of here before we get caught up in some sort of investigation," Dexter warned.

"Okay, but I don't feel much like any more touring, honey. Maybe we should just find a place to get something to eat, and get back to Uncle Landry."

"Ugh! That was really horrible to watch, wasn't it, baby?"

"It sure was… somebody's son, or daddy, or uncle is not going to be happy when they see this guy. Oh look! There's a guy coming towards us. Come on … let's get out of here now, Dexter."

"It's too late for us to get out of here. He is heading towards us now. Let me see what he wants. Don't say anything… let me do the talking."

"yes sir!"

"Hello sir… how long have you been sitting here?

"Maybe ten minutes, that's all."

"Okay, I need to have you and your wife… is that your wife?"

"Yes, she's my wife…"

"Well, I need you to come over to the station to answer a few questions for us."

"Why do you need to ask us some questions? About what, officer?"

"Sir, you were a witness to what just happened out here with the officer and the prisoner… you and your wife both, are considered material witnesses. What we need for you to do is come in and make a statement as to what you saw happened."

"Look officer, we're not from around here… we were just passing through your town. We really don't want to get involved in anything. We'll be leaving in a few days, and we just rather not make any statements or anything like that," explained Dexter.

"Sir, I understand you are passing through here. At the same time, there's going to be some charges filed concerning this incident. Our camera saw you parked across the street… so obviously, you were a witness to the fact that our officers were reacting to control the prisoner. It won't take long. Just come with me."

Norma spoke:

"Honey, is this the right thing to do? Shouldn't we have a lawyer... just in case?"

"There won't be no need for a lawyer, maam. You are witnesses-not suspects! You understand that, right?"

"Yes, we do understand that. But I think we do need to consult with a lawyer concerning our rights, officer. I'm sure you can understand that as well, right," insisted Dexter.

"Well, why don't you come on in and you can use our phone to call whoever you want. Just follow me in here and you can use the phone at my desk."

Dexter nodded to Norma to secure her agreement. They parked and locked their car at the rear of the station and went inside.

"Who should we call for advice, honey? Do we know anybody here, or should we call someone back home?"

"Let me call Uncle Landry first. I think we should let him know where we are, at least. He may also know somebody we can talk to as well.

"Good idea," said Norma. "Officer, will you give us a couple of minutes?"

"Of course... take your time. I'll be at this desk over here filling out this paper work."

"Who was that fellow being arrested?" asked Dexter.

"He's almost a regular around here. It's almost every year this kid gets hauled in for some criminal activity. His name is Jason... Jason Fontenot."

"Okay, let me make this call."

Dexter called his uncle. He spoke:

"Nonc, this is Dexter."

"Hey Dexter, how ya'll makin it?"

"We're okay Nonc. Listen, I need to ask you something. You got a minute?"

"Yeh, sho!"

"Norma and I were driving around town taking a survey of everything, when we came upon the police station. There was an officer who was

133

arresting a young black kid about 19 or 20 years old. Now we witnessed the kid kicking the officer when he was being taken out of the back seat. Then we saw about four officers who came out of the station and they beat this kid pretty badly. Now the reason I'm calling you is to get some advice from you."

"No problem… what you need?"

"Well, the police want Norma and me to sign a statement as witnesses to what happened. We think we need to get some advice from a lawyer before we do."

"You probly should. If I was you… and you wanted my opinion, I wouldn't sign nothin for the police. They been treatin these black kids pretty rough around here. But I ain't no lawyer. You know you got a cousin who is a lawyer… well she's almost one. She waitin on her test result. But if you want to talk to her, I got her number in New Orleans. Do you know who the kid is?"

"Yes, the policeman say's his name is Jason Fontenot."

"Jason Fontenot?"

"Yes, that's the name!"

"Jason Fontenot is my grandson, Dexter. That's my daughter's middle son—that's your cousin!"

"Oh my God! …Oh my God! …my God!"

"What is it Dexter? What did he say, sweetheart?

Quietly, Dexter told her:

"Jason Fontenot is our cousin!"

"You mean this young man we saw in the…"

"Yes, baby. Uncle Landry said it's his grandson. Well, it's obvious that I am not going to sign anything that's going to incriminate him."

"What are you going to do, honey?"

"We must remember that we are not the suspects here. We didn't do anything wrong. They can't make us sign anything, or make a statement if we don't want to. I'll just tell them that we're not going to make any statement."

"Can we do that? I mean can they force us to make a statement?" asked Norma.

"I am not going to! We are not going to sign anything."

The officer requesting them to make a statement returned to his desk where Dexter had used his telephone. The sergeant in charge entered into the station. He joined his junior officer, who walked away from Norma and Dexter. They were obviously discussing the situation at hand. The sergeant straightened his belt as he returned to the Simons. He knew he was on sandy ground in trying to force a statement. He decided to get some general information on Dexter and Norma, and then let them go.

"You're Mr. and Mrs. Simon, right?"

"That's right, sir."

"And you said you're in town for a few days?"

"That's correct," said Dexter.

"Where are you staying while you are here Mr. Simon?"

"We're staying with my uncle… Landry Simon."

"Oh… Mr. Landry Simon is your uncle?"

"That's right. We're here visiting with him for a few days."

"Mr. Simon is a good Christian man. Well sir, if you will just let me see your drivers' license, you can feel free to leave after that."

"Okay… you are not insisting we give a statement or anything like that?"

"No sir. I'll just take your information from your license and you both are free to go."

"I can do that… here you go!"

Dexter and Norma walked out of the station as nervous as they have ever been. How much can one take in one's life that would be considered 'enough is Enough'? The last month has been quite a test of faith for them both. Just how much can this mind take before loosing itself? Dexter thought.

"That's what we prayed about last night," Norma shared with Dexter. "There are so many things that comes into our lives that confuses us, and knocks us off course, that we can't figure out how we got into it, or how to get out of it. Without the guidance of the Holy Spirit, we would be totally lost."

"I'm leaning on the Lord in this situation, babe. Who would have thought we would be a witness to an incident that would involve a relative of ours? And not only that, what prompted Jason to kick that officer in the first place? Whether we like it or not, we're going to have to come to the aid of that young man. But, I don't think everything's going to go in his favor."

"We need to find out what happened before he got to the station that caused him to react that way," reasoned Norma.

"That's going to be a problem, honey. We just can't get into another family problem, while we are so involved with Brian's situation. I think we need to let our cousin know what we saw, and let them handle this one. I just can't get wrapped up into another criminal case. In fact I'm about as stretched as far as I can possibly be. I'm **razor thin** right about now!"

Chapter 23

D exter and Norma decided to head straight for Uncle Landry's place, instead of stopping to get something to eat. When they arrived, there were 3 other cars parked in his long gravel and grass driveway. There was almost an eerie quiet hovering over the house. No one came out to meet them. It was no accident that these cars are here, Dexter reasoned. Uncle Landry must have summoned them to his home to discuss the incident involving Jason. Norma wanted to remain in the car for a few moments just to get her wits about her, and to prepare to meet some additional relatives of Dexter. She was truly sorry it had to take place under these sad circumstances.

"*Okay honey, I'm ready,*" said Norma. "*But let me say this; Even though none of what's going on is familiar to us, you can count on me to support you on what ever comes up. If it means this is going to cost us more time and money to help them get this resolved, I will trust you to make that decision, and I will go along with your decision, okay?*"

"*Thanks you sweetheart. I know you are there with me. I just need to try to get a handle on what's happening, and we can go from there. I really don't expect it's going to cost us money, but I might have to come back. But, we'll see,*" said Dexter.

"Oh wait honey-there's another car pulling up behind us," said Norma.

"It's okay... we can go in. Come on."

"Ya'll doin alright?" asked the stranger.

"Doing very well, sir. How are you doing," responded Dexter.

"Well, the way I look at it, as long as you got your health, you got the most important thang you can have. Thank the Lord I got that!" The stranger said, laughing. "Ya'll go on in."

The stranger, dressed with a short-sleeved white shirt and open collar; with tight khaki pants and wore soft black shoes, resembled a local government official to Dexter. His hair was closely cut; clean shaven and he looked slightly tanned, and a bit over-weight. He followed Dexter and Norma into the back door of the house.

"You know Landry Simon?" asked Dexter.

"Sure do... he's my nonc."

Both Dexter and Norma expressed quiet surprise at hearing that. This man looked to be white to them in every way. Certainly, if he lived in any other part of the country, with his fine grade of hair, he would have no problem with being perceived as white. No one would even question who his people were.

Uncle Landry was quietly sitting on a large comfortable box chair, in his small living room. The window air conditioner was turned all the way at full speed. A couple of the persons in the house had pulled chairs from around the kitchen table, and situated themselves against the inside wall, next to the china cabinet. A dimly lit light strained to reveal all the strange faces present in the room. Now, with Dexter, Norma and Uncle Landry's other nephew joining them, there was hardly any space left to squeeze into.

"Como Savoy, everybody. Nonc, how you doin? Hey Shirley, Pinky, CeCe, Teeta. Listen, I was at my office when I got word about Jason. 'Teeta', I know how you feel being Jason's mother and all. But, we all feel bad with you, cause we know how you been struggling with dat boy. We *gon be there with you through this whole deal, okay? Anybody heard what happened?"*

Nonc Landry spoke:

"Okay! Listen ya'll. Dis here is yo' coozans Dexter and his wife fom Shreveport. Day da ones dat saw what happen and call me. Da seen what Jason did... and day saw da police beat 'em. Dexter, dese yo coozans Shirley, Pinky, CeCe, Teeta and Calvin."

"Hey, you guys. This is my wife here, Norma."

"Hello everyone... nice to meet you all," said Norma.

Everyone responded by getting up from their seats and extending their arms to welcome them, and to hug them both.

Calvin spoke:

"Nonc, I left the office with a rookie. I got ta git back. Listen, I'm goin call ya tonight Teeta, so you can tell me what we need ta do. I can talk to Judge Babanaux about what we already talked about. I saw him in his office today. But you tell me, if you want me to! ...Nice to meet you 'coozans'... Dexter ...Norma. I'll see you tomorrow...ya'll goin be here?"

"Yes Calvin, good to meet you too. And, we'll be here for a couple more days-until Friday ...probably."

"I'll see ya'll before ya go for sure. You play some dominoes, Dexter?"

"Yeh, sure. In fact, a guy named... I think they say his name is tea-spoon, invited me to come over to his house."

"That's me. I'm tea-spoon. Well, that's what they call me around here. We call him June-bug," said Calvin.

"Okay, that's right...I'm sorry."

"No problem. We play tomorrow night. I'll come pick ya up 'bout 8. Okay, see you then."

Calvin left. Dexter moved back into the living room where the conversation was continuing concerning Jason. Dexter decided to sit back and listen to how this family would handle this traumatic incident in their lives. He joined Norma in sitting on the edge of her chair as Teeta, Jason's mother, began to speak.

"Daddy, you know every since dat boys daddy died, I been havin

trouble wid him. I am so sic of goin down dere ta da police station, bailin him out of trouble. He don wanna work… he don wanna go ta school. He just layin 'round da house waitin for me ta go ta work, den he bring in his friends to play video games all day long. Dat grandson of yours gon be 17 years old next month… hell, he grown, an I can't do notin with him. Like I said befo, I think he be better off if he join the National Guard."

"Oh come on Teeta! *You know what my husband said 'bout the National Guard… Dey don killed and wounded so many dem troops in Iraq, Bush takin up all da National Guard dat joins. He said for sho, if he join da National Guard, he goin to Iraq as soon as he git out a trainin,"* said Shirley.

"Dat ain't even a choice rat now, Teeta with a record like he got. Ain't nobody gon take him wit all dose **misdemons** *on his record,"* advised Pinky.

"For goodness sake Pinky, if you gon **indike** *da boy, ya ought ta least git his record straight--It's* **Miss-damentors** *he got,"* clarified CeCe.

Norma reached for Dexter's hand and squeezed it- trying to hold back a chuckle. They could appreciate the enormous task they had ahead of them, and decided to give them a pass on correcting their language.

"Nonc, Calvin mentioned something about a Judge Babanaux before he left. What was that all about?" asked Dexter.

"Well, he spoke to da Judge the las time Jason got arrested and the Judge told him if he wanted to join da National Guard, and try ta make sometin outa his self, he would get his record cleaned so he could join. He tol him if he din't, and he got in trouble again, he wus gonna thro da book at 'em. It sho don't look too good dis time. Dis time, we gon hav ta git a lawyer for dat boy. It sho looks lak he don mess up good dis time. It sho do look lak it," lamented Nonc Landry.

"I know one thang, we can't leave dat boy up dere in dat jail house. We got ta go see him and git him to a doctor," said CeCe.

"Yeh, you right CeCe," said Teeta. *"When yo husband getting home fom work?"*

"Bout 6 if he don't stop off at Freeda's place."

"I think he, Tea-Spoon and Nonc need to go up dere together and talk to a lawyer first, and den to Judge Babanaux," advised Teeta. "Da ain't gon listen to no woman tryin to talk to dem."

"Listen," said Dexter. " I would be happy to join them when they go to talk to a lawyer. Do you already have one in mind?"

"Well daddy, you know dat white lady who got a son in Lafayette. You know who I'm talkin 'bout?" asked Shirley.

"Yeh… his name is Chase Abbott Pierce. That's ol lady Mary Frances Pierce' oldest son. He spose ta be real smart. He got his degree fom LSU, and another one fom Simon Business School, where his uncle was a teacher. I think he got his Law Degree fom Xavier in New Orleans, too."

"He don't sound lak somebody we can afford," said CeCe. "He sound lak he **too** smart, wid all dem degrees."

"Well, let's start out by contacting him, first," said Dexter. "In fact, I'll contact him, if you don't mind. I could try to have an audience with him, after we visit with Jason. Is that okay with you, guys? Nonc…is that okay with you?

They all agreed. Dexter looked at Norma, who gave him a smile and held his hand. Dexter understood that she was in agreement with his offer.

"First, we need to get something to eat… Norma and I are a bit hungry. Perhaps we can hook up with Calvin and your husband after he gets off from work tonight. Would that be alright?"

"Dat's fine, Dexter. Dat's sounds real good. We goin down dere to see Jason, and we let you know how he doin, daddy."

"Alright… ya'll call me when ya can."

For the next couple of hours, Dexter and Norma spent their time at nonc Landry's home, relaxing. They had a full day of activities without taking in some protein for their bodies. As they rested, they mulled over the situation the family faced. The sisters had returned to their individual homes to freshen up before they met at the police station. Of all the reasons they could have had too come together, this one was not priority on none of their lists. It became a cycle about every three or four months, that a family issue would come up, which required their collectiveness to solve it. At 4:45 PM, Dexter was asleep in the big box chair in the living room, while Norma was resting across the bed in the room where they slept the night before. Dexter's cell phone rang. After the second ring,, it jarred Dexter from his slumber. He looked around, collecting his wits, then reached into his pocket and answered it.

"Hello, this is Dexter Simon!"

"Hello Dexter, this is Marvin Klein… from Klein Invest…"

"Oh, yes… yes, hello Marvin, how are you?"

"I'm well… you got minute?"

"Yeh, sure. What you got?"

"Well, I got a lot… and there's a lot more out there."

"Really!"

"Yes sir, I'm afraid so. But first let me tell you this…Your brother is considered in the business to be dirty."

"Please, Marvin, explain that to me."

"That means that he has his hands in something that's illegal. He's been in it for over 10 years. He's listed with the FBI, DEA, ATF, Homeland Security and the local police. He's been surveyed by the local police for the last 2 years. You didn't know any of this?"

"NO, I swear… I mean I guarantee you I knew nothing about anything he might be involved with. That's why I hired you, remember?"

"Okay, but the investigation also has a brother involved to a lesser extent. I suppose you're saying that's not you, right?"

"Absolutely!"

"Absolutely what?"

"I mean absolutely not! But I do have another brother, though."

"Oh!"

"Yes, he's my youngest brother, but I can't see that he's…"

"Listen Dexter, I don't make this stuff up. I allow the information to drive the investigation. Not the other way around… you understand?"

"Yes I do... I do. Listen; have you any information where my brother is right now? Remember I said they-the hospital-moved him last week."

"No, the hospital didn't move him. He was moved by the ATF and Homeland Security ... for protection."

"For protection? ...From whom?"

"I can't tell you the details at this time. I do have some more information but, there are some other things I need to check out to be sure. I should have it by tomorrow. You want to come by here tomorrow afternoon?"

"No, I can't. I'm out of town... on vacation... I won't be back until Monday."

"Okay, that's fine. I should have even more info for you by then."

"Wow! ... this is unbelievable. I mean totally unreal! Thanks... thanks Marvin."

Dexter closed his phone and stared at it. Norma had been listening to him as she rose up from her nap. She spoke:

"Not good, huh?"

"Nope...not good at all. In fact, it's about some of the worst news I can get... just about the worst; not **the** worst, but some of the worst." said Dexter. He prayed:

"Have Mercy dear Lord."

Chapter 24

June-bug wasted no time in getting over to nonc Landry's house to escort Dexter to the shed at the rear of his house. Dexter had spent some quiet time with Norma, and assured himself that she would be fine with him leaving her with his uncle. All the boys had congregated about 8 PM, and one of them had started cooking something in a large cast iron pot, located in the corner of the small shed. By the time Dexter arrived, whatever it was, it was almost done, and produced a wonderful aroma.

"*Heeey, dere he is... come on in Jack... we been waitin on you... how ya feel? ...Da food bout ready... you hongry?*"

"*Thank you ...thank you, fellows. Something sure smells good. What is it?*"

"*Listen,*" said Calvin. "*You don really want ta kno. If you hongry, grab a bowl.*"

It took no time at all for Dexter to meld into the environment of the evening. Everyone introduced themselves. The gaming table was set up for dominoes and Teaspoon, Prince, Dale and June-bug pulled their chairs up to the table to scramble the pieces. Dexter was not shy, so he took a bowl; scooped up some rice, and filled it with the mystery dish. June-bug pulled a chair from the side of the wall, and placed it next to him, for Dexter. While Dexter ate, the rest of the foursome

144

divided up the bones, and began to play. Dexter started with a half bowl, but decided to get a top-off before he sat down to eat. The smell made it alluring.

"Wow, this is good stuff, guys. Really, what's in it?"

"Well, you got chicken in dere, sausage, pork, squirrel, and a little bit of turtle in dere too." said June-bug.

Dexter started to feel warm. He had not put any hot sauce into the bowl, but sweat beaded on his forehead.

"Aaaha! Okay... I think I'll just eat the sauce and rice and maybe I'll have a piece of chicken, if you don't mind. Prince, you want the rest of this if I can't eat it all?" asked Dexter.

"No, not yet. You ain't got 'nough in dere for me, man. You sweatin, too. You goin be alright?"

"Ohhh weee! This has some real kick to it... but it's good, though," declared Dexter. *"So, this is where you guy's hang out during the week, huh?"*

"Dis is where we hang out, period," advised Prince. *"We probly over here almost every evening. We just play dominoes, eat, drink our beer, and talk about the news. Did ya'll hear dey gon close da crawfish pond?"*

"Naw," said Calvin. *"When you heard dat?"*

*"Hit wus on da bulletin board today. Day say da got da **white spot syndrome virus**. Dere wus four ponds altogether 'long south Louisiana,"* reported Prince.

Do any of you guys work in the crawfish industry?" asked Dexter.

"Just me," said Prince. *I supervise a bunch a guys at the processing plant."*

"Where do the rest of you guys work?" asked Dexter.

Calvin spoke for the group.

"I work for the city; Prince drives truck; June-bug and Dale work off-shore... What do you do, Dexter?"

"I work for a GIS company. That means Geographical Information Systems."

"What in da world is dat," Prince asked.

"Well, it's all about satellites, and about the information they gather," said Dexter.

"Oooh, sounds like some government spying or somethin. Is it like that movie called… what's the name of dat movie June-bug? You know, where the government wus trackin Will Smith with a satellite!"

"Oh, you mean 'Enemy of the State'."

"Yeah, dats what it sounds like."

"Well, I saw that movie, too," said Dexter. It was a good one. But it's not quite the same as that…Hey, Is it my turn yet?"

"Yeh, git up Tea-spoon--You low man. Sit down Dexter."

As Dexter sat down to play, he felt the time would soon be right for him to engage in conversation about their families and their spiritual beliefs. He wanted to get a few more minutes of sparring and small talk on the table before he started that line of communicating. He was an invited guest, he reminded himself. Things would not always go his way. He would give it a try and see what would happen. They played their hands.

"That's **20**," said Prince.

"Oh, you think you got somethin, huh? Give me **25**!" demanded Dale, slamming the bones onto the table.

Play continued in this way until Tea-spoon slammed down the final score of 15, to claim that he won that round. Everyone released an audible sound to show their dissatisfaction. Calvin pushed from the gaming table and headed towards the dish for the evening, to get something to eat. The rest, except Dexter, joined him.

Dexter spoke with confidence. "All I needed was 25 more before I would have won."

"Yeh", said Dale, "that's what they all say."

They all had a good chuckle as they settled back down to eat and relax for a moment. The time was 10:41 pm. Dexter felt himself getting tired. He wanted to stay long enough to show his appreciation for the invite, but he also wanted to interject the subject of knowing Christ into the evening's conversation. At the same time, he did not want to appear condescending or lofty. What he needed to do was, speak to their needs as they revealed it to him. This would be his only chance to make his point for Christ, he felt. Therefore, it would be best to be patient about that. He spoke.

"*Say fellows, do any of you guys know about that lawyer over in Lafayette named Chase Abbott Pierce?*"

"*Yeh, we all heard 'bout him. Dat's 'spossed ta be a real sharp white boy. You kno he got his law degree from Xavier! But, mo dan dat, he don won a lot of cases for po people, over his own kind. Dat's one white boy other white lawyers don't want ta tangle wit.*"

"*Yeh, I heard da same thang,*" said June-bug.

"*Well, do you suppose if we contacted him to talk about Jason, he might be willing to take his case?*"

"*I thank he take anybody's case if da money's right,*" said Calvin. "*I thank he want ta win, moen he want da money, though. Dat's just my feeling.*"

"*Well, I'll be calling him tomorrow morning. I hope I can catch up with him before we have to go back home,*" explained Dexter. "*I want to do what I can before I leave, to help our 'coozan'. Based on what I saw, he's going to need a good lawyer to handle his case. By the way, has he been a hot-headed kid growing up? I heard he became this way sometime after his daddy died.*"

"*Ah, Jason's like most of the other kids 'round here. I tell you the truth, Dexter, he mo like his friend he went to high school with... Bailey Toussaint. Dey played football together; dey dated da same kinda girls together... and...*"

"*Excuse me, what kinda girls did they date, Dale?*"

"*Bailey's daddy owns a ice house. His daddy would set Bailey up with some of the younger girls dat hung 'round the place, and Bailey would turn Jason on to some of them.*"

"*Well, what kinda girls were they?*" asked Dexter.

"**Dey wus hookers... white hookers!**"

"*Bailey is white?*"

"Yeeessss!"

"Oh, I didn't realize that was the case. Sooo how did that go over with the great citizens of New Iberia who knew about this arrangement?" asked Dexter.

"Dats what started gettin Jason noticed by da police. Dey started watchin him after dat, and stoppin him for every thang when he drove his momma's car. Most of da time, he ain't done nothin wrong. Dey wus harrassin em for nutin. He probly wun'd doin nutin dis time, 'sept hangin wit ol Bailey and one of dem chicks."

"You mean he might have been arrested because of the people he hung with? How could that happen?"

"Listen Dexter, nobody want ta talk 'bout it but, dis Bailey kid been accused of bringing illegal drugs to town. But da police might bus Bailey, and den let him go. If Jason wus wit him, dey would work 'em over, and den take him to jail. So Jason gets beat up and da record, and Bailey gits the girls and da dough. Hit's messed up for sho, but what can ya do 'bout it? Jason just won't stay way from dat bad white boy."

"I will certainly keep that in mind when I speak with Mr. Pierce," said Dexter. "This all seems so unreal to me. I mean it's hard to believe that that sort of thing is still going on in this country."

"Dat ain't nothin. You stick 'round here for a week and you'll see a hol lot mo. Hit's lak we stuck in a glass bottle, and we cant git out. It feel lak somebody stedy porin water on top our hed, an we ar drownin. Jus 'bout da time we feel lak we 'bout ta drown, da pressue ease up and we can brethe agin," lamented Prince.

"Do you all feel that way?" asked Dexter.

"You damn right," answered Calvin and June-bug.

"Is it money or lack of it, or what?"

"Naw man-hits deeper den dat. I can't put ma finger on it, but hits kinda lak we inside a balloon, and somebody keep blowin us up, and den lettin da pressure out some. I cant lay it out lak I want to. But I guarantee you... I can feel it!

"I think I know what you mean, fellows. I really do. In fact, I have felt like that myself at a point in my past," counseled Dexter.

"You?"

"Yes, sir. In fact, I almost had a nervous breakdown, when it seemed as if everything around me was caving in. I felt as if I could not control anything I touched. I spent a lot of time trying to analyze my situation, and tried to logically work things out. The deeper the problem, the more I analyzed, and the less control I had. I truly felt hopeless, and weak. I felt as if I could not make intelligent decisions. I tried to withdraw myself from those I thought were causing me problems, and spent more time alone. Really, the more I tried to fix the issues caving in around me, the more out of control I felt."

"Dat's what it feels lak for me, too. I can't believe you had da same thang happen ta you, too? I mean you look lak you always had it together, man. How did ya finally git thangs fixed? What did ya have ta do?"

"I gave up!"

"Huh? You gave up what?"

"I gave up control of my life."

"Ta who?"

"When I was at my lowest point in my life, and could not control any facet of it, I gave control of my life over to Christ Jesus. The LORD was the only one who knew me, and knew my situation. Believe me when I tell you fellows, the moment I gave my life over to Christ; to live according to his plan for me, **everything... everything** turned around for me."

"Lak what? What changed for you?" asked June-bug.

"Yeh...dats what I wanna kno too," said Prince.

"I was able to release the pressure I felt trying to conform to what others wanted me to be. For the first time, I felt that God was listening to my pleas for HIS help. I felt comforted, as if I was being held in my grandmothers arms, as she rocked me and comforted me. I started attending church on a regular basis and genuinely started to praise and worship God. My conversations with HIM became personal between HIM and me, and I felt that the Holy Spirit was speaking directly to me on a daily basis. In other words, I was seeking after God for once in my life, and not trying to concentrate on me. I decided to place God on top of my priority list, and not just when I got in trouble. I began to pray for wisdom and understanding of God's word. I prayed for revelation of God's plan for me. That's when I began to see my life turn around. That's when I found my wonderful wife, Norma. I was a believer in God, but I did not place HIM first in my life. Now, when I place HIM where HE wants to be, HE opens up a road map in my life, and HE allows the Holy Spirit to guide me. Does any of this make sense to you guys?"

"Yeh, man. It makes sense to me," said Prince.

"Me too," said Calvin, June-bug and Dale.

"Do you fellows want me to pray with you right now?"

"Yeh Dexter, would you do that? I feel I need it," said Prince.

"Of course. Let me ask you all this—have you accepted Jesus Christ as your Lord and redeemer?"

They answered in unison—"Yes!"

"Okay then, let us pray."

"Dear Lord Jesus, I honor you as the Son of God. You are my Lord and Savior. You sacrificed your life so that all mankind would have the opportunity to be reconciled with the father. Lord God, your word tells us that if we lift you up, you would draw all men unto you. Lord I lift you up right now. I lift your name up to all men. May you be glorified throughout the earth. Lord forgive us for our sins that we have committed against you and others. We are truly sorry for our misdoings. Strengthen us to withstand the temptations of the evil one. May the light of Christ shine within us continuously. Make us worthy to be called the children of God--Make us worthy dear Lord. Now Lord, I pray for these my brothers. Lord you know them right down to the number of hairs on their head. You know their needs and their desires. Father I pray you will bless each of them individually. Lord, may this day be the first day, of the best days, of the rest of their lives. What ever they have done against your will, I pray you will forgive them. Let them feel your forgiveness, Lord. Father do not let them

leave this room the same way they came in. Make them stand up
for you; for themselves, and for their families. Lord, bless their lives,
their wives, and their children. May they become the peer pressure
and not succumb to it. Thank you Lord for all you have done for all
of us. I pray this prayer in the name of our Lord and Savior, Jesus
the Christ...amen!"

"Amen...amen...amen!" said June-bug. "Thanks for dat Dexter. Man
I feel so much better."

Dexter, smiling, reached out to shake the hand of June-bug, as
Prince, Calvin and Dale came over to hug him. They all began to cry
as they never have before. To Dexter, it seemed as though a river of
tears, backed up since they were boys, was being released down their
faces. They needed no words to be spoken, as much as they needed the
flood gates to open. They hugged each other tighter and cried more
and more freely. Dexter invited the presence of the Holy Spirit.

**"Receive their cries Holy Spirit. Touch each one and accept them
right where they stand.** *Yes, release those feelings; my brothers... release
them into the arms of Jesus. Come on... let it go...let Jesus handle your
burdens as only he can."*

"I kno I ain't been all dat I could 'a been for ma family," said June-bug,
sobbing ..."I ask da Lord ...ta forgive me for dat."

"I ain't 'tended church lak I shoulda ," confessed Calvin. "I ask da
Lord ta forgive me."

There were no dry eyes in the little smoke house. Here were five
grown men wiping snot running from their noses, onto their shirt
sleeves and the back of their hands. After about four or five minutes
of getting themselves back together, each one tried to get back into
character by clearing their throats and shaking each others hand.

"You alright, Dale, Calvin, Prince?" asked June-bug.

"Yeh, thanks ta Dexter and his prayer. I feel different now. I really do;
I feel loose and free."

"That's the power of the Holy Spirit, fellows. Jesus has set you free from
your burdens you've been carrying all this time. You now need to walk in

151

his love and in his Devine will for each of your lives. One thing you need to remember... Jesus is always there for you. No matter what you are going through... no matter what the situation is... you can always call on his name, and he will answer your prayer. He **will** *answer your prayer. Remember this scripture in Psalms 118:8 'It is better to trust the Lord, than to put confidence in people.'"*

"*You got dat right, Dexter. I agree wit dat,*" said Prince.

"Alright gentlemen, may God be with you. Keep the faith ...Listen, I've got to get back to my wife. What time is it any way?"

"It's 11:11 pm."

Chapter 25

Norma was still awake when Dexter returned home and eased through the bedroom door. Only a glimmer of brightness from a street light pole, shown through a divided Curtain which cascaded onto a mirror atop the thin white veneered dresser. The only other furniture in the room, besides the bed, was an antique four-drawer dresser used to store the everyday clothing for Dexter and Norma. It was the place where Dexter placed his watch and loose change from his pants pockets. After undressing for bed, Dexter climbed in beside Norma. It was sticky hot in the house, and Dexter decided to sleep without the top sheet. He kissed Norma on the forehead and said a short prayer over her. Shortly, they were fast asleep.

During the night, Dexter was awakened by a tapping sound, coming from within a few feet of where he laid his head. He lay stilled by the rhythm of the tapping trying to determine what it was, and where was it coming from. Dexter's' eyes surveyed the darken room to no avail. The tapping continued. He wanted to arouse Norma, but decided against it for fear she would be startled. Dexter saw no figure, nor the outline of one. But he knew something in the physical world was responsible for what he was hearing. More and more, he was tempted to reach for the light sitting atop the dresser, but was afraid to extend his arms. The sounds continued, until Dexter could not take it anymore. He decided to slowly extend his hand to the lamp, and turned the light on. He hurriedly withdrew his arm, then raised himself to a defensive, sitting position. He looked left; then right; up; then down. Norma stirred from her sleep and asked:

"What's the matter honey?"

"Baby, did you hear that tapping sound coming from over there on that dresser?"

"No, I was asleep!"

"I was too, before I heard a tapping sound coming from right in this area," said Dexter. It continued to tap until I turned the light on."

"Where did you say it came from?"

"It sounded as if it came from right here!" said Dexter, pointing to a spot on the edge of the dresser.

"Well, the only thing that is there is your watch sitting on top of some of your coins," said Norma.

"Exactly! ...It had to be my watch. I wonder what time it is anyway. ... Honey, do you see this? My watch has the time of 3:33 am."

"Baby, what is it with these number combinations? Have you figured that out yet?"

"I have no idea what's happening with that. I left June-bug's house last night at 11:11 pm; remember nonc Landry gets up at 5:55 am. He worked at the lumber yard for 33 years and 3 months. I have been seeing number combinations like that for the past month or so. Do you remember Brian was in room 333? I also found a paper on the first floor of the County Hospital with those same numbers on it.

Then I walked outside and looked at my watch, and it was 3:33 pm.

It seems like somebody or something is trying to tell me something through numbers. Sometimes I feel a spiritual connection to them. I sometimes think the plan for me and my way of living has something to do with these numbers--especially three numbers," explained Dexter.

"Well, we need to get some sleep, honey. I'll keep my ears open to see if I hear anything, okay?" assured Norma.

"Yeah, I do need to get some sleep too. Don't mention anything to nonc, *okay. I don't want to get him excited by this… whatever it was,"* asked Dexter.

Norma curled up in Dexter's arms. He was still warm from an accelerated heart rate and rapidly rising temperature. He loved his wife with all his heart but, he was not ready to have her body heat meld with his own, right now. Gently, he turned to his other side and told his wife he loved her, as he said goodnight. She repeated the sentiments and tried to get into a comfortable position to get back to sleep.

The next morning, Dexter and Norma convinced nonc Landry to have breakfast with them at a local restaurant frequented by many of the locals in the community. The item everybody recommended was the country breakfast. It was bold and heaping- enough for any hungry giant. Dexter ordered it, but because of the enormous amount of food, he agreed to share part of it with Norma. Nonc Landry ordered a bowl of fruit, and biscuits with gravy on top. Dexter took the time to tell his uncle how much he appreciated his hospitality, and apologized for not having enough time to help him with some over-looked items around the house. Today, however, he wanted to help the family with the legal matter they found themselves caught up in. Nonc understood and appreciated Dexter and Norma's intentions but, he told them he preferred that he assist the family, by meeting with that young lawyer in Lafayette. The rest of the time spent together at breakfast was invaluable, Norma thought. They could communicate again, the way they did the first day they arrived.

"Uncle Landry, have you seen a big visible change in the way people are today versus the way they were, say 40 or 50 years ago?" asked Norma.

"U'm goin ta tell ya the biggest change dats happen since dat time, sugar. Da biggest change dats happen is with da **Black man**. *He used ta be a workin man dat took care his family. No matter what happen, we make sho we was dere to put food in da family stomach, and clothes on dere back. Da black man don lost his way. He don lost his stiffness when da goin got tuff. If he got fired off a job, he went out and got 'nother one. His family was number one, even befo his own self. If his kids needed som*

shoes, and he only had a copula dollars, he would go almost barefoot his self for dem kids. I tell you 'nother thang 'bout how da black man changed. He don give up on God. He thank he can workout all his problems by his self. He used to pray over his family… for protection 'gainst evil men who wanted ta keep him down. Den, he got high an mighty with education; he started following the way of the white man, wit all dat hustling and bustling, and he forgot 'bout God. Now he don got all confused and lost his way. Da ones who came up taday got further and further from his fathers way. Now, what you think he got to teach his boys? Dem boys ain't got no man to show 'em da right way in da home. His momma got her hands full wit raisin all her chillen. She doin her best to keep 'em in line. But, most of 'em can't control dat boy when he gits ta be a teenager. Where's da daddy? Look how many of 'em don walked away from da family. Hit's a dad-gum shame da leavin da family unprotected like dat. Dat's 'zactly wat da devil wants, ya kno. Hit's da MAN dat God 'pointed to head da house. Now he don walked away fom dat 'sponsibility. How he goin lead a family, when he lost his self? What 'bout his boys? You look round now. Look at what we got for da future? …What we got? …We got draggin pants, wild hair style, getto talkin; no 'spect for da female, and not even fo old folk… hit don't look good, sugar. Naw sir, hit don't look good 'a tall. You ask me what changed, sugar- dat's it! Dat's it!"

Dexter wiped tears from his eyes. Norma sat silently with her hands cupping her flushed face. Nonc held his head down as tears traced down his cavernous face. He gritted his teeth as the muscles in his jaw tightened up.

"What do you see for the future, Uncle?" asked Norma.

"I don see hit getting better soon… We look lak a bunch a ants stumbling all over each other, tryin ta find our way. Da difference is, da ants know where he goin, and he kno what his purpose is. Ya see, he come here dat way-His purpose passed down ta him in his blood. Ever time we git a new birth in da family, many of dem struggle all da life trying to find da purpose. Dats how we loose generations, sugar. Cause, most of our people never find da purpose. We spen a whole life of startin over. We git goin dis way …and *when dat don work, we git goin dat way. Hit's true ya know, dat education is what we need. But education is just a tool ta help us find da way. It ain't ever thang by hit self. Once you find da way, God is da one dat goin give ya da increase, if ya lean on him, and not ya own understandin. We got ta break down da attitudes of high mindedness and lackadaisical attitudes befo we kin start ta change,"* commented Uncle Landry. *"But… we got two generations lost, already. We way behind time.*

Our leaders failed us too, ya kno. Fact is, we don lost our leaders when integration come along. We usta have our leaders' right dere in our own neighborhood. Day was da ones dat taught us in school; preached ta us; sold us our bread at da corner store; whipped us when we got outa line, and told our momma day did it by da time we got home.

They ain't been no leader since Martin Luther King died. Jesse Jackson give up on da people when he lost runnin for President, after he got caught foolin with dat woman dat wattun his wife. Can't nobody understand dat fellow from New York… Sharpman, Sharp…"

"You mean Al Sharpton, nonc," said Dexter.

"Dat's him. He don't make no sense ta me. He talks too high for me ta understand him. Den you got dat new guy… he's a Senator fom Chicago…"

"Barack Obama?"Asked Dexter.

"Yeh, him. He just popped up on da scene. Ain't nobody heard a him befo. Now he wanna be President of da hole United States. Dat sound funny ta me. He ain't done notin for us Black folk, far as I kin see," admonished Uncle Landry.

Dexter had composed himself and spoke.

"You know nonc, I understand what you're saying, and I agree with you. I've talked with Norma about this for some time now. I truly believe what it says in Ephesians 5:23. The husband is the head of the wife, as Christ is the head of the Church. But equally as important is what it says in verse 25. It says a husband should love his wife as much as Christ loves the Church. Now that makes for a powerful combination if we can get that right. But, you're right- we have gotten away from what God tells us in his

word. If we can get ourselves right with God, then get ourselves right, we can then get our families together! ...so goes the family, so goes the world, they say. If the family is sound and safe, we don't really need political leaders to do for us do we? Because everybody would be doing the right things-living Godly lives!"

"You don hit da nail right smack on top of da head wid dat, Dexter. When ever thang fall in place, dat mean puttin God first, dis will be a much better world."

"But how do we start, Uncle? Where do you think we should begin to accept the changes that are necessary? Whose responsibility is it to begin the dialog-to start the personal responsibility change we all must adopt, in order to get ourselves back on track?" asked Norma.

"Hit got ta start with me, and you, and Dexter. In other words, everbody dat hear dis word, got to 'ceppt the truth in it, and decide ta do his part. We gotta come ta beleve and 'ceppt dat we don strayed 'way from God, and we got to ask God to 'ceppt us back. He been dere all da time-we da ones dats left. I beleve when we do dat, dat would be da greatest blessin since Christ rose from da dead," said nonc Landry. "Yes sir...dat would be a great blessin."

"So you agree that we have walked away from the Lord, and we must return to HIM before HE will heal our families, finances, health, relationships, marriages, communities, churches, government, children, schools... and everything else, as it said in Hosea 6?" asked Dexter.

"I know I do," agreed Norma. "I see no way any of this can fix itself without each of us doing our best to know the Lord, so he can refresh us like rain."

"Dats for sho. I tell ya sometin else too. Da one dat got da 'tention of da people ever week is who?" asked Uncle Landry.

"The Preachers," answered Dexter.

*"Dare ya go! ...Da Preachers got ta tell it like it tis. Dese times gotta have a different kinda preachin, if ya goin reach da people taday. If he is truly of God, he will warn da people dat Gods angry 'cause of dere sins, like **Jeremiah** did in Chapter 6 and 7. He can see all da problems goin on*

*in da community... Getting 'em to live Gods way is da 'portant thang. Savin souls is da challenge. But, people gotta kno dere purpose **after** da ben saved, and hit ain't raisin money fo no Pastor's Anniversary. Da gotta be real with da word...make it real to da people and da will respond by cummin to Christ... Anyway, God's got plans fo all us. He got a future fo us dats good, not evil. Dats what I see when we return to HIM in Chapter 29:11,"* instructed nonc Landry.

"Nonc, let me ask you something else. Knowing what Jesus told his Disciples to do with the Gospel-go into all the world and preach the Gospel-when do you do what he said about leaving that town and dusting off your shoes? I mean, even in our own family, there are those who do not want to hear what you got to say, and it's hard for me to keep coming back... do you understand what I mean?" asked Dexter.

"What do ya thank Jesus would say?" answered nonc Landry.

Norma spoke.

"If you don't mind me giving my opinion first, I would think Jesus would say speak the word as you have been taught and let it fall where it will. I think he would ask us to take another look at the parable of the sewer."

"That's what I would say too, sugar. Hit don't matter who it is... if da don't want ta hear, let dem live in darkness, and da suffer da consequences... no matter who it is." advised Nonc.

"But, I just can't help feeling that maybe I didn't do something that I could have done to help my brother, or sister, or anybody accept Jesus Christ, and start living a Christian life." lamented Dexter. ..."*Would you excuse me...I need to go to the restroom. Where is it nonc?*

Nonc pointed to the direction of the restroom. Dexter took off his light weight jacket and placed it on the back of his chair, before heading in that direction. He was gone for no more than a minute when Norma heard a ringing sound coming from Dexter's' jacket pocket. It was his cell phone he had left in his interior pocket. By the time Norma got to it, it had stopped ringing. After taking a look at the caller ID, she could tell it was a call to him coming from back home.

She laid it on the table beside Dexter's plate. Dexter returned minutes later. Norma spoke:

"I tried to answer your phone when it rang while you were in the restroom, honey. It stopped ringing before I could get to it. It looks like somebody from Shreveport calling you."

"Thanks babe. I think I'll call them back after we finish our meal. Whatever it is can wait, I'm sure."

Dexter's phone rang again. He picked it up to see who was calling. He answered it.

"Hello, this is Dexter...Yes sir...when?...where?... Oh my God, have mercy. Well, we are planning on being back there by tomorrow night. Tell me this sir; is he going to make it? I mean just how bad is that?... Well, thanks for calling to let me know. We will continue to pray for him. How is his wife doing, do you know?"

Norma sat with her mouth open as she listened for more details from Dexter's conversation. She felt a heavy weight on her spirit, anticipating the word about Brian to be depressing.

"Thank you sir, for your call. If you see any of our family, please tell them we'll be in tomorrow night."

It was nearly 10am. A uniformed officer entered the café to have breakfast. He looked around the café and greeted everyone he saw with a nod of his head. Nonc Landry spoke:

"You see dat one dere? Dat's the meanest one on da police foce. Da say he da one dat beat up da ones he 'rest. I betcha he did sometin ta my grandson, too!"

"Let's get out of here, and go see Jason. I need to make sure he's okay before I call Mr. Pierce," said Dexter.

Dexter laid a twenty dollar bill on the table to cover the tab for all of them.

"You better give it ta da watress ta git yo change back, Dexter," advised Nonc.

"I'm okay, Nonc. She let us sit here for a long time...that's covers my rent."

"You sho"?

"Yeh, I'm fine, lets go!"

As they passed by the officers table, Nonc greeted the officer with a salute and nod.

"Sheriff!"

The officer stared at Dexter as he wiped his mouth and returned the greeting to Nonc.

"Mr. Landry... ya'll doin alright?"

"We fine, sheriff...just fine!"

"Ya'll stay outa trouble, ya hear?"

Staying out of trouble was not Dexter and Norma's issue. Their issue was the trumped-up trouble their cousin was in, based on what Nonc had explained to them. Dexter spoke while opening the door to his car for Norma.

"You know, all of this is so unreal to me. It brings back images in my mind of the old movies about the Klu Klux Klan, and the involvement with the sheriff, and how they abused the black folk in the woods and burned down their houses and came back the next day to warn the survivors to be good, or else. You remember those movies, honey? I do not like this guy at all."

"I agree, honey. He does have a suspicious nature, doesn't he?"

"Can't nobody prove it... but I thank dat stuff still goin on round here," said Nonc Landry. *"Black folks round here know dere place, pretty much. Dey jus go ta work and ta church and pretty much min dere own business. Ever once in awhile dey stir up sometin 'round here. Hit ain't been notin lately, till Jason's situation come up."*

Dexter drove to the jail and parked his car on the side of the building. The three of them went into the front and walked slowly to the counter. Dexter felt uneasy, but tried not to show it to Norma. Nonc Landry spoke to the woman in civilian clothes typing behind a disk.

"Cuse me! ... Cuse me , madam," interrupted Nonc.

"Oh, I'm sorry-can I help you?"

"*We're here to see Jason Simon*", announced Dexter.

"*I believe you mean that young boy they brought in yesterday. Are you any kin ta him?*"

"*Dat's ma grandson,*" replied Nonc.

"*I'm sorry 'bout that…he's been transferred to Lafayette General Hospital this morning.*"

"Oh my God!" Norma shouted. "*Is he going to be alright?*"

"*I can only tell you what I know, miss. They needed to get him some medical attention, and that's where he is. If you want to call them, I'm sure they can tell you more' bout his condition, okay?*"

"*Let's get back to your house Nonc, and call Shirley. She might know what's going on. I just can't make that trip to the hospital if I am going to visit with Mr. Pierce.*"

"*Can you tak me by her house,*" asked Nonc.

"*Yes, that's a good idea. I'll do that.*"

This was not considered good times for Norma and Dexter. In fact, these were some of the worst times they had seen since they moved back to the south. Not withstanding the trials the family was having back in Shreveport, this visit with his relatives in New Iberia was more disheartening, and spiraling downward fast. Dexter felt he was getting so deeply involved in Jason's life, he would soon lose the management of his own. How far should he go, he wondered? At what point should he disengage himself from their lives and reconnect with his own? What would they do if he was not there at this time? He felt weak in his knees and in his gut. He felt as if he would become a failure if he tried to take on the local politics of the law in New Iberia, and was resigned to simply carry the message of concern to the young lawyer in Lafayette.

"*Nonc, Norma and I will take you home. We'll get in touch with the hospital for you and find out what's happening with Jason. But after that, we're going to have to go see that lawyer.*"

"*No problem Dexter… I know you gotta go. I 'preciate what ya'll done fo Jason so far. Ya'll go on and take care of dat business in Lafayette wid dat lawyer. We gon be alright here. Don ya'll worry 'bout dat."*

After visiting for almost three days with his family in New Iberia, Dexter and Norma's trip was coming to an end. They had no more time to help nonc Landry do a little fixing up around his place; they could not widen their involvement with Jason's case, but resigned themselves to try to make contact with the young Attorney Pierce in Lafayette. Dexter had briefed Norma concerning what happened at June-bugs place the night before, and she was excited about the success he had in emphasizing the amazing love of Jesus. She considered his prayer to be just what Christ had ordered for some men who had temporarily lost their connection with the Savior. Surely, she uttered, that must have been part of the plan for this trip, and she would be forever thankful to God for the opportunity her husband took advantage of, to refresh the belief's these men had, thereby denying Satan the opportunity to cast doubt within them. Now, it would be up to the Holy Spirit to grow the seeds that were planted into their fertile grounds.

They came to Shirley's house and parked in the gravel driveway. They exited the car and headed towards the front door to the house. Shirley came out and met them as they approached the porch. Two chickens sprinted across the porch being chased by a large white rooster.

"Watch out for that rooster, ya'll. I think he might chase you guys if he thinks you might try to take his girls," said Shirley.

"Shirley, do you know about Jason? Have you heard from him at the hospital?" asked Dexter.

"Yeah, they called me at the hospital and told me they thought he had a broken rib."

"My God, Shirley... I am so sorry for you and for Jason. Would you mind if we prayed with you before we leave?" asked Norma.

"Please come on in, ya'll. I don't mind at all. Daddy, you look bad. Are you constipated again? Did you eat yet? Did you take your medicine?" probed Shirley.

"I'm fine, I'm fine. Go on in so dey can lev to get back home."

Pressed for time to get everything done before they left, Norma led the family in a prayer that asked God for forgiveness and for mercy. When they finished, they all exchanged goodbyes and hugs. Since Dexter and Norma had packed their clothes the night before, there was no need to return to Nonc's place. Instead, Shirley agreed to take him home after they left. By mid-day, the family visitors were off to Lafayette.

Chapter 26

A rriving in Lafayette during the high traffic time presented a special challenge for Dexter and Norma. Feeling a bit anxious to get their business done and get back home to Shreveport, they had to slow down to a crawl to make way for a caravan of football fans riding through the town before a game with a rival team. They had called Chase Pierce's office on their cell phone but was unable to speak to him. He had experienced an upset stomach after eating some bad oysters for lunch, and went home to take some medicine and get some rest for a couple of hours. Obviously pressed for time, Dexter preferred to wait in Chase's office until he returned. They entered into the front door.

"Hello, we're Dexter and Norma Simon. We are here to see Chase Pierce," said Dexter.

"Yes… I see you made it in. Would you like to have a seat in the conference room? Mr. Pierce should be here in about thirty minutes or so. Can I get you something to drink?" asked the secretary.

"How about some water," asked Norma.

"I'll be right back… please have a seat"

It was hard to miss all the certificates, awards and photo's on the walls in the conference room. Sitting prominently above a set of legal books encased in a glass door bookcase, was a one-hundred year old rifle with an inscription below it that said… "Presented to Chase from Grandpa". Norma was in awe of the old photos of seemingly rich white men with guns, and appearing to be hunting in the woods. Dexter saw photo's of Chase's graduation from college and presentations being made by national, state and city officials. How could such a young man be so well connected and successful as this, they wondered within their minds.

"Here we go… here's your water. Make yourself comfortable… it won't be too long." said the secretary.

"May I ask you, who is that black person in the picture with Chase, with the little kid?" asked Dexter.

"That's Mr. Fulton, that's Mr. Pierce-that's Chases' daddy. The black man is Mr. Panky Simon from New Iberia."

"Panky Simon! Panky is my grandfathers name. That's my grandfather, honey. Wow! …I wonder what that photo is all about? Who is the kid?"

"You have to ask Chase about that. I don't know."

The telephone rang, interrupting the conversation between them. It was Chase calling to report his estimated time of arrival would be in five minutes. Dexter and Norma reclined at the conference table to await his arrival. They were both impressed with what they saw. There seemed to be a whole history of the South displayed within this one room. The door opened as Chase entered, removing his coat.

"I'm sorry about that folks. I apologize for being late. How are you? How are you maam?"

"We're fine…thank you for asking. We understand you got a little under the weather during lunch. Are you gonna be alright?" asked Dexter.

"Yes, I'll be fine. I took some of my daddy's home remedy and laid down for a minute. I'm okay. You can bet I'll ask how fresh those oysters are the next time I eat out."

"Mr. Pierce…"

"Please call me Chase!"

"Okay, Chase. May I ask you who those people are in that picture over there?"

"Right here?" Pointing to the photo.

"Yes!"

"That's my dad, back about 45-50 years ago. The black man right here is Panky Simon and his son. I think his name is Avery."

"My grandfather was Panky Simon!"

"Really! Well that's a picture of your grandfather, right there. That must be your uncle then."

"I never heard of Avery before... How did they happen to be taking a picture with your father, though?"

"Dad was his lawyer... He represented him in a suit against a man who killed his wife with his truck."

"What! Someone killed his wife? What wife was that?" asked Dexter.

"Well, I would have to take a look in the old files to be able to tell you those details, Dexter. I can have my secretary take a look for me... Hold on a second."

Norma and Dexter sat back into the black leather chairs around the oblong oak conference table. Dexter clasped his hands and raised them to his chin. He took a deep breath and then released. He looked at Norma as she reached out to touch his hand. She smiled at him.

"Baby, are you following this as I am? Are you seeing something in that photo that you didn't know about before?" asked Norma.

"You know it. **I never knew my grandfather had another wife...** That never came up before... I never knew I had an Uncle named Avery, either...I think I'm going to have to do an ancestry search and find out just who is in my line of DNA."

Chase returned to announce that they had moved the old files to a warehouse, and he would not be able to get to them right away. He promised Dexter that he would get the file if he wanted him to look into it further.

"You bet I do. I'll gladly pay you for your time, of course."

"Okay, I will get that information to you. Make sure we get your address and phone number before you leave. Now, what was the other reason you wanted to see me today?"

"Okay, I really don't know how to start this… except to say that I am here on behalf of my relatives in New Iberia. Let me tell you the quick story…"

For the next fifteen minutes, Chase allowed Dexter to recount the events that occurred with their cousin Jason. He felt the need to express his concern for his overall safety, in light of the assault they witnessed in front of the jail house.

"Are you telling me you saw them hitting and kicking him while they were dragging him out of the car?"

"Yes!" answered Norma. It was horrible to watch. In fact, he's in the hospital now with broken ribs."

"Alright, let me ask you. Why do you want me to represent him in this case? Why not get somebody in New Iberia? I know there are some good lawyers there who happen to be black. Why not them?"

"Actually, we don't know anyone in New Iberia except our relatives, who without hesitation, told us to contact you. Apparently, they feel you were the right man to represent them. They told us that you had represented several others who were mistreated by the justice system, and that you were very aggressive, respected and very talented."

"I'm truly humbled by your words, Mr. Simon. And, I appreciate the confidence expressed by your relatives. But I must tell you that a case like this could take some time, and could be very costly. Who is going to be responsible for my fees?"

"Can you give me some idea of the amount of fees that might be involved?" asked Dexter.

"I would have to hire a Private Investigator; get some folk subpoenaed; do some research on case law; my office time and so forth and so forth… You could be looking at as much as 150 to 200 hours. My fees are $150 an hour if we don't have to go to court. If we have to sue, then you're talking about $250 an hour for that time."

"I will be honest with you Mr. Simon, I don't know if we can afford that. In fact, I know we can't. Is there anything else we can do to get Jason the help he needs?"

"Sure, you can hire a cheaper lawyer!"

"Let me be truthful with you Mr. Pierce..."

"Just Chase, please!"

"I seemed to have inherited the burdens of several of my relatives, lately... none of this has anything to do with me and my wife. It seems that no matter where we go, there is trouble following us. We got a cousin in New Iberia with this legal problem; a brother in Shreveport with a life and death issue; my wife and I are trying to get pregnant and she has to take fertility treatment for the past year... I make good money, but I just can't carry all this on my shoulders. Do you see where I'm coming from, Pierce?"

"I do! I see it clearly, Dexter. I'll tell you what I can do for you... I will check out the situation with your cousin, and I will get back to you, after I have a chance to do a little investigation... How's that?"

"That's reasonable, sir. I can appreciate that. I'll leave my contact info with your secretary. I appreciate you taking the time to discuss the case with me. I feel better about the outcome, just by talking with you."

"By the way, you mentioned your brother had a life and death issue. What's that all about?"

"He really was in serious condition before we left last week. When last I spoke with the investigator, his condition had gotten worse. That's why we have to get back as soon as possible."

"Does his family have legal representation?"

"I don't think so... not yet."

"Was he in an auto accident?"

"Yes, sir!"

"That's what I specialize in...!"

"Well... perhaps we should talk to his wife about hiring you to represent her and the family."

"Well... let me put it this way... I could very well represent both your relatives if we can work it out. That way, I could discount my services to both parties. . .you follow what I'm saying? In other words, I could suspend my fees on one, if the other one has insurance. Does either of them have insurance?"

"Yes, my brother had auto insurance."

"Great!" But who is this investigator you spoke about?"

"I don't think she hired him. I think he was trying to get a certain law firm to handle the case, but nothing's been done. . .I don't think!"

"I know you gotta go but let me say this. . . it would be in your best interest to convince your brother's wife to let us handle her case, along with your cousin. . .you follow what I'm saying, Dexter?"

"Why would it be in MY best interest?"

"I'm saying it would benefit ALL of your family members to have both cases handled by my office, because I would save everybody the extra cost of investigation, coordination, etc, etc."

"Yes I see what you mean. Well, we need to get back to Shreveport to find out what's going on. . .then we can address that situation with his wife. I think we can handle this with her. It makes sense. . .right honey?"

"It makes sense to me, babe!" We'll need to pray about that and get back to him next week, right?"

Chase reached out to shake Dexter's hand and placed his arm around his shoulders, while walking by his side towards the front door. Norma followed.

"Estelle, would you get Mr. & Mrs. Simon's contact information for me. And, enter a notation on their file that I need to give them a call by next Friday? That ought to give you enough time to talk to your sister-in-law, Dexter. Okay? . . .How's that?"

"Okay. . .that's fine. I really appreciate you taking the time to discuss this with us, Chase. Thank you!"

"It's my pleasure. Good to meet both of you. Ya'll be careful driving back."

""Oh. . .on our way in to your office, we saw a cemetery, back about 2 or 3 miles from here. Is that an historical cemetery? I mean who might be buried in there?" asked Dexter.

"*That happens to be where my grandfather, father, uncle and many founding fathers of this community is buried. As a matter of fact, I think Panky (your grandfather) was buried in there as well.*"

"*I was just eleven when he died but I didn't know where he was buried,*" said Dexter.

"*You would be well served to pay a visit there, if you can. Like I said, there is a lot of history in that old graveyard. Good luck*".

Dexter and Norma carefully maneuvered their way to the 10 acre cemetery which had it's beginnings as far back as 1811. They stood at the entrance which had a rusted wrought iron gate, weathered, pealing white paint and leaning from the weight of time and weather. A large, grand old oak shaded the first twenty-five feet to the entrance, where they stood to survey the monuments and head stones. Silence was the sound of the morning, pierced by the swishing of the wind as it danced with the massive branches and leaves of the trees. A lone care-taker was seen clipping the grass between headstones housed within a gated area with two concrete vaults. Where were they to start, they wondered. What should they be looking for, and who could they identify?

"*Do you want to try to find your grandfather, honey?*" asked Norma.

"*Yeh...I would like to , but where in heaven's name do we start?*"

"*Maybe with that care-taker over there... he might know where everybody is buried.*" Said Norma.

"*Let's try it...sounds like a good idea.*" agreed Dexter.

As they made their way towards the place where the care-taker was located, they could see sites which had sunken in and some had stones turned over because of the shifting of the earth under them. They looked left and right at the names and dates on some of the stones.

"*Born 1818... Nate Clemmons- Died 1866. I wonder if he was in the Civil War between the states?*" questioned Norma.

"*Look at this one born in 1801 and died in 1812. This was a child who probably died of a disease. Looks like his name was...what does that say?*"

"*Looks like Carter or Cartier...I can't tell. Oh baby, look! The caretaker is coming this way. He's waving at us.*" reported Norma.

"*Hello!*" yelled Dexter.

A small framed, old man with a thinning face and neck, approached them with a weed-eater in his hand. The old man was smiling as he spat out some chewing tobacco through his missing teeth. Although it was a hot day, the man was fully clothed with a long sleeve shirt buttoned all the way to his neck.

"Como Savoy". He greeted them.

"*Hello, sir. My name is Dexter Simon and this is my wife, Norma.*"

"Hello ma'am".

"*Sir, we are looking for my granddad who was buried here in this graveyard. His name was Panky Simon. Have you heard this name before, or know where he's buried?*" asked Dexter.

The old man smiled again and bowed his head.

"*I apologize for bothering you and taking you away from your work, but we were trying to find my grandfather's grave before we left town. I understand he was buried here some time ago. Are you aware of where he was buried?*"

The old man grunted and shook his head, no.

"*Are you saying you don't know, or are you saying he is not buried here?*" asked Dexter.

"*No!*"

"Norma spoke. "*Honey, I don't think he can talk very much. At least I don't think he can understand what you're wanting from him. Try it again.*"

"*Can you tell me sir, do you know if Panky Simon is buried here?*"

"*No!*"

"*Honey, I think...*"

"*That's alright ...I got it! That's alright sir, thank you... thank you*". exclaimed Dexter. "*Let's go see what we can find, baby. I don't see where we're going to get any where with this gentleman. Thank you again, sir! Thank you!*"

Dexter took Norma by the arm and led her away to another place within the cemetery, away from the old man who stood there watching them. As Dexter and Norma decided to split up to search separately, the old man went back to care-taking of the graves. Dexter felt certain that the old man understood him because he spoke in French when he first greeted them. But suddenly, he went dumb when he heard who he was looking for. Without some guidance, Dexter felt they would be there for hours. Nevertheless, they both continued their searching. Periodically, each of them stopped and pondered the information they found on certain grave head-stones, then they continued. Norma, kept one eye on the old man as he concentrated on a specific area as he was trimming grass. Norma kept walking and looking at the old man. He was spending a long time at the same location as he seemingly continued to catch the eye of Norma. She wondered if he was trying to communicate something to her about the area where he was spending a lot of time. Norma was certain he was saying something to her as he seemingly bowed his head at her several times. When she gazed at him for an extended period of time, the old man walked away to another area.

"HONEY!"

Norma yelled to get Dexter's attention. She waved her hand in the air and pointed toward the area where the old man had just left. Dexter pointed in agreement and they both headed towards that area.

The old man headed towards the entrance to the cemetery and stopped under the majestic oak. He watched as Dexter met Norma in the area he just vacated. Norma arrived first. Her eyes were fixed on the grave marker, barely standing, and leaning to its side. As Dexter met her at the area of focus, he too could see the words "Panky Simon 1901-1973".

"But why is the grave sunken like that? Where is the casket that's supposed to be here?" asked Dexter.

"That's a good question" responded Norma. *"It sure looks like somebody has removed the casket from his grave."*

They looked up to see where the old man was, to ask him the question. He was gone-vanished in the middle of the work-day.

"HELLO!...SIR, ARE YOU STILL HERE?... *What the heck... Where do you think he went, honey? HELLO! HELLO!*"

Dexter ran to the area where he last saw the old man behind the big oak tree. He was gone. Dexter turned to survey the graveyard. He saw other open graves in spotted places. No doubt these graves also housed caskets which had been removed.

"*Baby, this is too unreal. WHAT'S THE DEAL? I think I need to check into this some more. I think we need to go back to Chase's place and see if he knows what's happening here. My gut tells me something smells to high Heaven. Let's look around a bit...how long do you think this grave's been empty like this?*"

"*You know what honey, I am not feeling well. I think we need to get back on the road and head for home,*" pleaded Norma.

"*Okay, okay sweetie. Let me take a look at these other open graves... this one looks kinda fresh too. Look...look at that one over there... what happened? Where did they go? I'm counting...one...two ...three"...four... five! There's five open graves with head stones.*"

"*Honey, I've been getting upset stomachs for the past hour or so. I don't want us to lose the effectiveness of that last fertility treatment, remember? Can we go now? It's getting dark too. I think it's going to rain.*"

"*Okay babe, you're right. We do need to get going-- but I will get in touch with the people responsible for this cemetery and find out what happened, later. Let me get you home--easy, sweetie...let me help you get in the car... there. Are you alright now?*"

"*I'm alright now...let's go. This place is starting to give me the creeps!*"

Chapter 27

It was late in the evening when Dexter and Norma arrived back in Shreveport. They headed straight for his mother's house to try to get to her before she went to bed. Although recent storms had passed, the skies remained heavy with dark clouds and the air smelled fresh with ozone. Norma was feeling less faint, having slept most of the miles home. Dexter knew he had some tough questions to ask his mother, about his grandfather, but he didn't want to appear harsh and disrespectful. He and Norma said a prayer after entering onto the driveway. A dim light was on in his mother's bedroom, which was at the front of the house. They knocked on the door, while attempting to open it. Shortly, his mother came to the door and pulled back the curtains.

"Hey momma, it's us. You still up?"

Mrs Simon unlatched the lock and pulled the door open towards her. She had already prepared for bed and was waiting for her tea to finish brewing.

"Hey you two, ya'll made it back alright?"

"Yeh momma, we just made it back," said Dexter.

"Hey big momma, how you feeling?" asked Norma.

"I feel pretty good, sugar. 'Specially for an old lady anyway."

"Aw! You show me an old lady and I'll bake her a cake," joked Norma.

"You can bake me a cake anyway."

They all laughed and followed Mrs Simon into her bedroom. She sat on the edge of her bed and motioned for them to take a seat.

"How was everybody in New Iberia...? How was your uncle Landry?"

"Uncle Landry...Nonc...is doing real good momma," reported Dexter. "In fact, everybody is doing well except a couple of your kinfolk's boy... what's his name honey?"

"It's Jason...Jason Fontenot."

"Jason Fontenot?" asked Momma. "What happened to him? That's uncle Landry's grandson."

"We have heard some things about him getting into trouble a few times, momma. In fact, this boy apparently is trying to find his way in life. But anyway, we made contact with a lawyer before we left who will help him get back on track."

"A lawyer? Well, what did he do?" asked momma.

"I don't want to get you into that, momma. It's being taken care of by a very good attorney out of Lafayette." explained Dexter. "In fact, we want to see if he will be able to represent Brian if he decides to get an attorney... How is he doing, by the way?"

"Thay say he going make it! He may not be the same as before...but thank GOD he going to make it!"

"Thank GOD is right. Is he still in the same room at the same hospital?"

"Yeah, I thank so."

"Okay, I'll check on him tomorrow. Right now, I want to ask you a question about grandpop."

"Your granddad?"

"Yes...Panky Simon."

"What you want to know, Dexter?"

"I just want to ask you this, and I know there won't be time to discuss it all...but I want to know something about his marriage before he married your mother!"

"*Before he married my mother? What you know about that?*"

"*That's all I know! He had a son with a woman who was killed be a white man who ran over her in a truck. He killed the white man and went to court.*"

"*Where you getting all that mess, Dexter?*" *That ain't nothing but mess, you hear me? Did Landry tell you that? That's where you got that from… it nothing but mess, you hear me? You're right…there ain't going to be no discussion cause it's nothing but MESS. Now you take your wife on home and get you some rest…ya'll be careful hear! You go get you some rest, sugar, 'ya hear? Goodnight!*"

There was definitely a sensitive cord struck with his mother, thought Dexter. He had never witnessed her being so abrupt as she displayed tonight. How was he going to get the facts about his grandfather, and his uncle whom he never knew? Who would be willing to talk to him if his own mother would not? One thing was for sure, there were too many mysteries in his life, which needed answers. Perhaps not tonight, but he was going to get to the bottom of some of this… this nonsense.

Saturday morning found the Simon's still in bed at 9am. They woke to the sound of a lawn mower noise and men talking. Dexter turned over and met the gaze of Norma smiling at him.

"*Morning precious-you wake?*"

"*Mmm…just barely!*"

"*(Yawn) I need to get going… I got to check on Brian…I think I'll call Adam first (yawn).*"

"*Hey Adam, it's Dex. Yeah, we got back last night… It was good… different!... How's Brian?...really…yeah, I'm going over this morning…why not? …Where? … Oh my GOD. Why didn't you call me, Adam? Does mom know that? What about Sharon…is she alright with that?...man, I didn't know that. Can you come over? No, really, I need to talk to you about something…yeah, It's important. How about this afternoon about 2 or 3? Okay, I'll see you then.*"

Chapter 28

D exter decided to seek some professional help with sorting out the continuous series of numbers he had been seeing randomly. He wanted to find some relevance from someone. He didn't want to see a reader, or other questionable types. He wanted someone with formal training in theological Diaspora, or ancient writings on symbols. When Marvin overheard Dexter referencing the numbers he was seeing, and desiring to find someone to talk to concerning the same, he recommended a Psychologist he had visited in the past, while going through his last devorce. Marvin was sure she could help him at least come up with all the right questions, even if she didn't have the right answers.

So, you've been wrestling with this for how long now?" asked Dr. Richter.

"It's been crazy this past several months, that's for sure."

"And have you come to some resolve concerning these issues?"

"You mean concerning the numbers?"

"Well, yes."

"That's the reason I'm here, doctor. Do you have any experience with numbers and these types of combinations?"

"Yes, I have had some. But I am very curious about your feelings and

how are these repetitive visualizations affecting you. Why do you feel there's some relevancy to them?"

"Because I keep seeing them, doc. WHY?"

"Well, I can assure you that no one knows for sure...not even the so called Psychics."

"What's your best guess?" asked Dexter.

Dexter was in the doctors office for over 2 hours. She had cancelled the rest of her appointments for that afternoon, to spend time with him.

"I suspect you have experienced what we call...Psycological Historical Revisionism. (PHR). As you regress back into your past, you will experience some things that have previously occurred, either physically or within your mind. It works like this... Something occurred; you are aware of it; It becomes a part of you, and it recurs over and over in the present. In Religion, it is defined by some theologians as Generational blessings or curses...depending on whether they are positive or negative."

"Well, these things that have occurred in the past month or so are negative to me. So I guess these are Generational Curses."

"Lets explore this possibility further. I don't want to have to ask you about specifics that you are aware of, I just want you to talk to me about people in your past that you know something about their lifestyles, or character. Now, this will take some time, so don't expect that we will be able so complete this assessment today."

"Oh, no problem, doctor, I understand. So, where should I start?"

"How far back in your past can you go back? Like, do you know anything about your great-grandfather on either side of your family?"

"On my mothers side, I know that he was a tall heavy-set, half-French, half-Indian man who practiced some sort of rituals over people who were sick. He also was a drinker and quite a ladies man, too."

"What was his name?"

"Touque Ben, I heard my momma say."

"Tell me more about him. Was he married, where did he live, did he have any brothers or sisters, how many kids, that sort of thing."

"Well, I don't know if I'm the one to talk about him, really. My uncle would be able to tell you more, since he told me. But on my fathers side, now there's where the interesting characters come into my family. "

"What can you tell me about them?"

"Well, my uncle told me about my Great-great grandfather who was a slave owned by an officer in the Confederate Army, named Colonel Lea. His daughter became famous for marrying Sam Houston."

"Great...go on!"

"Well, this character had several boys by different slave women who were forced by the master to have sex with him. Apparently, he was about 6'-2" tall and light-brown skinned, and made some good-looking, strong babies . The way I understand it, one of those boys named Jack, was sold to a man by the name of Mason Stoneman, who treated his slaves with a degree of cruelty. Most of his slaves were under fed and over worked, six days a week. Well, what happened was, this Jack (Stoneman) became a run-a-way on many occasions, and wound up stealing chickens; watermelons; or whatever he could get hold of to survive. He was always tracked down and captured, then returned to the Stoneman plantation. He was beaten by the overseers and forced to work extra hard and longer than the ones who didn't run-a-way. Now, evidently, Jack grew up looking like his father, and became the same kind of a breeder that was forced on his father, even though he never had a face-to-face relationship with his father."

For two hours, Dexter recounted all that he knew about his past generations, as told to him mainly by his uncle. His intellect assured him that there would be a positive, understandable outcome, but he was not certain how they would get there. For now, he would let things flow and answer all the doctors' questions.

By the time Dexter returned home from his doctors' appointment, Norma was standing at the side door leading to the house from the garage. She could hardly wait for Dexter to come in and tell her all about the visit to the doctor. But, Dexter was not ready to recount all that he had discussed. Instead, he was willing to give her a broad outline of their visit, favoring to save the details for another time.

"Hey baby!"

"Hi honey, you hungry?"

"I could use a fresh cooked meal if you know where I can get one."

"Oh, I know exactly where you can get one, and it isn't here! We've got leftovers."

"You know honey, that will be alright. Even your leftovers taste like fresh cooked."

"You only say that because it's true! How did things go at the doctors' office?"

"They went fine but very intense. Honey, if you don't mind, can we talk about this tomorrow? I kind of have a headache right now. I don't mean that kind of headache...I mean my head is so full of stuff, I'm still processing all of it. I think I need to get beck down south to see if I can get more info on my past generations."

"You go into all that today, in two hours? I thought you were trying to get help in figuring out those numbers."

Yes, yes honey, I did. I mean I started the process, but there apparently is much more to all this than I, or any of us can imagine. In other words, it must be necessary to understand the past, to have an understanding of the present. She's taking me back to my great-great grandfather's time on my father's side. I was able to recount some things I had totally forgotten about."

While Norma prepared dinner for Dexter, he continued to talk about his past as he did with the doctor. He outlined the historical information until he came to the actions of Jack Stoneman. He paused...then said to his wife...

"Honey, do you remember when we were in New Iberia with Uncle Landry, and he talked about his Fathers brothers?"

"Yes, and other relatives of your father."

"Right. I need to know more about some of those relatives. There is something going on today that may have some connection with the past."

"Really! And what might that be?"

"That's what I need to find out."

The time is now 6:17pm and the home telephone rang. Dexter wiped his mouth and started to answer it when Norma motioned with her hand for him not to stop eating-she would answer it.

"Hello. Yes he is, but he's having dinner right now. Could you call back in about thirty minutes? Who shall I say called? ... Mr. Marvin, I will tell him."

"No, wait honey...let me talk to Marvin. Marvin, Marvin, how are you? No, no it's alright. I'm finished. What's been happening with my brother's situation? Have you found anything else? ...Sure I can. Of course I will. Sure...I can...I will...what time? ...I'll be there. Thanks Marvin, I appreciate your work."

Chapter 29

Marvin was sitting at a table outside of Starbucks, sipping on a large coffee when Dexter drove into the driveway. Dexter parked and walked over to him. Marvin stood and offered to buy Dexter a cup. Dexter agreed and went inside to order. They exchanged small talk until the order was ready. They returned to another table outside towards the end of the property for privacy.

"Okay Marvin, what you got for me?"

"What you want to know?"

"Everything!"

"You can't afford everything!"

"You are right about that! I guess what I want to know is anything you might know about the business my brother has and what was going on out behind his office. Why are there law enforcement officers all over the hospital where he lies in a comma? Just tell me why all this suspense and secrecy."

"Listen Mr. Simon, you've got a huge situation here with your brother- even your family. I probably shouldn't be telling you all this but you seem like a guy who is trying to do the right thing."

"I truly am."

"You should be prepared to hear some things you will not believe about *what's been going on in your family-especially with your brother and even your dad and other relatives."*

"What are you telling me Marvin? What in God's name could all this be? We are not a bad Mafia-type family going around shooting people and beating up people, right? Right?"

"Well, I'll let you be the judge of that."

"Come on, Marvin! I might have been away for some time, but I know better than that. Now, you gotta be specific for me. Go on…I can take it."

"Right now, the FBI has a 200 page file on your brothers; your father; uncles and even your mother."

"WHAT? …MY MOTHER? YOU HAVE GOT TO BE JOKING WITH ME, MARVIN! THERE IS NO WAY! AND MY BROTHERS; MY FAMILY TOO?"

"You forget Mr. Simon, this is MY business. I do not speculate about such important matters."

"Well, in what way are you saying any of my family is involved with any kind of crime, that includes my mother?"

"I didn't say your mother was involved in crime. I said that the FBI has a file on her as well as your brothers; your father and his father- even your uncles."

"How do you know this? What proof do you have that this is the case?"

"I have sources in all of law enforcement. I did not see the file itself, but I trust my sources."

"If my grandfather has been dead for over 40 years, are you saying they-whoever they are-were investigating him before he passed away-way back then?"

"If you knew who your grandfather was, you would understand why."

"Okay Marvin, what in God's name is that supposed to mean, huh?"

"Listen, All I can tell you now is that your brother might want to stay in a comma for a while. He's been deep into contraband, transporting between

the south and mid-west. He's been pretty smart about it too. He is rather low key and not flashy about his life-style, you follow me?"

"What exactly is he involved in Marvin? Just, just..."

""I told you in the beginning you can't handle everything right now-especially when it comes to the rest of your family."

"Oh my God! My God this is crazy! I can't believe any of this...I just can't believe it!.. And my MOTHER? What about her? What has she done to have the FBI keeping tabs on her?"

"Your mother has been an enabler, Mr. Simon. She has known for years about your brother; her husband; your uncles and the rest. She holds some deep secrets about what was going on out there off highway 35, and she knows all about the trafficking of contraband by Brian."

"What about my brother Adam? Has he been involved as well?"

"I think you must understand that everyone wanted to turn their backs on what they knew was going on. He certainly benefitted financially from some of the profits Brian has made over the years. He no saint in all this either."

"Well, if all this is true, why hasn't anyone been arrested—or charged?"

"Mr. Simon, take a deep breath. I gave you some info that could shut down all my sources. I'm giving you this info because I like you and want to help you. There is just so much I can share right now, but I guess you can see why there is such interest in your brother at the hospital."

"But he's in a comma. What do they want from him now?"

"They want to protect him!"

"From who?"

"Other people who know his game, and know that he knows theirs. They don't want him to come out of that comma and start ratting on them."

"Oh my God!"

"Well, tell me about the business he had. What was going on out there that caused such a great explosion? What was his business model? How did he make his money?"

"The business your brother is involved in is a family business, Mr. Simon! Do you understand?"

"No, I don't."

"I involves more than your brother, and it has been going on or some time now. In fact, it involves a number of funeral homes; junk yards; drugs and more. Now, don't ask me any ore questions about this because those who know about this in sitting on it until they complete the investigations."

"But you say..."

"I have said more than I should. Everything's about to come to a head when the investigation is complete. Let me say-and I've got to go-what they found out there will make some people question what happened to their buried loved-ones, who are no longer in their graves. And...how your brother was involved in their disappearance."

"You mean grave robbers?"

"You will be shocked at the news."

"Lord Jesus, help us!"

"The best thing you can do (right now) is keep out of the line of fire-so to speak-while the FED's do their jobs. There is nothing you can do at this point and time, except what? ..."

"Oh I know how to pray Marvin. And you can bet I'll be praying like I never have before."

Chapter 30

Dexter wanted to cry out loud to God but he felt he shouldn't. He wanted to try to see Brian at the hospital, but felt he couldn't. He wanted to go to his mothers' house to confront her about what he just found out but felt it unwise. His mind had him visioning in circles like a roller coaster. What should he do? What could he do with the revelations he had? Should he trust everything he heard from Marvin? Perhaps, he thought, he should discuss this with his pastor. No, he knew the family. He finally decided to make a call to someone who was not as close to the situation he was involved with, and someone who could be purely objective with any advice he gave. He pulled out his phone and called.

"Hello…may I speak to Mr. Pierce? …Yes, Dexter Simon from Shreveport… certainly I can wait, …thank you."

"Hello this is Chase!"

"Hello Mr. Pierce, this is Dexter from…"

"Oh yes, Dexter I remember…how are you? How's your brother doing?"

"We're fine, I mean I'm fine… my brothers hanging in there too. Listen, I won't take up your time, but I wondered if I can come down for an office visit to talk to you about some things?"

"Yes of course. Let me ask my secretary what my schedule looks like. When did you want to come in?"

"As soon as possible, really. I must start back to work soon and I'd like to come in before I get bogged down in all my paperwork that's piling up."

"Let's see here... I'm available on...well, I would say Saturday morning but I think I'll be fishing if the weather holds up, so..."

"Oh man, fishing? You mean on a boat-the kind that goes out into the gulf?"

"I have that kind, but I'll be doing some fresh water fishing this time. Like I say, if the weather holds up."

"Let me ask you, if you don't mind... I would love to go fishing. I've never been since I was a kid. Is it possible I can come down and go fishing with you? I mean we can discuss what I want to talk to you about while we are fishing. Is that possible?"

"Well, I don't mix business and pleasure, Dexter. I don't mind if you want to go fishing with me, but I gotta warn you...no business. Or, you can come in the first of the week in the afternoon and we can..."

"No, I rather come Saturday and fish, really. Is that alright with you? I hate to impose myself on you. Are you sure it's alright?"

"Hey, be at my office by 7am with plenty of warm clothes and you'd better pack a lunch. Don't worry about the drinks; I'll have plenty of beer."

"Well thanks, but I don't drink. I'll bring some bottled water. What about a pole and some bait, should I..."

"Nope, that's it. You remember how to get here, right?"

"I do."

"I'll see you then!"

Chapter 31

Allison Tate arrived at the office about 20 minutes later than she normally did because she had to detour around some downed telephone poles along the surface street she usually travelled. As she entered unto her office, Marvin slivered his way between several desks to talk to her before she could settle in to start working. Allison was a bit reserved as she just didn't want to hear any more bad news about Brian, which Marvin may have uncovered.

For his part, Marvin felt he was doing Allison a favor by trying to shield her from this 'schemer' and 'con-man', who was going down as soon as he was able to recover from his wounds and coma. No time was really right (in Marvin's eyes) to bring her the newest info he had uncovered, so she rushed right into her office space. She hung up her coat and sat down.

"Allison, how was your weekend?"

"My weekend was fine Marvin, just fine. Now what do you want on this Monday morning, when my nerves are fragile, and my feet are hurting cause my shoes are too tight?"

"I'm sorry about that Allison, but if you don't want to hear what I have to say, it's all right with me…I'll just go back to my office and leave you alone!"

"Okay, okay…what you got?"

"You want some coffee?"

"Yeh, that's fine!"

"Come on, I'll pour you a cup."

They both walked over to the break area where the coffee and other vending machines were housed. Marvin was silent as he retrieved a cup and poured Allison's half full.

"Here... Listen... I met with your Brother-in-law yesterday!"

"Who?"

"I mean Brian's brother, Dexter."

"Okay, let's keep this crap straight. I have no brother-in-law, okay?"

"Okay, okay. You know who I'm talking about. Anyway, I met with him and gave him some info that's going to hit the fan with everybody who has anything to do with Brian...I mean everybody, Allison!"

"Why are you looking at me like that? I already told you that I've had nothing to do with Brian for years."

"Are you sure? Did he ever give you any large sums of money; buy you expensive clothes or purses; take you on expensive trips or anything like that?"

"No!

"Are you sure?"

"Yes I'm sure, and keep your voice down... Listen, I have had NO relationship with Brian for over 10 years! What's going on Marvin? What kind of crap is he into now?"

"I really can't tell you, babe!"

"Like hell you can't! *I want to know since you keep bringing this mess up to me. You can't just leave me hanging like this! What has he done, Marvin?"*

Allison's supervisor passed by the break room... then backed up. She spoke:

"Aha...there you are, Allison-Good morning! Hi Marvin. When you finish your chat Allison, Mr. St. John wants to see you in his office."

"St John? What about?"

"Don't know! As soon as you can, okay? Thanks!"

"Marvin, what is going on here? What does the big boss want with me? Is it about this mess about Brian? …Damn you Marvin! …What have you got me into?"

"I swear to God, Allison…I have not spoken to anyone about this at this office-no one, you hear me! Maybe it's something else, or maybe he wants to promote you… Like I said-I don't know!"

Allison poured the rest of the coffee into the sink and returned to her desk. She surveyed the area to be sure there would be no criticism of her work station. She walked to another wing of the law office to Mr. St. John's office. She greeted his secretary:

"Hi Ms. Fisher. Mr. St. John wanted to see me?"

"Oh yes. I will let him know you're here."

"Pardon me sir-Allison Tate is here to see you. Thank you, I will."

"Have a seat Allison. He'll be right with you."

"Thanks."

Allison's heart was racing a mile a minute. Her mind turned over many scenarios as to what this was all about. It must have something to do with Brian's situation. But what does that have to do with her, she wondered. She wondered if Marvin, their chief investigator was truthful with her about keeping his information quiet to the powers that be. But, he works for this firm-he must tell them what's going on. He lied to me about not telling anyone. But what could it be? What could he have told them that concerns me? Oh God, please help me!" she silently prayed. The intricately carved double doors reaching to the top of the ceiling opened, as a tall thin man exited.

"You have a good day, Mr. District Attorney!"

"Thank you Ms. Fisher…the same to you."

"You may go in now, Allison."

Allison walked in silently holding her hands in front of her as she approached St Johns' desk. He was reaching for a file which was at the right side of his massive desk. It was the only file on the desk. Allison stood motionless as St John looked up at her.

"Oh hi there Allison, please have a seat."

"Thank you, sir."

"I suppose you are curious as to why I asked you to come to my office."

"Yes sir, I am."

"Please relax, you've done nothing wrong...to my knowledge anyway!"

"Oh, I didn't know... I mean I didn't know what to think, sir."

"Well, let me put your mind at ease. That was the District Attorney who just left my office. Mr. Thill has been notified that he will have a very valuable and hot case to bring to justice in the near future. He has been told that this case will make him a shoe-in should he decides to run for Mayor. Now I understand that you might have some information about some persons of interest in this case that could be very valuable to the district attorney' office. Now, I don't know exactly what it is that you have, or how you may be of assistance, but I want you to know that this is a very, very important case, and I want you, and everybody in this office to do what is necessary to facilitate this investigation. Now, I am personally going to authorize you to spend time away from this office to be available to the DA's office whenever they may need you. But more importantly, do not discuss any of this with anyone else in this office, or any other office, until this case is completely wrapped up and all parties have been properly adjudicated. That means, absolutely...NO ONE!"

Chapter 32

Allison did all she could to avoid Marvin and anyone else in her office who might have been aware that she was called into the big boss' office, or who knew anything about her relationship with Brian. For the most part, she was ineffective at work as her mind would not release her from what Mr. St John had discussed with her. All she knew was, she could not talk to anyone about this situation with Brian, and that she could talk to the DA's office. What kind of mess has she gotten herself into, she thought for the fourth time. She felt trapped in a web of mystery and suspense that even an enterprising spider couldn't get out of.

Everyone took notice of her not being engaging as she normally was, and their suspicion led them to stay away from her as well. Because of the tension thick enough to cut with a butter knife, Allison's supervisor gave her the rest of the day off.

At 3:15pm, Allison drove up to A. J. Spiller High School where Tara was a senior. The school bell would ring in 15 minutes and Allison was there to surprise Tara. She decided to take her daughter out to dinner and unwind from the days events. The air was cool so she left her car running to keep the heater going. The campus security guard approached her car from the rear and asked:

"Can I help you?"

"Oh, I'm here to pick up my daughter."

"Well, you can't stay here ma'am. This is where the buses come in. You have to wait for her over there in the parking lot."

Allison drove to the end of the drive-way, heading for the parking lot when she noticed Tara coming from a temporary building, which was her last classroom. Tara waived when she recognized the car her mother was driving. Allison saw her and pulled over to the side of the drive, motioning for Tara to come to her.

"Hey mom, what are you doing here?"

"I got off early today, and I thought I would take you out to dinner before we go home today. How about that?"

"Great! Where we going?"

"Where do you want to go? What do you have a taste for?"

"I like some Italian food."

"Let's go. Are you finished with everything?"

"I'm done."

The drive to the restaurant took a half hour, which gave Allison a chance to have some small talk with her daughter. Allison was beginning to look at her daughter with a deeper sensitivity, based on her intuition about what the future might hold for her. Tara could sense that her mother was making small talk, but wanted to have a more serious conversation with her.

Within minutes of their arrival at the restaurant, they were seated in a booth where no one was around them. This way, Allison could open up and share her feelings with her only child.

"You seem a little up tight, momma-like you are serious about something."

"Do I?"

"Yeah, why are you so serious today? Something bugging you?"

"As a matter of fact there is, baby. It's not about you though. I don't have a problem with you-You're fine."

"What is it then?"

"Baby, you understand that there are some things that happen to us
that we have no control over, right?"

"Okay."

"Well, some things are happening, concerning your dad that seems to
be getting out of control, even as he lay unconscious in the hospital."

"Like what?"

"I really can't talk about the specific's, sweetheart, but I can say that
there are some things that will be coming out that will not look good
for him."

"Like what?"

Tara was beginning to get emotional about the conversation she
was having about her father. She hated the fact that he was not in her
life since she was a little girl, but at the same time, she was defensive
about any negative conversation anyone was having about him. Her
eyes were filling up with tears as her mother continued.

"Baby, you are the only one I can talk to about this, so please make
sure you never repeat this conversation to anyone, okay?"

"What is it, momma?"

"No, you gotta promise me first!"

"Okay, I promise."

"I been thinking about this for some time now-every since your dad was
in that accident. Even though I have had no contact with him for over ten
years, apparently, he has been involved in some things that were not lawful.
I don't have the foggiest idea what it is, but all indications are that he has
been following a pattern of wrong doing throughout the years. Now, people
don't just start doing illegal things and continue the pattern on their own.
What I think is he must have seen something in his past, that he got from
someone else, and he's been following that pattern. It's called generational
curses. Somewhere in Brian's past, he decided he was going to follow a path
that maybe his father, or grandfather had. Is this confusing to you, Tara?"

"No, I understand what you're saying mom."

"Well, I'm trying to understand what's going on as well, and I want
to be able to explain what's happening to you. Now, I think your dad will

be in a world of trouble when he gets out of the coma, and heals from his wounds. Like I say, I don't know anything for sure, but the way things look, his world will be closing in on him."

"Well, what if he doesn't wake up from the coma? What would happen then? Would he still be in trouble then? What can anyone do to him if he was dead?"

"Oh baby, I don't think like that-you shouldn't either!"

"I'm just asking mom."

"I'm sure everyone's praying that he does wake up, honey. No matter what kind of trouble he may be in, I think his family especially would like to have him alive rather than dead."

"Do you know anything about his father or grandfather? Did they do some bad things that they passed down to my dad?"

"Oh honey, I don't know...I don't know anything about his family!"

"But how could he pick up the habits of his grandfather if he never saw him or grew up with him? I understand his father died when he was young so... he couldn't have been around him very much to pick up any bad habits or, what did you call it, generational curses?"

"Its very real that that can happen. I don't know if he knew about any of that, but the Bible talks about that. Something about the **"Sins of the Fathers"** can be passed down three generations. Some people can follow a pattern of crime, or activities that they never knew how they got started. Some families have a whole generation who seem to have what they call 'bad luck'. They seem to repeat the same patterns from father-to son-to grandson. But, the good thing is...those curses can be broken. Somebody has to break the curse. Somebody in that generation has to refuse to accept the 'demands' of the curse. Somebody who will flip that curse and go another way. That would be the way of the 'Cross' that Jesus bore."

"This all sound 'spooky' and ghostly to me!"

"It is spiritual, honey. This is not flesh and blood that you can openly see. But, make no mistake about it...it is Very Real! And, the thing most people don't realize, it affects 3 generations."

"If that's what's happening to my dad, do you know what generation he is in?

"I can't be the one to determine that, sweetheart…somebody else has to study their family history to find that out. But one thing is for sure, you can tell by studying the scriptures. I believe it's in the book of Exodus where it talks about 'The sins of the fathers will be visited upon the children, and upon the children's children, unto the third and forth generations.' It's all in the scriptures, and the curses are passed down through the ones who carry the seeds."

"The ones who carry the seeds?" Asked Tara.

"The ones who carry the seeds!"

Chapter 33

Chase Pierce took his fishing very serious. Fishing was in his blood as it was for the past three generations. Inland fishing was on the agenda this time, as his wife preferred the sweet taste of the Official State Fresh Water Fish-White Perch. The weather would be perfect to relax and let those crafty animals fill his large cooler. Dexter arrived at 6:45am at Chase' office. They wasted no time in transferring the rest of the supplies into Chase' SUV.

"So, it's just the two of us today?" asked Dexter.

"Yes-just the two of us. My nephew was going to go with us, but he was out late with his high school buddies last night, after the big game."

"Who won?"

"We did-28 to 10... Are you ready?"

"I'm ready. Where are we headed?"

"I have a great little fishing spot on the other side of Broussard. It'll take about an hour for us to get there. It's almost to New Iberia."

"Oh, I'm sure Norma and I passed by there when we came to see you. By the way, is this the road where that graveyard was you sent us to?"

"Yes, it's up here about three or four miles. Did you find your grandfather's grave in there?"

"We found the gravesite, but it was empty."

"What?"

"It had no body in the it. There was an old man there who was trimming the grass in the graveyard who ran away when we tried to ask him some questions about the empty site. In fact, we saw several other sites that were also empty."

"Waaiitt a minute! Wait a minute, Dexter. Are you telling me your grandfathers grave was empty-like no casket in it-like an empty hole?"

"That's what I'm saying. We couldn't believe what we were seeing. Apparently, somebody dug it up and made it vanish. I can't believe he just 'rose from the dead."

"I am aware of thefts of Urns that have brass on them. In fact, over in Florida, I read about the Police in St. Lucie County investigated the theft of about 15 or 20 bronze vases and placards. The cost on those items was about $300 apiece. But if they sold them for scrap, they could only get about a dollar a pound."

"But in this case, the whole casket or whatever they put them in when everybody leaves the site was missing."

"Wow...that's unbelievable. And you say there was somebody working there who didn't want to talk to you?"

"Right...at first he was friendly enough, but when my wife and I questioned him on where my granddad was buried, he went silent on us and took off. We searched around the rest of the graveyard and that's when we saw the marker but missing body."

"Now that beats all, Dexter. That is a serious matter, man! That's something I need to bring to the attention of our Sheriff and our Police Juror. Empty graves are out of the norm, and we need to be sure the Preservation Society is not involved before we start rattling somebody's cage. You follow me?"

"I do. I appreciate that. God knows I don't need another issue to deal with at this time."

"I know what you mean. Now, I said I was not going to deal with business but, tell me about your brother's situation. Did you find out if he had insurance?"

"Yes, he does."

"Has his wife hired anyone to represent him?"

"I don't think so, not yet."

"Oh you have not spoken with her as yet, you mean."

"I don't know where she is…I don't know where my brother is either."

Chase eased off the gas pedal and looked at Dexter out of the corner of his right eye. He tried to connect one and one to get two, but the numbers were not adding up. He inquired:

"Your brother was in the hospital in a coma, and now you have no idea where he or his wife is right now?"

"Right!"

"Is he still alive?"

"I don't know that either."

"Okay, what do you know?"

"Okay, my wife and I went to visit with my brother and his family and the Law Enforcement personnel had locked down the entire hospital. They were not allowing anyone in. If you were not a patient, everyone had to leave. We asked a police officer what was happening and he flagged us on-told us we had to leave. We found out that Homeland Security had taken over the hospital because they had exceeded the maximum by 30%."

"Homeland Security? What was that all about?"

"We were told by a guy that I hired to do some investigative work for me, that they were protecting my brother from some persons who might wish him never to come out of the coma."

"Do you know what you are telling me, Dexter? Do you know how serious all this is when you get these people (HLS) involved in your business?

"Well…"

"This is serious business my friend…I don't get much more serious than that. But why would they get involved in a routine accident case?"

"That's why I want to hire a good lawyer to take this case on. That's why I want to hire you, if your fees are affordable. This is much more than I can handle myself. And I've got to go back to work on Monday. Even so, this is way above my pay grade."

"*Above your pay grade, huh? This would be above anybody's pay grade except the insurance company's. If he has anybody except some discount pay-by-the-month for coverage insurance company, we can work with him. Do you know who the company is?*"

"*I don't, but I can find out. I'll give my brother Adam a call when I get back.*"

"*Listen Dexter, I will be willing to take on your brothers case as long as we're talking about representing him on his personal injury case. And...if he has a good Insurance Company. Now, if this case swells into something else...something involving a criminal case, we would have to take another look at that. In any event, we can get the ball rolling on what came first-the accident. Then we would need to find him and his wife to get her to sign the representation agreement. How long has it been since the accident, two weeks?*"

"*Yes, it's been about that time.*"

"*We need to get this started right away. I like to have my clients on board the following day after any accident, if not the same day. Now I don't want to waste my time on this so...do you think you can find your sister-in-law and get her to sign some papers as soon as you get back? I can get everything filled out and all she has to do is sign where I flag the pages. Can you do that?*"

"*Sure, If I 'legally' can do it.*"

"*Look, I know you don't want me to drive all the way to Shreveport and have to charge you for my time for a day. We can make this work for all of us. Don't worry about the legality of this...that's my job. All you do is deliver the papers and if she has any questions, you can call me. I can answer any questions she may have.*"

"*Okay. Okay!*"

Within an hour, Chase and Dexter had arrived at Chase' favorite fishing spot. They unhooked the boat and eased it into the water. The water was still and the sun glistened across the waters, causing them both to put on their shades.

"*You're sure there is fish in here,*" asked Dexter.

"Most of them were stocked by God himself."

"Well, I know what that means. I would be satisfied if I can at least catch one."

"I can almost guarantee that."

By 1pm, they had stashed 26 White Perch into their coolers. Dexter caught his share and was very satisfied with the results. Wrapping things up took much less time than it did when they started. Chase offered to process Dexter's catch, along with his, but Dexter wanted to take his home to show his wife. Back in Lafayette by 3pm, Chase invited Dexter into his office for a few minutes while he downloaded and printed the papers he needed signed as they had discussed. Dexter felt relieved that this situation was finally going to be placed in the hands of an expert, and he would not have to shoulder the burden as he has been.

"Okay, I will do what I can, Chase. I should get these to her by Monday evening and I will call you as soon as I do. I really appreciate you allowing me to go fishing with you. That was really a lot of fun catching all those fish. I really appreciate everything."

"You're welcome. You be careful on those slippery roads up north. I'll talk to you Monday."

Chapter 34

Dexter arrived home late, and Norma had already prepared for bed. She knew Dexter had been up since very early that morning and would need a good relaxing bath when he arrived. She had already learned that he had a successful fishing trip and was anxious to see them. Although they had not been cleaned, he simply bagged them and placed them in the meat-keeper portion of their refrigerator.

"Well, what do you think, babe?"

"*They are huge! You did good honey. I'm very proud of you. Now come on…I got your bath water ready. Take off those smelly clothes and put them in the wash room. You want to eat?*"

"*Naw…I'll just have some fruit and some hot tea. Do you have some of that Arizona Tea?*"

"*I do. You take your bath and I'll get everything ready for you.*" By the *way, when you get done, I want to share some good news with you. In fact, I want to share some great news with you.*"

"*I'll take the great news now! What is it?*"

"*Are you sure?*"

"*Yes, yes, I'm sure…what is it honey, come on!*"

"*We… are……*"

"*Ah baby, come on, what is it? We are what?*"

"P...r...e...g...n..."

"Pregnant? We are pregnant?" Yes...Yes...Yes! Thank you Jesus! Thank you Lord. We're gonna' have a baby!!! A Baby? I'm soooo happy!

"But wait...wait. we're gonna have **three** babies! Not **one**, but **three!**"

"**Oh my God...triplets? We're having triplets? Oh...my...God- triplets!**"

"Thank God the treatments worked! The fertility treatments worked on the 3rd try. Oh...my...God. **Bless the Lord! ...Thank you Lord.** ... Honey, let's pray and give thanks."

Chapter 35

L ife had been very hectic for the past couple of weeks for the Simon family. Tragic incidents were the highlights of all their lives, showing no sign of letting up. With the great news announced by Norma last night, they both decided to go to church to praise God-in his house of worship- for the blessings of new life he gave them. He wanted to go to the Alter, at the appropriate time, to offer their thanks. During the services, both Norma and Dexter caught each other wiping away tears from their eyes, having been overcome with emotions of gratitude.

The church was filled to capacity, as the pastor had announced last week that he was going to preach on the effects of 'the sins of our fathers', at the 8am service. They had not attended last weeks service, and had no idea that that was the title of the sermon for this week. Sitting together, with Dexter's arm wrapped around Norma's shoulder, they listened closely as the pastor began his sermon.

"*I want to invite you to go on a journey with me through a time in ancient past, when God's chosen people was experiencing a difficult relationship with Him. He was their creator... the one who gave them life, and sustained them through difficult times in the desert; the one who made a covenant with their fathers that he would eventually take them to a place where there was milk and honey flowing through the streets. And* all he required of them was to recognize what God had done for them, and worship Him, and Him only.

They had turned their backs on God, and failed to realize that God was a jealous God, who desired and required that his children obey Him.

Imagine, if you have children, that you have raised and nurtured them...you made sure that they had all their needs met, and everyday, you made sure that you told them, and demonstrated to them that you loved them, and that you will always love them, and all you required was for them to 'honor' you as their parent, ...and they turned their backs on you-disregarding anything and everything you had done, and anything you have to say. **Imagine that!**... How would you feel if that happened to you? Everything they owned, everything they needed was provided to them by you...and they have 'dispelled' you... disregarding any history...the thing that connected them to you...and have now gone their own ways!

Even as I say these words, I have to tell you that chills run up and down my spine, if something like that happened to me and my wife. I would be devastated-to say the least. And yet, ...they are our children and we brought them into the world, and fed them; taught them how to walk and talk; how to eat and what to eat; and educated them; clothed them with their Air Jordan shoes, and Dooney & Bourke purses, and yet...they have forgotten all that, and turned their backs on you. **How would you feel?**

Dexter listened intently to every word coming from the pastor's mouth. He was addressing exactly what Dexter was searching answers for, with the family drama he and Norma were going through. What more could he explain that could bring clarity to the complicated issues they were experiencing.

"So, what should be done about this state of rebellion? What would you as a parent do, about the continued disobedience from your children? Would you give them warnings of future consequences, or demand that they stop the disobedience or be grounded for a week? ...**What would you do?**

Warnings about the consequences came for many years to the chosen ones until finally, God decided to attach a lasting penalty to their wrongdoings. Look at the blessing God attached to the ones who loved him *and kept his commandments. Deu. 7:9 says: Know therefore that the Lord thy God, he is God the faithful God, which keepeth Covenant and mercy with them that love him and keep his commandments. Mercy with them that love Him …Mercy !…Mercy!*

Well now, what about those who have chosen the way of iniquity (sinful way)? What happens to those who do not keep the Lord's commandments? According to the text (Exo. 34:6), the Lord, The LORD God, is merciful and gracious, longsuffering, and abundant in goodness and truth. He gives mercy for thousands, forgiving iniquity and transgression and sin, and (v:7) 'passing' on the sins of the fathers upon the children, and upon their children's children… for how long? …Unto the third and fourth generation. So now, even though He is longsuffering and merciful; abundant in goodness and truth, He has attached a consequence to their sins… He will pass the sins (of the fathers) down into their third and fourth generations."

Dexter was receiving exactly what he was looking for in this sermon. So many of the clouded issues he was wrestling with were becoming clearer. He thought about his great-grandfathers ways, and the ways of his grandfathers-even his own father. Could it be that even he and his siblings were in the years of the fourth generation of his fathers? Perhaps much of the secrecy and wrong doing on his brothers part, as well as the unfortunate accident, adultery, and criminal activity seemed to be attached to their past (according to the sermon). Brian was always considered the one who lived on the edge of right and wrong. He (over the years) slipped back and forth into the hearts of his family and friends through his brushes with the legal system. But, he was always the one to try new adventures and always drug his younger brother into it with him. Did Brian even know the story about his great-grandfather stealing chickens and having his way with many women? Did he witness the actions of his uncles as they never seemed to hold down a steady job, but they always had money in their pockets? What about his cousin Jason Simon in New Iberia-could there be a generational curse attached to his activities? What will happen to Brian's son Greg he wondered, if Brian was part of the 'curse'? Should he expect that Greg would be part of that 'bad' seed from his dad? If so, what can be done about it? What about his own descendents-what could he do to be sure his children (yet to be born) were part of the 'blessing' instead of the curse? His mind had him asking many questions of himself, as he listened for the way out for his family. Something had to change. The only true change can only take place when one accepts the Lord Jesus Christ, who would give a new heart. He would give a new start after repentance and accepting Christ as their savior. Even though he has tried to bring that message to all he came in contact with, he knew all he could do was plant the seed, and allow God to produce the increase.

"And so my brothers and sisters, if you have been wondering why there seems to be a cycle of problems within your family or acquaintances or friends... have a look into their ancestry. Look into their genealogy to determine where the seed became corrupted. It's in the seed that generations are either blessed or cursed. Now if that seems to be what's happening in your family, I want you to come down here to the Altar for prayer. You may have been wrestling with this for some time, and you have not been able to figure it out. You may have thought the issues had to do with 'bad luck' or just being in the wrong place at the wrong time. Listen to me... this is not flesh and blood you are wrestling with. No, no! This is not of the carnal. You are in a spiritual battle, and you need to break that pattern of punishment of 'the sins of your fathers'. That can only happen when Jesus sets you free from your past. Don't let the pattern continue. Stop the pattern in your generation...whether you are the third or fourth generation...get it stopped now! Come forward and God will honor your obedience, right now. Come...Come now!"

Norma took Dexter's hand as they made their way to the Altar. Within minutes, the Altar was crowded with respondents to the pastors' call. Instinctively, they each joined hands as the pastor prayed for God's forgiveness and His mercy. He prayed that those who came forth will be forgiven for the sins of their fathers, and that they will follow the path of righteousness, for His name sake. He prayed that any future children will not be cursed, but rather be a blessing to their parents and to the Kingdom.

When the services ended, Dexter told Norma how blessed they both were to be in the house of the Lord to hear this very important message. He now could proceed with confidence that he and his family were on the right track, and they resolved to stay in the path of righteousness for the rest of their days.

Chapter 36

Police Jurors and Sheriff's have always been respected and appreciated by the white citizens--and many citizens of color--in Louisiana. Those not earning the respect in and around Lafayette, New Iberia and Abbeville, most often found themselves on the opposite end of the courtroom table, being sued by Chase Abbott Pierce. Chase found his counseling nitch with the oppressed and downtrodden people of the state. Perhaps influenced by misapplication of the law from what he observed from his father, (et al) he was particularly energized when he saw an opportunity to right a wrong against persons of color.

This was not the case with his father, who enjoyed a position of high authority with the powers that be. Old man Pierce was a close relative of the founder of the Simon School of Business, in upstate New York. Another Pierce relative ran a branch of the prestigious graduate school in Louisiana.

After Dexter left to return home, Chase mulled over the prospects of getting into a case with Brian, which could lead into exciting experiences, leading to some great outcomes. With his history of attending college with blacks, and joining one of their coveted fraternities (Alpha Kappa Psi), he knew if there was a case at all, it would lead him to a higher (National) level. If things develop as they could potentially, He could become a sought after attorney for the NAACP or the Urban League. He could even envision himself representing the NBA players Union or the NFL.

As he sat in his SUV outside his office, he thought about Dexter's Cousin Jason, who was taken to a hospital in Lafayette. He made a couple of calls to find out which facility he was in. Chase decided to drive to the Community Hospital to hear from Jason first hand, what happened to him.

Outside of Jason's room sat a uniformed policeman. When he saw Chase walking towards him, and gazing at each room while passing by them, he stood.

"Which room are you looking for sir?"

"Ah, there it is. This is the room right here."

"Wait...you can't go in there. This boy is in police custody."

"Like hell, I can't. That's my client in there and I'm here to consult with him. Now officer, if you don't mind ...My name is Attorney Chase Pierce."

"Hold on! I need to speak with the Sergeant first."

"You go right ahead."

"Nell, limme' talk to Sergeant Ledoux, please. ...How long? Okay, I'll wait... Just tell 'em there's a lawyer here to see the prisoner... Ask him what he want me to do. I'll wait!" ...Okay? ... Okay, I'll tell 'em. Okay, you can go in for a half hour... I'll be right outside here... You can leave the door open."

*"No, I will **not** leave the door open. Do you understand that I am an officer of the court, and I have Attorney Client privileges?"*

"What's that?"

"Never mind, ask your boss... I'm going in."

Chase moved quietly into the private room where Jason was asleep. Chase moved next to Jason's bed and sat down in a chair backed up against the window. The overhead light was off, but the window blinds were slightly open allowing daylight into the room. Chase surveyed

Jason's body with bandages wrapped around his body and head. Jason's eyes opened slowly. He spoke.

"Who are you, another doctor?"

"No Jason. My name is Chase Pierce."

"Well, who is Chase Pierce? What you doin here?"

"I am an attorney, Jason. Your cousin Dexter asked me to represent you."

"Represent me for what? …**Ouch!**"

"Be careful there. Do you need me to help you? You want to sit up?"

"Thanks. What cousin are you talkin 'bout?"

"He lives in Shreveport, and he came down to New Iberia last week to visit with your family—I believe your uncle."

"Oh yeah, I heard of him. I never met him though."

"Anyway Jason, he told me what he saw happen to you at the police station."

"He did? He saw those police beat me. Hell, there was a bunch of 'em. I couldn't fight 'em all. Too many!"

"Jason, I represent people who are mistreated by the police. What I need to find out is why the police did this to you. What caused them to do this?"

"You wouldn't understand…white folk never understand when their own kind beats a black man. They always think we musta' been doin something wrong. It's always our fault, 'cause the police say so."

"Jason, I don't know what all you heard before, but I am not one of those people who think like that."

"Oh no? Why not? …You are one of them …All you white folk stick together."

"Jason…"

"Go on, leave me alone…besides, my family don't have money to pay for no lawyer, anyway …**Ouch!**"

"What did they say were your injuries? What did they find?"

"My ribs; my head; my shoulder and my left wrist."

"I'll tell you what, Jason. I will let you get some rest and get better. I will come back to see you in a couple of days, after I visit with your parents. What's your dad name?"

"He's dead, you don't need to know his name."

"I'm sorry about that. How about your mother...what's her name? They live in New Iberia, right?"

"Yeah. Her name is Teeta Fontenot."

"We'll work this out Jason, but you gotta be honest with me and tell me the truth about what happened, okay? Not now, but when I come back in a couple of days, okay."

"Fine... cough, cough!"

Chase walked out after spending twenty minutes with Jason. The officer stationed outside of his room spoke.

"You done? You had ten more minutes, Mr. Attorney."

"Thanks, officer ... Looks like you wasted some pizza on you shirt there."

Chapter 37

Chase Pierce had been told he was a 'Type A Personality'. Among other things, he was a bit hyper, and was obsessive about understanding and seeing the full picture of everything. As he left the hospital from visiting with Jason Fontenot, he felt he needed to go to Jason's mother, to secure her permission to represent him, should he decide to file suit against the New Iberia Police. He needed more information about Jason's past however, and felt that Jason's mother was the best one to provide it.

In the meantime, he had some questions he wanted to ask of the local Police, concerning their side of the story with the Jason's injuries. He also wanted to talk to the local Sheriff about the empty graves as reported to him by Dexter.

He called his wife to report that he had finished with his fishing trip, but was headed to New Iberia to investigate some leads he had for a possible client. When he arrived at the home of Teeta Fontenot, he knocked on the front door.

"Mrs Fontenot—Chase Pierce, Attorney…May I come in?"

"Ooohh, you're that Attorney from Lafayette, right?"

"Yes ma'am, I am."

"Sure, come on in… Calvin, come in here—that attorney is here from Lafayette."

"*Thank you Mrs Fontenot...let me ask you this...do ya'll like white perch?*"

"*You know we do—yes sir.*"

"*Well, let me give you these fish I just caught this morning. I think I got about a dozen or so in my truck. You can have them all.*"

"*Oh my goodness. Thank you sir, I sure appreciate that. You came all the way over here to give us some white perch fish?*"

"*Oh, no ma'am. I wanted to talk to you about your son, Jason. I saw him at the hospital a little while ago. Now Jason's under age, so I needed to talk to you-his parent.*"

"*You think he need a lawyer? I mean, I don't have money to pay for a lawyer.*"

"*Well, there's no doubt he needs a lawyer...but let me get some more information about what happened to him, then we can talk about the cost. Actually, I was asked by your cousin, Dexter if I would represent your son. We may be able to work something out, so that you personally don't have to pay anything out of pocket. We'll let you know when we are able to work out the details. Now give me some of Jason's history, and I'll need you to sign some papers to get things started?*"

For the next forty-five minutes, Teeta relayed Jason's storied past to Chase. She was not proud of her son's history since his father passed. It seemed that he was rebelling against society, because his best friend was gone. Her major concerns centered on Jason's involvement with his buddy from high school, Bailey Toussaint and hanging around his father's ice house. Everybody knew there were drugs being sold and consumed there, and Jason would be tempted to get involved with the rest of them, she thought.

When Chase finished with his conversation with Teeta for now, he inquired as to the location of the local police station. Chase left after Calvin, Teeta's brother, thanked him again for the gift of the fish.

Chase arrived at the police station just as two civilian employees were leaving.

"*Pardon me ladies, can you tell me who is in charge here.*"

"*Sergeant Ledoux.*"

"*Thank you ladies-have a good evening.*"

"*You too.*"

Chase walked into the old building housing the police department, which was next to the city hall building. Some construction was going on outside and the station was a bit untidy inside.

"*May I speak with Sergeant Ledoux, please?*"

From the side office, Chase could see a uniformed officer look up from behind his desk. The booking officer did not speak but looked and pointed to his right, then looked back down to continue processing his reports. Chase walked to the side office door and asked:

"*Sergeant Ledoux?*"

"*What can I do for you, come on in.*"

"*Sergeant, my name is Chase Pierce, an attorney from Lafayette. I'm here representing Jason Fontenot.*"

"*Oh, wait…wait right there, Mr. Pierce. You don't want to talk to me…I believe you want to talk to the District Attorney.*"

"*No sir…I want to talk to you at this point. I just want to ask you a couple of questions about the incident that was witnessed outside of your jail.*"

"*Like I said…you don't want to talk to me. If you got a witness, there's where you need to get your information. Besides, that boy attacked my officer. I think he got what he deserved.*"

"*Really? You mean he should have gotten arrested, tried and sentenced right there on the spot by the arresting officers? Are you sure it's supposed to work that way Sergeant?*"

"*Like I said, you need to take this up with the DA.*"

"*Okay Sergeant, let me ask you this…do you know anything about the old cemetery called Lafayette Memorial Park where some of the old founding fathers and their families were buried?*"

"*I know about it-why do you ask?*"

"*This might be a strange question…but, are you aware that some of the caskets are missing from some of the graves?*"

"That doesn't surprise me... that might be the case in others as well."

"Why? Why would there be missing bodies?

"Who are you talking about? What bodies are missing?"

"I know of one named Panky Simon."

"Panky Simon, from New Iberia? His body is missing, too?"

"Have you known about others, sergeant?"

"Well, there has been a couple missing over in Abbeville, at St Paul Cemetery. I heard last year there was a missing body in Beau Pre, near Jeanerette."

"Anybody investigate these missing bodies? What's going on here?"

"All I know is, these are very old graves. I mean the people been dead a long time. We don't have a problem if they are running out of room and need the space-that's not who we protect and serve, you know what I mean? You need to go talk to the Funeral home people to find that out. We don't get into any of that. As far as I know...there is no crime."

Chase was making good progress in acquiring information on a variety of concerns he had. The funeral homes in the area would be on his list to investigate their policies relating to removal of bodies, due to lack of space. He had no idea how relevant any of this was, but there were open questions slotted into his brain—and they needed answers. He would then check that information against what the state's policies were.

For now, it was time to head home and get some rest. This indeed had been a very long day. By Monday, he would have a new list of things to get done. Not the least of which, was securing Sharon's signature, in order to start working on her husbands case. He reasoned that this case could become a landmark, in that a personal injury case could lead him into the halls of great intrigue and influences with other organizations. All he had to do was secure the necessary signatures, and get his investigations started. Although he did not attend his uncles' prestigious business school. He would make his mark on achievement within the family, by winning a highly visible case in another city, which held some great promises.

Chapter 38

Global warming was the blame for unusual weather throughout the entire country. There was no difference in climatic conditions around Shreveport during the late winter this year. People are less friendly when the weather is bad. They become selfish and self-centered. After suffering through bad weather for the past several weeks, Dexter was finally headed back to work. Few co-workers greeted him with open arms. Instead, most of the company's employees were attending a meeting in the large conference room located in the basement floor of the building. His supervisor waived at him, as he entered his office area, and motioned for him to come into his office. He was briefed on some new information about a new government contract when Dexter's cell phone rang. He looked at the number and asked his supervisor if he could be excused for a minute. He spoke.

"Hello, this is Dexter... Oh hello Chase, what's up?...This evening?... sure, sure, I can....you call me and I will give you the address. Okay... okay...I will. Goodbye!"

Dexter wanted to try to get to the bottom of all the problems, and all the confusion and suspicion over the past few weeks. With Chase coming to Shreveport to handle the business he asked Dexter to handle, was a good thing. But Dexter had to find out the latest on where his brother and sister-in-law were. He felt it to be unfair to try to accomplish all this while on the job. He owed it to the company to give them a full day's work. He would wait for his lunch break to make some calls to the hospital. In the meantime, he would let his supervisor know that he had some personal problems he would be wrestling with. Luckily, his supervisor understood and 'cut him some slack', concerning his first day back.

Three other calls needed to be made before the end of the day—one to Klein Investigative Services, one to Adam and one to his wife.

"Adam, have you heard from the hospital?...what did they say?...well, ***that*** *is good news. Will they let us visit him there? Is Sharon there too? ... How is he doing, Adam?...still, huh? Okay...is mom doing okay?...Okay. I've got a lawyer coming tonight to represent Brian. He's... No, he does need a lawyer...Yes he does, and so I have already talked with a lawyer from Lafayette...Yes, he'll be here tonight to get Sharon's signature...I think you should be there too...of course...good, I'll let you know when...I'll call you later...are you gonna be okay?...are you sure?...okay brother...I want to be sure you're not going to need a lawyer, too."*

Five o'clock came quickly. It was the end of the work day for Dexter. He hurried to his car parked in the garage. He called the number in his caller ID to give Chase a meeting location at the hospital where Brian was moved. He was still in a coma, but according to Adam, Sharon was with him and doing okay. He gave Chase the name of the hospital where they should meet. He then called Marvin Klein and spoke briefly concerning the meeting at the hospital. Marvin needed to attend this meeting, Dexter thought, in order for Chase to hear the latest from the expert investigator. Perhaps they could work together if Sharon agrees to give Chase the okay to represent Brian. Dexter called Norma's cell to tell her he would be home later than usual, because of the meeting he had scheduled. He drove directly to the hospital, using the directions he was given by his GPS. Upon arrival, he observed a black SUV circling the parking lot, which looked like Chase's vehicle. Dexter parked and waited at the entrance for Chase to catch up with him. They greeted each other by shaking hands as they walked inside. There, waiting at the information desk, was Marvin. After brief introductions, Dexter asked the receptionist if they had a conference room that was not being used. She directed them to a small office down the hall about 20 yards from the front. Dexter asked the receptionist if she would direct his brother to their meeting when he arrived.

"So, how long have you been practicing law, counselor?" asked Marvin.

"It's been 10 years next month, Marvin. …How about you …in your business?"

"Over 20, last year."

"Wow, that's some time. Do you have a card?...thanks."

"Are you affiliated with any specific law firm, or are you independent?" asked Dexter.

"I work for anyone who pays a check …Anybody who needs information …that's my boss."

"I know where you're coming from." said Chase. "Being a one man firm myself, I done my own investigations, so far."

"Don't worry, if you are in the business long enough, you'll need some outside help." admonished Marvin.

"Well gentlemen, the reason why we are here is because of my brother's unfortunate accident. Marvin, I met Mr. Pierce…"

"Please call me Chase."

"Okay, I apologize. We'll keep it on a first name basis…Oh, wait, here is my brother now… Hey Adam, I'm glad you could make it…meet Marvin Klein and Chase Pierce… Gentlemen, this is my brother, Adam."

"Nice to meet you, gentlemen. So, what you got, Dex? I'm on my way to the room to see Brian and Sharon?"

"Let me say this. I have been meeting with Marvin several times, Adam. He has information that is startling about Brian's business and…"

"What kind of information? Why has he been searching information on my brothers' business, Dex? He's laying up there in a coma, and Marvin here, has been investigating him and his business? …Come on, man!"

"Now wait a minute, Adam. Let's get to the main issue here, which is why Chase is here. Brian is going to need some legal representation for that accident. Surely, somebody is going to file a suit against him, or…or… he may need to file against the person that actually caused the accident. Now, Chase here came up from Lafayette. I met with him after he was recommended by all our cousins in New Iberia—even uncle Landry."

"Let me say this, Adam. If Brian's wife…what's her name?"

"Sharon!"

"Right …Sharon. If she would rather have someone else represent her husband after we have a talk, I will freely, go back home and she-nor anyone else-owes me anything."

"Well, I can't be a part of this. I told you to leave all this alone, Dex. What you doing is stirring things up for no reason. Brian's business is his business…you and Marvin here, need to stay out of his business, man. Just leave it alone…leave it alone. He may need somebody to sue for pain and suffering and all that…but that other stuff about investigations…man, leave all that alone… I got to go… I can't be no part of that… I'll see you later, Dex."

Dexter stood frozen as the others remained seated. Marvin knew why Adam wanted no part of 'all this', and so did Dexter. Marvin felt compelled to speak, as he wanted to expand his investigative business into Chases' territory. This was his time to show his skills as an investigator. He spoke.

"Listen, Dexter, as I told you. I let the facts drive the investigation. Now Chase, I told Dexter that his brother has been involved in some illegal doings that has caught the eyes of law enforcement all the way to the top."

"Really?" asked Chase. "How far is the top?"

"All the way …all the way!"

"What he shared with me is that there has been a business relationship between my dad, his dad, and my great-grandfather on my mothers side, as well."

"Which grandfathers are you referring to?"

"According to the files I saw, it has the names of Ben and the name of Simon." answered Marvin.

"What were the first names?"

"I was writing as fast as I could as I scanned the files. I was not supposed to see them. But, I believe the Ben sounded like it was Indian, like Tou... let me look in my file...I have it right here...Okay, yes his name was Touque Ben."

"That's the name of my great-grandfather on my mother's side."

"Now, that guy was a character. He worked for some local business owners in New Iberia who were in the alcohol business. Mr. Ben was the one who transported moonshine and other liquor throughout the Indian territories. He was part Indian and knew their ways, and spoke their language. It seemed that he brought other men in his family into the business, and they eventually broke away from the white men they were working for in New Iberia. The white businessmen didn't like that, so there were some white people who got killed. Ben and his family fled north and settled in Shreveport, and continued to traffic in any, and everything they could get their hands on, that the local law enforcement let them get away with. They knew what he was doing, but allowed them to continue as long as they were getting their cuts."

"How did the Simon's come into the picture" asked Chase.

"That Simon character was married to a woman who had the appearance of a white woman. They had a son and a daughter. He ran a funeral business and had some land where he buried folk between Lafayette and New Iberia. The woman he married was the half sister of Touque Ben. It was Ben who got Simon into using his funeral business to transport Ben's products into the southern areas of Louisiana. I mean, this guy was good."

"What was Simon's first name?" asked Chase.

"Okay...I have it right here...Panky...Panky Simon!"

"Oh my God...oh my God!" exclaimed Dexter. "Are you telling me that was the black man in the photo you had in your office with the little boy, Chase?"

"That was your grandfather in that picture, with his son."

"He was in the funeral business? Did you know that? Did you know about his business dealings?" Tell me, Chase. Did you?"

"No. No, I didn't Dexter. I knew my dad represented him in court about killing a man, but I didn't know anything else about him. That's the truth."

"Man, oh man. So that's the kind of 'fore-fathers' I have! I've got killers, drug-dealers, and who knows what else? Oh, man, this is too much...it's too much!"

The meeting between them had lasted over thirty minutes. The receptionist reentered the room to announce that the office manager for the evening shift would be coming in soon, and she would not approve of them being there.

"Okay, gentlemen, I...ah...I need to go up to see my brother and sister-in-law. Chase, if you want, you can come along with me as we discussed... Ah...Marvin, I need to get back with you tomorrow, if that's alright. I owe you more money, do I?"

"You can call me tomorrow... We can talk then."

"Okay, okay...thanks, Marvin...thanks for your time and... information."

Chapter 39

Sharon, Greg, Brenda and Adam were waiting silently in Brian's room when Dexter and Chase arrived. Adam turned away and looked towards the wall, knowing what Dexter was there for. He was fed up with Dexter's intrusion into his best friends' business affairs. Now, he has secured the services of an investigator, and an attorney, without Sharon's permission? Where will all this lead to, he wondered, as Dexter greeted them all?

"*Sharon, I am so pleased, and thank the Lord that things are alright with you. I heard about the mass confusion last week, and Norma and I were praying that you both were safe.*"

"*Yes, we're still here by the grace of God.*"

"*Oh Sharon, please meet Mr. Chase Pierce, an attorney from Lafayette.*"

"*Hello ma'am. It's a pleasure to meet you and your family. I am so sorry for the misfortune your family has had with your husband's accident. I know how devastating that can be.*"

"*Thank you Mr. Pierce…nice to meet you.*"

"*Sharon, there has been so much going on since the accident, and you know we all have been concerned for Brian, and we want to assist you in protecting his and your rights, as it relates to who's financially liable. That's why I visited with Mr. Pierce who specializes in this type of law.*"

"Yes I do, Mrs Simon. I'm really here to answer any questions you may have and to give you the best service I can to protect your family. Now, I don't have any of the particulars, but the way I work this is you will have to hire me to represent you and your husband--then I go to work to get all the particulars to give you the legal protection you need."

"I appreciate you Dexter. I want to be sure we are protected, but I need to understand something first. Can you tell me where all this is leading us? I mean, I don't understand why we went through what we went through last week, with the Police and FBI and everybody coming in and moving Brian over here in this LifeCare Hospital? Whey did they come in there like Rambo's and treated us like we were on some kind of special informants protection program or something. Why is Brian being guarded around the clock? I just want some answers to what's happening to Brian and us as a family, Dex. Can you answer that for me, Mr. Attorney?"

"Sharon, can we walk outside. I just want us to talk about these things in a quiet and peaceful manner. I do understand all your concerns, sis-in-law, and that's why Mr. Pierce is here. There's no doubt you'll need legal advice. If it's not him, you still need a lawyer."

"Okay, let's walk outside. I'll be right back you guys. You coming Adam?"

"I'm with you."

As the four of them left Brian's room, they observed a plain-clothed male sitting behind a counter across from Brian's room. His eyes were keyed in on their every move. Dexter motioned for them to move down the hall before they began to speak.

"Mrs Simon, I will caution Dexter and anybody else, from talking about your situation at this time. Are you willing to have me as your lawyer or not?"

"Yes, I'll hire you based on the recommendation from Dexter."

"**Great**! I need you to sign this agreement and I will officially represent you and Brian. That means, I will get all the answers you need, and I will be the one responsible for any questions anybody else may have concerning your husband, and any and everything the law enforcement people, or *anyone else, wants to do concerning your husband, they have to come through me. They can't move him; question him when he comes out of the coma...***nothing***...without coming through me!"*

Sharon signed the legal agreement and Dexter signed as a witness. Adam was a by-stander, choosing to remain silent throughout the entire conversation. Chase located a nurse on the same floor and asked if she would make a copy of the agreement. The plain-clothed person was observed using his cell phone during the entire mini-conference down the hall. It was not the time to try to answer all the questions Sharon had, Dexter thought. Perhaps tomorrow would be better. Tonight, he wanted to address the status of Brian with the hospital staff, and perhaps the doctor. Chase agreed to remain in town another day, to spend time with his new client. They all returned to Brian's room to spend time with the family while Dexter went in search of the nurse or doctor on duty. Earlier, several staff members came in to draw blood and monitor Brian's blood pressure.

The doctor came to Brian's room with Dexter, and reported to the family that everything was still the same with Brian's condition. He was encouraged that he seems to be stimulated by conversation. His heart rate increases when you talk directly to him. It appears that he is aware that something is being said and a part of his brain is trying to communicate that. Needless to say, that was great news for all the family to hear. They were encouraged that one day soon, they hoped, he would recover fully and they can take him home to become a husband, dad, and brother again.

"Sharon, we all have reason to celebrate tonight. God is still in the healing business and the prayers of the righteous still prevaileth much. If you don't mind, can we pray before we leave?"

"Please."

Dexter prayed a brief prayer for the family and for Brian's continued recovery. Chase was impressed by the closeness he witnessed between them, even though he got nothing but silence from Adam, and the siblings of Sharon and Brian. He was relieved that he had a new client, but he felt that this one was going to be one of the most challenging ones to date. Although his specialty was in Personal Injury cases, he was also qualified to handle criminal cases. Just how much of a criminal case was this going to be was way up in the air. He needed to make an agreement with Marvin as well, as he has apparently uncovered a host of information that would be needed when he finally met with Sharon later.

"Well, I need to get home, guys. My wife is holding down the fort 'till I get there. Chase, are you going to be able to find a hotel for the night, sir?"

"I saw one about a block away. But I think I'll hang around here with my client for a while, if I can Sharon."

"Yes, yes of course."

"Great, guys. Hey Adam, can you walk me to the front?"

"No problem. I'm going to be leaving too. Sharon, I'll talk to you tomorrow, okay? Greg-Brenda, ya'll take care your mamma, you hear? Everything will be alright. You ready Dex?"

Dexter and Adam walked out together. Dexter placed his arms around his brother's shoulder and squeezed him tightly. He whispered words of encouragement to ease the tenseness Adam displayed.

"Adam, I know your birthday is Thursday, but Norma and I would like for you to come over for dinner on Friday evening, to celebrate your 45th. Is that alright? Are you available?"

"Yeah Dex, sure. I appreciate that. What time?"

"How about 6?"

"Okay...see you then. I'll need to talk to you tomorrow though. It's about Brian and what we were talking about before we went into his room. I mean just the two of us, okay?"

"Absolutely, brother. You got it. I'll call you tomorrow. Hang in there."

Dexter headed home after a very long day that was as electrically charged as that running through the utility lines. But he felt that some of the confusing and secretive events of the day were finally getting resolved in his mind. The biggest accomplishment was getting Sharon to sign the agreement with Chase, and getting him started on representing them. But at the same time, he knew that there were going to be some real 'dog' days ahead as more of the secrets surrounding his family came to light. How would any of them be able to take the news about Brian's business dealings, and the other family members who are in the FBI files? He resigned himself to be the bearer of bad news and was determined to get to the bottom of all this as soon as possible. He placed a call to Norma to let her know that he was on the way home. Even though he was very tired and drained, he was uplifted that he was going home to his incredible partner and his wonderful gifts of life--his triplets.

Chapter 40

One of Norma's favorite programs was airing on television when Dexter arrived home. She motioned for him to come to her as she sat on the couch with a glass of orange juice, to give her a hug and kiss. Dexter knew not to disturb her when her program was on, so he obeyed like a good boy and left her alone until the program break. He went into his room to disrobe and put something casual on. At the break, she yelled out...

"**Hey honey, you're home**, aren't you?"

"*Who told you? ...Huh? ...How did you know?*"

"*How was your day? ...You hungry?*"

"*You bet, I am—what you got for me?*"

"*Well, we have baked chicken with Cilantro and citrus to flavor the chicken, with mashed potatoes and your favorite vegetables-broccoli.*"

"*Wow, what's the occasion for such a special meal?*"

"*You got your prayers answered, didn't you? You got, not one...but* **three!**"

"*I am soooo thankful, sweetheart. We are really blessed. But...I don't want to let anybody know until the doctor can detect a good heartbeat, okay?*"

"*I agree...I was talking to mother today, and I was sooo tempted to give her something to think about, but I thought better. She would have blurted out to my sisters, daddy, and I know he would have told his whole church."*

"Well I'm glad you didn't. Being a down-home type preacher, that news would have been right up his alley--to work that news into a sermon... Oh, there's your program coming back on. You go ahead...I'll get my dinner and I'll join you on the couch."

For the next twenty-five minutes, they both sat watching the CSI program that Norma had seen before, but she never missed an episode, no matter how many times it aired. Dexter ate his dinner sitting next to her, even if in silence. When the program ended, they settled into a comfortable position on the couch and Norma wanted to continue the conversation she started about speaking to her mother and father.

"Okay, mom and dad wanted me to tell you hello, and I spoke to daddy for a little while about the numbers you were seeing. I told him about the trip to New Iberia; the times when you looked at the clocks and they registered the matching numbers; and the time you left the hospital; and Brian's room number...all that."

"Oh...okay...what did he say?"

"Well, he thought about it for a while and then he told me to tell you to give him a call when you have time."

"Oh...okay. Did he seem like he had some idea about what they might mean?"

"He didn't lean one way or another. He just said, have you to call him."

"Great, I think I will. You think it's too late now?

"No. Daddy stays up late. Momma's the one that's in bed by 9 o'clock."

"Thanks honey I will do just that. I've got a lot to tell you about, too. I had a busy day at work and after. I'll tell you about it when I finish."

Dexter placed a call to his father-in-law in Mount Holly, North Carolina. Rev. Farrell and wife lived in a small town where the population was only ten percent black, but he was the pastor of a large church in Charlotte. Dexter knew he would have something to say that would shed light on the appearance of these numbers.

"Hey dad…how you been? …how's that gout you been suffering with?…you been taking medicine for that, too?"… I do understand… How's mom doing? Great. Tell her hello for me. Norma said she told you about the repetitive numbers I've been seeing…Yes, I've seen all the combinations… Well, I've seen 111, 222, 333, 444 and 555. I've even seen combinations like 1111, but only one time. The combination of 333 seems to be the most common. I've seen that combination all over the place…it doesn't matter whether it's morning or night…no, not at all. You heard of this before? … You have? …Is there some explanation for them…Well, I would be very interested to know what all this means.

Dexter listened intently while remaining silent. His father-in-law spoke to him about number combinations which were of significance. He explained that the 333 combination represented 'balance or completeness' and he gave some examples of it: He explained that the God-head was made up of the Father, Son and Holy Ghost. He said that Jesus Christ rose from the dead on the 3rd day. Three persons were crucified on that faithful day. Jesus told his accusers that if they destroyed his temple, he would rebuild it in three days. The Apostle Paul spoke of the greatest gifts in terms of 'Faith, Hope and Charity-The greatest being Charity'. Three men were thrown into the fiery furnace; the number three, and three days or three years was very prominent throughout the Old and New Testament. So, he explained, there is the Sun, Moon and Stars; there is Heaven, Earth and Hell; there's the Body, Mind and Spirit. That number, he concluded, is one of completeness. Everything's in balance with that number.

"Okay, I can see how that works … I can understand the balance for me."

"Dexter wanted to tell his father-in-law that he and Norma were expecting triplets, but he held back on making that announcement at this time.

"What about the other numbers I've been seeing. What do you think the relevance is with them?"

Off the top of his head, Reverend Ferrell said…

"Add 'em up! …see what they add up to!"

"Are you serious?" Dexter laughed. *"Just like that, huh? Just add 'em up!"*

"Go ahead and see what it totals. Let's see…1+1+1=3 okay 2+2+2=6 and 3+3+3=9 okay 4+4+4=12 and 5+5+5=15. Now add the 3+6+9+12+15=45. **Now,** *If that's all you have, you need to find the significance of* **45.** *Something that's going on around you that is tied to that number* **45** *has some significance. Now you will also see that, what's common between each set of numbers is what? …*

"Three!" *Three is the common denominator.*

"There you go… So that's why you see (3) **three** *more than any other set of numbers. It's the commoner, so to speak. That's what I think of when I think of you, Dexter. I see you are balanced; you have a level head; you are God-fearing and you have a balanced household. You and my daughter complete each other. In other words, I see you both as a complete package, together. God's plan is for a man to take a wife, and they have children together. That's makes the 3. Now if you can ever have children, then you will really be complete--as a family."*

"Okay dad!"

"I know …I know ya'll been trying. I'm just saying! We've been praying for you two, though. Don't you worry; the Lord will bless you two one day. Don't worry."

"Hey, you been very good help for me dad. I'll keep an eye out for the significance of the **45.** *I appreciate you, and we love you and mom, okay. Goodnight."*

Chapter 41

"Good morning everyone, this is Kitty Kincaid at KLAC with your morning news update. You may recall over two weeks ago, we brought you a story about an explosion that took place off highway 35. In that explosion, several persons were hurt and seven were killed. We have been investigating the aftermath of that explosion, and we have an update for you.

What we have found out, is the owner of that towing business was engaged in another business, where he was transporting vehicles from South Louisiana, to his location here in Shreveport. Now apparently, there were other things within those vehicles he transported, which is very bizarre. Authorities found some evidence of skeletons within the caskets. Now these remains appeared to be very old, in that the persons had been dead for some time. Authorities also informed us that the owner had been using illegal immigrants from Mexico in transporting those vehicles to his business location. All seven of the deceased in that explosion were illegal immigrants, as were the wounded.

Now, our sources also tell us that the owner of the business named Brian Simon is himself in the hospital, due to an unrelated accident. Mr. Simon has been in a coma since his accident, and the family is asking for everyone's prayers. Last week, the FBI and other law enforcement agencies took over the hospital operation for a day where Mr. Simon was in intensive care. Our sources further tell us that Mr. Simon has since been moved to another undisclosed location. We will, of course, bring you more up-to-date information when we get it."

Dexter and Norma were just finishing eating their breakfast and were on their way out of the door when that news flash came on the television. They sat through the entire report by Ms Kincaid in complete silence. The telephone rang. It was 7:20am. Norma answered it.

"*Hello... Oh, good morning Adam, how are you? ...Yes he's here, we're about to walk out the door. Okay, here he is.*"

Norma placed her hand over the receiver and said, whispering...

"*He sounds like he's been crying.*"

Dexter took the receiver and told Norma she should leave for work and he would speak to her later.

"*Good morning Adam, what's up? ...Yes we did. I know, Adam, but what can we do about it? ...I know, brother" ...I'm with you on that but, all that didn't come from any one that I know... Marvin wouldn't... No, I don't think that came from Marvin... Okay listen, I'm on my way to work. I can call you when I get there. We are getting together later, right? ...Okay, I'll call you later.*"

Dexter called Chases' cell number. After a brief conversation, Chase offered to buy lunch at noon--Dexter agreed. Dexter drove to the office with his stomach in knots. Now, the entire city knew who Brian was and many would know the connection he had with him. More importantly, the information released about his business dealings was devastating. He didn't want his mother to hear this before he had the chance to talk to her. He reasoned that this could cause her to have a breakdown, as her health was very fragile. What could he do at this juncture, to quell the tide of information being aired about Brian? Chase is needed to become the spokesman for his brother. And,

Sharon would probably be calling him next. Instead, Norma called him to find out what happened with the conversation with Adam.

"*Honey, did you make it to work on time?*" asked Norma.

"*Yes, I just got here. I was on the phone all the way with Adam, then Chase. I'm just going to have to wait this out, honey. I'll get back to you after I have lunch with Chase.*"

Dexter went into his office and began to work on his computer. Within the first hour of starting his work, his supervisor came in to make an announcement. Because of Dexter's experience and competence, he was selected to attend an industry conference to be held in eight days in Washington DC. He would have all expenses paid for the 3 day conference and he should contact the travel assistance office for scheduling. Dexter threw his head into the air and his eyes rolled up to the ceiling. He did not want the supervisor to think that he did not want to accept the assignment as this was an honor for him to be chosen.

"*Thanks, Chris. I feel honored that I was selected. I'll get in touch with travel and get things set up.*"

Nevertheless, he was in the middle of some serious issues with his family. He called Norma and informed her of his selection. Norma was pleased and encouraged him to go forward. Dexter made a call to the hospital to speak with Sharon. When he reached her in Brian's room, he tried to be upbeat with his greeting to test her reaction. She sounded livelier than she had the night before.

"*Good morning, Dex. Brian had a good night sleep and he didn't seem to stir as much as he had been. It gave me a chance to have some rest, too. By the way, I'm meeting with Chase in a few minutes. We are going for breakfast in the cafeteria down stairs.*"

"*Well, you sound good. I'm so pleased that things are getting better with his condition. You are going to have to get some relief so you can get some rest yourself.*"

"*I'm okay. Adam also called me and said he wanted to be here when*

Chase comes, so he can be aware of what's going on. He really is concerned about us. I appreciate what you brothers are doing for all of us, Dexter."

"Believe me, it's the right thing to do for anyone, Sharon. Since we are family, it's all the more important that we stay together, even through thick and razor thin-my mother always says."

"Oh, here he is now. Do you want to talk to him?"

"Just tell Chase to call me when you guy's finish."

Chase Abbott Pierce represented himself to Sharon and Adam as a man of confidence and integrity. His intent was to show Sharon how much he believed in fully representing his clients, even if it meant that he had to go against the big boys, like the government. He explained that he needed to have all the facts concerning the client that was available. He recognized that Sharon may not have been privy to the information presented by Marvin, and therefore he had to ease into the subject, with Adam standing near by.

"Mrs Simon, tell me what you know about the accident itself...where were you when Brian had this accident?"

"I was at home. I had just said bye to him as he left for the convenience store... we were finished talking about attending church and..."

Sharon recounted the events of the evening with Chase. When she told all she knew, he asked her about her knowledge of his business. Sharon was curious as to why he needed to know about her husbands business, as he was not working when this occurred. Adam interjected his objection as well. Chase explained that he needed to have full knowledge about his clients. He assured her that her comments were safe with him. She told him all that she knew--which was not much. After forty minutes of conversation, Chase felt that he had enough to get the case started with. His first efforts were to notify the insurance company that Brian was in an accident, and provide them with a copy of the police report. Much of this would be handled by his secretary. For the rest of the day, he needed to make contact with Marvin Klein, and work out an agreement to provide information to him. It was very clear to Chase that Marvin had uncovered some possible criminal activity which could enormously complicate his case for personal injury. Not that he would not mount a case against the responsible party but, it was wholly in order to integrate a defense for Brian. The insurance company had the money to pay for his services, but a criminal defense would require some up-front money from the family. He met with Marvin at his office.

"Counselor, do you know what you're getting into with this guy? I mean really?"

"Okay Marvin, that's why I'm here,. Let's talk. First, let's talk about our arrangement. What will be your fee for the information you already have?"

"Mr. Simon has already contracted with me to give him what I've already found. If he wants to give that to you is alright with me. Now, have a seat so we can talk about this situation."

Marvin held nothing back. Chase was given a clear picture of how far back Marvin's investigation covered. He assured Chase that his sources were sound and he has never been given incorrect info before. Chase was astounded that Government agencies were well aware of years of the Simon's involvement in criminal activities. No moves towards arresting anyone was made because they wanted to get to the top of the heap, which included in and out of state persons. This case is big-time, and Marvin could only warn Chase that he was no match for the feds. The best thing he should do would be to back out of the deal and let things fall as they may. Besides, Brian may not even recover from his injuries, and he may not have a client at all. Marvin's phone rang.

"Hello, this is Klein's Investigative Services—how may I help you?"

*"Listen Marvin, this is Zack Powder…what the **hell** is going on here?"* speaking in a low toned voice.

"About what Zack?"

I'm talking about the Simon case you asked me about. What tha hell is all that about on the TV? I told you not to let any of that information out, didn't I?" Didn't I Marvin? You let me down, bud!"

"*Wait a minute Zack, old buddy—I don't know what you're talking about. I didn't let you down pal, you know that. Never would I do that.*"

"*Where did all that detailed info come from, then if you didn't dive it to them?*"

"*Zack, look, I have only spoken to a lawyer and to Brian's brother about this case. That's it.*"

"*Who is this lawyer, and just what did you tell him, cause my tail is on the hot seat. You know everybody in this department knows about our friendship. Tell me you didn't give this lawyer any of the confidential information I gave you—please tell me that, Marvin!*"

Looking at Chase while he covered the telephone receiver, Marvin spoke.

Look, there's this lawyer that Brian's family hired to represent them on the accident. Now, he's gonna ask some questions and do some investigating for his client, right? So, Brian's brother hired me to find out about his brothers business and the two of them got together, and you know they probably exchanged some info about that. That would be it, Zack…I swear, my friend…that's it!"

"*Who is this lawyer, Marvin?*"

"*He's not even from here, Zack. He's from down south and just came up here to see his client, Mrs Simon.*"

"*Who is he?*"

"*Oh, somebody just came in, Zack. I'll have to call you back in a few minutes. Give me about 20 minutes…I'll call you right back.*"

Marvin turned to Chase and gritted his teeth while placing his hands on his hips. He felt trapped between two huge pillars, and now being squeezed. He knew the seriousness of the case the feds were developing and he did not want to be the person to cause the case to blow up. He wanted Chase to get out of his office as soon as possible. In fact, he wanted him to return to his home town, now.

"*Listen Chase, you just heard the conversation. This is exactly what I told you about this case. You need to drop this case and get the hell out of this town NOW!* **He wants your name!** *He wants to know who you* are---that's for a reason and I know how these guys work...you need to leave, man."

"Wait a minute Marvin, I'm not going to let anybody run me out of town...I have a job to do for my client."

Marvin picked up some papers off of his desk and handed them to Chase. He turned to his file cabinet and thumbed through his files until he came to the Simon file. He reached in and pulled out several pages. He gave them to Chase and grabbed his right elbow and started walking him towards the front door.

"You can have these papers Chase. They're my rough notes on my initial investigation. Here's what I want you to do for me...don't call me or ask me for anymore information on this guy, okay? It's not your fault, my friend...but I've got to call this cop back and give him a name. Now, I don't want to give him your name, especially while you're still in town. If you're going to represent Mr. Simon on the accident, I suggest you stick to just that—alright? Better than that, you need to just go back to Lafayette and forget about this case—it's not going to be worth your while, my friend."

"I appreciate your help Marvin...but, I'm not interested in letting anybody tell me who I should represent and who I shouldn't. I heard what you said...and I don't have a problem with you telling them who I am. I think I can take care of myself."

"Like I said, you obviously don't know the people involved here. I wouldn't put it pass them to have someone on their way to my office to see who leaves. Chase...you do what you want. I'm out of here. I'll get back to my friend later... Is this your car? Nice car...now get the hell out of town, okay? Have a nice day, Mr. Chase!"

"Pierce...it's Mr. Pierce!"

By the time Chase climbed into his one year old Chrysler, he looked into his rear view mirror to be sure no other cars were behind him. He was clear to back up from his parking spot in front of Marvin's office, but he noticed an unmarked car had come to an abrupt stop across the street from him. The two persons in the car sat without movement, looking in Chase' direction. Chase looked forward and saw Marvin move back into his office building. Chase drove off at a reasonable pace while keeping an eye out for the other car. He knew he was now being followed just as Marvin had warned. He decided that he would not inflame the situation by staying in Shreveport, so he decided to head south for Lafayette. By the time he reached the outside of the city, he noticed the unmarked car had stopped at a stop light as Chase continued on his journey. He felt relieved that he was no longer being followed. At the same time, he felt emboldened that he was right to want to represent his client, and that he needed to gather all the facts about the case, in spite of the threats he was sure to face. He continued his drive home ever mindful of the fact that this would truly be a case to be remembered, whether he decides to continue to represent Brian or not. About 20 miles from Shreveport, Chase called his secretary to find out if he had any calls, and to say that he was headed home. He relaxed to make the lonesome drive home when he noticed a shadow of a helicopter cross his path. It didn't alarm him until it passed over his car again, as it circled around to his right side. It was flying lower than he thought it should. He could see that the persons in the chopper were looking at him as they flew directly towards him, then peeled off to his left and disappeared.

Arriving home around 4:30pm, Chase stopped by his office to pick up the messages left by his secretary. He went to his credenza and unlocked the drawer on the top right side. He reached in and took out a 38 caliber pistol, he kept for his safety. He placed it in his briefcase and left the office. On his way home, he decided to go to the grave yard where Dexter told him that his grandfather was missing from. Chase arrived at the grave yard and turned off his engine. Since it was almost dawn, he decided to take his flashlight and his briefcase with him, as he surveyed the area. Walking slowly and reading the names from the headstones, Chase made his way to the center of the yard. He looked around and up at the towering oak trees, dripping with moss. It was still quiet—eerily so. He continued his slow walk until he tripped on a headstone half way buried in the ground. He pulled out his flash light and his pistol from his briefcase, and shoved them in his outside coat pockets. He came upon a large headstone that had an inscription that he recognized. It read Raymond Toussaint—a man who was close to his father, and a honored citizen of the Lafayette community. He kneeled down to read the--difficult to see--writing when suddenly…

"kaboonk"

Awakened by the ringing of his cell phone, Chase jerked at his chest. He half raised to his elbow to realize that his head was about to fall off. It was in fact pounding like never before. What the hell happened, he wondered. Oh, my God, he thought, somebody knocked me out. Who was it and why did they do that? He looked around and then scrambled to his knees before someone was trying to reach him on his cell phone. He retrieved it from his inside coat pocket and saw that the called ID showed his home number. He hit redial and his wife answered.

"Honey, I've been waiting for you. You said you were on your way home over 2 hours ago."

"Hey, babe…I…I…know…I was just reaching for…. I was just standing…."

"Honey, you don't sound right… where are you? Are you alright?"

"I'm okay… I'm alright… I'm trying to figure something out… just give me a minute, okay?… Oh, my head is killing me!"

"Honey, please tell me where you are. Honey I'm worried about you. Should I call the police?"

"No…no… I'm alright, babe. I'm alright. I'm on my way home… I'm not that far away. I'll be… right there, okay?… Don't worry."

Chase sat stunned at the fact that somebody had knocked him out cold. He figured he was out for at least a half hour. By now it was dark in the graveyard and the moon was the only light around. He could hear crickets singing and frogs courting, but nothing else. He felt his pockets and found his flashlight. He patted his right pocket and his pistol was missing. Was he robbed? Did somebody sneak up behind him to rob him of his gun? Or was it something else, he wondered?

Did any of this have anything to do with the unmarked car following him earlier; or the helicopter hovering over him? What about those missing graves Dexter told him about? Is this the time to continue to search or should he get out of here as fast as he could? He grabbed his case from the ground and started to walk towards his car. With his first step, something called his attention. It was his 38 caliber pistol that had fallen out of his pocket. He felt relieved that it was not a robbery as they didn't even touch his wallet. He reached his car and quickly slid unto the drivers' seat. He turned on the ignition and the lights came on, showing a note on his windshield. It read: **"The Law-Stick to the law!!!"**

Chapter 42

Chase Abbott Pierce was born into a family of means. During the cotton and sugar cane production years, the Pierce family owned most of the acreage south of Lafayette, and their relatives owned most of the rest. By now, most of the old guard has died out and passed the family wealth down to Chase's uncles and aunts. His grandmother--on his fathers' side--was alive at the age of 96, and still in her right mind. Although Chase enjoyed a good relationship with his mother, he had a better one with his grandmother. After he woke up from a hard night of rest, and still suffering from a headache from the blow to this head last night, he decided to pay a visit to his grandmother, to get some of her friendly advice.

"Ma Ma Sir, vous faites bien ce matin ? (You doing alright this morning?)"

"I can't complain, Abby. I'm doing better than a lot of folk my age."

"vos mains sont froides. (your hand feels cold)"

"Well, it's always that way son. That's what you have to look forward to when you get this old. Listen, you can speak English with me this morning... there ain't nobody else here.

"Aww grandma, I always slip into French whenever I see you. I keep forgetting you prefer English these days."

"What you doing over here this early in the morning? …Turn around, let me see something…why you got a patch on the back of your head?

"Oh, I had a little accident last night over at the graveyard where Mr. Toussaint was buried…you remember him, right?"

"Of course I do—who can forget him? …But what happened?…you want some tea?"

"No Ma, I'm fine. But I wanted to talk to you about something that I'm working on with a client."

"Come on in to the kitchen while I get me some tea, and we can talk in there. You still representing black people in your law practice?"

"I still am, and anybody else who needs me. I don't just work for black folks Ma."

"I was just wondering, son. I ain't saying there's something wrong with that…I was just curious."

"That's the something I wanted to talk to you about, Ma. Way back before I was born, when daddy and his brothers were in a business for themselves, what kind of business were they really in?"

"Well, they ran your grandfathers business, and he ran his fathers business. It was a family business passed down through the generations."

"But what did they do in the business."

"Why you asking about all that, Chase Abbot? …What that got to do with you representing black people?"

"I'm trying to see if there is a connection between the business daddy ran, and his parents, to a client I'm working on now?"

"How could it be? Your daddy didn't sell his business to nobody outside of the family!"

"Was he ever involved in the funeral business?"

"They owned five or six of them."

"Was he ever involved in the liquor business, too?"

"Chase Abbott…"

"I need to know Ma Ma. I understand that the family used to make moonshine liquor and sold it to some Indians."

"Your grandfather and his brothers had some property in the back *woods where they wouldn't let any of us know where it was. They might have been making moonshine. But, I know they did sell liquor to the soldiers who were stationed here in Louisiana. That's why they grew all that sugarcane."*

"Would they have done business with some black folks in the funeral business or with the moonshine business?"

"Now Chase Abbott, I'm an old woman...I ain't got long here... I don't want to raise up nothing that's already been buried... now, you asking me about something that been long gone...I ain't worried about nobody doing nothing to nobody cause they all been dead-a long time ago. But I would say it like this; your grandfather's father on down to your daddy had the same business. And, they had some blacks who worked in the business for them. Now, somehow, a white man got tangled up with a white woman cheating on their husband with a half-black man, and they got into a fight. The black man killed the husband and the black man and his family-- they ran out of town. They went up north, the way I heard it."

"You mean north Louisiana or to a northern state?"

"I heard it was around where the Cane River starts... somewhere around Shreveport."

"What about the funeral business?...did they have any blacks working for them in that business, too?"

"Oh sure, behind the scenes. They couldn't come out there where the white families were though--they were in the back doing the work. Then they drove the car to take the bodies to the grave, after they dug the hole... yes, they were in the business all the way."

Chase knew he had drained about all he could out of his dear grandmother. Oh, did she love that boy. He was the apple of her eye because of his dedication to becoming a lawyer and trying to do the right thing. She offered to raise him from age four, but his mother refused. He was an independent soul, who was focused and would never quit until he was satisfied with the outcomes. He was on to something now. He could feel it in his heart. There is a connection, he thought, between his past, and the past of Dexter Simon's family. The irony of it was that they were both on a discovery path, which would surely lead them to a place yet to be identified. Without appearing overly appreciative, Chase was ready to head to his office to get some work done. As was his usual gesture of saying goodbye, he stood, went over to his seated grandmother and kissed her on top of her head.

"Grandma is old, Abby… my days are short… You been a good boy all your life. I always knew you were a special boy. I always believed you'll do some great things in the law business. You got a good heart and a good mind. You keep on being that way. Don't let nobody make you compromise who you are. I don't want you to pattern yourself after my son—your daddy. He always took care of his family—you and your brothers. But I got to be honest with you; he sold his soul to the devil for some of that blood money. All those businesses he got into didn't do nobody good but the devil. And you should know, that all those politicians around here got in on some of that money too. The same thing happened to your grandpa. I want you to keep on standing for good, Abby. You stand for what is right. I want you to stay that way, you hear? …Now take care yourself… You know your grandma loves ya!"

Chase was flushed in the face-drained of warm blood, hearing this statement from his own grandmother. This news was a total shock to him as he never contemplated that his dad was anything but a good father and friend. He remembered how his dad took time with him and his brothers by going hunting and fishing. But he also knew that he never involved them in any of their businesses. It was a foregone conclusion that he was going to become a lawyer from the time he was a child. But his mother was the one that showed interest in his school work, and helped him get into the college he wanted to attend. But now it is a new day. He has been enlightened with some information that would guide his actions with his dealings with future clients as well as old acquaintances.

Chase arrived at this office by 10am. His secretary had a to do list that was a mile long. He gave her the new file of Sharon & Brian Simon for her to work her magic. He settled into his office chair and started thumbing through the phone messages. One message that caught his eye was from Dexter Simon. He felt that he really needed to talk to Dexter, in light of having to leave Shreveport as quickly as he did. He dialed his number.

"Hey Dexter, this is Chase Pierce, how are you?"

"Good Chase, I see you got my message--how are you?"

"I'm good...I'm good. I made it back to Lafayette last night."

"I thought you were going to call me after you finished with Sharon."

"Yeah, well...I'm here to tell you things changed real quickly after that. I'll have to tell you sometime."

"Okay ...did you get things accomplished as you expected?"

"I did...I did."

"Good, good. Listen Chase, I just found out that I'm going to have to attend a conference in a couple of weeks in Washington DC. I hope we can get some things accomplished before I leave...what do you think?"

"I think we can...I think we can. Dexter, can you come back to my office within the next few days? I think we need to talk about some things that's come up recently."

"I can come this weekend, Chase. I just came back to work so I can't take off the rest of this week."

"This weekend will be fine."

"What's up...why the sullen tone in your voice, Chase?"

"I just had an interesting 24 hours, that's all. When you come this weekend, I should have more clarity about some of my concerns."

"Okay. I can live with that. Say, if my brother Adam can come with me, will that be alright with you?"

"That would be fine. I know he has had some issues with me, and you and Marvin, right?"

"He does. But I think when he comes to our house this week for a birthday dinner; I think we can make some progress along those lines."

At 12:25pm, two white locals walked into Chase' office, dressed in slacks and long-sleeve shirts with open collars. Both looked over weight as they approached the front desk.

"Mr. Pierce, please."

"Okay, gentlemen, did you have an appointment with Mr. Pierce?"

"Yes, no…no we didn't. But, it was about lunchtime and we thought we could all go to lunch together. Can you get him, please?"

"Just a minute…I'll see if he is available… Have a seat, please."

She returned in a few seconds.

"He'll be right with you…would you like some water?"

"No thank you, ma am."

"Gentlemen, how can I help you? Come on into my office. What can I do for you?"

"Are you free to have lunch, Mr. Pierce?"

"No, I'm not having lunch today, gentlemen. I've been out of my office for a few days and I'm eating in today. But, what can I do for you?"

"You're Attorney Wayne Pierce's kid aren't you?"

"Wayne was my dad, yes."

"You're the lawyer who has been representing a lot of black folks, right?"

"Wait a minute…who are you guys? Do you have a card?"

"How was your trip to Shreveport on Monday, Mr. Pierce?"

Chase gazed into the eyes of both men as they sat across from his large desk. He was surprised at the question suggesting they knew of his visit with his new client in Shreveport. They did not resemble what he thought would be the 'Fed's' dressed in such casual clothes. He had not seen them around Lafayette. But it was evident that they came there for a specific purpose. He felt that he could not play dumb and act as if he knew nothing of which they spoke. He would not give them any information without getting some ID from them.

"Listen, gentlemen, I have no idea who you are--but you seem to be businessmen. If so, let me have your cards and I'll get back with you at another time. I usually work by appointment, and I would be happy to have my secretary set a time…

The man doing most of the talking reached into his back pocket. Chase tightened his grip on the sides of his chair. Both men stood in sequence. The leader took out a beige envelope and flipped it onto the desk. Chase followed the envelope's path, remaining seated. As they turned to leave, the leader spoke again...

"I heard you're a sharp lawyer, Mr. Pierce. I hope you understand the purpose of our visit. Have a nice day."

Chase followed after the men as they walked out of his office. He was more fixated on the two of them, rather the package they left on his desk. He stood in his doorway as they left through the front door without saying anything else. He observed the license plate holder on their vehicle that read: "Buy Local-Buy New Iberia".

"Were you going to lunch with them, Mr. Pierce?"

"Not today, Ms Guillory...not today!"

Chase walked back into his office and closed the door. He retrieved the envelope from his desk and sat down. His mind was racing with thoughts of what was in it.

He was not naïve--It felt like money. He slowly opened it and slid the contents out which was wrapped in paper. Written on the paper were the words: "The Law—stick with the law".

"Ms Guillory, who do I have appointments with this afternoon?"

"You have...one...two...three appointments. There is another man who called this morning and wanted to see you today, after he got off work, about 5:30pm. I told him he may have to wait till tomorrow. If you want to see him, that'll be four."

"It's okay, I'll see him. Are they all personal injury, including the man who still works?"

"Yes, sir. The man at 5:30pm was calling about his son."

"Okay...I am going to lunch and I'll be back about 1:30pm...will that work?"

"I'll make it work, sir."

Chase got into his car and sped off to see a friend of his who has been in the law business for over thirty years. He was a trusted lawyer and friend who has also stood up against the establishment on many occasions. By now, he felt untrusting of the local law enforcement, but at the same time, he knew he would have to go through them while representing his clients. Jason Fontenot was foremost on his mind as he yet lay in the hospital, recovering from his injuries. He needed to speak to his friend before he challenged the New Iberia police force directly, by filing suit against them for violation of Jason's human rights. He called his friend's cell phone while driving.

"Hey, Trever, this is Chase."

"Hey, Chase what you up to?"

"You been to lunch yet?"

"No, no not yet...what do you have in mind?

"Let's grab a sandwich at Gumbo-to-go over on Dragon St. I can pick you up!"

"Okay, are you on you way?"

"I'm about five minutes away from you."

"You have to wait about five more minutes--I'm just finishing up with a client."

"See you then."

Chase pulled up to the front of Trever's office and waited for him to finish with his client. While he waited, he relived the events which took place over the past two days which has him questioning his ability to identify all the players, and where will all the trails he has uncovered, so far, lead him. One thing was for sure, he was not going to give up representing his client in Shreveport, and he was going to investigate Jason's case, fully. Of all the clients he's represented, these two will be the most challenging. Trever came out of his office, swinging his coat over his right shoulder. He clawed the door handle on the passenger side of Chase' car and climbed in.

"Hey, man.? I ain't seen you in a while...you been busy?"

"That is not even the word for it, Trev. I've been smothered, how about you?"

"Same here, my friend. You got to make that money when you can make it, right?"

"So what's up? You sound like you got something on your mind."

"Yeh, I just want to get your opinion on a couple of things I'm working on."

"Yeh, sure...what you got?"

They arrived at the famous Gumbo-To-Go restaurant. There was a line of waiting patrons 20 feet from the front door. They were moving fairly well, but Trever got out to secure their place in the line, while Chase found a parking place. Chase joined Trever in line by the time he reached the front door.

"So what's up Chase?"

"Well, I've got this client I just signed up in Shreveport who was in an accident, right? Now he is in a coma and been there since the accident about two weeks ago. Now, he's got insurance and all that, and it looks like it's going to be a case that should be fairly clean."

"Okay."

"Well...the problem comes in where this guy owns a business that's been under surveillance for a long time by the Fed's. It has nothing to do with the accident, but now it looks like my investigation is going to cross over with what the Fed's are working on."

"I'm sure you can keep them seperate. I have that kind of issue sometimes... Oh, we're here--what are you gonna order?"

"I want to get a shrimp poboy, and a coke, please."

"I'll take the same...I'll get this Chase, put your money away."

"Thanks, Trev."

"No problem."

They move down the line while waiting on their order. Trever turns towards Chase with a look of confidence as Chase looked concerned. They were handed two glasses to get their drinks as Chase continued.

"So, I meet with this private investigator in Shreveport to try to work out an arrangement with him for information, when he gets this call from one of his sources, who is pissed at the investigator."

"What was that all about?"

"He thinks the investigator leaked some details of the investigation they were conducting on my client, to the local television station."

"Well, did he?"

"I don't know. But, get this...the investigator tells the source that he only told the clients brother...and an attorney!"

"That be you?"

"Right! But...he won't tell the source my name...and he insists I get out of town and drop the case with my client."

"Why?"

"Because the Fed's have been working on this family for some time, and they don't want anyone getting in their way."

"Well, they have a point there, right?"

"Yeh, sure...but, this poor guy is still in the hospital in a coma, and his poor wife is down to a frazzle. I can't just leave them hanging without getting involved to get some financial relief for his pain and suffering...I won't leave 'em there."

"Okay, here is our food... Let's sit down in the corner over there.

"Look Trever, you know me...I just can't cut my client loose, just like that. It's not me."

"What do you have in it, Chase? How much time and money?"

"Minimal, Trev. That's not my real concern. It's not about the money... you know that."

"I do know that. Let me ask you this...is it a black client?"

"What difference does that make, Trever?"

"Answer the question?"

"No...no I'm not answering that...I don't give a dam..."

"Hey, hey...I'm on your side, Chase...I'm not your enemy...you asked me for advice, right?"

"Yes...yes I did."

"Well, let me give it to you then..."

"But before you do, let me say this..."

"Okay."

"I...think I'm being followed."

"Really? Why?"

"I feel it has to do with this case. Somebody's been following me since I left Shreveport, in a car and then overhead in a helicopter."

"Whoa, Chase…back up! You mean you think all this is related to your representing this client…who is in a coma?"

"Listen to this… Something is going on around here, too."

"Around here…like what?"

Chase looked over his left shoulder and over the next. He leaned forward towards Trever and spoke softly.

"I got knocked out last night while I was looking at some greaves out at the old graveyard, about 4 miles outside the city."

"Knocked out? What tha hell…"

"Wait…when I came to and got to my car, there was a note on my windshield that said: 'The Law—Stick to the Law'".

"Gees, Chase!"

"Then…then, about an hour ago, two guys came to my office and left this on my desk…"

Chase pulled the envelope half way out of his coat pocket-still in the brown envelope. Trever stopped eating his sandwich and stared at the package. Chase returned it to his pocket.

"What tha hell, Chase? …What is that man?"

"Just what you think it is! And…and, there was a note on it that says: The Law—Stick to the Law. These guys probably came from New Iberia based on the license plate holder on their car. Do you see I got a problem here?"

"My god, my friend. I think you know the answer, already. Obviously, somebody don't want you to be involved in something!"

Trever's cell phone rang. He put the rest of his sandwich down-wiped his hands and answered it.

"Hello, this is Trever…yes I am…yes, sir…yes, I do know him…"

Trever winked at Chase and pointed at his cell phone. Chase stopped eating and listened intently to Trever's' conversation, trying to find a clue through Trever's demeanor to know what was going on. Trever continued…

"Yes, sir, go on…well, let me say this…I know him…he's a good man, and a damn fine lawyer…yes, sir he is…well, I can't promise you that, but I will get the message to him…yes, sir I sure will…goodbye!"

It was not easy for Trever to listen to the man on the other end of the phone call as he was given some instructions to be delivered to Chase. Chase knew he was the subject of that conversation, and he knew it had to do with his involvement with the Simon's. Chase appreciated Trever standing up for him, by calling him a good lawyer and his friend. But what is the message, he wondered. He wanted Trever to go ahead and tell him. They both were no longer hungry. Trever placed his right hand atop his forehead and rubbed it back and forth. Chase sipped on his drink as he waited for Trever to talk. They wrapped up the rest of their sandwiches as Trever spoke.

"You can fix this Chase… You gotta fix this before it gets out of hand, pal…you know that, right?"

Chase gazed at Trever with his arms folded on top of the table. His gaze turned into a stare. He wanted a response from his friend that would assure him that he was doing the right thing for his client, and for himself. He understood what Trever meant by fixing this. Oh yeah, he knew what that meant. But he was not about to compromise his principles, just because somebody didn't like his involvement. The hell with them, he thought. The hell with all of 'em. He was now ready to go. He said nothing…he got up from the table and started walking towards his car in a brisk manner. Trever followed.

"Hey, Mr. Pierce, wait a minute… wait a minute, will you?"

The restaurant patrons seated nearby, looked up at the two of them as Trever spoke louder than he would if they had no disagreement.

"Chase, let me talk to you man. You don't know what I want to say."

"You already said it. I can just drop my case, right? I can walk away from somebody who I agreed to represent for them to recoup their losses. That's what we lawyers do, Trev. That's what we are supposed to do, right?

That's what you've been doing for 30 years, and now you want me to drop it! You don't really know me, Trev. If you think I can abandon my client at the hint of a threat from a phone call..."

"Okay. You're right...seriously, you're absolutely right...I guess I didn't really know you. You've got more principles than I thought. I can understand how you feel...I really do."

Chase stopped at the sidewalk leading to the parking lot, as he turned to Trever. His face was flushed and his breathing was labored. He was mad!

"Listen, I came to you to get some advice on what I should do. Up until you got that phone call, I was beginning to think that you would give me an honest answer, after you had a chance to hear my whole story. You haven't heard my whole story and you already let me down. That disappointments me, my friend."

"Let me say something, Chase."

"Come on...let me get you back to your office."

Chase was silent as he drove Trever back to his office. Trever did the talking during the ten minutes it took them to return.

*"I am really concerned about you Chase. That's my worry, my friend. That call was from somebody who said he was calling for someone else. I have no idea who wanted you to have a message. All I know is they wanted me to tell you they wanted you to stick to the law. I knew you would identify with that from our conversation earlier. I just didn't want to spend a lot of time on the call because they had nothing else to say. How he got my number, or knew that I knew you, is beyond me. But, Chase, I really didn't know how this would affect you. I now see, and I apologize for what I said earlier. I apologize. I understand you better, now. Never...**never** will I underestimate you like that again. I will tell you this...if I can help you with this case or any other case...I would be honored to assist-Pro Bono."*

Chapter 43

exter was just about to hang the telephone up, when his front door bell rang. It was Adam coming for dinner for his birthday. Norma opened the door and invited him in. He hugged Norma and gave her his hat he always wore. She placed it on a soft chair in the living room as she escorted him into the den area where Dexter was talking on the telephone. Adam observed the new house she and Dexter had purchased several months ago. This was his first time in their new home, so he inquired whether this was the same size home they had previously.

"No, the other one was smaller and temporary until we finally settled in Shreveport. We looked all over and finally found a home here in Stoney Point that had some yard size, and a single story. In Chicago, we had none of that."

"This is nice…real nice, Norma."

"Thanks…we love it."

"Okay Sharon…that's sounds good to me. We will be there tomorrow at 10am for the meeting. You hang in there now, and remember that God is good…that's right…all the time. We'll see you then. Bye-bye. …hey Adam, how was your day? Happy birthday, brother!"

"Thanks bro…thank you. I had a good day…was that Sharon at the hospital?"

"Right. Did you talk to her today...about the doctor wanting to meet with the family tomorrow to discuss the prognosis for Brian?"

"Nooo, I didn't know about that. The doctor wants to discuss his what?"

"His prognosis...you know, what things look like as far as his recovery and long term health is concerned."

"Oh, oh...that's good. Will you be there? I gotta work."

"Yep. We'll be there. I'll call you after the meeting to let you know what he had to say, okay? Come on, have a seat brother—Norma's getting dinner ready and we can have a chat while we're waiting. Can I get you a drink? I got soft drinks, juice, water and oh, I can make you a smoothie, if you like."

Adam wanted to be on his best behavior as he respected his brother and sister-in-law. But he really wanted to have a real drink. Dexter didn't offer anything with alcohol in it, but that was what he wanted.

"I'll take a smoothie...that sounds good."

"Ooookay. Let me get that for you brother. Hey, I'm going down to Lafayette Saturday. I'd like for you to go with me...you got any plans?"

"What's happening in Lafayette?"

"Oh, I'm going to see Chase Pierce, that lawyer that..."

"Oh yeah, that guy. How long you gonna be down there?"

"I'll be back the same day."

"Okay, I'll ride down there with you."

"Hey Adam, do you like Brussels Sprouts, asked Norma?

"Do I have to be honest?"

"Yes!"

"Not really, but I'll eat 'em. You sure got something smelling good in there. What else you got?"

"It's a surprise."

"Okay, it sure smells good."

"Here you go brother...happy birthday!"

"Thanks bro—I don't care what they say 'bout you, you're alright in my books."

"Sooo, how old are you going to be tomorrow?"

"You know!...I'm gonna be 45.

"You hear that Norma? Adam's gonna be 45 tomorrow."

"Happy Birthday Mr. 45. That's gotta be a special day for you, I know... honey could you come in here for a minute?"

"Hey, bro, Can I use your bathroom?"

"Of course...it's right through that hallway and the first door on the right... Let me know if you need anything."

Dexter walks into the kitchen to answer Norma's request. He had no expectations about what she wanted. She kept her voice low.

"What's up?"

"Babe, you remember when you talked to my dad about the numbers?"

"Oh, yeh, sure!"

"Did you ever figure out about the number 45?"

"No, not yet...why?... wait...wait a minute..."

Dexter looks towards the den where he and Adam were lounging. He looked back at Norma and smiled as his eyes ranged from looking right to left and back again.

"Are you thinking the number 45 is tied to Adam?"

"Um huh. I don't know how...but I would be willing to hang this steak on it, that that number is tied—somehow--to Adam!"

Adam came out of the bathroom. Dexter met him at the couch. Although these were perfectly grown men who were blood relatives, and quite familiar with each other, they both were uneasy about this coming together. Dexter wanted to be gracious and show his brother a side of him he had not seen since he returned to Shreveport to live. For Adam, he sensed that there was something up Dexter and Norma's sleeves, and they were going to spring it on him sometime during the night. They sat looking at each other with their heads cocked to the side, as close friends sometimes do.

"So, what's up Dex? What's going on with everything? What's gonna happen to us?...what's gonna happen to Brian?"

His voice beginning to quiver…

"You know Adam, I really wish I knew the answer to that." He moved closer to the edge of the couch near Adam. *"You know all the things that have been up in the air since Brian's accident. I know we're all praying for his full recovery, and for him to get back to a normal lifestyle."*

"Man, it really don't look like he can be normal again. He's still in bad shape."

"Well, we'll see what the doctor has to say tomorrow. But, I'll tell you this; I firmly believe that prayer can change things, and God answers prayers. I've seen it in my own life."

"Man, I used to think like that. But I've seen too many things that happened that was bad and wrong, and I always asked where God was in that? I saw one of my co-workers get killed…with my own eyes. I was praying my heart out for God to save him--He died. I saw a kid get bitten by a pit bull, and that little girl died. Where was God? Can you explain that?"

"Hey guys, are you ready to eat?" asked Norma. *"Go ahead and get washed up and I'll have it ready by the time you finish."*

Dexter knew he needed a real miracle to happen tonight. He wanted his brother to ask questions about faith, and trust and even the sovereignty of God. He may not have all the answers, but he was going to rely on the Lord to supply what he needed.

"Okay, honey!… we better get washed up before she calls us again. She gets upset when her dinner gets cold. But, hold that thought, okay. I want to respond to your questions, alright."

"Yeah, I'll hold it, 'cause I want to hear your answer…nooo problem."

Norma asked Dexter to set the table with place mats and flatware. The meal would be consumed at a casual pace, and therefore they had to do the table settings. When they were finished, Norma brought the prime rib platter to the table while it was still sizzling. Adam took in a deep breath and smiled.

"*Now that's what I call some good eating. That looks and smells great, Norma.*"

"*Thank you, sir?*"

"*Hey, nothing but the best for my youngest brother turning 45. Wow! Should we sing happy birthday now, or when we have the dessert, honey?*"

"*Let's wait till dessert!*"

"*Good, let's get after it. You help yourself Adam.*"

Adam was not shy about eating. This was definitely 3 cuts above the fast foods he was so accustomed to eating most days of the week. His doctor had been ordering him to eat a healthier diet for the past several years to little avail. In fact, he was warned to lay off the booze as well because of his damaged liver. Adam simply switched from whiskey to gin. They continued their meal as they shared conversation.

"*You know honey, when we were young; Adam was a spoiled little brat.*"

"*No way!*"

"*Yes, way. You were the youngest boy, and momma had to hold you most of the time, because she didn't want to see you suffer like Brian.*"

"*Brian suffered? How?*"

"*Yeh, he was always sick with fevers, and mom was constantly having to take him to the doctor. Sometimes she gave him some home remedies, that I think was the reason he pulled out of a constant cycle of sickness.*"

"*I never knew that about Brian.*"

"*Oh yeah…mom will tell you. But, when we got older, you started attaching yourself to Brian because he was next to you in age and he was getting stronger to start going out to play. You and he were like two peas in a pod from about the time you turned 4 or 5.*"

"*Well, we've been close, that's for sure.*"

"*Do you remember when you were about 12 or so and mom wanted us to be in a church play, and Brian made himself sick because he didn't want to be in it? And you started crying cause if Brian was not going to be in it, you didn't either?*"

"I remember something like that…yeah, I do."

"You mean to tell me you refused and started crying because of Brian?" Asked Norma?

"Yeah, if he was not going to be in it, I didn't want to either. But, I guess we were that way all the way through high school."

"You guys are that way even now, commented Dexter. Whatever Brian wanted to do, there was you."

"Except when he started his business. I didn't get involved with him when he took over that towing business from dad.

"Why not? What happened that you broke away from him then?" asked Norma.

"I don't really know. I was having some issues with my second wife and our kid, and I was out of a job. I guess I was in sort of a depression. That's what I have heard from a friend I used to work with. She used to talk to me about going to church and letting go of my problems through Jesus Christ. I couldn't see that. Mom was all over me too. So, I just kinda went my own way for a long time. That's when my wife left me and took my son, and all the little money I had in the bank. That hurt me bad. I was really close to taking my own life, man. I was bad off."

"My God, brother, I never knew things were that bad with you. Every time I talked to mom before we decided to move down here, she would just say you're fine, Brian was fine, and that would be the end of it. I should have tried harder to keep in contact with you and Brian. That, I could have done better."

"They were worse than that."

"Oh my God Adam! Are you alright now?" exclaimed Norma.

"I'm better now. Oh yeah…a lot better."

"Thank God!"

By now, Dexter believed that this was the time to let the Holy Spirit lead the conversation. He quietly asked for the Spirit to take over the conversation and bring healing and salvation to his brother. Since he had him in his space, this time would be devoted to him exclusively. The home telephone rang. Dexter excused himself to answer it. He thought it strange that he asked the Holy Spirit to take over, and then the phone rang, breaking the flow of the conversation.

"*Let me get some more water.*" insisted Norma.

"*Hello!*"

"*Hello Dexter, this is Daddy Farrell, how are you?*"

"*Oh hey dad, I'm fine, how are you?*"

"*Fine…fine. Norma okay?*"

"*Yeah, she's fine dad, she's in the kitchen.*"

"*Well, the other day when we talked, you remember we talked about those numbers?*"

"*Oh yes, I remember.*"

"*Well, we got to adding everything up that came to 45, right?*"

"*Right.*"

"*I been thinking about those numbers, and I think I have the answer for you.*"

"*Great dad, great.*"

"*The number 3 was the one representing completeness, and balance, right?*

"*Right.*"

"*The 45 is not 45! The numbers must stand alone. You have the 3 and the 4 and the 5. I think each of the numbers stands alone. Now…I think the Holy Spirit is giving you a message concerning something that's going on with you and around you. Now let me ask you this…do you know who your great-grandfather was?*"

"*It's ironic you ask me that dad, because I have been talking about him even this week…yes, I know who he was…but wait, I think I want Norma and my brother to hear what you're going to say. I'm putting you on the speaker, okay?*"

"*That's fine, hello ya'll.*"

"*Hello, dad!*"

"*Okay, I was saying that the numbers mean something because of what you guys are going through now. Now Dexter, you said you know your great-grandfather. Okay, he represents your first 'base' generation; your grandfather is your first generation, your father represents your second, and you and your siblings represent the third. Now your children (when you have some) would be your fourth, and theirs the fifth. Now if you go back and take a look at your ancestors, you'll get to see who they were and what they did. I had something like this in my church a few years ago. This man's ancestors lived a bad life of drinking and carousing and none of the men in the family ever lived past the age of 55. I mean all down the generations, all the men in the family would die off before they reached that age. It was not until that member of my church came to me and we discussed it and found out that he was the fourth generation. He wanted to break that curse of the devil, so we prayed for him over three nights. Now he repented for his sins; the sins of his fathers and his fathers father who were inflicted with this curse of loosing all the men. Now that was about 15 years ago, and that man celebrated his 69th birthday. His brother was born a year after him on his birthday, and he is now 68. What I want ya'll to know is that there is such a thing as a generational curse and a generational blessing. What's happening in your life today could be dependent on what happened with your fore fathers—even down to your 3rd, 4th and 5th generations. So you take a look at what's going on in your life and know that you can be living in the blessings of God, or the curse of the devil—all the way down through future generations. But remember, that curse can be reversed—but one must repent, and pray for God's amazing grace to forgive the fore fathers for their sins. Alright, does that make since to you now?"*

"Wow... what can I say?... Wow... dad, you don't know how much I appreciate you. With all my heart I want to thank you and the Holy Spirit for that revelation. I really appreciate it."

"Yeah dad thanks. That sure gives us relief from seeing those puzzling numbers. We love you dad. Say hello to mom and I'll talk to her this weekend." said Norma, lovingly.

Dexter placed the phone on the pedestal as he looked at Norma. He then looked at Adam who was sitting at the table while the conversation was going on. He tried to understand what the conversation was about, but managed to understand the talk concerning the curses and blessings. Dexter knew the Holy Spirit answered his prayer. That phone call contained everything Adam needed to hear for Dexter to now zero in on him about his relationship with the Creator of the Universe. Silence filled the air, as Dexter rejoined Adam at the table along with Norma. They continue to eat their now warm meal, and when finished, Norma brought out the cake. They sang happy birthday and Norma divvied up the slices. For tonight, Dexter decided to let the information Adam heard, soak in. He was going to be with him again on Saturday, and that would be a good time to discuss matters of repentance and salvation on the way to Lafayette. For now, he would let the conversation flow as it would flow with Adam leading it. He felt relieved that once again, he could say that God answers prayers.

Chapter 44

ood morning everyone, this is Kitty Kincaid with KLAC
morning news. You may recall a couple of days ago we
brought you an update to the story we aired over two
weeks ago, concerning an explosion that occurred out on highway
1, where several persons died and several were wounded. This
evening at our 6 o'clock news, we'll bring you another update
which will highlight the owner of that business, and his dealings
in a bizarre business that you wont believe. Tune in to KLAC for
all the news and updates at 6 o'clock.

Adam was on his way to work when he heard this blast over the radio.
He was getting his car filled with gas and hearing this infuriated him. What
the hell were they going to expose to the whole world about his brother now?
He became agitated and ceased filling his car to call his brother, Dex.

"Hey, Dex, did you hear that news blast on the radio about Brian?"

"No, I didn't Adam. What did they say?"

"They are going to have a news update at 6 o'clock on the KLAC
television station. They are going to talk about Brian's business—talking
about it was bizarre."

"Well, what can we do bro? I don't feel good about what's happening,
but I'm afraid there's nothing any of us can do about it."

"I am sick of all this. You know momma musta heard about this by now."

"I'm on my way to the hospital now to have that meeting with the doctors. When I finish, I'll give Chase Pierce a call. Maybe he can call the station to get them to stop these news blasts—I don't know if that's reasonable or not, but worth a try."

"Okay, let me know what happens with the doctors, okay?"

"You know I will. Talk to you later."

Dexter decided to call Marvin Klein before he called Chase, just to see if he would give him any more insight into his brothers investigation. Marvin did not answer his phone and Dexter had to leave a message to call him back when he could. Dexter arrived at the hospital about fifteen minutes before the scheduled meeting time. He went into the hospital and down the hall to get into the elevator. As he was about to enter the elevator, he heard a voice calling his name. It was Adam.

"Adam, I thought you had to go to work."

"Yeah, but I think this is more important than going to work. I called in and told them I was having car trouble. I'll go in later."

"Okay...come on up."

As they reached the floor where Brian was assigned, Dexter stopped at the nurses' station to ask about Brian's status.

"May I ask you a question when you finish, nurse?"

"Yes, sure...what is it?"

"Can you tell me what Mr. Simon's condition is today?"

"Well, the doctor will be able to tell you that. It'll be a few minutes and he will be here, okay?"

"Okay, thanks."

Dexter and Adam walked into Brian's room and greeted Sharon with a big hug. Sharon looked tired and drawn from the long hours she had been putting in, by being at Brian's bedside since his accident. She was alone with Brian and was at this bedside stroking his forehead. Occasionally, Brian was able to open his eyes and close them right away. Otherwise, he was non-responsive to any of the conversations she had been having with him. She was anxiously awaiting the doctor's visit, and was very pleased to see her brother-in-laws. Their wait was of short duration. The doctor arrived by 10:05 am.

"Good morning everyone...how are ya'll doing?"

"Good, doctor...we're doing fine. We just want Brian to be doing fine and out of here." said Dexter.

"Okay, let's talk about Brian. Are you'll comfortable?"

"Yes, sir." each responded.

"Okay, Brian is technically in a coma. Coma is a prolonged unconsciousness that is considered a medical emergency, in that there is a traumatic injury to the head. The symptoms are closed eyes; depressed brain reflexes; no response of limbs; no response to pain stimuli, and irregular breathing. Now coma's lasting more than several weeks may transition to a persistent vegetative state. Also, depending on the cause of the coma, people who are in a persistent vegetative state for more than three years are likely never to awaken. Now, because Brian was treated soon after the accident, his brain was preserved and that improves his chances of recovering from the coma."

"So, you're saying that since he was treated soon after the accident, his chance for recovery is good?" asked Sharon.

"Basically, that 's what I'm saying."

"If you put a number to his chances of recovery, what would that be, doctor." asked Brian.

"As far as I can tell, the doctors who saw and treated him when he first came in did a fabulous job. They did what they needed to do in a case like this. So, if that question is answered in the affirmative; I would say it's now up to Brian to eventually come out of it. It is now up to him and the good Lord to have him come back to us. So the number is 50/50."

"Is there anything we can do to help him, doctor? I mean help him to come back?" asked Sharon.

"Talk to him. Tell him you love him...tell him you want him back...

just talk to him as you would when he could answer you. That's about all you can do. Oh, if you wish…you can pray for him, too."

"So, what's going to happen to him, now? asked Adam.

"He's going to be moved to a rehab unit of this hospital. You know that he has around the clock security, right?"

"Yes, we know about that…for his protection." said Dexter.

"What did you hear about that, Dexter?" asked Sharon.

"It's for his protection."

"Oh, Whatever!"

"Okay, do ya'll have any more questions for me?"

"I want to know if you think he's in any pain doctor." asked Sharon.

"No…he's in no pain right now. He's pretty medicated to relieve the pain."

"Okay, good."

"Well, thank you doctor for your time and all the info you gave us. We appreciate it." said Dexter.

"Ya'll have a nice day."

Dexter reached out his arms to surround both Adam and Sharon. He told them that he was pleased that now they know what the prognosis was and they could go forward knowing what the chances of Brian's recovery. Sharon was a realistic person and she simply responded that she thank God that he was still alive. She knew that she might have to care for Brian in a vegetative state for the rest of his life. That was the only issue she had and just wanted him to live.

"Sharon, have you been watching the news, lately?" asked Dexter.

"Off and on…I haven't been looking at much, why?"

"I was just wondering if you saw anything on the news or not."

"I try not to…the news is too depressive for me."

"Good!" responded Adam.

"Why you ask? What's going on in the news?"

"Nothing that's noteworthy." exclaimed Dexter…"have you had breakfast?"

"Yes. I'm okay. I got to go to the tax office to pay for the tag renewal for Brains' car. You think I should tell them the car was wrecked?"

"Yeah. You may not have to pay for the tag if the cars wrecked." explained Adam.

Dexter's cell phone rang. He looked down to see who was calling him. It was Marvin returning his call. He answered it.

"Hey Marvin, how you been?... good,,, I wanted to ask you about something...hold on! ...I'll see you guys later, okay? Sharon, you know we love you, okay? Keep the faith."

Dexter walked outside of Brian's room, leaving Adam and Sharon alone with Brian. Sharon felt conflicted that she must leave Brian for a brief time. Adam decided to leave and head for his job since the meeting was over and Sharon was in a decent place in her spirit. But once again, Adam felt that he needed to brace himself for any news sure to be coming from the conversation between Marvin and Dexter. He went to the side of the bed and began to rub the arm of Brian as he spoke healing into his unconsciousness. He wanted his best friend back. He wanted Brian to regain consciousness and defend himself against all the accusations being hurled against him.

"Wake up Brian, wake up!"

Outside of the room and down the hall from Brains' hospital room, Dexter was talking to Marvin on his cell phone.

"Did you see the news this morning, Marvin?'

"No...what happened?"

"I'm wondering where this Ms Kincaid is getting all her information about Brian and his business. They will be coming on with more details this evening at the 6 pm news. Marvin, do you have any idea where any of this information is coming from?"

"Well, I would start with their Journalist who are investigative reporters. That's their job to get information and develop a story for the 6:00 o'clock news."

"You think that's where all this is coming from and it didn't come from you?"

"That's right. But...there's going to be more...much more to come out as time goes on. Your brother had a thing going for a long time. The best thing for you is to lay low and let the info flow...if you know what I mean."

"How can I, when you are talking about my family, including my own mother?"

"You remember I told you that they have files, right?"

"Right. But what does that mean when it comes to my mom particularly?"

"They are looking at all possible parties involved in this operation... whether they were actively a part of the crimes or facilitators."

"So you're saying my mom is a facilitator?"

"All I know is that I saw a file on her, okay?"

"I think I will go over and speak to her about this."

"I would suggest you say nothing Mr. Simon—are you listening to me?"

"But, like I said, you're talking about..."

"Leave it alone, Mr. Simon. The case is developing and you don't want to be the one who is accused of tampering with potential witnesses, do you?"

No, I do not."

"Nothing more need be said. You have a nice day. By the way, you need to send me another check for three hundred-fifty dollars. I'll send you an invoice, alright?"

"Okay, but hold off on any new investigating until I get back to you ."

"You're the boss!"

Chapter 45

The weekend weather came with a roar. Once again, the bad weather plaguing the northern part of Louisiana for the past three weeks, returned. The wind blew from the south and carried moisture from the gulf, meeting up with the cold air from the north, producing thunderous downpours. Norma wondered if it would ever ease up and go away. She decided to sleep in and catch up on some much needed rest, while Dexter prepared to leave to pick up his brother at his house to start their trip to Lafayette. He drove into Adam's driveway at 7:10 a.m. He honked his car horn once, prompting Adam to come out of the rear door carrying his jacket and a small container.

"Morning Dex!" Adam greeted.

"Morning Adam...how did you sleep last night?" Dexter asked.

"When I finally got to sleep, I slept good. I was up late with my daughter and her friend. She calls herself baking a cake for my birthday and we had a little celebration," said Adam.

"Well, that's great, Adam. Girls seem to always pay attention to their dad, huh? Dexter said.

"This one does...the other one...well...her mother has her brand on her. I don't want to talk about her just in case she's listening," said Adam.

"Okay, let's get this show on the road," said Dexter.

Adam settled in for the long drive, knowing his brother was a talker and would surely keep him awake most of the trip. For Dexter, he was confident that this would be a trip that was sure to open Adam's eyes to much of what Dexter was trying to get across to him. Dexter started the conversation about Brian.

"Listen Adam, are you comfortable with everything you know about Brian?" Dexter asked.

"What do you mean?" asked Adam.

"I mean about what you've found out lately?" said Dexter.

"Well, I still have a problem with getting into Brian's business. I just don't think we need to expose him that way," said Adam.

"Expose him in what way, bro?" Dexter asked.

"What I mean is, he's in a coma and can't defend himself, and everybody going through his business with a fine tooth comb," said Adam.

"Yeah, I understand that too. Now here's my question… what kind of business has he been involved in that would have everybody investigating it? I mean, you said you didn't even know what he did for a living and you're his best friend. Now we find out that there is much more to his business than even you knew," said Dexter.

"It's always been that way, Dex. I never figured he was doing anything wrong. I still don't believe he's been doing anything wrong. As far as I'm concerned…he's doing what dad was doing before he died…towing cars!" responded Adam.

"I think that is part of the problem, Adam. I think Brian took over a family business that involved something else besides just towing cars," said Dexter.

"Like what?" asked Adam.

"What do you think all that was about on the television a couple of days ago? What was that about when we went out to Brian's business and got chased by someone? What was it about when the cops stopped us and you wound up getting beat up by one of the cops? You never told me why that happened to you. When I hired an investigator to help Brian with his accident liability, you didn't want to even hear what he had to say … I

272

mean, ever since I've been back, there has been nothing but secrecy and silence about everything," said Dexter.

"Well, we've always been staying out of everybody's business, that's all," said Adam.

"But in this case, we're just postponing the inevitable. There are some things going on that involves Brian and other family members as well. There is some information that will probably come out, that everybody's going to know about. The veil of secrecy is going to be blown away, and there's nothing we can do about it," said Dexter.

"This is hard to hear, Dex. I'm trying to get this in my mind. It's almost like some movie I've seen before," Adam said.

"You want to know the potential, here? The potential is that we are all going to be effected by not only what Brian may have done, but also what our dad and his dad did," Dexter said.

"What the heck is that all about, Dex? How can anybody be punished for something a dead person has done?" Adam asked.

"What I'm saying is that we in this generation may be punished because of the sins our forefathers have committed. It's like a curse upon this generation that has been passed down through the ages," said Dexter.

"Yeah right! ...I heard your father-in-law say that the other night...do you really believe that stuff, man?" asked Adam.

"Listen, it's in the Bible. It's all over the Bible that God has allowed the sins of the fathers to be visited upon generations to come. It's in the Bible man, and I believe the Word of God..." said Dexter.

"Hey, let's stop in there and get a cup of coffee, you mind?" interrupted Adam.

"Oh sure, no problem. But here's the thing Adam- I want you keep an open mind this weekend. This attorney (Chase) is a really good one. I mean he's dedicated to fully representing his clients and he comes highly recommended. Did you know that he joined the Kappa's when he was in college?...Let's get a sandwich while we're at it, okay?" said Dexter.

"That's fine. I can't believe he joined a black Fraternity," said Adam.

For the next several hours, the brothers conversed about their family situation. Dexter wanted to get Adam to the point where he understood the seriousness of what was soon to come. He thought it best to hold some of the details about what he learned from Marvin until their return trip home. In the meantime, he was resigned to let Chase Pierce press the case about what was involved in the accident case. Perhaps being away from his home turf would demand Adam's attention and understanding the complexities of the case for personal injury. And perhaps he would come to understand what the issues of generational curses were in the interim.

Dex, I really want to get all this shi ...uh, I mean this case about Brian's business behind us. I want Brian to get well, man. I just want my brother to recover and we get back to the life we had before all this happened. I can't believe that he is still in a coma...I just can't believe it," said Adam.

"Be careful with that coffee...its hot!" warned Dexter.

"Yeah, I got it...," said Adam.

"Lord, I thank you for this food we are about to receive, may it be used for the nourishment of our bodies ... Amen," said Dexter.

""Do you always have to bring religion into everything you do, Dex," asked Adam.

"Yes...yes I do. It's not religion per se, Adam ... It's asking God to bless the food like we have always done...even when we were kids. You remember when we did that at home, right?" Dexter reminded him.

"Yeah, but you seem to go overboard with that religious stuff. It makes you look like you're perfect compared to the rest of us," said Adam.

"Perfect? No way, brother. Let me explain something to you... You remember when we were young and were forced to go to church and participate in plays, and singing in the youth choir, etc.? We'll, that was playtime for me. I never really took things serious as I have come to understand since I fully accepted Christ into my life. I did what I was told to do and I thought that was the right thing to do because I wanted to please mom. You remember that, don't you?" Dexter asked.

"Yeah, I do. I was just following what you and Brian were doing," said Adam.

"But, I met Norma at an expo in Chicago 15 years ago, and she was the one who helped me see the missing link in my walk through this life," said Dexter.

"What link are you talking about?" Adam asked.

"She helped me to see that all I was doing was living without a purpose. I wasn't concerned about anybody else. I wasn't even concerned about what was happening to me, as long as I had money in the bank, a job, and I could take vacations when I wanted to. I had girlfriends when I wanted them and a couple of friends I could hang with. Man that was my life, until I found out that that was all a fallacy. I got my bachelor and master's degrees thinking that would make more money for me, and make me happier. My life had no meaning or purpose, no direction. I could feel it in my whole body. I never knew my life could be directed for the good, not only for the sake of myself, but for others as well," said Dexter.

"So, what happened that made you realize what you were doing was wrong?" Adam asked.

"Well, it took me some time to come to the realization that I could have my life directed for good, by simply accepting Christ into my life. Norma helped me get to that point," said Dexter.

"That's it? You just accepted Him?" asked Adam.

"I actually asked Christ to come into my life and become the director. It was like I asked him to take control of this steering wheel and I moved over to the passenger seat and let him drive. Ever since I did that, I have confidence that I have a purpose and I'm being directed by The Holy Spirit for God's purpose," said Dexter.

"You know brother, you almost persuade me to accept Christ," Adam said.

"You are not persuaded by your own power my brother, but by the revelation of the Holy Spirit of God. All you need to do is invite Christ to be your Savior and repent of all your sins. Adam that is all you need to do for you to be accepted into God's Kingdom and to be saved to live with God in eternity. It's really about having a personal relationship with Christ. When he comes into your heart, you become a brand new creature...I mean brand new! Everything in the past is washed away. It's like...poof... you're free from your past sins--the ones you've committed and those that have been passed down from our forefathers. What happens is you stop all the wrong things and start doing the right things. It is truly amazing how that happens. You can do it Adam—the question is...will you accept Christ to become your Savior?" Dexter invited.

"Like I said, I am almost...**almost** persuaded!" Adam said.

Dexter's cell phone rang.

"Good morning, Chase. You up already?"

"I've been up. Are you on your way yet?" Chase asked.

"Oh sure, we're almost there--Probably about another thirty minutes or so. Are you at your office now?" Dexter asked.

"No, I'm headed to the meat market to pick up a few things. That's what happens around this town on Saturday mornings. Say, do you like boudin?" asked Chase.

"Oh, you know it... hey Adam, do you like boudin?" Dexter asked.

"I love it when I can get the real thing," responded Adam.

"My brother Adam wants to know if it's the real thing?" asked Dexter.

"It's as real as it gets. Say, why don't you guys meet me here, and then we can go to my office from here," said Chase.

"That's fine...what's the address?" asked Dexter.

"You got your GPS with you, right? It's... hey Paul, what's your address?... okay, Dexter, it's 8690 Highway 12. You can't miss it. I'll be here waiting for you, alright"

"I got it. See you soon--bye," Chase said.

"Aaww look Dex, we gotta wait now—a funeral's coming, and it's a long one," said Adam.

"Yeah, and it looks like a military one--Probably a kid killed in Iraq. We'll just have to wait," said Dexter.

"How come you never went to the military, Dex? Didn't you ever find a war that you liked?" Adam said.

"As a matter of fact, I never did. I would have served if there was a *draft, Adam. But I was too busy living my life. I was like most of the other guys around my neighborhood that was going to school—we had other things in mind. You know, like girls and parties, and trying to make it. Military was never in our family, and so we never had the tradition, right? Why didn't you join?"* Dexter asked.

"The same. I was too busy chasing, man—you know what I mean. Besides, I saw too many guys get messed up coming back home. They lost their arms, legs, their minds and like this guy—their life," responded Adam.

'I don't know if you know him or not, but we have a cousin in New Iberia who might be forced to join the National Guard. His name is Jason. Have you heard of him before?" Dexter asked.

"Naw, I really don't know any of our family down here," said Adam.

"Well, he's been getting in constant trouble and the judge in New Iberia has threatened to put him in jail or force him to join. As a matter of fact, he's here in Lafayette in the hospital, recuperating from injuries he suffered when the police tried to arrest him," shared Dexter.

"So they beat him up trying to arrest him?" Adam asked.

"Norma and I saw it happen with our own eyes. That's how we came to know Chase Pierce, because uncle Landry and Teeta, his daughter and Jason's mother, highly recommended him," said Dexter.

"I think we can go now—it looks like the last of the cars is about to pass," said Adam.

"You're right. We are not far from the meat house. You know, I didn't even get the name of the place. Let me call him back and let him know we are almost there and I can get the name at the same time," said Dexter.

By the time they arrived at Croute's Meats and Grocery store, many of the locals filled the front section. Some looked as if they had just gotten out of bed, and some were dressed as if they had come out of the fields. Some were black residents and more were white—at least they looked to be white to Adam. They took numbers from the young lady behind the counter as she called out their names while handing them their orders.

"Number 67, Mr. Pierce, your order is ready," the server called out.

Dexter spotted Chase on the opposite side of the store. He waived and headed through a maze of people towards him. Chase made his way to the counter where Dexter and Adam joined him.

"Morning! I'm glad you two made it before everything was gone. How are you doing Adam?" Chase asked.

"I'm doing fine...doing fine! Where's the boudin?" Adam asked.

"Oh, here you go. This is for you guys," Chase said.

"Wait, Chase." interjected Dexter. "Is this all we can have? I mean I can eat all this by myself."

"Oh, no you can have more...that is if they have any left by the time your number comes up. I apologize...I should have asked you how many pounds you wanted... You go ahead and get your number. Imagine this... they make about 2,000 pounds of this stuff for Saturday, and it's all gone before noon," said Chase.

Chase spotted Mr. Latham Dupree from the Cane River Creole Community. Mr. Dupree was on his way back to Natchitoches after visiting his daughter and son-in-law in Lafayette. Chase had represented his daughter in a discrimination lawsuit and won some $67,000 for her--last year.

"Dexter, will you pardon me for just a moment. I need to talk to that gentleman there before he leaves. I'll be right back," said Chase.

"No problem, you go ahead. Adam is in line to get some more boudin," said Dexter.

Chase was with Mr. Dupree for 10 minutes. Dexter surveyed the rest of the store while Adam stood at the counter, waiting for his order. Chase returned to Dexter with a sad look on his face.

"Is everything alright, Chase?" Dexter asked.

"Aw, that was one of my client's father. He just gave me some sad news about a kid he knew who was killed in Iraq," said Chase.

"Oh my God...was he buried today?" asked Dexter.

"No...SHE was buried today!" responded Chase.

"Oh precious Jesus, have mercy!" said Dexter.

"Yeah, it's a sad situation. I still don't understand why they let women serve in a combat zone. War is not supposed to be for your mother, sister or daughter...**damn!** I just can't wrap my arms around the thought of it," Chase said.

"Adam and I passed by that procession on the way here. It was huge and looks like they were headed in the direction of the old cemetery where my grandfather was buried," said Dexter.

"I think so...I really think that's where she will be buried." agreed Chase.

"Hey Adam, are you ready? Did you get the order?" Dexter asked.

"Yeah, I got it. I'm ready. Where are we headed?" Adam asked.

"To my office guys...just follow me," said Chase.

Chapter 46

C hase rolled into his parking lot with Dexter and Adam following closely behind. Starting out as a cool and overcast day, the weather turned into a warm, but breezy afternoon. Chase inserted the key into the front door lock to enter. The door was unlocked. His movements slowed as he eased the door open. He looked backward to catch the eyes of his clients. He raised his right hand to his lips to signal them to remain quiet. As he moved into his front office, he scanned the area. Some of the file drawers behind his secretary's desk were slightly open. Chase became eerily tensed. He eased forward and into his office. His door also was unlocked. He wondered if he forgot to lock his door, and perhaps if his secretary had left the file drawers open. He couldn't recall if that had ever happened before. Just as he arrived at his desk area, he noticed that his middle drawer was open and the contents missing—including the package of money he placed in it until he could figure out what to do with it. The answer to that was now obvious—it was gone. Who did this, he wondered. Perhaps it was the two men who visited him earlier and gave him the money.

"Chase, this does not look good. Are you going to report this to the police?" Dexter asked.

"I need to take a good look to see what's missing before I do that. I had some money in my desk that's missing. I can't prove that, though. I need to see what else is missing first," said Chase.

"You keep money in your desk?" asked Adam.

"Not usually. I was holding some money for a client," said Chase.

Chase resumed his search for other missing items. He could find none. Apparently, whoever did this, knew what they were looking for and found it. No doubt, this was the men who gave him the money in the first place.

"I'm not calling the police--there's nothing to report. Come on in and have a seat gentlemen. We have a lot to talk about. I apologize for the delay 'cause I know you've got to get back home...listen...what I want to talk to you about is your brother. I know you know the complexities of the case. Number one, your brother is still in a coma, and we can't find out from him exactly what happened. Near as I can tell, he was the one who ran the stop light. Regardless of who's at fault, there is a case to be brought to justice. Secondly, your brother has been under surveillance by the Feds. Best, as I can tell, he will be indicted when he recovers. Now, under normal circumstances, I would not have a problem with any of these issues but, I want you both to know what we're up against," said Chase.

"Oh, so now you **don't** want to represent my brother, huh?" asked Adam.

"No that's not it. You need to know that some others don't want me to represent him. I have an idea who it might be, but I can't put a face on them," said Chase.

"On them? ...Chase, where is this coming from?" asked Dexter.

"Listen, I usually don't get into details with my clients but, things started happening when I was in Shreveport. I've had some people following me in cars and helicopters as well," said Chase.

"What! You mean because you are representing my brother?" asked Dexter.

"Dexter, you remember when we talked about the missing bodies in the graveyard just out of town?" asked Chase.

'Yes, I remember," Dexter responded.

"I went out there to investigate your claim myself and guess what..." began Chase.

"What?" Dexter responsed.

"Somebody came up behind me and knocked me out. When I woke up, I found a note on my windshield that in essence said for me to stick to the law," shared Chase.

"What the hell does that mean?" asked Adam.

"That was the same note passed on to me right here in my office, along with the money that's now missing... so listen, I visited with a good friend of mine who got a phone call that he was told to pass on to me," said Chase.

"What was that?" the brothers asked in unison.

"They wanted me to drop my representation and investigations surrounding all this...are you guys following what I'm telling you about what's happening on this case with your brother? And I haven't even talked about your cousin from New Iberia, yet," said Chase.

"So what are you telling us, Chase?" asked Adam.

"I'm telling you that things are going to get ugly. I'm telling you that because I don't scare easily, there's probably going to be trouble brewing for everybody involved. I'm telling you that I haven't even scratched the surface with both these cases and somebody wants me to stop. Anybody going to the extent of becoming violent with me, and making phone calls to get me to stop, has got to be dangerous. You brothers need to know what might be involved so you can prepare yourself and your families...you follow me? I want you to be comfortable with your decision, because it's a serious situation. You may involve your relatives in New Iberia with Jason, and what your PI tells me about your brother, and other relatives," warned Chase.

"So, it is true what Marvin has said about my family members? I mean my uncles and father and grandfather?" asked Dexter.

"What are you talking about Dexter? What did he tell you about our relatives?" asked Adam.

"Apparently so. But...but, I have not had the time to do my due diligence yet. My best guesstimate is, if I am going forward with both cases, it's going to take a lot of time and money, not to mention the resolve it's going to take to withstand the pressure that's sure to come. Are you up for this? I mean are you really up to the pressure that's sure to come?" asked Chase.

"Oh, yes...we have to do this, Chase. We know Brian needs help and he can't do anything to help himself. Jason is definitely going to need help, as his life is just getting started. He could be lost in the system if he can't straighten himself out now," responded Dexter.

"Well, I'm mainly interested in getting Brian what he needs. He's my main concern...I don't even know Jason. I know he's my cousin, but you understand what I mean? But, I don't want to see anybody get in trouble, either. I just don't want anybody getting hurt," declared Adam.

"Listen Chase...I think we're in agreement about going forward with representing Brian and Jason. I think we need to do both, Adam. Now, I know you must protect yourself too. I certainly will pray for you and for all our protection. I know it's going to cost money and I can write you a check for a thousand dollars today. I'm going to do that for both of them. It's not much now, but I'll get back to you when I return from Washing D.C. in a couple of weeks. Please go forward and we'll be watching out for each other, okay? Will that be alright?" Dexter asked.

"Are you sure about that? You want to go forward, no matter what?" Chase asked.

"We want to go forward, right Adam?" Dexter asked his brother.

"Yeah...go forward!" said Adam.

Dexter went to his car to get a check from the glove compartment of his Jeep Cherokee. When he returned, he pointed to the photo on the wall, picturing his and Adam's grandfather. Adam moved closer to get a good look. Dexter wrote the check and gave it to Chase. Chase asked if he could send a receipt on Monday when his secretary returned to work. They agreed. The time was getting late and Adam wanted to get back to Shreveport before night fall. Chase shook hands with his clients and walked them to the front door. Dexter turned to Chase again and asked if he wanted to call the police. Chase declined and waved goodbye.

"Say, I think I will pass by the old graveyard so I can show Adam where his grandfather was buried," said Dexter.

"I would be careful if I were you. You know what happened to me out there. I would just be careful, that's all," warned Chase.

It seemed as if this weekend was one devoted to funerals, visits to graveyards and hospitals. After Dexter left Chase's office and headed towards the old graveyard he previously visited with Norma, he remembered that Jason was in the local hospital and they had not seen him since his incarceration. Since the GPS showed that the hospital was just a few blocks off the path to get to the graveyard, he asked Adam if he would not mind if they stopped to see him for a few minutes.

"I guess it's alright since we're not going to get back to Shreveport before dark...why not? But, when we finish, we need to get something to eat, don't you think?" asked Adam.

"You mean that boudin won't fill you up?" Dexter said, while smiling.

"I'm keeping this 'till I get home. It sure smells good, huh?" said Adam.

Earlier weather forecasts warned of some severe conditions moving in from the west about 8 p.m., and lasting until midnight, around Lafayette. Dexter's intentions were to get to see Jason and then drop by the graveyard before heading back home. They arrived at the hospital about 5:15 p.m. The air felt like it had cooled at least 5 or 6 degrees. They hurried to the front entrance and inquired from the receptionist which room Jason occupied.

"He's in the cafeteria right now. I saw him and an officer pass this way about 10 minutes ago. You can find him right through there," said the receptionist.

"Thank you ma'am. Is the food any good in there?" asked Dexter.

"Today they have crawfish etouffe over brown rice with vegetables. I think you'll like it," she responded.

"*Thanks, ma'am. Let's go so we can spend some time with him before he has to leave, Adam,*" said Dexter.

"*I'm with you,*" said Adam.

"*Over there...that's him sitting with the police officer,*" pointed out Dexter.

"*Hello, Jason.*"

"Step back... this man is a prisoner!" warned an accompanying officer.

"*I do understand officer, he's also our cousin. Can we just have a moment while he eats?*" asked Dexter.

"*You can't talk to him while he's eating. You have to wait till he gets back to his room in 15 minutes,*" said the officer.

"*But we're from out of town, sir...we're leaving tonight and we just wanted to say hello before we go,*" said Dexter.

"*Alright...I'm gonna sit right here...go ahead and talk for a couple of minutes,*" said the officer.

"*Hey Jason...how are you feeling?*" asked Dexter.

"*I'm alright, who are you guys?*" Jason asked.

"*Oh...this is my brother Adam, and I'm Dexter from Shreveport,*" he said.

"*You was the one that was here a couple of weeks ago? You tha one who saw the cops beat me up, right?*" Jason asked.

"*My wife and I saw the incident--yes. Listen Jason, we hired a lawyer to represent you when you go to court,*" said Dexter.

"*You hired that white lawyer?*" Jason asked.

"*His name is Chase Pierce. He has a great reputation, Jason...even from your mother and grandfather. You need to be sure you cooperate with him because you're really going to need his services,*" said Dexter.

"*Yeah, right!*" Jason said, defiantly.

"*Hey, this is the first time I've seen you son.*" advised Adam. "*But what I heard, you're going to need some help. One of the things you can't do is fight with the police, man.*"

"*You don't even know anything that they did to me, man. You don't even know what they been doing to me for the last year,*" said Jason.

"*What? Why don't you tell me about it!*" Dexter prompted.

"*I ain't telling you nothin with this cop sitting right here. They just want to hear me say something so they can lock me up and throw away the keys,*" said Jason.

"*Who told you that?*" Dexter asked.

"*He did. Didn't you?*" Jason said, confronting the officer angrily.

"**Okay, that's it... it's time to go back to your room.** *This conversation is over, gentlemen!*" said the officer.

"*Okay...okay sir. Jason, we want you to know that we are praying for you, okay? You just cooperate with Chase Pierce and everything is going to be alright...okay? ...Hang in there, little cousin!*" said Dexter.

"*That's cool. I 'preciate that,*" said Jason.

Dexter and Adam watched as the restraining officer led Jason back to his room. He placed no cuffs on him but he held him by his left elbow. Jason walked haltingly, so it probably would not be in the cards for him to try to run away in his condition. After Jason was out of sight, Adam looked at Dexter.

"*Man, that kid needs a lot of help if he fought with the cops. I know what these cops will do to make sure they throw the book at you, whether it's legal or not,*" said Adam.

"*I understand your feelings, brother... but I think Chase will do a good job for him...I really do ...You ready to go?*" asked Dexter.

"*Wait, what about eating here, Dex? That etouffe sounds good to me,*" said Adam.

"*Okay but, we only have about a half hour before it starts getting dark. We still have to stop by the graveyard so I can show you the open graves,*" said Dexter.

"*Aw, we got time. I'm in no hurry,*" said Adam.

"*Okay...I don't want to hear any complaints,*" said Dexter.

By the time they both finished their cheap, but tasty meal, the time was 6:00 p.m. Dexter looked at his watch and signaled for Adam to hurry. They said goodbye to the receptionist as they exited the hospital front door. Adam complimented her for a good recommendation for dinner. The atmosphere was heavy with moisture and it began to drizzle. Dexter unlocked the car and turned on the ignition and wipers.

"Turn on the heater too when it warms up. Man, it's getting chilly out there," said Adam.

"Give me a minute and it should be warm enough. You want to hear some news or music?" asked Dexter.

"Lets hear some of that Zydeco/Creole music they play down here. Man that music sure makes you rock. I love to see the real Creoles dance that French La' La... Hey, let the good times roll, shah!" said Adam.

"You sound just like one of them ...But try not to rock the car, okay?" said Dexter.

By the time they reached the graveyard, there was a faint light shining at the entrance. This light flickered on and off as the winds blew. Adam questioned whether they should go forward as he was always scared of the dark, especially in a graveyard.

"Adam, you need to face your fears, brother. Besides, there is nobody out here to harm you—they are all dead. Look in that glove compartment and hand me that flashlight, will you," said Dexter.

"I don't see one in here," said Adam.

"Oh, I forgot I left it in my garage. Well...that's alright. Come on-- we can see some with that light up there," said Dexter.

The wind whistled through the old oaks, just as they do every night. But the air was turning cool and moist, giving them a reason to spend as little time as possible among the sites. Adam followed behind Dexter while looking backward every few steps forward. Dexter remembered the trail he and Norma took and he tried as best as he could to follow it.

"Okay, be careful around here, Adam...there are some holes in the ground and you could step in one of them. Stay close to me," Dexter warned.

"*Don't worry...I'm right behind you,*" said Adam.

"*Okay...somewhere about here... there was a grave... Wait!...*" said Dexter.

"*For what? What is it?*" asked Adam.

"*Hold on Adam...did you hear something?*" asked Dexter.

"*What tha hell you talking about, Dex? All I hear is the wind blowing! Don't try to scare me, man!*" said Adam.

"*No, I did hear something that sounded like... wait, did you hear that?*" asked Dexter.

"*I heard something, but what was it?*" said Adam.

"*I don't know...come on...let's keep going,*" said Dexter.

"*Keep going? What tha hell Dex. If you heard something, I am not going any further. Let's get out of here,*" said Adam.

"*Wait a second...just stand still for a second...don't move!*" said Dexter.

Adam was frozen stiff. He recalled another time about a month ago when Dexter had him in a scary position like this when they went to investigate Brian's business. And once again, he was scared out of his wits. Only this time, he was in a graveyard and throughout his life he was never certain if there were ghosts hanging around graveyards or not.

"*Alright, let's go this way.*" whispered Dexter.

"*Dex do you know where you're going, man? Why don't you show me what you want me to see from here?*" asked Adam.

"*It's not far... let's keep going this way. I can see from my car lights over this way. I promise we won't be long... watch your step...,*" said Dexter.

"*Oh Lord Jesus, please help us.*" prayed Adam.

"*I stand in agreement with that prayer, Adam. Lord, hear our prayer,*" said Dexter.

As Dexter lead Adam approximately 30 or 40 feet further, he came to the indentation in the ground where a grave would have been.

"*Here... this is the one I'm talking about ...This is where our grandfather's grave was,*" said Dexter.

"What do you mean where it was? Did somebody dig him up?" Adam asked.

"Yeah they did ...or moved him some place else, without the families permission. He's not the only one that's been moved or dug up, either," said Dexter.

"There's some more like this one?" asked Adam.

"You bet...com on, let's go over this way," said Dexter.

"Wait, Dex. Man, do we have to go further? ...I can't see any lights back in there. I can take your word for it... don't you think we should go?" asked Adam.

"I just didn't want to have to come back here later. If we can take a picture of the empty graves, we can get this info to somebody to investigate what's happening out here. I left my camera phone in the car. I'll need to go back and get it...Do you want to stay here or...?" asked Dexter.

"Hell no! I ain't staying out here, and when I leave, I ain't coming back, either," said Adam.

"Well come on with me then—It'll take a few minutes," said Dexter.

Adam grabbed onto Dexter's arm as they starting walking back towards his car. Suddenly, a single shot cracked the sounds of the night.

Blam!

"Dex! That was a shot! Somebody's shooting at us!" yelled out **Adam.**

"Get down, Adam... *get down here!"* cried Dexter fading his voice to a whisper.

Both men scrambled to hide behind a grave marker that yielded little protection. Dexter was leaning against the marker with his back to it, as Adam squeezed against Dexter's chest kneeling in a fetal position.

Blam!

"Adam, I don't think they are aiming at us. That is probably a poacher hunting for a deer or something," reasoned Dexter.

Blam!

The next shot ricocheted off the side of the marker where they were hiding. They laid deeper into the ground where a grave was once occupied. Both were breathing heavily. They knew the shots were meant for them, now. For Dexter, nothing like this had ever happened to him before. He was now coming face-to-face with evil. He believed that we should love our brothers, but this was taking things too far. How was he going to get himself and his brother out of this situation? he wondered. He heard three shots and things went silent. Were they waiting for another shot? The last one came so close; the shooter obviously could see them even in the darkened night.

"Adam, do you feel that?" Dexter asked.

"What?" asked Adam.

"Something is warm and wet on my leg," said Dexter.

"I'm sorry man... I didn't mean to pee on you, but I couldn't help it... I'm sorry, but what are we going to do?" Adam asked.

"I only heard three shots, right?" said Dexter.

"Yeah, why?" asked Adam.

"I think that's all... I don't think they're still there, or I don't think they are going to shoot at us again," said Dexter.

"How tha hell do you know that?" asked Adam, unconvinced.

"I don't... but it seems quiet now. Maybe if we get up from this muddy ground and make a dash towards the Jeep, we can get out of here," said Dexter.

"Man, you been watching too many movies. Somebody shoots at us in the middle of the night and the third shot almost takes our head off, and you want to make a mad dash for the car... You gotta be smoking something... **you** make a dash for it and see what happens," said Adam.

"Okay, you get off my legs, and keep your head down... I'm going to run to the car. When I get there, I'll turn the engine on and you come running," said Dexter.

"Not on your life are you going to leave me here...I'm going with you," said Adam.

"Okay, let's go!" Dexter said.

Running in a zigzag pattern, Dexter and Adam ran low and fast. Adam made it to the passenger side ahead of Dexter. He grabbed at the door handle and his hand slipped off. He grabbed again and opened it. He jumped in and slumped down under the dash. Dexter jumped in and searched for his keys. He found them on the seat.

"Hurry up, Dex. Let's get out of here... Come on start the car," said Adam.

"I'm trying...I'm trying!" said Dexter.

Red and blue lights flashed behind their car. Another car with lights flashing pulled in behind the first car. It was the local police from Lafayette. Dexter looked in the rear view mirror and then the side mirror.

"Good Lord, what now?" said Dexter.

"What is it? Who is... Oh hell... what is going on now?" Adam asked.

"You, in the car...turn off your engine and throw the keys out the window...now!" the voice of an officer rang out.

The officers exited their cars with their guns drawn to a firing position. The officer in the first car approached the Jeep on the driver's side and the one in the second approached on the passenger's side.

"Open your doors and both of you get out with your hands up!" the two officers warned.

"Do what they said Adam... Let's not get ourselves shot. **Okay officer... we're coming out with our hands up, okay?"** *said Dexter.*

As strange as it seemed, Dexter and Adam were being caught up in a law enforcement web just as they did a month or so ago. This time, guns were pointed at them in the dark of night and any wrong moves could result in their being shot. They knew they were innocent of any wrong doings, but at the moment, they needed to follow the directions being given by the men behind the guns. Dexter knew how his brother could be and he hoped and prayed that he would restrain himself so that cooler heads would prevail when they finally were able to tell their story.

"Turn around and lean against the car...both of you!" said one of the officers.

As soon as commands were given, they both complied. Adam hoped they would not command him to do anything he found offensive, as he could loose his cool. It was still getting cold and the rain was falling in a drizzle. Nonetheless, the ground was wet and soggy, and he hoped that he would not be forced to kneel.

"Place your hands behind your head and get down on your knees!" he ordered.

"Hey, wait a minute officer..." responded Adam.

"Get on your knees, now!" he demanded forcefully.

"Okay, okay officer... get down Adam...do as he says," said Dexter.

The officers approached the two of them while they were down in the puddles of water forming around their car. Dexter decided to remain quiet and let the police do what they thought they needed to do to feel safe. After all, it was dark and he wanted nothing to go wrong that would give them a reason to pull their triggers.

Both officers placed handcuffs on each of them and then ordered them to get up.

"What ya'll doing out here in this graveyard at this time of night?" one of the officers questioned them.

Dexter spoke first.

"I am glad you asked, officer. We actually came out here to see our grandfather's grave before we went back to Shreveport. We were running late from visiting with our cousin who is in the hospital. We were about to leave at the time you stopped us," said Dexter.

"So, why were you shooting out here?" one of the officers asked.

"That was not us, you nits. Somebody was shooting at us...we were trying to get away from them!" said Adam, with irritation.

*"Somebody was shooting at **you**? ...You expect us to believe that? ...you boys need to lean against the hood over here. Do you mind if we search your car? You got any weapons in there or on you?" the officer asked.*

"Oh no, officer...we don't carry weapons. Sure you can search the car... we've got nothing to hide." answered Dexter.

*"Dex, you don't have to **let** them search your car. They have no probable cause. Don't let them do it, man!"* Adam said.

"It's alright, Adam. I've got nothing to hide," responded Dexter.

"I'm telling you man...they don't need to search your car without a reason, and we haven't given them a reason. They can't just stop somebody and ask if they can search your car!" Adam said with increasing alarm.

"I know, but it's really okay...go ahead officers...you'll see...there nothing there!" said Dexter.

"Dex!" Adam shouted out.

"Adam, please!" Dexter said.

The second officer acting as the back-up, pointed to the hood of the car. Dexter was already sitting on the front of the hood and Adam moved next to him. The first officer went to the passenger's side and started searching. He looked into the glove compartment, and then under the seat. He found nothing. He then looked over the rear seat and saw the small container Adam had brought with him for the trip. The officer went to the rear passenger door and opened it. He leaned in to capture the container which had a zipper on the top side. He unzipped it and looked in. He saw a vial containing medication for Adam's medical condition. On the inside of the container was a zipper which had a bulge protruding. He unzipped it and reached in to extract a small caliber pistol. The officer raised up and looked at his partner who was standing in front of the brothers. They caught each others eyes. The searching officer raised up the pistol and nodded to his partner. The search officer pressed the button on his radio and requested assistance of a supervisor. He joined his partner at the front of the car.

"Okay, you want to take these handcuffs off of us now, sir and let us explain what happened?" asked Dexter.

"Not yet. I want you to explain something for me...whose container is this?" asked the officer.

"That's my container, damn it! You have no right to search his car without probable cause...that is the law, sir!" said Adam.

"But you say this is your container...is this also your weapon in here?" the officer asked.

"Wait a minute...what weapon are you referring to? There's no weapon in my car," said Dexter.

"What's this?" said the officer, holding up the gun.

"What? ...I, ...I, Adam, is that...? Oh no...I knew nothing about that... Adam, don't say anything else ...Just don't say anything else," said Dexter.

"I tried to tell you they could not search your car if you didn't give them permission... I tried to tell you!" said Adam.

"I wish you had told me you had that, and what for?...**man!**" Dexter shouted.

"Do you have a permit to carry a weapon, sir?" the officer questioned Adam.

"Adam, I think it best we do no more talking as we have not consulted with an attorney," said Dexter.

"Sir, we have not charged you with anything... I merely asked if you have a permit?" the officer asked again.

"Do you Adam?" Dexter said, turning to his brother.

"Sure do," said Adam.

"You do? Well show it to him then. Man, I didn't know all this...go ahead and show him so we can get out of here," said Dexter.

"I don't have it with me...I left it at home," said Adam.

Another police car arrived on the scene and stopped behind the second car. This was the sergeant on duty. She exited the patrol car and communicated with her base that she had arrived at the scene. She walked to the front of Dexter's car where all lights were shinning on them.

"What you got here officer Wayne?" she asked.

"Well, I was patrolling the nearby area when I heard several gunshots. After the third shot, I could tell it came from over here in this area. I drove *in and found these gentlemen trying to hurry to get into their car. I called for back-up and we engaged them. I asked why they were in here at night firing a weapon. They said they heard somebody shooting at them. I asked if I could search their car and the driver answered affirmative. Now the passenger wanted him to decline. I searched the car and found that the passenger was carrying this weapon. He said he had a permit, but he didn't have it with him," the officer said.*

"Listen ma'am, officer, sergeant, I can explain everything, please," said Dexter.

"*I will give you the opportunity to do that, sir. Just hold on for a minute and I'll be right with you. Wayne, come over here with me. Officer Drake, you keep an eye on these gentlemen for me, please," said the officer.*

The sergeant in charge and the responding officer discussed the situation for about five minutes and then returned to the brothers.

"*Sir, are you sure you weren't firing your weapon at a deer or some other animal there in the woods?" asked the officer.*

"*I can assure you sergeant, we did not fire any weapons. You can probably smell the gun to see if it was fired…I guess you can tell… can they Adam?" Dexter asked.*

"*Yeah, sure…the last time I fired it was at the range about…four months ago," said Adam.*

"*Check it out Wayne. Don't touch the grip," said the officer.*

"*No, I can't smell anything fresh," said Dexter.*

"*There you go… I told you it wasn't us!" said Adam with glee.*

"*I think we better get you gentlemen inside a warm dry place so you can tell me your story about what happened out here. Because there were shots fired, there's going to be somebody reporting that they heard them and we need to have an explanation for them, that's all," said the officer.*

"*Well, can you remove these cuffs, please?" asked Dexter.*

I could, but just for your protection and ours, let's just get you to the station first and we'll take them off," said the officer.

"*Well how do you expect us to drive over there with these on?" questioned Adam.*

"Don't worry, we'll get you there," said the officer.

"Oh man, you mean you're treating us like criminals, sergeant. We are not criminals, I can assure you. Would you please allow us to drive to your station? I promise we will not give you any trouble," said Dexter.

"I'll tell you what, your passenger can ride in the back of Officer Wayne's car and you can drive your car between Officer Wayne and Officer Drake. I'll follow behind you all. Okay, take the cuffs off and let's get to the station," the officer ordered.

Chapter 47

Sergeant Paula Stratham, a ten year veteran of the force, violated the policy of the LPD by allowing a detainee to drive himself to the station, while removing the handcuffs from the detainee riding in Officer Wayne's car. If anything went wrong on the way to the station, and either of them was to break free from the arrangement, she could be severely reprimanded. She decided to turn on the emergency lights and ordered her subordinates to do the same. Dexter saw the lights flashing and thought this was excessive show on her part and it made him feel like a criminal. This had never happened to him before and he prayed for God's protection. He knew that his faith would help him get through this ordeal and there must be a reason God has for him to be here at this time. All he thought about was that this was a test of God's purpose and it will somehow be revealed. In no time, they pulled into the rear of the station and parked just outside of the rear door. Other officers were on their way into the station and held the door open when Adam was taken from Officer Wayne's car. Dexter exited his car and jogged into the station unescorted. Sergeant Stratham wanted it to appear that she was bringing in two suspects for questioning. She ordered them into an interrogation room.

"Have a seat in there. Do you want some water or a soft drink?" she asked.

"Oookaay...I'll have a coke." said Adam.

"I'm okay... I don't want anything. Thank you, though. Can we tell you our story Sergeant, so we can get on the road to Shreveport?" asked Dexter.

"Oh, you're from Shreveport, huh? ...both of you?" she asked.

"Yes, we're brothers. Do you want to see any ID?" asked Dexter.

"That would be good. Officer Wayne will take those—you know what to do Wayne," said Sgt. Stratham.

"Yes Sergeant... I got it," said Officer Wayne.

"Okay now; I want to hear your story about being there in the graveyard--how did that happen?" asked Stratham.

Just as Dexter and Adam were about to tell their story, two officers were struggling with a middle-aged man who appeared intoxicated and acting belligerent. His slurred voice filled the station and drowned out the casual conversation they were having in the side room with the door open.

"Hell, I ain't drunk.... I was... I was... dancing...," the man said.

"Yeah, I know Pete---you can dance here for a while, like you did last week," an officer responded to him.

"Let me close this door so we can hear each other ...Now where were we on your story?" asked Sgt. Stratham.

"Okay, Sergeant, we are visiting here from Shreveport. We have a cousin in the hospital here and we visited him for a while, before we decided to go by the graveyard to visit our grandfather's grave. Unfortunately, it was getting late and we needed to hurry before it got too dark. We didn't make it in time. But, we thought we could still see with my car lights," said Dexter.

"I'll be honest with you... I was scared to go in there but my brother knew where his grave was so I went on with him. That's when somebody started shooting at us." admitted Adam.

"You mean somebody was shooting at **you**?" the sergeant asked.

"We heard the first shot and we ducked behind a marker. After the second one, I thought it might have been somebody trying to shoot at a deer or something. By that time, the third one hit the marker where we were hiding. We knew then that someone was shooting at us," continued Adam.

"But why? Why would anybody do that?" asked Sgt. Stratham.

"I wish I knew! In fact Sergeant, we have a lawyer friend who told us that somebody knocked him out one night when he was out there," said Dexter.

"What was **he** doing out there?" the Sgt. Stratham said with a questioning tone.

"Okay, here it is… He, as well as we, were there trying to find out what happened to our grandfathers casket. There are some missing graves out there Sarge," reported Dexter.

"Missing graves?" Officer Wayne questioned.

"Yes ma'am, at this yard, we counted at least 6 or 7 … Dug up… gone!"

"I see. Well… let me see what Officer Wayne's got. We'll go back out there and check things out when this rain stops. Let me get you that drink and I'll be right back. You gentlemen just relax for a second," said the sergeant.

"Do you mind if I make a phone call to my wife back in Shreveport, sergeant?" said Dexter.

"It's okay, you go ahead," the sergeant said.

Sergeant Stratham joined Officer Wayne at the computer located towards the front of the station. She asked Officer Drake to get a coke from the kitchen and give it to Adam.

"Okay, what you got, anything?" asked Sgt. Stratham.

"I checked the first one… Dexter R. Simon. He's clean… I can't find anything on him," said Officer Wayne.

"What about his brother?" the sergeant questioned.

"This one (Adam T. Simon) is strange… he got a code 6 on him out of Shreveport," she responded.

"Code 6? That's …that's with **Homeland Security** … What tha hell?" the sergeant said alarmed.

"That's a "detention if necessary" order with their codes, right?" she asked.

"Let's look at the new codes... just to be sure... if that brother has a gun and he don't have a permit, that code means we got to detain him. You get the new codes for me and I need to call the Lieutenant... Drake, come here... you go back in there and just tell them we'll be right with them—it'll be just a few more minutes and you stay in there with them... gimmie tha code book Wayne!" the sergeant yelled.

Dexter made the call to Norma to tell her that he and Adam would be home later than anticipated, but not to worry. He did not want to alarm her unduly and explained that they were investigating the situation at the graveyard. Norma expressed that she wanted him home as soon as possible, but she wanted them to be safe.

Chapter 48

When the weekends come to a southern town below Interstate 10, the powers-that-be like to participate in community events which includes; crawfish boils, bar-b-que's and Commission Meetings. This Saturday night, Sergeant Paula Stratham felt the need to call Lieutenant Alfred, who was participating in a meeting of the Commission on the Needs of Women. The lieutenant was not on the agenda to speak, but he was deeply concerned about this commission and its work. When his cell phone vibrator went off, he looked down to see who was calling. Since he recognized that the call was coming from his sergeant, he decided to leave the meeting room to answer it.

"This is Lieutenant Alfred."

"Lieutenant, this is sergeant Stratham at Precinct 3."

"Yeah, Paula what you got?" Lt. Alfred asked.

"I've got a Code 6 situation with a man from Shreveport, and the code book is not quite up to date on what we are supposed to do with him-- besides detain him. He had a gun in his car when we searched it and he didn't have a permit with him. What do you think I should do with him?" said Sgt. Stratham.

"Hold on… are you saying that the code book is not up to date?" asked Lt. Alfred.

"Well, *its dated six months ago, and I know there was some new directives that came in from Homeland Security, but it's not in here*," Stratham responded.

"Well, *you have to go by what you have now, Paula. What was the reason for the search and seizure?*" he asked.

"*Officer Wayne heard shots being fired out near the old cemetery, and he determined that they were coming from their car...at least he thought they fired the shots*," she said.

"*The old cemetery is not in your precinct...what was he doing out of the precinct?*" Lt. Alfred asked.

"*This is our weekend to cover for the sheriffs in the Parish. You remember our agreement to cover for them to save money?*" Stratham reminded him.

"*Okay, I got it. Well, let me ask you this...did you find out who did the shooting?*" Lt. Alfred asked.

"*Not yet. We brought them in to find out their story...!*" said the sergeant.

"*Who are* **they**? *I thought you said you had a suspect!*" Lt. Alfred said.

"*It's his brother that was driving. He didn't know about the gun, apparently*," the sergeant said.

"*What's their name?*" Lt. Alfred asked.

"*The older one that was driving the car is named Dexter and the one with the gun is named Adam Simon*," said Stratham.

"*What was the last name?*" the lieutenant asked.

"*Simon*," Stratham answered.

"*Wait a minute, these guys are from where?*" Lt. Alfred asked.

"*Shreveport*," the sergeant responded.

Sergeant ... you have persons of interest in a much larger case ... Listen... I want you to hear me clear ... I want you to book them under suspicion of carrying an illegal firearm... Now, its very important that you follow this exactly as I'm telling you... do not, I repeat... do not allow them to make any phone calls... take away their cell phones, and do not

allow them to call anybody. Since it's the weekend, I can't talk to anybody
at Homeland Security. We'll have to wait 'till Monday. Do you understand
what I'm saying to you Paula?" Lt. Alfred asked.

"Yes sir...I understand," Stratham said.

"That last name is hot! There's something going on back there in
Shreveport that's so hot, we could get our heads rolled if we don't handle
them right. So we got to get some directions from HLS. So just book 'em
for the weekend, until Monday," the lieutenant said.

Sgt. Stratham hung the telephone up and leaned back in her chair.
Officer Wayne came to her and asked how things went. Sergeant
Stratham could not tell him all that she heard, but decided to give him
some simple instructions.

"You and Officer Drake take the two of them to the booking area and
process them. Tell then its LPD procedure to go through this process until
they can get them cleared through the system. Place them in the holding cell
for now. I need to make a call to a friend of mine in Shreveport to get some
more information. Okay, you got that?" said Stratham.

"Got it," Officer Wayne responded.

When Officer Wayne got to the interrogation room where Dexter
and Adam waited for their return, Dexter was just hanging up from
a call he had placed to Chase Pierce to let him know about the delay
they had on their return trip home. He left a message on his cell phone
that they were being held and questioned at LPD.

"I need you gentlemen to come with me, please," said Officer Wayne.

"Where we going now, Officer?" asked Dexter.

"We are going to the processing room. It's just our policy to go through
the fingerprinting process to get you cleared through the system...this way
gentleman," Officer Wayne responded.

"Hold up, officer...what are you saying? Why do you have to process
us? I do not like what I'm hearing here," responded Dexter.

"Sir, we heard shots out there. You say it didn't come from either of you.
We don't know where it came from. For all we know, you may have thrown
the weapon into the woods before we got there. It's raining out and we can't

find out until we get some daylight. We need to hold you at least 'till daylight and we can get you cleared through the system. In the meantime, we have to do this. Now please, follow me," Officer Wayne repeated.

Dexter was getting to the point of wanting to blow off some steam. He was not accustomed to being placed in a situation where he had no control. They had to be processed in the system like they were criminals. How long would his patience last, he thought, before his faith in God would be severely tested? He did not want to lose it, especially with his brother looking on. It was unbelievable for him to tolerate what he was being put through right now. He prayed.

"Lord, I trust you to get us through this ordeal. I do not know what your purpose is right now, but I am going to remain silent and let your Holy Spirit work this out for your purposes. If I must endure this for your purpose, let me be your instrument for good, in spite of these negative circumstances. I ask it in Jesus' name, Amen," Dexter prayed.

"Amen…what are we going to do, Dex? Adam asked.

"We are going to obey the authorities, Adam…that's all we can do at this point," Dexter said.

"Man, I don't believe this…this is for the birds… How long are you guys going to violate our right as citizens of these United States, huh?" I guarantee you there's going to be some calls made to the Civil Rights Commission, the NAACP and Jessie Jackson… I don't believe this, Dex," said Adam.

"I do think we need to make a call to our attorney, officer," Dexter said.

"I am sorry 'bout that. I need your cell phones as well." said Officer Wayne.

"Why?" asked Dexter. "If you are going to detain us, we should have the right to an attorney. Now I need to make that call."

Sorry… You need to empty out your pockets and give me that phone… and yours too. Now, if you gentlemen want to play hardball, I can go there." ordered Officer Wayne.

At the moment the two brothers surrendered their phones, Dexter's phone rang. The detaining officer looked at it and placed in into a plastic bag. He did the same with Adam's phone. After three rings, the phone went silent. Adam's phone rang within a minute of Dexter's. Officer Wayne ignored both calls.

"Sir, those calls were probably our family trying to find out when we will be home. Now I need to at least call me wife back as she is pregnant with our triplets," said Dexter.

"What? Dex, you and Norma are going to have triplets? …how come you guys didn't tell me, man? You are finally going to have a kid, huh? Not one, but 3? Congratulations bro," said Adam with excitement.

"Thanks Adam. We wanted to wait to tell everybody when we had our next doctor's appointment," said Dexter.

Officer Wayne continued to process them with fingerprinting and photo ID. He was seemingly not deterred with Dexter's announcement as he was following orders from his sergeant. Dexter's phone rang again, but to no avail. Both pleaded for the use of their phones for one more call, but were refused. When the processing was completed, the brothers were placed in a holding cell, along with Pete, the drunk who was brought in earlier. Pete was asleep on one of the medal benches attached to the wall. The small 10' by 10' cell smelled so bad Dexter almost threw up the meal he had earlier at the hospital. The thick metal door slammed shut behind them.

"Dex, man I'm sorry I got you in this mess by bringing my gun. I always carry it with me and I just didn't think anything about having it with me this time. But still, this is Bull shi#@!!!" Adam said in frustration.

"That's not going to help us brother. What they need to do is get back to the graveyard and see that there's damage to that marker. But Adam, do you see what's happening here? I mean, there are too many things that don't add up here. You got the missing graves, the explosion back home with skeleton bones found in the warehouses behind Brian's business, people shooting at us in the dark of night, Homeland Security investigating our own brother and other family members, Chase getting knocked out being in that graveyard, the old man care-taker disappearing when Norma and

I were there. Something has been happening here and in Shreveport that is not right. And…and, somebody does not want us to find out about it. Now listen Adam, I need to know if you know anything about any of this… anything at all…we've got to get to the bottom of this before somebody else gets hurt. What do you know, brother?" Dexter prodded.

"All I know is Dex, that Brian had a contract to transport cars, trucks, whatever from southern Louisiana back to Shreveport. I know he was getting paid for his work and he was putting it away," responded Adam.

"Was he only hauling or transporting cars and trucks?" Dexter asked.

"Whatever they wanted him to haul. You know that was the business dad had before he died, right?" asked Adam.

"I thought he ran a tow truck business, yes.

"Did you ever participate with him in his business, Adam?" asked Dexter.

"I rode with him a couple of times, when he came down to New Iberia and Abbeville," said Adam.

"What was he hauling when you came with him?" asked Dexter.

"I couldn't say…he picked up trailers that were covered tightly with a tarp. All he did was hook onto it and delivered it to the warehouse behind his shop," said Adam.

"Well, could it have been caskets in those trailers?" asked Dexter.

"Caskets?...hell, I don't know…I guess it could have been…it was big enough for one, two, maybe up to four to fit in it… wait, you think Brian was hauling caskets in his business?" asked Adam.

"I'm thinking that there is a possibility…and it could be he was getting them from somebody who would be in the burial business," said Dexter.

"You mean funeral homes?" asked Adam.

"Exactly! But, what would be the purpose of having Brian haul caskets from southern Louisiana back to northern Louisiana, as well as daddy? You would think they would use a hearse or something like that," said Dexter.

"I remember daddy used to travel down here on a regular basis when we were kids," said Adam.

"I remember that, too. So what was his business when he came here?" wondered Dexter out loud.

"Did you guys… say something 'bout … a funeral home or graveyard?" asked Pete, as he woke up from his sleep, with his voice wavering. "I used to …work …work at a …funeral home… I was the main…main man…I took …took care of every …everything…I know about funerals… nobody can tell me nothin 'bout funerals… that I don't already know… that's for sho," said Pete.

Pete faded back into his slumber. His statement got both their attention. They looked at each other and moved to the bench where Pete was laid out. In his present state, Dexter knew he would not get coherent statements from Pete about what information he had, but he gave them enough to ponder over until he sobered up somewhat.

"Adam, did you hear what Pete said about having full knowledge about funeral homes? Do you know how valuable he may be to give us some insight about those missing graves, and what that means?" asked Dexter.

"Yeah, I heard him. But he may just be talking out of his head. I know how that can be. I been there myself a couple of times," said Adam.

"Yes, but suppose he does have information about what goes on at those gravesites. Suppose he knows about other sites that may have missing bodies as well. I'm just saying…suppose he does! A lot of questions could be answered," said Dexter.

Sergeant Stratham made a call to the Shreveport Police Department to find out if there was any information pending on a case involving The Simon brothers. The night shift civilian operator took the call.

"Shreveport Police Department…can I help you."

"Yes, this is Sergeant Paula Stratham from the Lafayette Police Department…I'm calling to speak to your officer in charge for this evening… who is that?"

"That would be Sergeant Eddie Thomas, but he's busy with an interrogation at this time. Would you like to speak to his assistant?"

"Yes, thank you," said Sgt. Stratham.

"Hello this is Officer Harley…how may I help you?"

"Officer Harley, this is Sergeant Stratham in Lafayette, how are you?"

"I'm great sergeant, how can I help you?"

"I have a situation down here involving a couple of citizens from your fair city, and I was calling to find out if you can give me some info on them," she said.

"Sure, what you got?" asked Officer Harley.

"I have a Code 6 on an Adam T. Simon who has been brought in for suspicion of carrying an illegal firearm. Do you have anything in your files that explains what the Code6 from Homeland Security is all about on him?" she asked.

"Sergeant, you called the right person...you need to know that this brother has a Code 6 because he's part of a very important investigation up here involving drug trafficking and other substances. Now this brother is not the main target-- The main target is in the hospital in a coma. HLS has control of the investigation, and they think it's bigger than these small potatoes. I think you got some big fish from around the state at least. But, they don't want to spring the trap until this brother comes out of the coma he's been in for over a month. They go back awhile in their investigation and it looks like the father and his other relatives were also involved—it's a generational crime family, but they are low keyed. I think you got a small potato in your custody there. I just think HLS want to bust the big ones first and they are working with the departments all over the state—even in your town. Somebody there should know about this...You should ask your chief...I guarantee you he knows what happening. Listen, I got to go...I hope that helps." reported Officer Harley.

Chase Pierce, his wife and daughters were leaving the barbecue get together at his friend Trever Levy's home. Even though it was only 9:30p.m., Chase never wanted the girls to stay up longer than 10 p.m. on any night. He had not missed his cell phone he usually carried on his hip, until he got back in his car to head home.

"Okay, let's buckle up girls...daddy got to get you home before daddy goes to sleep at the wheel," said Chase.

"*Honey, you want me to drive?*" asked Clair, Chase' wife.

"*Naw...I only had a couple of beers...I'm just feeling tired tonight...I'll be alright,*" he responded.

"*Did you know you left your phone in the car? It looks like you missed a call.*" said Clair.

"*I sure did...I didn't even miss not having it, either. It felt good not to hear that thing ring for a while...Let me see who called... Dexter Simon... Probably calling to tell me he made it back to Shreveport... okay, I'll call him tomorrow... Is everybody set? ...here we go,*" said Chase.

It only took 15 minutes for Chase to arrive at his home. Although the rains had stopped, he still had to navigate through puddles of rain water to get to his front door. Chase got the sleeping girls into the house with his wife's help. He went back to his car, parked outside of his garage to bring in the containers of food he brought back from the get-together. He realized that he left his phone on the seat where it was when he left Trever's house. He looked at the caller ID again, and zeroed in on the time of the call. It was 7:38 p.m. He questioned himself as to the time that Dexter and Adam left his office. He realized that if Dexter called at that time, it would not give them time to get back to Shreveport. He opened the phone to voicemail to hear the message. He was shocked to hear that they had been taken to the police station for questioning.

Chase went into his home to let his wife know that the call was one of distress from his client, Dexter. She advised him to go ahead and make the call, but he needed to stay home to get some rest. Chase returned the call. There was no answer. He hung up and called again—no answer. Conflicted with whether he should try to find them by going to the station or keep trying to call. He decided to call the station to find them. His second call was made to Precinct 3 where Officer Wayne answered.

"Hello sir, my name is Attorney Chase Pierce. I'm trying to find a client of mine whose name is Dexter Simon. Do you have him at your Precinct?"

"Hold on... what was your name again?" Officer Wayne asked.

"Attorney Chase Pierce."

"Hold on a minute sir... just a minute," said Officer Wayne.

"Sergeant, there's an attorney on the line asking if we have a Dexter Simon in custody," she said.

"What tha! How did an attorney know that we got Mr. Simon here? Didn't I tell you not to let them make any calls, Wayne?" said the sergeant.

"I took their phones, sergeant. I did what you said...they didn't make any calls when I took the phones from them. Maybe they made the call before I got to them," Wayne said.

Sh@#, Wayne, you're gonna get our asses fired... tell him no. Tell him we don't have anybody here by that name," said the sergeant.

"But, what if..." responded Officer Wayne.

"Just do it Wayne...we'll worry about what if's later," said the sergeant.

"Sorry sir, we have no one by that name," lied Officer Wayne.

"Would you do me a favor officer? ...would you check the other precincts for that name? ...I would certainly appreciate it," said Chase.

"Give me your number and I'll check and call you back," said Officer Wayne.

"337-313-4444. that's Chase Pierce."

"I got it...we'll check it out," she said.

Chase sat up in his living room chair waiting for a call back. He dosed off several times before he finally slumped into a deep sleep, when no one returned his call. When he heard his grandfather's clock gong on the hour of 11 p.m, he was jarred awake. He checked his watch and realized that an hour or so had passed and no phone call back. Perhaps, he thought that they had already left and were no longer in the system. Regardless, the message left by Dexter was clear enough. He had to find out where he was now, before he went to bed. He called his friend Trever's phone. Trever's party was still going on.

"Hey Trev, you still got your party going on?" asked Chase.

"*Yeah ...are you coming back? We're doing the 'letric slide.*" said Trever.

"*No man, I got a situation I need to deal with.*" said Chase.

"*At almost 11:30 at night? Come on Chase. You need to relax bud. It's time to have some fun and let your hair down.*" invited Trever.

"*I got a situation I need your help with, Trev ...Can I come back to talk to you,*" Chase said.

"*Hey, you and Clair are not having a fight are you?*" asked Trever.

"*Oh no, nothing like that.*" responded Chase.

"*Okay, come on back...I'll see you in a few minutes,*" said Trever.

Chase arrived at Trever's by 11:30 p.m. Most of the guests were still there, but he could see that the party had slowed. The women were sitting down talking near the outdoor kitchen and the men were gathered around the tractor and trailer used to harvest hay from Trever's 50-acre homestead. Chase waved at the women when he passed by, and joined the men. Trever offered Chase another beer, but he refused.

"*Trev., can I talk to you now? I hate to take you away from your guests, but I need your advice, man.*" said Chase.

"Yeah sure bud, come on over here by the barn. What's bothering you, Chase?" Trever asked.

"Listen, something is going on with my client I told you about—the Simon's," Chase said.

"I remember...I told you I would support you, man. You can count on me; you know that...I will," Trever said.

"That's fine, that's fine...but here's the problem. I think they have been detained by LPD and their rights are being violated." said Chase.

"Why, what's happened?" Trever asked.

"*I got a voicemail while I was here from Dexter Simon to let me know that they were still here and were being questioned by LPD,*" said Chase.

"*Questioned about what?*" asked Trever.

"*I don't know. When they left me this afternoon around 3 or so, they*" *were going over to the old graveyard, where his grandfather's grave was open and he was missing—you remember old man Panky Simon, right? Now, I was out there earlier in the week trying to determine what was going on for myself. That's when somebody knocked me out before I could get a good look around. Now if Dexter and his brother went there, they might have suffered the same fate,"* said Chase.

"You think they might still be out there, or what?" asked Trever.

"No, no I don't. I think somehow, they got in the hands of LPD and they are not allowing them to contact me or any other lawyer. You know how those sons of bitches make up lies to protect their system. I called around to several precincts and they told me they had no one by that name," said Chase.

"But what would they be trying to hide?" asked Trever.

"They are trying to hide something that's going on in that damn graveyard! There's something happening with those missing bodies out there, and I think there's a connection between there and what's going on in Shreveport," said Chase.

"You been working this thing, haven't you Chase? There's something going on in Shreveport that you're working on, too?" Trever asked.

"I told you about these guys' brother who is in a coma and had this business that…" Chase continued.

"Oh, yeah I remember. So what about your client who left you a message…what about them?" asked Trever.

"I think they were on to something that seems to be something big. Now I didn't tell you about the investigation that has been going on by the HLS and that bunch, did I?" Chase asked.

"You talking about Homeland Security?" Trever asked.

"Yep…according to some reliable information I got when I was there, they think this brother Brian and his relatives that are deceased, were involved in drug trafficking out of south Louisiana into the Shreveport area," said Chase.

"So what does that have to do with the brothers you're trying to find here?" Dexter asked.

"They are all under suspicion, Trev. I think these brothers, and I, were getting too close to HLS's investigation, and they are trying to neutralize them and me, until they pull this thing off. See, I think there's going to be a big bust, Trev. I think there's some folk all over this state who have their hands dirty and it's been that way for some time. I think it's a generational crime scheme, and the Feds are about to bust it wide open. Now Trev... I'm going to let you in on something ...I think my dad and granddad had something to do with it as well," said Chase.

"Do you know what you are saying, Chase? Do you know what your mother and grandmother would say if they heard you say this?" asked Trever.

"Yeah, I know what my grandmother would say... She would say my great-grandfather's iniquities were passed down through the generations. And the way I see it, the Simon's worked for them in the funeral business and running bootleg liquor into Texas and Arkansas. So the Simon's are still in the funeral business, and my family still runs the largest wine and spirits business in the state. How many funeral homes are there right here in Lafayette, huh? However many there are, most are black-owned and operated. Now here's what I think... I think that all the old graveyards are used by these funeral homes to not only bury the dead... but I think they are being used to bury the drugs, until the right time comes along to dig them up and get them distributed across the states," said Chase.

"I believe this brother that's still in a coma was part of the distribution system. I believe the Mexicans found a way to get the drugs across the border and into the hands of the funeral homes. Then, when there was no heat in the air with the Feds, they would get the drugs where they intended for them to go in the first place. I think sometimes the drugs are in the ground for years, waiting for the right time.

Now, if I'm right... if I'm right Trever, when the crap hits the fan, you're gonna see a bust that's going to take down the heavyweight's in this funeral business, including some powerful people all over Louisiana," said Chase.

"Chase... listen, if you are right... if you are right, you better stay the hell far, far away from the kitchen. If the kitchen is going to get that hot, you stand to get burned as well, you know what I'm saying? I don't want to see you hurt, my friend. That would be my good advice for you. Stay away from them; at least until this thing blows over. If you get too close, you could lose your license, you know," Trever said.

"Are you going to lecture me on doing the right thing or not doing the right thing for my clients?" Chase asked.

"You do the right thing, bud—always. I'm saying, be more discerning. Choose your representation that will benefit you in the long run. Like I said before, somebody wants you to stick to the law and they are willing to resort to some degree of violence for you to get the message. Suppose your clients are in the LPD and they told you no, they were not ... Suppose they are holding them away from some impending action because they don't want them to be in the way. Maybe they were keeping tabs on the graveyard where the bodies are missing and these guys were going to cause something to go wrong. They could be doing that you know!" Trever said.

"They could... but does any of this make sense to you?" asked Chase.

"It does, bud. You may be onto something ...But I guarantee you, none of this is going to put any money in your pocket. You need to make some money, man. I know you still have your eyes on that big 55' fishing boat, right?" Trever asked.

"So what do you think I should do?" asked Chase.

"Go home and get some rest. You look bushed, bud. Call me tomorrow after church, and I'll go with you to see if we can find your clients, alright... seriously!" Trever said.

"Yeah... I guess you're right... I guess you're right! ... I'll call you tomorrow," Chase said.

"Goodnight!"

Chapter 49

At the stroke of midnight, while Adam was lying asleep next to Pete, who was sleeping off his intoxication, Dexter was on his knees meditating and praying. He had resigned himself to remaining in the jail holding cell until the next morning when he hoped that his attorney would come to their rescue. He felt the weight of sleep as well but, was compelled to have communication with his God. His head dropped many times while praying, but each time he would continue his quiet meditation.

Officer Drake was on duty for the night until morning, and decided to check in on the three men being held in the holding cell. As he peered into the cell through the glass window, he saw Dexter on his knees, appearing to be praying. Around his body was an iridescent light which seemed to pulsate bright to dim. Officer Drake was astonished at what he was seeing. He wiped his eyes and gazed in again. It appeared to him that the light moved away from Dexter and was hovering in the air above him. Officer Drake rushed to the front desk area when he engaged the receptionist on duty to come take a look. They both came at a fast pace to the holding cell and looked in. The light had disappeared. Officer Drake assured the receptionist that there was a light glowing over and around Dexter. They went back to their duty stations as Officer Drake secured his keys to his patrol car. He was going back out on patrol and thought this might have been simply an illusion. He shook his head and walked out the rear door to the parking lot. He climbed into his patrol car and started the engine, where he sat for at least a few minutes, pondering what that light could have been. He was a Christian man and he was familiar with some of the Bible stories. He recalled that the Apostle Paul was incarcerated once and had a spiritual experience with an angel appearing within his cell. He recalled that Paul was praying and praising God, when the cell doors opened and the shackles fell off.

Naw, he reasoned, that was in the old days—I must be seeing things, Officer Drake thought to himself.

He turned off the engine and jogged back into the station. He slipped by the front desk receptionist and eased back down the hall to the holding cell. He again peered in through the glass window. The light was back and now hovering over Pete and Adam. Dexter was now asleep on the floor. Officer Drake used his cell key to slowly open the door while continuing to look at the light. He eased the door open, trying not to disturb the detainees and hoping not to cause the light to go away. The presence of the light was strong and forced him to his knees. He felt he was in the presence of The Holy Spirit. He started to pray.

"Oh God, forgive me for my sins. I am sorry for all my wrong doings… forgive me for sins I have done against you and my fellow man. I ask Jesus to give me a clean heart, and strengthen me to be a better person. I ask this in Jesus' name…Amen," Officer Drake prayed.

Dexter opened his eyes at the time Officer Drake completed his prayer. He reached out his hand to him while offering a prayer of blessing.

"Bless you officer, in the name of Jesus. By the power invested in me as a believer and follower of Jesus Christ, be blessed in His name," prayed Dexter.

Adam awakened from his sleep and saw Officer Drake on his knees and he saw the light within the room. He instinctively shook

Pete, who had slept off much of his alcohol effects. Pete woke up and gathered his wits about him to see the same scene.

"What's going on? What's happening, fellows?" asked Pete.

Dexter and Officer Drake were still shaking hands as Dexter reached out to hold the hand of his brother. Adam asked what was happening. Dexter smiled and asked that he join hands with Pete. Dexter prayed.

"Father God, I honor you at this time…you are Awesome in every way. Father, I ask that you forgive all our sins…we are not worthy to be called your children, but through your son Jesus, you have accepted all of us who confess Jesus as your son who came to save the world, and He is the Lord of the all. Lord, I pray that you honor this moment as a confession of sin and acceptance of your Son who shed His blood for us, even when we did not deserve his sacrifice. As we each confess this, I ask that you accept our confession and accept us into your Kingdom. Do each of you make this confession?" Dexter said, after completing the prayer.

"I do…" said Officer Drake.

"I do…" said Pete.

"I do…" said Adam, crying …*"I want to say Lord that, I have not been the man I need to be to my family; …my wives; …my children and to you. I …I know I need to do better about going to church and serving you… forgive me for my drinking …and cussing… I just need you to help me to be a better man. I want to be a better man … Amen."*

"May the Lord grant you the desires of your heart my brother. As Christ would say go, and sin no more," proclaimed Dexter.

"I appreciate that prayer, man. I need to stop drinking, too. I don't need to be getting high every week like I do, either …What's your name?" asked Pete.

"I'm Adam, and that's my brother Dexter. He's the Christian who actually lives the life. …Really, I want to be like him…," said Adam.

"Do ya'll know what happened when ya'll were asleep?" asked Officer Drake.

"What happened?" asked Adam.

"When your brother was on his knees praying, I saw a bright light hovering over him. I couldn't believe my eyes so I went to get the receptionist to come see. He came back here to see, but the light was gone. I then left, thinking that I must have seen an illusion. When I got to the car to leave, something told me to come back to see if the light was still there. It was there, but this time, it was over you two. It felt like it was the Holy Spirit telling me to open the door and come inside. I am telling you, I have never felt anything like that in my life. It was a strong feeling drawing me in," said Officer Drake. "I've been a Christian since I was about 12 years old, but this is the first time I felt the Spirit like that."

"Here's what I know..." said Dexter. " God is a merciful God. He blesses us even when we don't deserve it. I know that I didn't want to be placed in anybody's jail house, but I asked God to help me to endure whatever I had to go through for His will and purpose to be done ... Adam, we were supposed to be in here at this time, for God's purpose. Now what we all must do is...walk in God's grace and in His purpose. Don't let the devil trick you into believing that this whole experience was a fluke. He will try to plant those thoughts in your mind. But know that this experience is meant for each of us to walk in the ways of God...turn away from evil... and never, never look back, or go back to our former ways...right? ...right?" ...Praise the Lord!" Dexter shouted out in praise.

Officer Drake righted himself and shook the hands of his detainees. He walked out of the cell with a smile, whispering praises to the Lord. He locked the door as he suggested that they all get some sleep. Things would be better in the morning, he promised. For Dexter, his body had little strength left in it. They all found a place on the bench to stretch out and close their eyes. Officer Drake returned with three blankets and pillows for them. This time when he left, he said 'PTL?"

Dexter answered with... "Praise The Lord!"

Chapter 50

Sunday morning after church, and after getting his family home, Chase called Trever and asked that he meet with him to find out where his clients Dexter and Adam were. Trever agreed to meet him, but after he made an appearance at the political fundraiser for a lawyer friend of his, Theresa Rene Malveaux.

Attorney Malveaux was running for the long held position of district attorney for Lafayette Parish. The incumbent had held that office for over 20 years and was nearing retirement age. Nevertheless, he wanted to run again for four years and had a bundle of cash in his campaign fund. Trever knew Ms. Malveaux would need all the help she could get financially to even make a respectable showing. The good-old-boy network was very solid in that town and newcomers would have little chance of success. Even though this was her first time running for any political office, she pulled out all the stops in asking everyone she knew to come to her Sunday afternoon rally at the Westend Community Center. Trever met Chase at the Center and they walked inside together. Ms Malveaux was seated at the head table with several other first-time candidates and was about to be introduced by the director of the Center when Chase and Trever took their seats near the front.

"Good afternoon ladies and gentlemen, thank you for being here. We

want to also thank the good Lord for this fabulous weather and sunshine...
right? It's been a long time since we have had sunshine over the last couple
of weeks.

"That leads me into the introduction of our main speaker for this
afternoon. You will see that she is a breath of fresh air and bright sunshine
that we need in this parish. By now, many of you know her to be a woman
of excellent character and high morals, who is dedicated to providing
passionate and honest legal representation. She has been acting as an
officer of the court for the past 12 years in Lafayette. She has served on
many boards—too numerous to mention—and currently serves as chair
of the Commission for Women's Needs. Ms Malveaux is running against
the incumbent, Mr. Toussaint, who has been the District Attorney for far
too long. Ladies and gentlemen, please show a warm welcome to our next
DA for Lafayette Parish...**Ms Theresa Rene Malveaux.**"

Approximately 150 persons attending the fundraiser stood to
their feet and warmly applauded Ms Malveaux as she came to the
podium. Family members and friends passed out flyers and campaign
information printed on refrigerator magnets. Ms Malveaux was a
41-year-old former crawfish festival queen whose parents were born
and raised in the 'Cane River' area of northwestern Louisiana. She
gazed over the crowd as she began to speak.

"Good afternoon and thank you very much for that wonderful
introduction and warm, heartfelt welcome. I greet all of you on this sunny
Sunday afternoon, and I especially want to recognize some of my colleagues
and associates who are in the audience today. First, let me introduce you
to my mother and father who are here from Natchitoches, Louisiana...
mom and dad won't you stand... Mr. and Mrs. Belardaux. Without them
of course, I wouldn't be here... next, let me introduce you to a good friend
and associate from the great state of Louisiana, and the great city of
Alexandria... Attorney Trever Levy.... And he has his friend from this
fair city of Lafayette, Attorney Chase Abbott Pierce.... I also want to
recognize the mayor of New Iberia, Mr. Wayne Toussaint, Jr. and his lovely
wife, Nancy. Now I couldn't overlook my friend and military advisor to

my campaign from the Louisiana National Guard, Colonel Jimmy Rideau. Now there are a whole lot more of you that I see in the audience that time will not let me call you by name. But I want you to know that I consider you true friends and I cherish all of you from the bottom of my heart. Again, thank you for being here.

As most of you know, I entered this race because this parish is in a crisis. For far too long, there has been a cover up of crime in this parish, dating back for many years...back long before I was even born. I don't mean petty crimes, such as those filling the court dockets in our parish today...no, no...I mean crimes that have been committed by certain of our forefathers, which have been continued down through the years. There are persons right here in this parish, who have gone unpunished for the unlawful acts that have been committed against our law abiding citizens of all races. As an officer of the court, I see crimes committed every day that if I am elected as your next District Attorney, I will bring those responsible to justice. It has been the policy of the present DA, to look the other way, and pretend that the lesser crimes are the cases he should pursue. I am here to tell you ladies and gentlemen, he is part of the problem and needs to be run out of office by the end of this election, and that is exactly what I intend to do--with your help...I will stand for right, and I will bring justice back to this parish, by weeding out the real criminals who have perpetuated the good-old-boy system way back since the state became a part of the union. If you will work hard to help me get elected to this highly esteemed office of District Attorney, I promise you that I will make you proud, and every other parish in this state, will look upon this parish as the model parish, and you will be proud to call Lafayette Parish your home...**I promise you that...I promise you that**... But we will need your sweat, your communication skills, your prayers, **and** your money...Can we count on you for that? Will you stand with us all the way to the election and beyond? I promise you that if you do, **Theresa Rene Malveaux** will stand by you, and represent you, and make you proud!

Thank you all...Thank you for your support...Thank you... thank you!

The crowd was energized to hear such an electrifying speech from such a promising young lawyer. In the history of politics in and around Lafayette Parish, there had not been a candidate so well qualified and so well spoken as her. The local politicians of her party felt that they really had a winner, who could actually do what she said she would do, and clean up the corruption that had gone on under the noses of so many for so long. She was sparking a core of volunteers who vowed to make history by helping her win over a long-time politician, who made promises to certain 'old guard' constituents at the expense of the average middle-class and poor.

Till now, Trever thought she was a very capable attorney, but this was the first time he had the opportunity to hear her speak to a large group of people. Judging by the large grin on his face, Chase felt that she was going to get a contribution from him and his vote.

"*Wow, what did you think of that?*" asked Trever.

"*She really knows how to excite a crowd,*" answered Chase.

"*Let's go up and shake her hand. I have a check for her as well but, I'm going to tear it up and write out another one,*" said Trever.

"*I got my checkbook with me as well. I think I can make a donation for a couple of hundred,*" said Chase.

"*Hey, if she wins this election, you're gonna wish you had added another zero behind it. You need to make sure she remembers you, my friend,*" reasoned Trever.

Trever led the way through the crowd to Theresa's parents. He greeted them and introduced Chase. They responded with smiles and thanked them for supporting their daughter.

"*We know she comes from good stock when her parents were born and raised in and around Cane River…Ya'll have a lot of rich history in that area.*" said Trever.

"*We know she got a big job going up against the big boys down here… we hope and pray ya'll gonna take care her, and don't let nothing happen to her,*" said Mr. Belardaux.

"*She is tough…everybody can see that,*" said Chase.

"*Well, ya'll take care…we want to congratulate her and give her a little cash,*" said Trever.

"*Thank ya'll very much, hear. We know she appreciate that!*" said Mrs. Belardaux.

Trever and Chase made their way to the front of the audience where Theresa was shaking hands. Standing only 5'2", she looked solid as a marine just out of boot camp, next to Colonel Rideau. She looked at Trever standing to her right and gave him a big smile. They hugged tightly. Then she shook Chase's hand tightly. He handed her a check. She took it in her left hand and looked before she gave it to the Colonel. It was for $1,000.

"*Oh my… Thank you Chase…that is really appreciated…thank you!*" she said.

She handed the check to the Colonel who was acting as her treasurer for the day. Trever handed her his check. It was for $2,000.

"*Trever, you are such a jewel. I am speechless! …Colonel, I think we are off to a **great** start, don't you?*" said Theresa.

"*I need to get a calculator. I can't keep up with it all in my head. Thank you both for giving us a jump start,*" said the Colonel.

Chase's cell phone rang. He reached down to see who was calling. The number was not a local area code. He excused himself and answered it.

"*Hello, this is Chase.*"

"*Mr. Pierce, this is Norma Simon in Shreveport.*"

"*Yes, yes, hello Mrs. Simon…how are you?*" Chase asked.

"*Not good, right now…have you heard from my husband, Dexter? Do you know where he is?*" Mrs. Simon said.

"*Well, I…I got a message from him last night that he was still in town. I was actually going to meet with him today… in a few minutes…I will be leaving a meeting to meet with him,*" said Chase.

"*Well, It's not like him to not call if he was going to be delayed. I mean he did call to say that he was delayed, but he didn't come home and I have* been calling his cell phone but no answer--the same thing with his brother's phone. It's getting to be a little worrisome, you know?" said Norma.

"Yes ma'am, I understand. But listen, I'm about to leave this meeting and I promise you I will get back with you as soon as I am able to, okay?" said Chase. "Now don't you worry, okay...I'll call you back shortly, okay?"

"Thank you Mr. Pierce." said Norma.

"Please call me Chase, Mrs. Simon."

"I'll be waiting to hear from you, Chase," said Norma.

Chase walked back to Trever with some urgency on his face...

"Are you going with me to find out where my client is...that was his wife in Shreveport?" asked Chase.

"Oh, yes I am...I forgot... we need to go... Theresa, we got to go! ... If I can do more, you just let me know, okay?" said Trever, walking out. "Sorry 'bout that, partner... that slipped my mind...let's go in my car over there ...I'll bring you back here when we finish."

They climbed into Trever's Mini Hummer and drove off. Chase wanted to go to the nearest precinct to start their investigation. That was Precinct 2. The sun was still shinning and the temp was in the 60s. Chase took off his jacket as Trever rolled down the windows. After driving for 15 minutes, they arrived at the precinct. They both got out of the car and parked at the front entrance and walked into the station. One of the officers leaving through the front door recognized Trever and stopped to talk to him.

"Hey Trever, what are you doing out on a sunny day like this?" the officer asked.

"Oh, hey Gus, how are you? Listen, this is Chase Pierce. He's an attorney, who is looking for his client. Do you know if you have a detainee by the name of... what's the name Chase?" Trever asked.

"There's two of them ...they are brothers named Dexter and Adam Simon. They might have been detained yesterday around 5:30 or 6 p.m.," said Chase.

"Hey, I don't recognize the name but, come on in and let's ask the front desk. *How you been Trever? Your kid gonna play baseball this year for the team?" asked the officer.*

"Yeah, he's been down at the batting cage almost every other day. He's getting good. How about yours?" asked Trever.

"Same here. I hope I can get a chance to see 'em play sometime…you know how it is with working the night shift," said Gus.

"I feel you." responded Trever.

"Okay, here we are… Dispatch, do we have a couple of gentlemen being detained by the name of Simon?" asked Gus.

"I'll check that for you…give ma a sec…! …. No, no one in by that name. Have you checked the other precincts?" asked the dispatcher.

"No, not yet. We were closest to you and we thought we would check here first. Are you able to see who the other precincts are housing?" asked Chase.

"Normally we could but, my computers are not acting right. I'm waiting on them to send somebody over. It's hard to find IT people when you need 'em. Do you know where 3 is?" asked the dispatcher.

"Yes, we do. We'll check with them. We appreciate your help, though." said Trever.

"Not a problem," the dispatcher responded.

"Thanks Gus, I'll see you around when the season starts," said Trever.

"Ya'll be careful, ya' hear? …nice to meet you, sir!" said Gus.

"Yes, you too Gus. Thank you," said Chase.

Chase and Trever walked back to Trever's car and got in. Trever knew the route to Precinct 3, but he asked Chase to put the location in his GPS for the fastest driving time. The whereabouts of his clients was on Chase's mind. He felt badly that he was not able to answer the phone when Dexter called last night. But his voice message did not sound as if he was in a panic. Nevertheless, he wanted to get to him soon to find out what happened and get him released.

For Trever, his thoughts were on the political scene, and getting his friend elected to DA. Although Trever has been practicing law for many years, he wanted so see some of the old farts he has had as clients replaced with some new people. To get Theresa elected was going to be the start of cleaning house of the old guard, and putting some new blood to work. In fact, the start of the replacement was when he assisted the new mayor of New Iberia, Wayne Toussaint, get elected last year. Wayne was the cousin of the present DA in Lafayette. The two cousins never had a close relationship, and were members of differing political parties.

Because Trever had been on the scene for a long time, he was quite familiar with the aspirations Theresa spoke of in her speech. If she was dedicated to seeing things through to the end, he would stand by her, all the way.

"Hey Trever, are you still serious about being behind me?" Chase asked.

"You mean on representing your client in Shreveport?" answered Trever.

"Yeah… and being there for me as a mentor. You know, if I need help with the locals around here who want to see me somewhere other than on the cases that I'm working on," said Chase.

"My friend, I need to tell you like a good friend of mine told me a long time ago… if you were in Africa and trying to survive as a gazelle… you better be faster than the fastest lion who wants you for dinner… Now if you were the lion, you better be faster than the slowest gazelle, if you want to survive… around here, everybody has staked out their territory. Everybody knows what they can do with whom, and what they cannot do. If you decided you wanted to move into some established territory, and you didn't get permission, every lion in that territory would be on you like the craw on fish. You couldn't survive long unless you became a slave to the pride. In other words, you would have to become just like them. Now, near as I can tell, you are stalking in their territory. You gotta be willing to fight—and I mean really fight, if you want to stay in their territory. Now you want me to be honest with you, right?" asked Trever.

"Yeah, of course." said Chase.

"It goes back a long time ago. I mean right out of slavery, when the Whites who lost the battle to keep slavery as their way of life had to redirect their activities in other ways. Many of them in Louisiana were already involved in illegal trade and prostitution, smuggling and the like, while slavery was still going on. So when they lost their legal rights to continue, they went underground -so to speak- and never missed a step. Some of them were involved in moonshine distribution out of the hills of Kentucky and Tennessee, hauling wagon loads all the way down here, so they could sell to the Indians and to the soldiers who were fighting them. Now there were some strong relationships established between some of the slaves who were trusted and given passes to go through other territories to haul that moonshine and whiskey all the way back here. So, when Louisiana became a part of the Union after the French and Spanish sold out, the Whites continued in the same businesses. This state was not allowed to sell liquor, but that didn't stop those enterprising souls from branching out into other areas. They went into politics, cotton farming, raising sugar cane and transporting it to New Orleans for shipment overseas to Europe. Even the sweetest tobacco and Indigo were grown up around the Cane River area. So, they always held onto the land, and some of them sold some land to their trusted slaves to grow crops for them... Are you following where I'm going with this?" asked Trever.

"So you're saying that they passed all those business down to their descendents. That's not so bad, is it? ...I mean the legitimate ones," asked Chase.

"The legitimate ones...no! But remember, there were a lot of businesses that came out of the illegal ones. It's like getting dirty money and laundering it through a good reputable bank. Is the money good, now? No... because it was tainted by the way it was obtained in the first place," said Trever.

"Okay...so you have all these businesses that sprang up that had nothing to do with the dirty ones from the past, what should happen to them? Should they have to lose their business because their grandfathers got their money through prostitution and other contraband?" asked Chase.

"Who's to decide? ...you... me... local government... the church... the state… the federal government? I couldn't answer that, could you? But… I can say this, I have a strong feeling that the big boys are watching. By that I mean the FEDs. There are enough indications that something's going on that some people right here in this state are getting nervous, and they don't want anybody to start stirring up the water. That's exactly why the politicians have so much money in their re-election kiddies. Hell, they all know each other, and they know how they all got to where they are. But I feel that there's going to be a generational curse to hit certain people in this state that any politician who has been in office for more than 10 years is going to be affected by," Trever said.

"Oh, we are here. Listen, I want to continue this conversation later if we could, Trev. This seems to follow the same ideas I have about all the secrecy around here and even in Shreveport. I just don't know the extent of it just yet and all the intricate details of it," offered Chase.

"Let me ask you this before we go inside… did you know your daddy was involved in some of that… and your grandfather?" asked Trever.

"It may surprise you that I knew that already Trever. I won't ask you why you didn't tell me that before now," said Chase.

"The reason…" Trever began.

"No, that's alright Trev, I do understand. I guess the question is what do I expect because of it, huh?" Chase said.

"Let's go on in my friend…let's see if we can find your clients, okay?" said Trever.

They both exited the Hummer and walked to the front of the station. The time was almost 2:20 p.m. A flight of helicopters flew overhead, carrying dignitaries from Homeland Security. Trever noticed the emblem on the side of the lead chopper.

"What do you think that is all about that they are here?" asked Chase.

"Probably want to make sure we're ready for another disaster when it comes. Hopefully it won't be like that Cat 2 a few years ago, huh?" responded Trever.

"Hopefully! But why do they need three choppers, I wonder? That's where they waste a lot of our tax dollars, right?" said Chase.

"Here we go… Excuse me ma'am…I'm Attorney Levy and this is Attorney Pierce… we are looking for a couple of clients who may be here in your precinct. Can you check on that for us, please?" asked Trever.

"Sure I can. What was the name, sir?"

"Their last names are Simon…they are two brothers," said Chase.

"Oh! ..Uh huh…well, I will be right back with you. Just have a seat and I'll be back with you in just a second…have a seat," said the dispatcher.

The dispatcher faded into the back of the precinct. Sounds were coming from the area where the prisoners were housed. It was obvious to any visitors that they did not want to be locked up on such a nice spring-like day. The dispatcher returned. She reported reluctantly that they did have the two mentioned by them, but they were not listed as prisoners. They were just being detained.

"So, you do have them…That's what we want to know…Great! That's great. Okay, they are our clients and we want to see them, please. Do you have a room we can sit and talk to them over here, perhaps?" asked Trever.

"Well, that's the problem…they are not allowed to talk to anyone at this time. They have a special status that says they cannot have communication with anyone until tomorrow, when we can get clearance," said the dispatcher.

"Clearance from whom?" asked Chase.

"I can't say Attorney, sir. I was told that by the sergeant. I'm following an order, that's all.

"Okay… I need to speak with your sergeant ma'am. I need to see my clients now!" said Chase.

Down the hall, Dexter could hear the voice of someone that sounded like his attorney. He quieted the conversation in the holding cell to listen more intently.

"Adam, hold on…I think I hear Chase," said Dexter.

"We'll let's let him know that we're here...**Hello Chase...we're here!**" yelled Adam.

The dispatcher excused herself again to speak with the sergeant. Chase and Trever waited until she was out of sight and decided to ease down the hall where they heard Adam's voice. Other detainees saw the attorneys moving briskly down the hall and came to the front of their cells. Differing voices were heard asking if they were attorneys coming to get them released. Some asked if they had a cigarette and something to drink. They made it to Dexter, Adam and Pete's holding cell.

"Hey Dexter...man I am sorry about last night. I am really sorry that I was not able to get your massage until late last night and I tried to find out where you were then," said Chase.

"Praise God you are here now, though. You know this is all wrong, Chase. They have us in here illegally. There is no way they should be holding us...all due to a mistake," said Dexter.

"What was it Dexter? What happened to you?" asked Chase.

"It was the same thing that happened to you in the graveyard. Only this time, they were shooting at us?" Dexter said.

"You were shot at in the old graveyard?" Chase asked.

"Yes!" Dexter said.

"**Counselors, do you two want to join these men in that cell?** You are in violation of a lawful command. You are not supposed to be in here talking to any of these men. You must go now!" said the sergeant in charge.

"What tha hell are you holding my clients in here for sergeant? You can't hold them in here without charge...and you know that. You have nothing on them and you know it!" said Chase.

"Get us out of here, Chase. Man we need to go home. We haven't done anything for them to keep us in here. The food is nasty, and it's cold and stinky, too. Use your attorney powers to get us out, okay?" said Adam.

"They refused to allow us to talk to anyone, Chase...not even to call home or even to call you. The last time I checked, we were still in the USA, right?" asked Dexter.

"Counselor, if you are not out of here in 10 seconds, I will be placing you two under arrest. What's your choice?" demanded the sergeant.

"We're leaving! Dexter…Adam, we got you covered. We're going to make some calls and get back to you soon. By the way, I told your wife that I would let her know when I saw you… we're leaving Sarge…hang in there fellas. We'll get back to you as soon as possible," said Chase.

Trever and Chase left after leaving their business cards at the dispatcher's desk.

"We will be back Sergeant, and I don't think you're gonna like the papers we'll have with us when we do. You are illegally holding our clients when they have asked for their attorney. That is called 'Due Process' in case you didn't know," said Chase.

They walked just outside of the precinct front door when Trever pulled out his cell phone and called the Assistant District Attorney at home. He was not able to reach him as he was on a conference call with his boss, the DA and the Mayor. Trever was fuming mad that his and Chase's status as officers of the court were being ignored. Somebody would see him in court over this terrible act of ignorance of their rights to see their clients. Little did he know that the third day of Dexter's and Adam's detention would prove to be a defining one. Everything that had happened so far would be explained on their third day of detention.

Meanwhile, across town, there was a Funeral Directors mini-conference going on and about to end at the Comfort Inn and Suites Hotel. Attendees were from all over the state. The front desk clerk brought a note to the registration booth and handed it to the person in charge. The registration supervisor looked at the note and looked at the intern working for them, signaling for him to come see. The intern was given the folded note and told to take it to the man sitting at the end of the head table inside the conference room. The intern made his way to the front table and handed the note to a Mr. Palou from Eunice. Mr. Palou read the note and looked around the room to determine what he should do with it. The person he was looking for was out of the room. Mr. Palou left the front table and made his way to the registration table, and asked the supervisor where this note came from. The supervisor told him from the front desk. Then he asked if she saw Mr. Doucette, the conference president. She told him he was talking on his cell phone down the hall. Mr. Palou walked briskly down the hall to find Mr. Doucette. When he came to the area outside, next to the pool where Mr. Doucette was talking and gesturing with his hand, it was evident that he was visibly shaken.

"*Well, what tha hell for, Gene? What we gon do about it*"? *...did you talk to Lester, yet?*

...Well call him and tell 'em... dammit 'tha hell... I can't believe this is happening!" *...You call me back today after you talk to him... I got to finish up this conference... call me back, 'ya hear?*" ordered Doucette. He closed the cell phone and responded to Palou's presence.

"*Yeah Palou, what you got?*"

Mr. Palou handed him the note and said nothing until he read it.

"*Where 'tha hell did this come from, Palou?*" *Doucette asked.*

"*It came from the front desk, and the intern brought it up to me at the head table,*" *responded Palou.*

Doucette could not talk for a few minutes. He had to take it all in. He knew something was coming down that would not be good. And this note was not making things any easier, either. However, he would rather get a heads up rather than be caught off guard. Although he was needed in the conference room to close things out shortly, Mr. Doucette needed to make one more phone call before he went in. He called the number he had for his brother-in-law who was trying to repair some of his heavy equipment he used in his logging business. The first call rang four times and went to voice mail. He did not leave a message, but hung up and called again. The second time he called, Jimmy Allen answered.

"*Hello,*" *Jimmy answered.*

"Jimmy, listen, I been trying to call you...listen have you heard anything about tomorrow?" asked Doucette.

"I ain't heard nothing about nothing Douce, cause I been trying to get this truck fixed for my crew to get some trees cut tomorrow. What was I supposed to hear?" asked Jimmy.

"Listen to this Jimmy... is there anybody with you?" asked Doucette.

"Yeah, my mechanic," said Jimmy.

"Can he hear you talking?" asked Doucette.

"No," said Jimmy.

"Okay, I got a note here that does not leave me with a good feeling. It says...

"3/3/03 ShreLongTex."

"What 'tha hell does that mean, Douce? You mean that scares you?" asked Jimmy.

"You dummy...that's gotta be a code name for something that's gonna happen tomorrow," said Doucette.

"Well, it don't mean nothing to me...I guess you better call your Governor again, huh?" Jimmy said.

"I guess you're right Jimmy...I guess you're right!" said Mr. Doucette.

Chapter 51

8:25 p.m. on 3/2/03: Governor Katrina Brulongo was setting foot onto the boat dock, with several of her aides in toe. She had been touring the waterways in and around Baton Rouge to see first hand, how the recent oil spill from a Russian tanker affected the Mississippi River shore lines. Overhead, two helicopters from HLS were coming in for a landing on top of the heli-landing pad atop the Governor's statehouse.

"*Are these the same choppers that came in earlier, Henry?*" asked the Governor.

"*I don't think so Governor. The other ones were from HLS and they are already here for your meeting tomorrow. I don't see any markings on these,*" responded Henry.

"*Check on it and find out who these guys are. I don't want people flying around my state without me knowing who they are,*" said the Governor.

"*Yes ma'am, I will,*" he responded.

8:40 p.m. on 3/3/03: The Governor was back in her office. The Land Commissioner was holding on the line for the Governor. The Commissioner wanted to know if they should file a letter of protest with the State Attorney General to get the U.S. State Department to ask for clean-up monies for the Russian tanker oil spill.

"*I don't think so, just yet,*" replied the Governor. "*I want to bring that* up with the HLS people I'm meeting with tomorrow. I wonder what they are going to be doing the rest of the time after we finish our meeting. Henry, do we have their itinerary for tomorrow? If we meet with them from 10-1:30 p.m., where are they scheduled to go after that?" asked the Governor.

They are headed for Lafayette and Shreveport, and then they are out of our state...heading back to D.C., I guess," reported Henry, the chief of staff.

"What is on their agenda for those two cities?" asked the Governor.

"It's not listed. We don't know," answered Henry.

"Well, we need to make sure the Mayors know they're coming. You better call both of them...just to be sure," ordered the Governor.

"Will do, ma'am," said Henry.

9:00 p.m. on 3/2/03: Governor still in her office, but sent her staff home to be with their families for the remainder of the evening. Her cell phone rang. She retrieved it from her desk and answered it. Since it was her private cell phone, she knew she could be casual with her greeting.

"Hello," said the Governor.

"Hello Governor, this is Eddie Doucette, in Lafayette," the voice said.

"Oh hello Eddie, how did the Conference go today? ...It was today, right?" asked the Governor.

"Yes ma'am, it went fine...everything went just fine--good turn-out," said Doucette.

"Oh, good. Well, what can I do for you Eddie? ...I don't need any money right now...the election is not for two years," said the Governor.

"Oh, I just wanted to know if you are aware of the Homeland Security people coming to our state tonight. We saw several helicopters this afternoon and were wondering if anything was going on maybe we should know about?" he said.

"Ah Eddie, you don't have to worry about anything...we're meeting with them in my office tomorrow to talk about some state business. Why do you ask?"

"Naw, I was just curious why so many of them came in flying over our *hotel on their way towards Baton Rouge. Then we saw another two pass over later. That was it. Some of my members were asking me and I told them I would call and find out. That was it…they were curious…that's all,"* said Doucette.

"Are you sure, Eddie? I hear a little tenseness in your voice," said the Governor.

"No, I'm fine. It's been a long day, that's all," said Doucette.

"Oookay. By the way, they will be meeting with your mayor tomorrow after they finish with our meeting. So you might want to put your ear plugs in when they come back… Okay, listen, I gotta go. Say hello to the wife. I'll see you at the Fat Stock Show kickoff, right? That's next week isn't it?" said the Governor.

"Yes, I believe its next Thursday," he said.

"See you then—goodnight Eddie," said the Governor.

"Goodnight Governor."

9:22 p.m. 3/2/03: Governor Brulongo decided to call the mayor of Shreveport to access his level of knowledge of the visit by Homeland Security tomorrow. Mayor Ken Midway was in his office but had placed his phone on silence while he met with members of his staff. One of the staff members saw the light on the phone blinking. He notified the Mayor, but the Mayor decided to let it ring, as he needed to finish the meeting he was having without any more interruptions. Besides, it was Sunday night—who could be calling who was more important than a meeting about waste management contract negotiations, he thought. The Governor left a message that she was checking with him concerning his Hurricane Readiness meeting tomorrow.

9:30 p.m. 3/2/03: The Governor's driver appeared in her office and told her he was ready anytime she was. She left her office for home.

10:10 p.m. 3/2/03: Back in Lafayette, Chase went to his office after leaving Trever Levy, to prepare a writ of habeas corpus, ordering the police to release his clients from jail due to unlawful detention.

11:09 p.m. 3/2/03: Officer Drake came into Precinct 3 to end his shift. Before he removed his uniform and changed into his civilian clothes, he went to the holding cell to check on his new friends, the detainees. Dexter and Pete were asleep, while Adam was awake and staring into the ceiling. He saw Officer Drake and gave him the thumbs up. Adam raised both arms as in surrender and shrugged his shoulders. Officer Drake clasped his hands together and bowed his head towards Adam. Adam responded likewise.

12:00 midnight 3/3/03: The holding cell was lit up again as it had been the night before. The light was bright enough to wake up Dexter. Dexter eased off the bunk where he was sleeping and got down on his knees to pray. Adam woke and so did Pete. They all bowed down to pray in their own ways. A humming sound was heard inside the cell while they prayed. Prisoners across from them could hear the sound and saw the light emanating from their cell. Some of them yelled out for them to turn off the light, as they were trying to get some sleep. When they finished praying, and climbed back into their bunks, the light went dim and then out.

7:00 a.m. 3/3/03: Shift change for the precinct and the start of a new work week for the jailers and administrative staff. Coming into his office early was Lieutenant Alfred, expecting to make contact with officials in Washington D.C. He had no specific person in mind, but he asked the operator to connect him with the Department of Homeland Security. After speaking with the Coordinator for Strategic Planning for the Southern Region, the Lieutenant learned that the person responsible for code assignment was currently in the State of Louisiana, and would not be available until Wednesday. But, he explained, the code is only assigned to persons associated to targeted persons of specific investigations, and was meant for the department to be able to know all the players in any one investigation or operation.

"May I ask what operation you are specifically talking about?" asked the Lieutenant.

"Yes…you may ask, Lieutenant…but it's given out to those who have the need to know."

"Well, can you tell me if there is an operation being conducted in Louisiana this week by HLS," asked the Lieutenant.

"You will know when it happens, where ever it happens…if it ever happens, Lieutenant."

"I appreciate your help. What was your name?" asked Lieutenant Alfred.

"My name is Will Spenser, sir."

"Thank you Will. I appreciate your speaking with me," the lieutenant said.

"You're welcome sir…goodbye," said Spenser.

8:00 a.m. 3/3/03: Lieutenant Alfred called the shift captain into his office. He instructed him to brief his patrol officers on the fact that there might be some unusual situations happening in their city this week. He told them that he was not certain of anything specific, but he wanted them to keep their eyes open for anything that might look suspicious. If they found anything that didn't look normal or was out of the ordinary, they were to call him directly on his private line. After their brief conversation, the shift captain left to spread the word to keep their eyes open.

8:25 a.m. 3/3/03: Lieutenant Alfred retrieved the cell keys located behind the dispatcher. He shuffled them until he found the one to the holding cell. He felt that he had satisfied his curiosity concerning the Code 6 on Adam and it was now okay to release him and Dexter from detention. We would not apologize for the detention, but would just explain the department's policy, regarding carrying a non-permitted firearm.

8:30 a.m. 3/3/03: Dexter, Adam and Pete were finishing up from eating their breakfast of oatmeal, orange juice and bread. The Lieutenant opened the cell door and walked in.

"Morning gentlemen…ya'll ready to go home? …Bonjour, Pete…you sobered up yet? …You want to go home to your family now?" Lt. Alfred greeted.

No one said a word. It was a feeling by all of them that they were there because of the Lieutenant's orders. Lt. Alfred advised them that they were all free to leave and they could retrieve their belongings from the front desk. He also advised Adam that they would have to retain the weapon until he could show that he had a permit.

"Dexter, you ready to go?" asked Adam.

"Not yet... I got to finish my breakfast first...how about you Pete...you ready to go?" asked Dexter.

"I'm in no hurry... I ain't had oatmeal like this in a long time. I think I want to finish this up before I leave for work," said Pete.

The three men had formed a bond between them and it was evident to the Lieutenant. He again told them that they could leave when they finished their meal and he would leave the door unlocked for them. When they did finish eating, they walked out of the cell and turned to their right to view the other cell's holding other prisoners. Dexter motioned for Adam and Pete to follow him down the hall. They stopped in the middle of the other four cells and Dexter began to speak.

"All of you were in here over this past weekend, just as we were. Each of you would probably tell me that you didn't deserve to be here, just as we would. But before we go, I wanted to tell you that I, for one, am glad we were here for the past three days. You see, while we were here, we all experienced a miracle through God's good grace and mercy. God has forgiven us for all our sins, and we have each made a commitment to follow after God and his righteousness, rather than after the world. We now have confidence that we are in the will of God, and each of us has now committed to walk according to God's plan...whatever it is. So, in the name of Jesus the Christ, I leave you with this...Seek first the Lord in your life, and accept his Son Jesus who suffered and died for you, you, you and me. But the good news is that He rose from the dead and now reigns as King of Kings. Accept him and let him lead you in all things...and He **will** direct your life.... okay? Ya'll be blessed!" said Dexter.

9:00 a.m. 3/3/03: Dexter, Adam and Pete walked out of the

Precinct from the rear exit. Dexter promised to stay in touch with Pete as he went on about his life. Pete assured them that he was never going to get drunk again. In fact, he asked the Lord to take the taste of alcohol away from him. He was now going to attend a church and start his life over again. They hugged each other and got into Dexter's car. Dexter had agreed to give him a ride home before they left town for home. Dexter called to speak with his wife who answered the phone on the first ring.

"Hey baby, how are you? I'm so glad to hear your voice, sweetheart. We're on our way home… yes, Adam and I are on our way, now. We should be there in about four hours… I've got so much to tell you, but I'll wait until I get there, okay… good, are you okay?" asked Dexter. Okay, I'll see you soon. Love ya, babe."

Dexter dropped Pete off at his house and said goodbye. Pee's wife had already left for work. She was accustomed to this type of interaction and knew her husband's pattern of living. Adam and Dexter said goodbye, and headed home after filling their tank with gas. On their way, Dexter called Chase's cell phone to let him know they had been released.

"Hey Chase, we're out and headed home," said Dexter.

"Finally. I am in my office right now getting ready to head over there to the jail with a writ. When did you guys get out?" asked Chase.

"About a half hour ago. That was an experience I must one day tell you about, my friend. But, it's over now and we're on our way." said Dexter.

"Did you call your wife, yet?" Chase asked.

"I did…she knows we're coming," said Dexter.

"Did she tell you about the press conference coming on this afternoon by the Attorney General's Office?" asked Chase.

"No, I didn't want to let her talk too long on the phone. What's that all about?" Dexter asked.

"CNN announced this morning that the Attorney General's Office was going to have a major announcement during a press conference this afternoon at 3:00 p.m. They have been speculating that it will have something to do with HLS. *Different reporters are speculating that it has to do with some investigations they have been conducting in the south,"* answered Chase.

"I have felt that something's about to happen haven't you? Adam and I were talking about that coming down here. I can feel it in my spirit, but what, who, how?" asked Dexter.

"Stay tuned my friend...and drive home safely," said Chase.

Adam was ready to lower his seat back to sleep as Dexter drove home.

"Do you want me to drive, Dex?" Adam offered.

"I'm good, bro. You go ahead and rest. Do you mind if I listen to the news a while? Will it bother your sleep?" asked Dexter.

"Nothing will keep me awake when I get sleepy...go for it," said Adam.

For the next few hours Dexter listened to any station he could get on his car radio to find out if there was any more info concerning the impending press conference. No further information was forthcoming.

1:00 p.m. 3/3/03: Dexter drove into Adam's driveway. Adam woke up and yawned. He shook his brother's hand and told him how much he appreciated him and his leadership.

"You gonna go see Brian later on?" asked Adam.

"I think we will. I do want to catch the press conference at 3 today," said Dexter.

"What do you think it's all about, really?" asked Adam.

"I think it involved our brother, Adam. I think I want to be there in his room just in case, you know what I mean?" said Dexter.

"Okay, I'll be there too," said Adam.

Dexter left for home which was 20 minutes away from Adam. The weather was clear and there was a cool breeze blowing when Dexter arrived. He parked his car in the driveway and Norma came out to greet him. She rushed to embrace him in the front yard and gave him a big kiss. Dexter was relieved to be back in her arms and would show her how much he had missed her when he got inside. He wanted to take a shower, eat a light lunch, and make love to her before going to the hospital to see Brian. Norma felt his desires and was in-tuned with them. Not much was spoken about his trip at that time. Dexter knew there is a time for everything--this was a time for some cherished, intimate interaction with the one he loved.

2:30 p.m. 3/3/03: Dexter and Norma left home for the hospital. They chatted about the trip and some of the incidents they encountered. He reserved the details for a later time when he could share everything with her. They arrived at the hospital, parked and went inside. When they entered Brian's room, all of Brian's family was there with him, including Adam. Dexter was a little surprised to see everyone and asked how they were all doing. Norma went to Sharon and hugged her, while touching the hands of the others. Sharon spoke for the rest.

"*Well, we have a wonderful blessing to tell everyone. I wanted the family to be here when I let you all know that Brian opened his eyes last night and smiled at me,*" said Sharon.

"*Praise the Lord… Oh what a blessing… That's a miracle,*" several of them said in unison.

"*Sharon, let me ask you… when was it that he opened his eyes and smiled at you…what time was it?*" asked Dexter, looking at Adam.

"*It was exactly at midnight, ya'll. He was stirring around and I woke up to see what was wrong with him. When I went to his bed and looked at him that was when it happened. It seemed that he had a glow over him, and I felt warm all over my body. That was when he opened his eyes and smiled… why did you ask about the time, Dexter?*" asked Sharon.

"*Adam, you tell them,*" said Dexter.

"*Well, first I want you all to know that I have accepted the Lord as my Savior,*" said Adam.

"*Praise God…Halleluiah… Bless the Lord,*" said several in the room. They surrounded Adam and hugged him. Adam continued.

"*Second, last night exactly at midnight, Dexter, me and Pete were in a police station on our knees praying. I specifically was praying for Brian and*

342

that God would spare his life and heal his body. I felt good after my prayer and I know Dexter did too. I just think that God heard my prayer like he never heard it before," testified Adam.

"Praise the Lord...Bless his name...," said some clasping their hands.

"The Lord is good. Let's praise him for who he is. Let's give him a hand clapping praise," said Norma.

Dexter looked at the clock on the wall. The time was...

3:00 p.m. 3/3/03: "Good afternoon everyone... This is Tom Apple from CNN. We want to interrupt our regularly scheduled programming to bring you a special press conference from the office of the Attorney General. We announced to our audience earlier today that the AG's office requested this time to make a major announcement. As soon as he starts we will of course take you to the podium for the entire press conference. In the meantime, I want to go to our political and legal analyst, Porter Gannett for his comments on what we can expect from the AG's announcement. Porter, what have you heard?"

"Well, Tom my sources tell me that there has been an ongoing investigation in the southern region of the U.S. involving crimes that have been on the books for a long time. I understand that it involves the HLS, FBI, DEA, as well as several police forces in several large cities in the south. I also understand...," said Porter.

"Sorry to interrupt you Porter, the Attorney General is at the podium now... let's go there!"

"Good afternoon ladies and gentlemen. I have a brief statement to make to you and afterwards I will allow questions to be asked of me, as well as of representatives of the departments I will mention in my statement.

First, let me say that today's announcement is the result of outstanding work on the part of many dedicated and professional civil servants who have put their personal lives on hold and their families have suffered to a great degree for their dedication to this operation over the years. At the beginning of my stewardship of this office, I was made aware of generational crimes occurring within certain parts of the country involving families of powerful means and some of lesser means. These families have been observed through the Department of Homeland Security, Federal Bureau of Investigation, Drug Enforcement Agency and the Alcohol/Tobacco/Firearms agencies. We have also partnered with certain local police departments and others.

Through our investigations, we have uncovered the illegalities in the funeral businesses, disturbance to the dead and transportation of their corpse illegally, transportation of massive amounts of drugs through the distribution areas assigned, illegally acquisition of alcohol and distribution to areas forbidden by law, human trafficking of illegal aliens and the intent to enslave, prostitution and cover-up of these activities by elected officials dating back to the late 1800s, and continuing to today.

These crimes were begun with several families, and over the decades, have spread to multiple families across the south. The operations we have launched today, as I speak, are called '**Operation ShreLongTex** and **Operation AlMon**'. Right at this moment, the Department of Homeland Security is carrying out arrests in several major cities in the states of Louisiana and Texas. The operation is centered in the northern part of the states, and is intended to break up a longstanding business in the areas mentioned above. Those cities are Shreveport, Louisiana, Longview, Texas and Texarkana, Texas. At precisely this moment, Operation AlMon is carrying out arrest warrants in Alexandra, Louisiana and Monroe, Louisiana. Now ladies and gentleman, this is a major accomplishment of many persons and is the beginning of more to come. Never before has such an enormous operation taken place in this country, involving over 1,000 people. I will have another statement to make tomorrow, and subsequent days to let you all know of the progress of warrants and arrests. We will in all cases respect the innocent until they are proven guilty in a court of law. We will do all we can to minimize the impact these arrests will have on families, local governments and state governments. Finally, let me say that if you are involved in any kind of illegal activities, this will be your notice. We will not rest until you are caught and pay for your crimes, and even the crimes you have inherited from your fathers ...I will take any questions you have now."

3:33 p.m. 3/3/03: Everybody in Brian's hospital room looked at each other and said nothing. Some had their hands over their mouths and eyes wide open. Dexter looked at Brian who was situated facing the television. Everyone in the room looked at Brian. Brian's eyes opened wide and stared at the television. His face slowly widened to a smile. He began to make moaning sounds as he seemed to respond to the news being broadcast over the television. Sharon moved to his side and stroked his forehead. Adam moved to his left side and grabbed his brother's hand. Dexter touched his feet which were covered by a light blanket. Brenda and her husband moved up to Sharon's back and Brenda laid her hand on her mom's shoulder. Greg touched the right side of his father's face. Norma held Dexter's hand. Brian was still smiling and began to scan around the room. The television caught his attention.

A reporter asked the Attorney General this question: "You say there were hundreds of persons involved in this investigation and you named several agencies, and then you said you were assisted by 'others'. By that, do you mean **informers** who were **undercover**, who were not in the government?"

"Without their help, our investigation would still be going on... the answer is **YES.**"

Dexter looked at Brian and asked *"Can you understand me?"* Brian nodded his head...yes. Dexter asked... **"Brian, are you one of ...the others?"** Brian nodded...**YES!**

Just as the weather began to clear and warmer air entered into the atmosphere around Shreveport, Dexter began to receive clarity in his mind about the misperceptions and family secrets he had encountered over the past few months. No amount of study at any of the universities or sustained study of the Scriptures would have given him the depth of understanding he had gained through these overall experiences. Recognizing the pain associated with all of it, he was convinced down to the core of his being, that he now knew what his purpose was on this earth. He had found the Maker's perfect will for him. No more questions for him to ask. No more doubts about the motives and intentions of others. He had learned how to **major** in the **major**--not the minor. Realizing that he cannot control the actions of anyone but himself, he now knows that it is himself that he has to work on. It is more than a duty to become all God has planned for him to do. It is more than coming to a realization that he must have a renewed mind—he must now work it out to where it becomes part of his being. He will soon realize too that, when he gets to the place where he should be, in knowing who he truly is, he will find that the relationship he desires with his God will automatically appear--it's always been there.

This was his biggest stumbling block in his relationship with his brothers. He wanted to be sure he got this one right, so he repeated it: "I need to be the light of Christ—I need to reflect what I believe, through the way I walk and talk everyday. It is I who need the mirror. I can move nothing or no one—it is the power of the one I reflect from within me, who will make the difference." As his spiritual maturity continued to emerge and he believes that God is the Head of his universe he realizes he must allow God to work on him for proper positioning. He also understands now, that his family represents the third leg of the triangle. Part of the plan is to have a family nucleus that would honor God and nurture the youth to become strong believers in their Creator. That's it! It's all in the numbers—1, 2, 3. God, self and family. When the numbers are aligned, God will be honored and **blessings** will flow for generations to come—not **curses**.

So, what about the repetitive numbers of 333, 444, 555, etc.? Dexter now realized that it was not the total of the numbers themselves—it was the numbers in three's that has meaning. There were 3 numbers (that he saw) to the puzzle. They were constantly reminding Dexter that he had to get the numbers right. If he didn't, maybe he would be continually out of balance in his life, and would miss God's plan for him altogether. Seeing these groupings of numbers over and over again in different places and under different circumstances, made Dexter believe that he had received his revelation. He felt that he understood the significance of the numbers, and would never allow room for misinterpretation again. He repeated:

God first; …then self …then family.
God first; …then self …then family!
God first; …then self …then family!

The End

Author's Note

When my father-in-law was alive, I used to visit with him in Eunice, Louisiana. I was particularly grateful for the times when he drove me to the countryside to visit some of his relatives. Some of the ones I met were just good old, honest country folks who had a good heart and a dedication to their kinfolks and friends. I saw many ideas for stories in the lives of those folks. I wrote short poems about them and took pictures to include in some of my paintings.

In this book, I have included some of the spirit of those good natured folk I met, and everybody else are merely fictional characters—conjured up out of my mind, so to speak.

I have also taken liberties in all of the events created in the book, and there is no connection with the truth and any of the businesses mentioned.

I want to thank the people I consulted with who acted as ghost readers for some of my chapters in an effort to give me feedback on the storyline and character development. Much love and appreciation to my good friend, Diane Tezeno, for her expert editing and subsequent PR work for the book. I particularly want to thank my wife for being my harshest critic and keeping me motivated night after night.

C.A.S.
April 3, 2011